COP TO CORPSE

COP TO CORPSE

Peter Lovesey

WINDSOR
PARAGON

First published 2012
by Sphere
This Large Print edition published 2012
by AudioGO Ltd
by arrangement with
Little, Brown Book Group

Hardcover ISBN: 978 1 445 82817 6
Softcover ISBN: 978 1 445 82818 3

The moral right of the author has been asserted

All characters and events in this publication, other than those clearly in the public domain, are fictitious and any resemblance to real persons, living or dead, is purely coincidental

British Library Cataloguing in Publication Data available

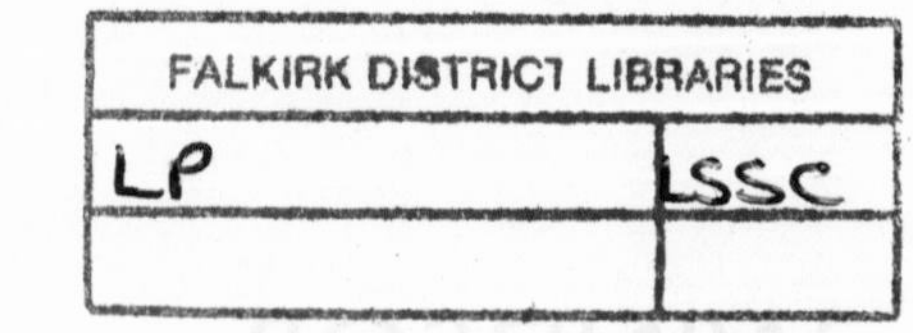

Printed and bound in Great Britain by
MPG Books Group Limited

CHAPTER ONE

Hero to zero.

Cop to corpse.

One minute PC Harry Tasker is strolling up Walcot Street, Bath, on foot patrol. The next he is shot through the head. No scream, no struggle, no last words. He is picked off, felled, dead.

The shooting activates an alarm over one of the shops nearby, an ear-splitting ring certain to wake everyone.

Normally at this time on a Sunday morning—around 4 a.m.—the streets of Bath are silent. The nightclubs close officially at three. The last of the revellers have dispersed. PC Tasker was on his way back to the police station after checking that Club XL was quiet.

His body lies in a bow shape under the light of a street lamp on the flagstone pavement, a small puddle of blood forming under the head. His chequered cap is upturned nearby.

Harry Tasker is the third police officer murdered in Avon and Somerset in twelve weeks. The others, like him, were shot while on foot patrol. A huge operation to identify the sniper has come to nothing. All the police know for certain is that the victims were shot by someone using a high-velocity assault rifle that fires 5.56 × 45mm cartridges. The killings and the hunt for the so-called Somerset Sniper have been splashed in headlines across the nation.

Nobody else is on the street at this hour. This is the pattern. The killing is done at night. The victims are discovered eventually by some early riser, a milkman, a dog owner.

But today there is a difference. In a flat above one of the shops in Walcot Street, a hand grabs a phone.

The 999 call is taken at the communications centre in Portishead, logged at 4.09 a.m.

'Which service do you need: police, fire or ambulance?'

'Ambulance, for sure. And police. There's a guy lying in the street here. I heard this sound like a gunshot a minute ago and looked out and there he was. He's not moving. I think he's a policeman.'

Another police officer. The operator is trained to assess critical information and act on it calmly, yet even she takes a sharp breath. 'Where are you speaking from?'

The caller gives the address and his name and in the emergency room the location is flashed on screen. An all-units call. Within minutes all available response cars and an ambulance are heading for the stretch of Walcot Street near Beehive Yard.

A new shooting is terrible news, but the speed of this alert gives the police the best chance yet of detaining the sniper.

Walcot Street was created by the Romans. It is believed to have formed a small section of the Fosse Way, the unswerving road that linked the West Country to the Midlands. It runs north to south for a third of a mile, parallel to the River Avon, from St Swithin's Church—where Jane Austen's parents were married in 1764—to St Michael's, where it morphs into Northgate Street. Located outside the old city walls, Walcot was once a village independent of Bath and still has the feel of a place apart. It was always the city's lumber room, housing, in its time, tram sheds, a flea market, slaughterhouses, a foundry, a women's prison and an isolation hospital for venereal diseases. Now it goes in for shops of character and variable charm such as Jack and Danny's Fancy Dress Hire; Bath Sewing Machine Service; Yummy House; Bath Aqua Theatre of Glass; and Appy Daze, Bath's Premium Hemporium.

The first police car powers up the street, blues and twos going. By now some local people in nightclothes are grouped around the body. Two officers fling open their car doors and dash over to their shot colleague as more cars arrive from the other direction. The ambulance snakes through and the paramedics take over, but anyone can see Harry Tasker is beyond help. His personal radio, attached to his tunic, eerily emits someone else's voice relaying information about his shooting.

A real voice cuts in: 'Let's have some order here. For a start, will somebody stop that fucking alarm.'

Ken Lockton is the senior man at the scene and must direct the operation. 'Senior' is a contradiction in terms. Inspector Lockton is not yet thirty, came quickly through the ranks and passed his promotion exam at the end of last year. He wouldn't be the first choice to deal with a major incident, or the second, or even the tenth, but he's the man on duty. As the uniformed inspector lowest in the pecking order he gets more night shifts than anyone else. He knew Harry Tasker well and is shocked by the killing, yet can't let that affect his handling of the incident. Lockton knows he must suppress all emotion, lead by example, and set the right procedures in motion. Inside him, every pulse is throbbing, and not just because another policeman has been shot. His strap-brown eyes are wide, eager. He doesn't mind anyone knowing he's a career man, a high-flyer aiming for executive rank. This is a thumping great chance for glory, the best chance anyone has had to bag the sniper. And he hasn't got long. As soon as Headquarters get their act together they will send some hotshot detective to take over.

The men available to Lockton aren't exactly the A team. Like him, they happen to be on the night shift, almost at the end of it, ready for sleep, stumbling bleary-eyed out of patrol cars and minibuses uncertain what their duties will be. He must make effective use of them.

He gets one success. The jangling alarm is silenced.

He grabs a loudhailer and begins issuing orders. No one must be in any doubt who is in charge.

The first imperative is to seal the crime scene. A stretch of the street for about a hundred yards is closed to traffic by police cars parked laterally at either end. Cones and police tape reinforce the cordon. While this is being done, Lockton assesses the location. If the sniper is still in the area, the local geography will hamper him. Behind the row of small shops on the side where PC Tasker lies is the river, deep and steeply banked. Not much chance of escape there. On the other side of Walcot Street is a twenty-foot-high retaining wall. Above it, on massive foundations, are the backs of Bladud Buildings and the Paragon, grand terraces from the mid-eighteenth century sited at the top of a steep escarpment.

The armed response team arrives by van. They were sent automatically when the seriousness of the alert was known and they are here in their black body armour and bearing their Heckler and Koch G36 subcarbines. Ken Lockton, glowing with importance, tells the senior man he wants stop points on all conceivable escape routes from the sectioned-off area.

He also has work for his sleep-deprived army of unarmed men and women. Residents disturbed by the noise and coming to their front doors will find officers standing guard. They will be told to lock up and stay inside.

Another group is sent to make a search of Beehive Yard, on the river side.

Do Not Cross tape is used to enclose the area around the body. Later a crime scene tent will be erected. The police surgeon is already examining the body, a necessary formality. He's a local GP. The forensic pathologist will follow.

The 999 call originated from a flat above a charity shop and Lockton goes in with a female officer to question the informant, a first-year undergraduate.

Ponytail, glasses, pale, spotty face and a wisp of beard fit the student stereotype. The young guy, who gives his name as Damon Richards, is in a black dressing gown. The questioning is sharp, considering that he raised the alert. Lockton knows that people who call the emergency number are not always public-spirited. They may well be implicated in what happened.

'Take me through it. You heard gunfire, right? Where were you—in bed?'

'Actually, no. I was at my desk, studying. If

I wake early, that's what I do. I had a book open and I was making notes.' He is tiresomely slow of speech.

'What woke you—a noise?'

'If you really want to know, I needed a pee. Then I was awake, so I started to work. Ten or twenty minutes after, I heard the shooting.'

'Where were you when you heard it?'

'I told you. At my desk. Over there by the window.'

The room is typical of early-nineteenth-century Bath houses, high-ceilinged, corniced, spacious. And typical of the twenty-first century, it is in use as a bedsit, crammed with self-assembly furniture. The desk is hard against the sash window and books are stacked on it. One book is open and there is a notepad beside it.

'With the curtain drawn?'

'Yes. I heard the gunfire and didn't know what it was so I pulled back the curtain and saw the guy lying there. He wasn't moving. That's when I phoned. I didn't go out to him because I was scared, to be honest. Is he dead?'

'You heard more than one shot?'

'I think so.'

'What do you mean—"think so"? You'd know if there was more than one.'

'There could have been an echo.'

'Do you have any sense of where the shooting came from? Was it close?'

'It sounded bloody close to me. Other people must have heard it.'

'The difference is that you were already awake. Was the gunfire from out in the street, would you say?'

'Well, obviously.'

'As distinct from one of these houses?'

'I get you. I couldn't say that. How could I tell?'

'Do you remember if there was a vehicle nearby?'

'There are some parking spaces that get filled up quickly. Otherwise it's double yellow lines all the way.'

'I'm not talking about parked cars, for God's sake. Did you hear anything after the shots, like a car or a motorbike moving off?'

'I don't remember any. I could be wrong. I was in shock, to be honest.'

'You keep saying "to be honest". You'd better be honest with me, young man. We'll need a written statement from you. Everything you remember.' Lockton nods to the constable and leaves her to start the paperwork.

It is still before 4.30 a.m.

Reinforcements are arriving all the time. Lockton knows he could find himself replaced any minute as the Senior Investigating Officer. He needs to make his opportunity count, and soon. He moves over to where the police surgeon has now stepped back from the body.

The shooting fits the pattern of the previous attacks. The entry wound is above the right ear. The bullet must have fragmented inside the skull, shattering much of the opposite side of the head. It's not a sight you want to linger over.

'Nothing I can tell you that isn't obvious. A single bullet wound.'

'We think there may have been more than one shot,' Lockton says.

'Have you found other bullets, then?'

'Not yet. Other priorities. Is there any way of telling the direction of the shots?'

'Depends where he was when he was hit. The bullet entered here, quite high up on the right temple, and you can see that most of the tissue damage is lower down on the opposite side. That could be an angle for you to work with.'

'You're talking about the trajectory?'

'That's for you to work out. I'm only here to examine the body.'

'A high-velocity bullet?'

'I'm a doctor, not a gun expert.'

Ken Lockton goes into deduction mode. 'It's unlikely the shooting was from ground level, so it's a good bet he fired from above us, like a window over one of the shops.' He's pleased with that. CID would approve.

'In that case, he would have been walking away from the town centre, towards Walcot.'

Lockton isn't sure now. He betrays some of the tension he feels by chewing his thumbnail. 'The right side, you say.'

'You can see for yourself.'

Actually he's seen more than he wants to. He doesn't need to look again to know where the bullet entered. He gives a nervous laugh. 'His shift was nearly over. He should have been heading the opposite way, back towards Manvers Street nick.'

'So?'

'If you're right, the killer wasn't on the shop side. He must have been somewhere behind us.' He turns to look again at that massive brick rampart along the west side of the street, a far cry from the cleaned-up stone structures that grace most of the city. Blackened by two centuries of pollution, the wall is tall enough and grim enough to enclose a prison.

A disused Victorian fountain is recessed into the brickwork under an arch flanked by granite columns. When the market across the street thrived, the trough must have been a place where thirsty horses were watered after delivering goods. Its modern use is as a flowerbed—with insufficient cover for a gunman to crouch in.

'I'm leaving,' the police surgeon says. 'I've pronounced him dead. There's nothing more to keep me here.'

Lockton is too absorbed to answer.

Left of the fountain his eyes light on an ancient flight of steps leading up to Bladud Buildings. Is that where the shot was fired from? The gunman could have made his escape up there and be in a different street.

His heart-rate quickening, Lockton crosses for a closer inspection, runs halfway up the steps and at once discovers a difficulty. It is far too narrow. To have fired from a height the sniper needs to have been at least this far up, but the tall sides mask the view. You can't see the fallen man from here. The sniper would have needed to wait for his victim to draw level across the street. The shooting from the steps didn't happen.

Cursing, Lockton descends, returns to the middle of the street, stares at that long expanse of wall and gets a better idea. Up to now he has accepted the structure without fully taking it in. Now he can see that the brickwork isn't entirely solid. At intervals there are cavities where entire bricks are missing. Maybe they are meant for drainage. They look like spy-holes.

Or sniper points.

The holes go in a long way. Beer cans have been stuffed into some within reach. You could put your whole arm into them. It's hard to tell how far back they go.

He has assumed up to now that solid earth is behind the wall. Still thinking about the possibility, he steps back for a longer look and some way to the right of the fountain notices a door and window spaces.

A lock-up. It belongs to a local firm that salvages and retails masonry and statuary.

His spirits surge.

Padlocks and hasps would be no great problem for a committed assassin.

He orders two pairs of armed officers to force the lock-up door.

The window spaces would be ideal sniper points, allowing a clear view of the street and a human target walking by.

Overhead, the police helicopter hovers, more proof of the seriousness of this operation. This is the biggest moment of Ken Lockton's career. All of this is under his command, the chopper, the cars, the bobbies stepping down from minibuses, the gun team yelling, 'Armed police!' as they storm the lock-up.

The doors are kicked in and the interior searched by flashlight. In a situation as tense as this, violent action is welcomed by the team. Inside are large chunks of masonry and statuary harvested from old buildings all over Somerset, griffins, dragons and hounds. Several are large enough to hide behind.

But it ends in anticlimax. There's nothing to show that the lock-up was entered recently. The team steps out, deflated.

4.40 a.m.

Lockton feels the pressure. For all he knows, the sniper could be inside one of the shops or flats holding people hostage. Each dwelling will need to be checked, every resident questioned as a possible witness, but unless something happens quickly this will have to be a later phase in the operation, after he hands over responsibility. Headquarters have already radioed to say CID are on their way and will take over.

He stares at the wall, the sodding great wall. Logically that was the side the bullets came from if one penetrated PC Tasker's right temple. Or was he facing the other direction for some obscure reason?

His gaze travels up the rows of blackened bricks. There isn't enough daylight to see properly and the height goes well above street-lamp level. He asks for a flashlight and picks out an iron railing along the top. 'What's up there, Steve?' he asks Sergeant Stillman, one of the patrolling drivers who had answered the all-units call. The two were sergeants together for four years. Stillman is worth his stripes, but in Lockton's opinion won't ever make inspector. No officer qualities.

'Behind the rail? Gardens. They're all the way along. They belong to the houses in the terrace.'

'Gardens?' Fresh thoughts stampede Lockton's brain. He can't see anything except overhanging foliage from down in the street, but he is visualising a gun position.

'They'll be roof gardens really. Just a few feet of soil.'

'How would he get up there?'

'He wouldn't, unless he lived in one of the houses. He'd have to come through someone's flat.'

'Drive me up there.'

'Now?' Stillman doesn't appreciate that Lockton wants a personal triumph out of this.

'Get the car, for fuck's sake.'

He could just as easily run up the steps. It would be quicker. Sergeant Stillman decides this is about power. Ken Lockton is asserting his rank.

A silver-haired sergeant is deputed to take over at street level.

Without another word Sergeant Stillman fetches the car and does the short drive as ordered, ignoring the one-way system by turning at Saracen Street and back down Broad Street to park on the front side of the terrace, level with the cast-iron bollards at the top of the steps—the same steps Lockton could have used in half the time.

To the right of the steps is Bladud Buildings. The Paragon is to the left. There's little difference. It's all four or five floors high and Georgian neo-classical in style: entablatures, pediments and cornices.

Lockton stands by the car with arms folded, trying to understand how this building is grounded on the steep slope. It isn't easy to visualise from this side. 'There have got to be basements,' he tells Steve Stillman. 'The ground floor is going to be above the level of the garden.'

He steps up to one of the entrances and looks at the array of bell-pushes on the entryphone system. Each terraced house must have been a sole residence once. Now there are flats on all floors. Beside each button is the name of the tenant. He tries the lowest.

Through the grille a weary voice says, 'Chrissake, what time is this?'

'Police,' says Lockton.

'Fuck off,' says the voice.

'That's what we get for safeguarding the great British public,' Lockton comments to Stillman. 'We'll try another place.'

Stillman is frowning. 'It could be him.'

'I don't think so. He wouldn't answer, would he?'

There was some logic in that.

They study the bell-system two doors along. Someone has been efficient here. Each name is typed on white card rather than handwritten on odd scraps of paper. 'Not this one,' Lockton says.

'Why not?' Sergeant Stillman is starting to question Lockton's deductive skills. By his own estimation, the house must overlook the place where Harry Tasker's body lies.

'Because it's not what I'm looking for, not what the sniper would look for.'

He finds it at the next house, handwritten names for flats 1, 2 and 3 and a blank for the fourth, the lowest. He presses 3.

After a long pause, a woman's voice. 'Who is this?'

'The police.'

'How do I know that?'

'Look out of your front window. You'll see our car.'

'Hang on a mo.'

Presently they are admitted to apartment 3 by a young woman in blue winceyette pyjamas. She rakes a hand through her blonde hair and tells them it's early in the day.

Stillman bites back the strong comment he'd like

to make after being up all night.

Lockton asks who occupies the flat below.

'Nobody,' the blonde says. 'It's been empty some time, far as I know.'

'You haven't heard any sounds?'

'Tonight?'

'Any time.'

A shake of the head. 'There was a noise like an alarm down in the street a short time ago, or I think there was. It woke me. Then I drifted off again.'

'How do we get into the basement?'

'The what? Do you mean the garden flat? The stairs in the hall.'

The two policemen find their way down. The door is locked.

'Force it, Steve.'

Sergeant Stillman aims a kick at the lock. The door gives at the second try. 'Shouldn't we get armed assistance?'

Lockton doesn't listen. 'Give me your torch.'

He's already inside, still living his dream of instant fame. The place has the smell of long disuse and the lights don't work. He senses that the sniper isn't here. Through what must be the living room—though the place is unfurnished—he can see a small sunroom, too poky to call a conservatory. Beyond is the garden, overgrown, a fine crop of stinging nettles waist-high and bedraggled with the overnight dew.

He steps through the sunroom and notes that the door isn't bolted from inside. Not a huge security risk, but any landlord worthy of the name would surely take the trouble to secure an empty flat.

If nothing else, he'll get a view of Walcot Street from the end of the garden. Parting the nettles, he moves on, following the torch beam, and then stops.

'Jesus.'

Ahead, resting against the railing, is an assault rifle.

CHAPTER TWO

'Don't touch it.'

Sergeant Stillman knows his crime scene drill. You don't handle evidence. You don't even go near it.

Like a kid caught at the fridge door, Lockton swings around and shows the palms of his hands. He has stopped short of handling the gun, but only just. This is his find. The excitement is all over his features. He tries to sound cool. 'I wasn't born yesterday, Steve.'

'Okay.'

'Quite some find.'

As if by mutual consent, they stand for a moment, in awe that the sniper was here in this small overgrown garden.

Stillman says, 'We'd better report this.'

'Quit telling me my job.'

There's tension between these two. They were sergeants together for a long time. Stillman is experienced, steady, able and, if truth were told, more savvy than Lockton. He just didn't bother to go for the promotion exam.

Rank must count here, rank and procedure.

'Our first duty,' Lockton says as if he's lecturing recruits at Peel Centre, 'is to assess the scene. The sniper obviously left without his weapon. But why? All the action was down in the street. He should have felt secure up here.'

'That shop alarm went off.'

Bloody obvious. The thing must have been loud even this far off. It was ear-splitting at the scene and Lockton has already dismissed it from his mind. He says a grudging, 'Okay.' And tries to gloss over his lapse. 'When you're in charge of an operation this big, taking decisions, your thoughts are all about what happens next. Getting back to the sniper, he hears the alarm and leaves in a hurry, not wanting to be seen with the weapon.'

Stillman says nothing.

'That's the way I see it,' Lockton adds.

'Yes?'

'You don't sound convinced.'

'I'm thinking if it was me, I wouldn't leave the gun here. Maybe he means to come back for it.'

This is another thought that hasn't dawned on Lockton. 'Just what I was about to say.' A gleam comes into his eye. 'We could trap him.'

'Just you and me? I don't think so. We need back-up.'

Lockton ploughs on as if he hasn't heard. 'To come and go, he'd need a key to the front door. He must have got hold of one to let himself in.'

Stillman shakes his head, disturbed by what is being proposed.

Lockton thinks the issue in doubt must be his theory about the key. 'Or he could have walked in when one of the residents was coming or going. Or a friend of a resident. In places like this people don't necessarily know each other. You hold the door open for someone else thinking they must be from one of the other flats.'

'Someone else with a gun?'

'Guns like that fold up. You can get one into a bag, no problem. It's feasible.' Lockton peers at the rifle again. 'I don't know much about firearms, but this looks state-of-the-art to me. Telescopic sight.'

'We knew he was good.'

'He'll be gutted at leaving it behind. I think you're right. He won't want to leave it here for long.' The opportunity is huge, irresistible. Lockton can already picture himself making the arrest—and tomorrow's headlines. 'He means to come back for it.'

'One thing is certain,' Steve Stillman says in his downbeat tone.

'What's that?'

'He won't come back while our car is outside.'

'Christ, yes.' Pause for thought. The blue and yellow police car in front of the house is a glaring giveaway. 'Move it.'

'Leaving you here?'

'Someone's got to be here. I'll stay hidden.'

'I don't advise it.'

'And I don't take advice from you, sergeant.'

The 'sergeant' and the way it is said is a low blow from an old colleague. A muscle twitches at the edge of Stillman's mouth. With an effort he stays civil. 'You'll need back-up. D'you want me to radio for a couple of firearms officers?'

'I can do that. I've got my own radio.'

'Shall I call Headquarters to let them know what we found?'

'Leave that to me.'

The two men eye each other. The mistrust is palpable. Lockton is hell-bent on making the arrest.

'As you wish,' says Stillman.

* * *

Because of its sheltered position, Walcot Street is slow to emerge from darkness. The tops of the stone buildings are getting a glimmer of natural light, the first of the day. The place is waking up to a street killing. Despite the best efforts of the police, nervous tenants are at their front doors demanding to know when it will be safe to go out. Almost without the order being given, the house-to-house questioning is under way. A number of the residents claim to have heard the shots or the alarm and gone to their windows, but no one has seen the sniper.

Being Sunday, there isn't the influx of working people you'd get on other days. Even so, at either end of the cordoned-off area, a few early risers are demanding to know what is happening. More persistent are television staff and pressmen trying to negotiate a better view. The news of the shooting has already broken on twenty-four-hour TV.

The police are adamant that no unauthorised person gets admittance, and as some of them are carrying guns, the warnings are heeded.

A large forensic tent has screened off the body of PC Tasker. A Home Office forensic pathologist is now at work making a taped summary of his findings. His crouched figure is silhouetted on the tent by the arc lamp inside. SOCOs in white zipper suits are coming and going.

The sergeant left in temporary charge of the scene has now been supplanted by CID officers. They have ordered a sweep search of the gardens between the shop backs and the river. Dogs are being used to check the outbuildings. It's a rare luxury to have enough personnel to mount an operation on this scale.

Officially the night shift will end at 6.30, but a major incident like this alters everything. When enough of the next shift—the early turn, as it is known—are bussed in, it's possible that the sleep-starved will be laid off. Until then they remain on duty.

Sergeant Stillman has moved the police car from its conspicuous position in the Paragon and parked it on the lower level, outside the taped-off section of Walcot Street. Being a wise old hand—and exhausted—he has decided to have forty winks—or a few more than forty. If he is needed, he'll find out. A personal radio with the volume on full is better than an alarm clock. He's at his post and on duty and you can't ask more from a man who's been up all night. His head lolls to one side until it finds a comfortable position against the car door and he drifts into a shallow sleep.

Meanwhile the whizzkids from CID have gone through the same process Ken Lockton did earlier, calculating the probable direction of the fatal shots. The pathologist has explained about the bullet's angle of penetration. The armed police inform them that a search has already been made of the lock-ups along the wall. It's deceiving, that vast wall. Daylight has to strengthen before someone looks higher and decides to order a search of the elevated gardens.

This time enough men assemble outside Bladud Buildings to make a near-simultaneous entry to each house and garden. By now hardly anyone in the neighbourhood can be unaware of what is going on, so there's no difficulty gaining admission. Most of the garden flats are occupied and the small gardens easily searched. There's just the one that Lockton and Stillman entered earlier. 'Someone forced this,' the officer says at the bottom of the stairs.

'Hold it, then,' his colleague says. 'We'd better bring in the armed response lads.'

It doesn't take long. The firearms team have driven up in their Trojan Horse van. They can't wait for some action.

They crowd the narrow staircase in their body armour and ballistic helmets. More are detailed to enter from the gardens on either side. The object: to terrorise any intruder into submission by letting him discover he's under attack from all sides.

'Armed police!' goes up the shout from the loudhailer. 'Drop your weapon and lie face down.'

This is the drill. If no one is inside, the anticlimax can be a real downer.

The first pair kick the door inwards, enter the flat and take up offensive positions. More follow. It's a show of strength designed to intimidate.

They move forward, checking each room in the basement flat. The search is simplified because the place is unfurnished. In seconds they are through the building.

'Stand by, stand by,' a voice says into all the earpieces. 'We have a sighting. Garden, right-hand side almost against the wall.'

A sighting.

This is the adrenalin moment they train for.

The movement forward is stealthy now. The only cover in the garden is a rich crop of weeds, and weeds don't stop bullets.

'Give him the message again.'

'Armed police! Drop your weapon and get face down.'

A long, tense pause.

'Result,' says another voice. 'The tosser has surrendered.'

Sure enough, a dark figure at the right of the garden is among the mass of thistles, prone. No obvious sign of a weapon.

The black-clad officers take no chance. You don't mess with a killer. They 'stack up' at strategic points, guns at the ready, covering the two senior men who must approach the suspect from behind and handcuff him.

It's swift and efficient. The pair go in at the charge. The first flings himself across the suspect's back to be sure he can't move while the second applies the cuffs. There's no resistance.

'Cool.'

Except that the man on top presently says, 'See what I see?'

'What's that?'

He stabs his finger at the two silver pips on the epaulette the suspect is wearing. Then at the mass of blood at the back of his head.

CHAPTER THREE

'You can stand down, super. The Serial Crimes Unit is on the case.'

Without a second look at the lanky young guy in leather jacket and shades who had just appeared on the scene, Detective Superintendent Peter

Diamond said, 'You could have fooled me.'

'I'm the first to arrive.'

'Hundred and first, maybe.'

'The first SCU man.'

'And you are. . .?'

'DI Polehampton. The others will be here shortly.'

'Having a late breakfast, are they?'

'Traffic, I expect.' Irony was lost on this guy. 'As the first at the scene, I'm taking over.'

'Oh, yes? You and whose army?' After almost twenty years in Bath CID, Diamond wasn't being given the elbow by a twit who looked as if he was straight out of training school.

'In the name of Chief Super Gull.'

Supergull.

Diamond filed that one away for future use.

Polehampton said, 'He heads the special team co-ordinating the hunt for the Somerset Sniper.'

'Special I'll give you,' Diamond said.

'I hope you're not being sarcastic.'

'It's just that I find you hard to believe, Inspector Hampton.'

'Polehampton. You can speak to Headquarters if you want.'

'Too busy,' Diamond said. 'You speak to them. They'll tell you this is my patch. The men you see around you are my people and they were first on the scene—fact. They've been here since first thing dealing with the murder of a close colleague. None of us are walking away from that.'

'I can understand that. If you want to stay and observe, you're welcome, but kindly update me first.'

There was a pause while Diamond reined himself

in. Far more was at issue this morning than a spat over who was running the show.

'Here's your update,' he said. 'Two officers attacked, men we work with every day. One dead and the other may not survive.'

'*Two?*' Polehampton blinked. 'Nobody reported a second attack.'

'He's just been found, that's why. Ken Lockton, a uniformed inspector with a serious head injury.'

'God Almighty—another shooting?'

'Bludgeoned, they're saying. The ambulance is on its way. I'm cordoning the area in hope of snaring the skunk who did this.'

'You'd better carry on, then.'

Diamond walked away, speaking into his personal radio, with far more on his mind than Inspector Polehampton. 'It is secured? . . . And the garden? . . . Is there any hope he's still alive? . . . Don't move him. Make sure his airways are clear and wait for the paramedics.'

At times like this, the basics of first aid leave you feeling more helpless than the victim.

He sprinted up the flight of steps to see for himself. Sprinted up the first ten or eleven, anyway. There were fifty-six and he felt about fifty-six pounds overweight. After emerging at the top, gasping, he turned right, towards a cluster of police vehicles. This second crime scene was in the garden of a house in the Paragon, a mid-eighteenth-century terrace where in less dangerous times Jane Austen had stayed on her first visits to the city.

Just as he arrived at the house, so did the ambulance, siren blaring.

He stepped aside for the two paramedics and their stretcher and followed them through the unlit basement flat to the back. You couldn't call it a garden. There wasn't a flower in sight, just a mass of weeds, much trampled. Near the front a huddle of armed police stood over a dark shape.

Lockton was face down in nettles.

All Diamond could see of the injury was a matted mess of blood and hair. It was obvious the man was out to the world, but the gravity of his condition was impossible to tell.

Suffocation is the commonest cause of death after a head injury. If the victim is unconscious his tongue relaxes and may block his throat. The paramedics checked this, even though the firearms team said they had already done so, putting two fingers at the angle of the jaw and two at the point and opening the mouth.

They went systematically through the standard tests for signs of life. There seemed to be hope. They applied a mask, lifted him on to the stretcher and carried him through the house to the ambulance.

For everyone left in the garden it was like the hiatus after a funeral. Some of the gun team had removed their helmets and goggles. These men who thrived on action seemed uncertain what to do next until Diamond broke the troubled silence. 'It's up to the doctors now. If there's a chance of saving Ken, they will. The rest of us have work to do. It's just possible there's evidence here that hasn't already been trampled over, so watch where you walk. Leave by the same route. Step one by one towards the wall and go through the house and return to your duties.'

His own duties kept him in the garden longer, assessing. The plot was roughly square, not more than ten metres by ten. Some overgrown roses along the side walls were the only indication that this had once been cultivated. He edged around to the iron railing at the end to check how much he could see of the scene below. From this height everything was scaled down. A diminished Polehampton was in the middle of Walcot Street gesturing to other people, looking about him, trying to appear as if he was in charge. More interesting to Diamond was the clear view of the forensic tent directly across the street. No question: the shooting could have been done from up here.

So many had invaded the small plot, crushing the crop of weeds, that it was impossible to work out where the gunman might have taken aim. Nothing so helpful as an empty cartridge case was visible.

He walked through the musty flat and told the constable on duty at the front to prevent anyone from entering or leaving the building except the crime scene investigation team.

'Including the residents, sir?'

'Especially the residents. Are they getting stroppy?'

'Some are. The armed response lads went through all the flats searching for the sniper.'

'People don't take well to that sort of invasion. Okay, if anyone wants to know, we'll be interviewing them all shortly. Do you know the injured man, Inspector Lockton?'

The constable nodded. 'Quite well, sir.' A pause. 'D'you think he'll pull through?'

'We can hope. Popular with the lads, is he?'

'He got promoted recently.'

'That isn't the same thing.'

A faint smile.

'He's mustard keen,' the constable said in an effort to be fair. 'He does a good job. He was here first thing, sir, in charge of it all. I mean down in Walcot Street where the shooting happened.'

'How did that come about—a newly promoted man in charge?'

'As duty inspector, on the night shift.'

'I get you.' The lowest in the pecking order gets the leavings. 'If he was directing the operation, what induced him to come up here?'

'I couldn't tell you, sir.'

'You were down there, weren't you?'

'All I know is he was there one minute and gone the next. Someone else took over.'

Diamond radioed for CID assistance and got his deputy, DI Halliwell, the man he trusted and relied on. 'Keith, I'm at the house in the Paragon. I want the people who live here turned inside out as possible witnesses. It seems likely the sniper fired from this garden and Lockton worked it out and came up here to investigate and was knocked cold. Someone let him in, someone clobbered him. And someone may have seen the attack.'

'I'll sort it, guv,' Halliwell said. 'Was Lockton working alone, then?'

'Apparently.'

'Strange.'

* * *

Diamond took the fifty-six steps down and was approached by a crop-headed muscleman he knew to be Supergull, Jack Gull, head honcho of the Serial Crimes Unit. Exactly how Gull, who wasn't much over forty and looked as if he chewed car tyres, had made it to chief superintendent was an unsolved mystery. A show of civility was inescapable.

'How you doing, Jack?'

'We're taking over,' Gull said.

'Fine.' Diamond refused to rise to the bait. He had his own way of dealing with situations like this.

'Fine' wasn't the reaction Gull had prepared for. 'Polehampton tells me you're pissed off about it.'

'Did he get that impression from me?' Diamond said. 'He's no mind-reader. What's the plan, then? Do I stand my people down and leave it to you guys?'

'You know that's not the way it works. We need them and we need you.'

'Some of them are still here from the night turn. They can't stay on their feet much longer.'

Gull wasn't interested in human frailty. 'What did you find up those steps?'

Diamond told him and played the trump card he'd saved for this. 'So we've got two crime scenes. Who do you want up there?'

Gull hesitated.

'Between ourselves,' Diamond said, 'Polehampton doesn't fill me with confidence. I already have a top detective at the scene briefed to interview possible witnesses.'

'Who's that?'

'DI Halliwell.'

'Halliwell can carry on,' Gull said as if he'd known Halliwell all his life. 'Would you oversee it? I need Polehampton down here.'

'If you insist,' Diamond said, suppressing the smirk that wanted to appear.

* * *

All this climbing of steps would either make him a fit man or bring on a coronary. Back at the house in the Paragon, Keith Halliwell had already singled out a key witness. 'I think you should speak to her yourself, guv. She opened the door to Ken Lockton and he wasn't alone as we supposed.'

'I'll definitely speak to her.'

'I'd better warn you. She's not the sharpest knife in the drawer.'

She was the tenant of the ground floor, a cello-shaped blonde of around twenty called Sherry Meredith. She'd made up—eyes, lips, the works—and was in white jeans and a low-cut black top with glittery bits that seemed out of place before eight in the morning. In matters of fashion Diamond was way behind the times.

'They called really early when I was still in bed,' she said. 'I buzzed them in.'

She already had his full attention, and not for how she looked or what she was wearing. 'Trusting.'

'I wouldn't have, except they said they were police and when I looked there was a police car outside.'

'You said "they".'

'Yes. Two of them.'

'Are you sure? In uniform?'

She frowned. 'I don't know.'

'Of course you know.'

'I didn't know what they were wearing. I know now, but I didn't when I looked out of the window. All I could see was the car. I'm trying to be truthful.'

He nodded, accepting the logic. He wished he

hadn't asked. 'After you buzzed them in, you saw the uniforms?'

She had to think about that. 'Yes. The one who did the talking is the man they just carried out on the stretcher. The other one was a sergeant. Three stripes on his arm—would that be right?'

His patience was being stretched. He nodded. 'Did you find out the sergeant's name?'

'If he mentioned it, I didn't take it in. I was still in pyjamas, not made up or anything.'

'What does that have to do with it?'

'It's embarrassing. How would you feel if you were me? I'm telling you why I couldn't think of much else.'

'Can you remember what the inspector said?'

'You're joking.'

'Do I look as if I'm joking? Try. It's important.'

'I told you I was in my pyjamas.'

'Miss Meredith—'

'Sherry.'

'Sherry, I've never believed those stories about dumb blondes. I can tell you're a smart girl. We need to know. He must have had some questions for you.'

The flattery worked. 'He asked me who lived in the flat downstairs.'

'And?'

'He called it the basement. I told him it's the garden flat.'

'Go on.'

'I said it was empty, been empty for years. He goes: have you heard any sounds from down there and I'm, like, no, nothing. Then he asks me the way down and I tell him about the stairs in the hall. That was it. Oh, and he said to lock my door.'

'I expect you watched what was happening from your back window.'

She blushed and ran the tip of her tongue around her lips.

'Understandable,' he said to relax her. 'Anyone would.'

'They pushed through the weeds to the far end where you can see down into the street.'

'And then?'

'They were talking.'

'For long?'

'Not long. They seemed to be arguing. The sergeant looked kind of, well, miffed, if you know what I mean. He came back through the flat and drove off in the police car.'

'Alone?'

'Yes.'

'You're sure? Did you actually see him get in the car and drive off?'

Her cheeks reddened again. 'From my front room.'

'So you moved from the back of the house to the front to see what was going on? And then?'

'Nothing. When I looked out the back again, the boss man wasn't in sight.'

Inwardly, he was cursing. She'd missed being a key witness to the assault on Ken Lockton. 'What did you do—go back to bed?'

'No, I wouldn't have got to sleep again after an experience like that. I showered and got dressed.'

He'd coaxed about as much as he was likely to get from Sherry Meredith. 'Who lives above you?'

'Mr and Mrs Murphy. They're old.'

'And above them?'

'Mr Willis, some kind of civil servant.'

'How long have the old people lived here?'

'Since it was built, I reckon.'

'About 1800?'

She giggled. 'I could be wrong about that. A long time, for sure. They know everything about the place. They're lovely, the sweetest people you could hope to have as neighbours. They take things in for me when I'm at work.' Her eyes widened. 'Oh, no, I've just remembered.'

'Something important?'

'I have a Sunday job at Waitrose. Will I be allowed to go soon?'

'A job doing what?' He couldn't picture her coping with the checkout.

'Round the back, preparing chickens for the spit.'

'And what do you do in the week?'

'Cosmetics—in Jolly's.'

Out in the street in front of the Paragon, he briefed the scene of crime team who had just arrived and were getting into their blue protective suits. The vacant flat had to be gone over in case the sniper had spent time there. And there were two possible incidents in the garden to investigate. First, he suspected the sniper had been there and fired from the railing at the end. The spent cartridge cases might well be waiting to be found. In addition, he hoped for powder residue that might be used in evidence. Second, some time after the shooting, Ken Lockton had been hit over the head and there ought to be traces of his attacker and possibly the implement he'd used.

The CSI team leader was confident of results until he saw the state of the garden. He commented that it looked as if a tank regiment had been through pursued by a herd of buffalo.

Diamond wasn't in a mood to smile. 'Come on—it's no size. It's a postage stamp.'

'A well-franked postage stamp.'

He turned away, shaking his head.

Keith Halliwell came down from interviewing the sweet old couple, the Murphys. They'd slept through everything until the firearms unit went through their flat. Hadn't heard the shooting, or the sirens. The presence of four heavily armed men at their door had come as a strong surprise. The armed officers had failed to get across the reason for their visit. Sweet old Mr Murphy kept a shillelagh behind the door. He'd bruised a few legs, he claimed. Probably the firearms lads were ashamed to admit to the assault.

The old couple could be ruled out as principal witnesses, but they had intriguing information about the civil servant who lived above them. Sean Willis had occupied the top flat for two years. He worked in the Ministry of Defence and belonged to a gun club in Devizes.

This had to be followed up fast.

'We'll see him together,' Diamond told Halliwell.

They marched straight into Willis's flat. There was splintered wood where the door had been forced. 'Anyone about?'

The tenant was slow in answering and when he did he was unwelcoming. 'Who do you think you are, invading my home?' Thirtyish, tall, lean, tanned, and with a black ponytail, Sean Willis wasn't the popular image of a civil servant. Sunday gear for him was a sleeveless black top and matching chinos.

Diamond told him who they were.

'That doesn't give you the right to walk in here without so much as a by your leave. I've taken photos.'

'Of what?' Diamond asked.

'The evidence.'

'Are you telling us you have evidence in here?'

'Of the wreckage after your heavy mob went through my flat.'

Diamond said in a few sharp words that a police officer had been murdered and he was making no apologies for the armed search. 'For all we knew, the killer could have been in here with a gun at your head.'

'In which case, I'd be dead by now,' Willis said. 'Your people weren't exactly subtle. The way they burst in would put the frighteners on anyone.'

'Leave it,' Diamond said through his teeth. 'We've work to do. I'd like to see the view from the back of the flat.'

'And I'd like you to witness the damage they did, because I fully intend to sue.'

Inside, the reason for Willis's outrage became more clear. He was a compulsive personality. The place was tidy to the point of obsession. It would have been immaculate before the armed response unit went through. Pictures and mirrors shone. Books were displayed according to size and colour, magazines stacked like a deck of playing cards on a shining glass table. The carpets must have been vacuumed the previous evening. All this made the open cupboards and their avalanche of contents spread across the floor, clearly dragged out by the gun team searching for the sniper or his weapon, look more of an outrage than it was.

Diamond wasn't being sidetracked. The windows

that interested him were at the back of the house, with original sash frames, two in the sitting room and one in the bedroom. All three would provide a direct line of sight to the stretch of Walcot Street where Harry Tasker had been shot. He checked the sitting-room windows and—as you would expect with such a fastidious owner—each moved so well it could be raised with one finger on the brass fitting.

The bedroom looked like a hotel room after the maid had been through, everything folded and in place. Except that the lower section of the window was pushed up.

'Why is this open?'

Willis said as if to a child, 'Airing the room.'

'Anyone airing the room would pull the top window down. You were watching what was going on.'

'That's no crime.'

'Did you hear the shooting?'

'I'm a heavy sleeper. The first I knew was all the sirens going. Shops, ambulance, police cars. They'd have woken anybody.'

'Were you conscious at any time of other people in the house?'

Willis rolled his eyes upwards. 'These are apartments. Other people live here.'

'Unusual sounds?'

'No.'

'You're a marksman, I heard.'

He hesitated. 'Who told you that?'

'Is it true?'

'Shooting is a hobby of mine, yes. Competition shooting.'

'What are we talking here—a rifle?'

'Mainly.'

'So you own one?'

'Three, in point of fact.'

Diamond kept the same even tone of voice. 'Where do you keep them?'

'Not here. That would really play into the hands of you people wanting a quick arrest.'

'I'm ignoring that remark,' Diamond said. 'Answer my question, please.'

'Under lock and key in my club at Devizes, twenty miles' drive, whichever route you choose.'

Keep the pressure on, Diamond decided. This man isn't as calm as he wants to appear. 'You have a car, then? Where is it?'

'Where I left it, I hope, in Beehive Yard.'

'Key, please.'

'I don't think you have the right.'

'If we aren't given the key, Mr Willis, I'll tell you what we do have—a small spring-loaded device that smashes car windows.'

The threat of more damage to his property was too much for the over-particular civil servant. He handed across the key and volunteered the make, colour and registration.

As a gun owner living in this house with a sight of the street, Willis had to be treated as a suspect. If he had the means and opportunity, his motives could be probed later. Who could say what was motivating the Somerset Sniper to pick off his victims? Contempt for the police? A personal grudge? The power thing you get from handling a precision weapon? Or was it just boredom from shooting on a range? A live quarry was a different challenge from paper targets.

'Have you lived here long?'

'Just over two years.'

'And you're in the civil service, I was told. Ministry of Defence.'

He glared. 'You've been talking to my neighbours.'

'Is it top secret, then, your work?'

'Not at all. I'm an office worker. I don't like being talked about, that's all.'

'Do the talking yourself, then. You're single?'

'Yes. It is allowed.'

Diamond waited for more, and eventually got it.

'In case you're wondering, I do have women friends, and they sometimes stay the night, and that's allowed too, even in the Paragon.'

'Were you sleeping alone last night?'

'Unfortunately, yes. But I expect you got that already from my talkative neighbours.'

'Actually, no. There was no gossip.'

'Otherwise I'm a model of respectability, educated at Sherborne and Oxford, a non-smoker, vegetarian, church-goer and I serve the community as a teller at elections.'

'Where did you learn to shoot?'

'The school rifle club, along with most of my contemporaries. It's not unusual in public schools.'

'He's smooth and he's smart,' Diamond said to Halliwell on the way down the stone steps. 'I don't expect to find anything in the car, but some of his prints will come in useful.'

CHAPTER FOUR

Any policeman will tell you the worst duty of all is informing the next of kin. Traditionally the young bobby straight out of training gets the job and his more experienced colleagues tell themselves they had their turn when they were recruits and can delegate with clear consciences.

Peter Diamond bucked the tradition. Years ago as a fresh-faced rookie in the Met he'd served his rites of passage, knocking on a door in Hammersmith to inform an elderly couple that their only son had been killed in a hit and run. In those days you were given no advice how to break the news. You improvised as well as you could. With mixed results. He'd done it ineptly. The parents had assumed the worst when they saw him in uniform solemn-faced at the door, yet, after repeatedly rehearsing what he would say, he'd stumbled over the words and—sin of sins—got the name of the deceased wrong, calling him Mike when he should have said Mark. 'That isn't our son,' the man had said, clutching at any straw. Diamond had been forced to stumble through his piece again, causing even more distress. That night he'd drunk himself legless. The memory was still vivid and painful. He'd resolved never to ask an inexperienced officer to do the job.

In the near-panic after the Walcot Street shooting, with every available officer called to the scene, no one had visited Harry Tasker's next of kin. The thing had to be done urgently, before the story broke in the media.

Others may have thought of it and kept quiet. Diamond was the first to speak out.

The uniformed sergeant he raised it with said, 'God, yes. We should have done this an hour ago. I'd better find someone.'

'Do we know who the next of kin is? Was he

married?'

'Married, yes, or in a partnership for sure. He lived near the old gasworks off the Upper Bristol Road.'

'I pass there on the way to work,' Diamond said. 'Is there anyone on the strength who would know the partner?'

'Unlikely. Harry was a quiet guy. A bit of a loner, in fact. We'll just have to send one of the young lads he worked with.'

'We won't.'

'No?'

'Get me the address. I'll break the news. I've done this before.'

His part of the investigation was on hold. Each of the potential witnesses in the Paragon house had been seen and Keith Halliwell was interviewing the neighbours. Until the search of the basement flat and garden was complete, little else could happen. Nothing would be gained from standing over the crime scene investigators.

* * *

The Upper Bristol Road is busy, dirty and noisy and has some oddly named addresses, like Comfortable Place, which has the look of an almshouse and actually houses a fitness centre. Just behind Comfortable Place stands Onega Terrace, where Harry Tasker lived. The row of small houses has a view from the back of the last remaining gasholder of the old Bath Gas, Light and Coke Company, a mighty drum in its supporting framework with a majesty all its own. It was 140 years old. Diamond often passed it and marvelled at the way it had rusted to an umber shade not unlike the stone for which Bath was famous. But not everyone appreciates industrial architecture so close to home, so the proximity of this giant relic must have depressed house prices and made it possible for a constable on Harry's modest income to pay the rent. The seven houses of the terrace, built probably in the 1890s, were accessed along a narrow pathway blocked with refuse sacks on the day Diamond arrived. Each house had its own bay window and most of them had satellite dishes.

Her name was Emma, he had learned from the office, and yes, they were married. She was Harry Tasker's wife turned widow, a change of status she had yet to find out. She came to the door in a red zipper jacket and jeans, in the act of wheeling out a bike. She was small, with large, intelligent eyes and shoulder-length black hair. 'I'm sorry, but you've chosen the wrong moment, whoever you are,' she told him. 'I'm on my way out. And I'm already late.'

She had probably taken him for a doorstep evangelist. Not many other callers wear suits and ties.

'It's about Harry,' he said. 'I work with him.' He showed his ID. 'May we go inside?'

The colour drained from her face. 'Something's the matter.'

He nodded.

She leaned the bike against the wall of the hallway and stepped back for him to enter. 'Tell me.'

'You'd better sit down first.'

Shaking her head as if she didn't believe this was happening, she opened a door into a small living room and sat on the edge of a short leather sofa.

The homely setting, the wedding photo and the family pictures over the fireplace made the task of breaking the news all the harder.

'He's dead, isn't he?' she said.

He nodded. 'I wish there was a gentler way of telling you. It was very sudden, early this morning while he was still on duty.'

'How?'

'He won't have known anything about it. He was shot.'

She took a sharp breath and didn't speak. She blinked several times and her front teeth pressed down on her lower lip. A shock as terrible as this takes people in different ways. Emma Tasker was internalising it.

What can you do to ease the agony for the suddenly, violently bereaved? Diamond's way was to fill the silence with information. 'We've got every available officer hunting for the gunman. It happened about 4 a.m. in Walcot Street, at the end nearest the city centre, two or three shots from high up when Harry was on his way back from checking one of the clubs. There had been no reports of trouble. This seems to have been unprovoked. Take it from me, ma'am, we'll find the scum who did this. You know how we feel when one of our own is murdered.' As his words tailed off, he watched her, prepared for an outpouring of grief.

It didn't come. She was silent, immobile.

Some seconds went by.

'Do you have any brandy in the house?' he asked.

He could have saved his breath.

'Whisky?' he said. 'Sometimes it can help. Or I can make tea. How about tea?'

No reaction. Her brown eyes could have been

painted, they were so still, so inscrutable.

'I'll shut up, while you take it in,' he said, easing a finger around his collar, remembering his own darkest moment. The difference was that when Steph had been murdered, he'd found out for himself. He'd attended a crime scene and had the unendurable shock of discovering that the victim was his own wife. It had all been so traumatic he still didn't have any memory of how he had reacted. One thing he did recall from the days that followed: no one had been capable of comforting him.

Would it be any different for Emma Tasker? He guessed you couldn't generalise.

If she had screamed, or fainted, or burst into tears, he would have coped better. He was in two minds whether to find the kitchen and make mild, sweet tea, that old remedy. He didn't dare leave her at this moment. Instead, he turned and looked out of the window, waiting for whatever would happen next, be it an eruption of grief or a quiet request for him to leave.

Minutes passed.

The phone rang. It was on a low table beside the sofa. Automatically Emma Tasker put out a hand.

Diamond moved fast across the room. 'Leave it,' he said, his hand closing over hers as she reached for the receiver. 'This will be the press.'

The contact brought a response from her, one he didn't expect. Her eyes blazed hostility. 'Don't touch me.'

'Sorry.' He withdrew his hand.

The ringing stopped.

She rubbed at the back of her hand as if his touch had been contagious.

'I didn't want you picking it up,' he said.

'*You* didn't want?' She was angry, galvanised. 'You think you have the right to tell me what to do? This is my home. It's my phone.'

'True.'

The simple argument about the phone was the tipping point. She vented all the anger she'd been suppressing and Diamond took the full force. 'You bastard! You come in here and flash your warrant card at me and tell me the worst thing I could hear and then you expect me to jump to your commands. Mister, you don't impress me at all. I don't care if you're the chief constable. I could spit in your eye. I've only got to look at you to know you sit behind a desk ordering good men like my Harry out on the streets at night dealing with drug dealers and drunks and gang members.'

No use telling her he was CID and Harry was uniform. Her ferocity wasn't amenable to reason. Better let this storm blow itself out.

She continued with the rant. 'He never got any credit for all the policing he did. He would have stayed a constable for ever. People like Harry don't get promoted. They do their work and all the overtime keeping the streets safe without complaining while the creeps and arse-lickers put all their energy into sucking up to the likes of you. I know what I'm talking about. I was in the force for three years until I couldn't stand it any more. That's how we met. Are you a Freemason?'

'No, ma'am.'

She wasn't listening. 'The Brotherhood, he called it. Great if you're a member. He was never asked. He wouldn't have joined, anyway. He had principles.' She glanced at the wedding photo on the wall showing a tight-lipped Harry standing rigidly to attention beside herself, his radiant, smiling bride. 'Did you know him?'

'Not well,' Diamond was forced to admit. 'I work from a different office.'

'Don't you listen? He didn't work in an office,' she almost screamed at him. 'He was pounding the streets while you had your feet up. Why the hell did they send you if you hardly knew him?'

'No one sent me. I volunteered to come.'

'That beats everything,' she said. 'What—do you get a kick out of giving bad news to people?'

In this situation the bereaved can say whatever they want and there's no comeback.

He shook his head. 'I'm here because I know what you're going through. Four years ago my wife was shot and murdered in Victoria Park.'

She gave a sharp, impatient sigh. 'I've got my own cross to bear. I can't find sympathy for you.'

'I'm not asking for any,' he said.

'I hate the bloody police and all they stand for.'

'There are times when I'd agree with you. Look, I really think you should drink something. You've had a terrific shock. Shall I make tea?'

She stabbed a finger at him. 'Don't even think about stepping into my kitchen.'

He'd not expected hostility like this. She'd taken against him and nothing he could do or say would alter that. The only way now was to find someone she was willing to relate to. Then think of an exit line.

'Is there anyone you'd like me to contact? A neighbour? A friend? I'm thinking somebody should be with you.'

Those fierce brown eyes rejected the suggestion outright, but she relented enough to say, 'Someone should tell them I won't be in for work.'

An opening. He went for it. 'Fine. Where is it? What's the number?'

She was a supervisor at Playzone, the children's activity centre, she told him before giving the details. He couldn't help wondering how small kids fared with this pent-up aggression. Maybe she was totally different with them. He called the place and said Mrs Tasker had suffered the loss of a close relative and might not be in for a few days. When he finished the call she was no longer in the room.

He heard a kettle being filled, so he followed her into the kitchen, defying her order to keep out. She had her back to him yet she must have heard his approach because without turning to look she said, 'I'm just so angry. He's been on nights all week. We've scarcely seen each other.'

'And there are things you wish you'd said?' He was speaking from painful experience.

'I feel cheated.'

'You have every right. Believe me, we'll pull out all the stops.'

She snorted at that. 'If you want sugar, it's in the cupboard behind you.'

While this embodiment of fury busied herself with milk carton and teapot, Diamond was bold enough to seek information. He asked if Harry had been threatened by anyone, recently or in the past.

'Apart from me, you mean?' she said without a glimmer of irony. 'I gave him hell on a regular basis. No, he was too easy-going to make enemies. Mind, he didn't tell me everything. Harry wasn't much of a communicator. He kept his feelings hidden. If I asked about his job, he'd say there wasn't anything worth mentioning.'

'I don't have to tell you police work is like that a lot of the time,' Diamond said. 'Loads of boring stuff you wouldn't want to hear about.'

'You don't get it, do you, bloody man?' she said, widening her big eyes. 'Anything is better than silence.'

Lady, you're going to get a lot of that in the weeks and months to come, he thought. 'I'm asking these questions because we have to be certain he wasn't shot by someone he knew.'

'He was killed by that madman who's been targeting policemen, wasn't he?' she said. 'I've forgotten what they call him.'

'The Somerset Sniper. That's a strong possibility. If so, it was almost certainly done because Harry wore the uniform, nothing more. He was a cop, so he was fair game. Doesn't make it any easier to accept.'

'To come back to your question, I can't think of anyone who hated him enough to kill him.'

'Did he have any interests outside the police?'

'Fishing.'

He took this as another rebuke. 'I'm doing my job. We need to know.'

'I said. He fished, with a rod and line. Is that clear enough for you?'

He gave a faint, embarrassed smile.

She added, 'He didn't get much time for it.'

'You must have gone out together sometimes. Where did you go? A favourite pub?'

'You've got to be joking. If we went out more than twice in the past year I can't recall it. All he ever wanted was to put his feet up and watch telly. It was the job. It tired him out. If I go out, it has to be with the girls, my buddies. That's all the excitement I get.'

'This being a murder enquiry, you're going to have to put up with any number of questions like these. We'll need to look at everything connected with Harry, bank statements, phone, address book, diary, computer. It's a huge invasion of your privacy, but necessary. I'm telling you this so that you're prepared.'

'You're not,' she said. 'You're telling me so that the copper who gets the job doesn't get the blasting you've just had. You're shell-shocked. You look worse than I do.'

* * *

Whatever his condition, he needed to drive into the city again. On the car radio the local news reports were coming in of the fatal shooting of a uniformed policeman in Walcot Street and they were linking it to the two previous shootings. He'd completed his next-of-kin mission in the nick of time, even though it hadn't been the sympathetic heart-to-heart he'd planned. He'd left Emma Tasker in the care of a policewoman trained in helping the bereaved. She would surely cope better than he had. Next-of-kin interviews were never easy, but that one had shaken his confidence. He didn't have time to dwell on it. Soon the media tsunami would swamp everyone. Good thing Jack Gull was in charge.

In the Paragon, the house-to-house was under way. Keith Halliwell had finished interviewing the close neighbours and nobody had spotted the sniper. Some had reacted to the sound of the shooting by going to their windows. So thick and high had been the crop of weeds that a gang of gunmen could have operated from that garden and not been seen.

'Getting on for five hours since the shooting,' Diamond said to Halliwell. 'If he's got any sense he'll be miles away by now.'

'Unless he lives here.'

'Right. What's your take on that civil servant, three-gun Willis on the top floor?'

'In the clear. His licence has been checked. Each of those rifles is registered. The Devizes gun club confirms that all three are in their armoury, secure. There's no way he could have used one this morning and got it back to Devizes by the time we interviewed him.'

'An unlicensed gun?'

'If there is one, we didn't find it. His flat was well searched.'

'He wouldn't have it in his flat after using it, would he? He's a careful bugger. Willis is still top of my list. That bedroom window.'

Halliwell gave a faint grin. 'If he's as careful as you say, he wouldn't have left the window open. The thing is, he may be nicely placed to have carried out this morning's shooting from his bedroom, but what about the earlier killings in Wells and Radstock?'

'Trust you to sabotage a good theory.'

* * *

Diamond went through the house to the garden and stopped short of the stinging nettles. 'Any joy?' he called to the senior crime scene man.

For an answer, a transparent evidence-bag was held up. Whatever was inside was too small to make out.

'What is it?'

'A cartridge case. A shot was definitely fired from here.'

'Only the one?'

'I'm told two were heard. He could have tidied up the first and missed this one. He's usually more careful. Now we're checking the brambles for fibres. It's going to take some time.'

'Rather you than me. Good find, though.' He stared up at the top flat, where Willis lived. A shell case ejected from that height could have dropped anywhere in the small garden. And that window was now closed.

* * *

Out in the street, a patrol car joined the row of parked police vehicles just as Diamond emerged from the house. A uniformed sergeant got out, spotted him and shouted, 'Mr Diamond, sir.'

The big man waited with arms folded.

The sergeant looked like a man who has been told he has a terminal illness. 'Sergeant Stillman, sir.'

'I know who you are,' Diamond said. 'Is there news?'

'I thought I'd better speak to you. I just heard about Inspector Lockton being injured.'

'You're the last, then. We found him all of two hours ago.'

'It's serious, isn't it?'

'Serious enough to have put him in intensive care. He took a blow to the head. What's your interest in all this?'

'I drove him up here.'

'This morning?' Diamond's attention quickened. 'You must be the second man.'

'Must I?'

'A young blonde woman in pyjamas opened the door to Ken Lockton and a mysterious sergeant in uniform. If that was you, you can't have forgotten.'

'That was me, yes.'

'Where have you been all this time?'

'Asleep in the car, I'm sorry to say.'

'Sleeping on duty while a full-scale alert is going on?'

'Technically, yes.'

'What do you mean "technically"?'

'Ken Lockton dismissed me, so I drove back to Walcot Street and parked by the barrier for a short nap. That was the intention. I was flaked out from night duty.'

'Let's rerun this from the start. How come you teamed up with Lockton?'

'Pure chance, sir. He caught my eye in Walcot Street when he had his idea. He told me to drive him up here because he reckoned the shooting must have come from this direction. We buzzed a couple of doors and he was interested in this house because the basement flat wasn't occupied. The blonde in pyjamas let us in. He asked me to force the basement door.'

'That was you?'

'My big foot. We went through the empty flat and found the rifle in the garden.'

The hairs rose on the back of Diamond's neck. 'What rifle?'

'The sniper rifle propped against the railings at the end. You must have found it by now.'

A slow shake of the head. 'You'd better describe it.'

'I don't know much about them. Black. About this length. Telescopic sight, I think. A box-type magazine that curved a bit. We didn't touch it, sir. Kept our distance. Ken Lockton was chuffed to find it. I remember saying if I was the gunman I wouldn't leave it there. I'd come back for it. Ken agreed and said it gave us a chance to nab him. He was raring to go. Then I reminded him that our car was still in the street out front—something he hadn't thought of.'

'Advertising your presence?'

'Exactly. He instructed me to drive back to Walcot Street. I asked if he wanted armed back-up and he said if he did he'd use his own radio.'

'You didn't report any of this?'

'Ken was the SIO at the time—before anyone more senior got there—and he made it very clear he intended to make the arrest himself.'

'He wanted the glory?'

'He didn't use those words.'

'But that was your understanding?'

Stillman nodded.

'Is this the first time you've mentioned it to anyone? Does Chief Superintendent Gull know any of this?'

'Not yet.' He blushed scarlet at the prospect. 'Should I . . . ?'

'Get some proper sleep, in a bed. I'll fill him in.'

Diamond had some sympathy now he'd heard the tale. If anyone was to blame for what had happened, it was Ken Lockton, and he'd paid heavily for his overambition. Presumably the gunman had been nearby when the police arrived, hiding in the basement or the garden, and had attacked Lockton from behind. True, it would have been helpful to have known for sure about the gun two hours ago, but in the bigger picture it might not matter.

But give Lockton his due, he thought: his theory had been correct.

Diamond's own pet theory—that Willis fired the shots from his bedroom window—now felt less appealing than it had a few minutes ago. Maybe the civil servant had preferred a closer range from the end of the garden. The problem with this was that leaving the murder weapon propped against the railing didn't chime with Willis's fastidious character.

The time for theorising ended. Keith Halliwell sprinted towards Diamond. 'Radio message from Jack Gull. A suspect has been sighted. There's a stake-out in Becky Addy Wood.'

'What am I supposed to do about it?'

'He wants you with him. He's about to leave.'

CHAPTER FIVE

'This is the breakthrough. I feel it in my bones,' Jack Gull told Diamond, seated in the back of a BMW response car with lights flashing, siren periodically screaming, as it powered over a mighty hill known as Brassknocker, the quick way out of Bath to Avoncliff and Becky Addy Wood.

'Bully for you,' Diamond said. All he could feel in his bones was the lurch of the suspension on the winding roads. What was going on in his stomach mattered more to him. He hated being driven fast. Embarrassing, in his job. A few of his team knew of this frailty. Gull did not.

'I heard about the cartridge case being recovered,' Gull said, expecting a businesslike exchange of their findings, even at this speed. 'And we picked up one of the discharged bullets. Would you believe it was lying in six inches of silt at the bottom of a drain? I guess it bounced off the wall into the gutter and dropped out of sight.'

'It's gone for examination, has it?'

'Don't get your hopes up. It impacted with stone and is well mangled. If nothing else, ballistics should be able to tell us which kind of rifle he used. It sounds like a semi-automatic again.'

'The rifle. I must tell you about that,' Diamond said and was forced to go silent again as a field to his left reared up like a tidal wave, threatening to tip a flock of sheep on to them. Coming down Brassknocker the contours were fearsome.

'Go ahead. I'm listening.'

By fixing his gaze on the driver's headrest, he regained a measure of self-control. Staccato-style, he reported the gist of what he'd heard from Sergeant Stillman. He left out plenty, including how and when the information had reached him.

So when Gull said, 'What a tosser,' he meant Ken Lockton.

It seemed fair enough that Lockton took all the blame. His ego trip had ruined a real chance of catching the sniper.

'Do we have ballistics evidence from the earlier shootings?' Diamond managed to say.

'Yep. Some of the bullets hit soft earth and were in good enough shape to check the rifling,' Gull said. 'No cartridge cases. Usually he's careful to pick them up. He uses a Heckler and Koch G36, same as the police-issue weapon.'

'That's rich, killing our people with one of our own guns.'

'There are thousands out there.'

'As many as that?'

'They've been manufactured since the nineteen-nineties. It's the frontline assault rifle of the German army and several of the NATO countries. Are you armed?'

'Right now, you mean?' Diamond admitted he was not.

Gull shook his head in disbelief that anyone could be so ill-prepared. 'Bad move. This guy is a cop-killer.'

'Good move actually. No one would be safe if I had a gun in my hand.'

'Even so, you should be wearing body armour. It's a good thing I have a spare set in the boot. Pity you're not armed, though.'

Diamond was starting to wonder if he should have come at all.

'No sweat,' Gull added. 'We'll have the Wiltshire armed response lads in support.'

'That's all right, then,' Diamond said. The car briefly became airborne going over a hump in the road. 'Strewth!' With a supreme effort to sound untroubled, he came out with a question worthy of a job interview. 'When did you first get involved in this operation?'

'After the Radstock shooting, when it was obvious we had a serial sniper murdering policemen.'

'Is the MO similar in each case?' He had an

inbuilt dislike of abbreviations, but at high speed the Latin was too much of a mouthful.

'Same fucking gun, never mind the MO,' Gull said. 'The rifling on the bullets is identical. But, yes, he likes to get to a high position and lie in wait. In Wells, he used a kids' tree house overlooking the street. In Radstock, he was on some scaffolding up the side of a new building.'

'Fingerprints?'

Gull shook his head. 'He's a careful bastard.'

'Obviously a planner.'

'Has to be. Not only does he find a good vantage point, it must be a street where one of our boys is on foot patrol. He must suss out the location days if not weeks ahead.'

'But any copper will do as the target?'

'That's become obvious. We researched the backgrounds of PCs Hart and Richmond, the first two victims, and there's no reason anyone would want to kill them for who they were.'

'No connection between them?'

Gull shook his head. 'It's mindless carnage, no different really from IEDs.'

After the mention of the MO, Gull must have thought Diamond was up with all abbreviations.

'IEDs?'

'Roadside bombs.'

'Got you.'

They'd almost finished the rollercoaster descent down Brassknocker. The traffic lights ahead for the A36 were on red. Their driver gave a blast on the siren, veered into the oncoming lane, swung right and joined the main road.

The straight stretch ahead was no relief for frazzled nerves, just a chance to pick up speed.

'So what's the thinking?' Diamond asked over the surge in revs.

'About the killer?'

'His motive.'

'He must hate us. Some bad experience in the past.'

'I expect you checked recent releases from prison.'

'You bet. And not just Erlestoke, Pucklechurch and Horfield. The whole goddamn country. An embittered ex-con would be the prime suspect. Too bad no one fits.'

'Unless he got out years ago and it was festering all this time.'

Gull looked away, out of the window. 'You're a real comfort. How could we possibly know that?'

The road ahead was mercifully free of traffic, a steep climb up a stretch overhung with tall trees. The engine needed a lower gear and Diamond recovered enough to say, 'Another angle would be the trigger-happy young hoodlum out to impress his mates.'

'You're not telling me anything.'

'I'll save my breath, then.'

'Trust me, some good minds are working on this. We're using a profiler.'

'What for?' He'd had enough of Gull's putdowns.

'Don't you believe in them?'

'I believe in them. I've met them.'

'This one is on the Home Office list. He's good. He suggested possible areas where the sniper might live.'

'Like midway between Wells and Radstock? Say, Chilcompton?'

Jack Gull turned to glare at Diamond. 'How did

you know that?'

'You only have to look at a map. I'm not a big fan of geographical profiling. I was reading about a serial killer in America who had the profilers going spare. Each time they settled on a location, he popped up somewhere they hadn't thought of. Turned out he had a motor home.'

Gull wasn't amused. 'I believe in using all the help going. If you can come up with a theory, I'll even listen to you.'

'What if the killer was one of our own, then?'

Another glare. 'A cop, you mean?'

'A bad apple. I've met a few.'

'He'd have to be psychotic.'

'Are you saying the sniper isn't? An evil cop would know how to get hold of that police-issue sniper rifle you mentioned. And he'd have inside knowledge of local foot patrols.'

They were still climbing steadily, and now overtaking all the way. Diamond was thinking it only wanted one dozy truck driver coming towards them and three more of Avon and Somerset's finest would join the list of dead.

'The bad-cop theory was raised at one of our brainstorming sessions,' Gull said. 'Personally, I don't buy it. If he was picking off hard bastards like you and me, maybe, but these were foot soldiers killed because of where they were, not who.'

'All right,' Diamond said. 'Try this for size. It's rare, but not unknown: the guy fixated on guns and killing.'

'Yeah?'

'He isn't content with bagging rabbits and pheasants. He kills with the indifference of a marksman hitting clay pigeons. It's his sport. He's out of his mind, but that's how he sees it, picking off policemen.'

After a pause, Gull said, 'Wild.'

'Too wild?'

Gull shrugged. 'It's one we haven't talked about, I'll give you.'

They left the A36 at the top of the hill and swung left. In a few hundred yards it was white-knuckle time again, one of those West Country lanes no wider than the car and without passing spaces. High hedges added to the claustrophobia. On went the siren.

Soon after, the lane opened up to a street with terraced cottages and a few parked cars.

The driver said, 'Almost there, gentlemen. Hold on. It gets a little hairy going down to Avoncliff. They use it for motocross.'

A bend that was a virtual hairpin started them down the scarp of the Limpley Stoke valley and into Becky Addy Wood. Grit-bins at intervals testified to the steepness. The road surface was potholed and the wood so dense that headlights were needed. Mercifully they didn't have far to go before reaching a glade where a number of police vehicles were parked.

It was bliss to get out. Diamond's legs felt unsteady, his arms ached from being flexed, but his stomach rejoiced.

Someone yelled, 'Why isn't that man wearing body armour?'

'Does he mean me?'

Jack Gull opened the car boot and handed Diamond the protective jacket and helmet. 'As you're not armed you'd better not get close to the action.'

'Are we expecting some?'

'That's why we're here. Shots were heard from the woods over the last couple of days. Not unusual in these parts, but this isn't shotgun fire. This scumbag uses bullets. A tree was used for target practice.'

Two people-carriers delivered more coppers for the stake-out, all in their protective Kevlar jackets. Most were from the Wiltshire force, for the wood was just across the county border, a remnant of the ancient Selwood Forest which had stretched from Chippenham to Cerne Abbas, fifty miles south on the Dorset Downs. The air of excitement was tempered by the sight of the terrain, dark and difficult to penetrate. This would be no walk in the park.

Gull made himself known to the local chief inspector directing the operation and made it clear he wasn't aiming to take over. 'Treat Mr Diamond and me the same as any other members of your team.'

Diamond doubted if that was a wise offer.

In a few minutes the small army, about forty of them, drew close to get instructions. Barely forty minutes ago, the chief inspector told them, an Avoncliff resident walking her dog had seen a figure in black running through the wood with a rifle. In view of the reports of gunfire in recent days and bullets embedded in trees she'd phoned the police. Becky Addy Wood had good possibilities as a hideout for the Somerset Sniper.

A few officers had gone ahead to scout the area where the gunman had been seen. Cordons had been set up at the obvious escape points. The entire wood was not large—barely two hundred yards across and half a mile in length—but difficult. For a start, it was on a steep escarpment of the Avon valley. Little had been done to manage the dense woodland except clearing the rutted motocross tracks. Thick scrub and fallen and rotting timber was everywhere. In places the search party would be knee-deep in leaf mould. As if that were not enough, the remains of a stone quarry were sited at the near end. A tramway had once delivered the precious limestone blocks down the steep gradient and across the Avoncliff aqueduct to a wharf where they were dressed and loaded on to barges and transported along the Kennet and Avon canal. Little of this industrial history was visible any longer. The trees, blackthorn and nettles had taken over. But hidden blocks of stone and open mine workings presented extra hazards.

The searchers were to spread out across the strip and advance slowly from west to east looking for signs of recent activity, in particular small fires, encampments and evidence of shooting. At any point if they sighted the suspect, they were to take cover at the nearest available place.

'No problem,' Gull said to Diamond.

'Hitting the ground, you mean?'

'Finding some cover. All these fucking trees.'

'It is a wood,' Diamond said.

'I hate them. I could take a chainsaw to them.'

Diamond quite liked trees usually and they were here in variety, oak, beech, larch, fir, pine and spruce. Unfortunately many were dead. The place had a neglected look. Maybe Gull was right and some felling was wanted.

Staying upright would be a challenge. The body armour made him top-heavy, a novel experience for him. The ceramic shield inside the Kevlar padding was like a ton weight. Still, it could be a life-saver. The pockets at the front contained helpful items including a torch, a taser and, not to be thought about, a personal first aid kit, for use by medics if he was injured.

He and Gull were side by side, twenty feet apart, in the line that presently started a slow rake through the wood. He had mixed feelings about this search. It was difficult to understand why the sniper would have thought it necessary to hide in Becky Addy Wood when no one knew what he looked like. Instead of skulking in this godforsaken place, he could have taken tea in the Pump Room without any risk of being recognised provided he tucked the gun out of sight.

'Where's the tree?' he called to Jack Gull.

'What do you mean—"the tree"?'

He'd touched that raw nerve again. 'The tree he's supposed to have used for target practice.'

'Why ask me? They must know.'

The voice of the chief inspector told them to shut their faces. A reasonable request in the circumstances, if crudely expressed. They'd asked to be treated like everyone else. Or Gull had. But there were respectful ways of saying it.

Five minutes in, and Diamond was ready to defect. He'd twice tripped over roots and once nearly lost his shoe in thick mud. Everyone else was in boots or heavy-duty trainers. If he'd known how this morning would turn out, he'd have dressed for a hike through the woods. He was still in the oxfords he wore for the office. And his second-best suit. He'd sometimes remarked to friends that his job was never boring. You couldn't predict from one day to the next where you would be and what you would investigate.

Suddenly the people on the left stopped and gestured along the line for everyone to halt. They'd reached a thickly wooded stretch where it was impossible to see more than two of the searchers to right or left. The rule of silence now was too much to hope for. The news of a find was soon passed along. There was evidence of a tent being pitched and the ashes of a wood fire.

'That's it, then,' Diamond said. 'He's upped sticks and gone. He'd be a fool to come back.'

'It's got to be taped off for checking,' Gull said. 'We could get his DNA. This could take some time.'

'I'm going to have a look,' Diamond said.

'We're not supposed to break rank.'

'Stuff that.'

He strode off to see what was happening. He hadn't come here to make up the numbers. If Jack Gull chose to toe the line, that was his loss, Diamond decided. The stride became a swagger, but not for long. The going was rough and made worse because of the downward incline. Soon his steps were more like stumbling. Once he caught his foot in a rabbit hole and landed on all fours. He got up, rubbed his hands and carried on, watched by more of the team waiting compliantly for the order to move on. They didn't question his insubordination.

Presently the ground dipped and he looked down on a sunken section formed possibly by quarrying and protected on three sides, yet entirely grassed over, a perfect hideaway. The CIO from the Wiltshire force was standing on the opposite bank overseeing police tape being staked around an area where a flattened square was clearly visible, as were the holes made by tent-pegs. The embers of a fire were still giving off faint wisps of smoke.

'What do you reckon?' Diamond asked.

The CIO looked up, surprised that someone had left his post. Seeing that it was Diamond he didn't make an issue of it. 'Not kids, for sure. No fag-ends, no beer cans. Looks to me like one careful camper was here last night.'

'Careful in what way?'

'Not to leave any rubbish behind.'

'The sniper, sleeping rough?'

'We'll find out, won't we?' The CIO's beady eyes were more than just hopeful.

'Why would he have returned to the wood this morning?'

'To bury the murder weapon is my guess. Easy to cover with leaf mould. Very difficult for anyone else to detect.'

Diamond needed more convincing. 'Where's the tree he's supposed to have used for firing practice?'

'There's no "supposed" about it. Someone fired bullets into it. About thirty yards behind us. An oak.'

'Have you recovered any?'

'They were all embedded in the tree.'

'How about the bits the rifle ejects?'

'The cartridge casings? No, we haven't found any. He had time to pick them up.'

'Do you think he's still about?'

'We've got to assume he is. Our first response car got here within fifteen minutes of the 999 call coming in.'

'What exactly did the witness see?'

'A figure running or jogging across the road close to where we all parked. Not much of a description, I'm afraid. Dark clothing, possibly black leather, but—this is the clincher for me—definitely carrying a gun.'

'A rifle?'

'Not a handgun, for sure.'

'Was he aware of being spotted?'

'She doesn't think so. The running wasn't an attempt to get away.'

'Hair colour? Height? Build?'

'Uncertain. Difficult to tell under the trees.'

Too vague for Diamond. The tree interested him more. 'While you're finishing off here I'll take a look at that oak.' He moved off in the direction he'd been told.

This one stood a good thirty feet high and the trunk must have been three feet in diameter. He saw the bullet holes. In its long life this tree had never suffered such injury, nor been given so much attention as a result. Blue and white police tape deterred anyone from approaching within six feet. Even in his present defiant frame of mind, Diamond conformed. Some restrictions had their point. It was likely that the gunman had stepped up to the tree to see the pattern of his firing. Footprints were a real possibility.

The bullet holes had ripped through the grey crevices of the bark at head height. They formed three parallel lines, each formed of about eight shots. Three bursts of rapid fire, he guessed. The depth of penetration was impossible to judge from this distance. Certainly more than a couple of inches and perhaps several times that. Recovering them without further damage would be a challenge for the ballistics team. The striations on the sides would be the key to matching them to a particular weapon. It might be necessary to fell the tree and saw off the section of trunk and remove it to the lab.

Those bullet holes impressed him more than anything he'd seen or heard in this wood. Signs of someone sleeping out could be open to mixed interpretations. This was beyond argument. A gunman had fired at the tree, a gunman who was no beginner.

Chilling.

The link between this and the murders of three policemen was as yet unproved, but what justification would anyone have for using a gun—almost certainly an assault rifle—in a Wiltshire wood?

The line of fire was obvious, the range less so. By standing level with the bullet holes and with his back to the tree Diamond made a significant discovery. In this dense wood the gunman had found just about the only possible sight-line of fifty yards or more. Trees and bushes blocked every other angle. He'd found a shaft between them as narrow as a laser beam. It ended at another massive oak maybe sixty yards away, approximately the firing distance of the shot that had killed Harry Tasker in Walcot Street.

Impressed without really wanting to be, Diamond started walking dead straight in that direction, an obstacle course over fallen trees, holly, brambles and springy beds of leaves that were liable to give way and leave him ankle-deep in mud. His dogged character wouldn't allow him to find an easier route. He persevered at some cost to his suit trousers and shoes until he reached the second oak and was able to turn and still have a finger-thin view of the target tree.

This was even more clever than he'd first appreciated, for the second oak had wide-spreading branches low enough to be climbed. It wouldn't require much athleticism to scale it. From high on an upper bough the gunman could have simulated the angle and distance required to shoot Harry Tasker.

For Diamond, the climb would have to be taken as completed. He was damned if he would attempt it dressed as he was, with the extra burden of the body armour. But he firmly believed that was what had happened. He'd suggest it to the chief inspector. In the upper branches they might well find fibres torn from the killer's clothing.

Crime scene procedure had not been at the forefront of his thoughts until now. With more consideration for the men in white coats and their painstaking methods, he chose a different line back. It really was a path of sorts, perhaps a badger-run.

Progress was easier this way. He stepped out briskly, with more enthusiasm to rejoin the dragnet. They might be moving on by now.

He'd walked not more than twenty yards when he heard a snapping sound.

He halted and listened.

Woods can be like that, silent as the grave and then surprising you. This wasn't of his own making, he was sure. A dead branch falling off a tree?

Subdued voices carried to him from some distance ahead. The police line, he decided. The sound had been closer. He could just hear the Avon passing over the weir deep in the valley.

There was no wind. Everything around him was still.

He moved on.

Immediately he heard two loud mechanical rasps followed by an engine blast. From the ground in front of him a black dome surfaced. The helmet of a motorcyclist. A crouching, leather-clad rider. A large machine, accelerating and bearing down on him.

How the bike had materialised from the floor of a quiet wood he had no time to discover. It was about to strike him. At this speed there was no escape.

CHAPTER SIX

Diamond could do nothing to save himself. There wasn't the split second needed to leap clear of the oncoming motorcycle. An Olympic athlete wouldn't have managed it, let alone a portly middle-aged detective. Yet there was time enough to know his number was up. The body may be slow to react, but the brain is super-fast in life-threatening moments.

A massive impact.

For a moment he was airborne and then he hit the ground like a tenpin, spinning with the force of the contact. No way out of this, the brain insisted. Fatal, such force, such weight. He resigned to being run over by bike and rider.

Lying helpless on his back, eardrums at bursting point, he glimpsed the black network of branches swaying high overhead against the grey of the sky. The last image he would ever see.

Not so.

The killer crunch from the bike didn't happen. The roar of the engine continued some seconds and then reduced. The note changed from a blare to a wail to a buzz. He heard it recede down the valley.

The branches overhead continued to stir in the wind.

Spared, then?

He didn't know how.

Every part of his frame felt numb. Impossible to tell the extent of his injuries. Unwise to investigate yet. He lay motionless until the engine sound was a hiss that merged with the distant swish of water from Avoncliff weir. Only then did he truly believe he might be safe.

The motorcyclist must have made a last-second decision to swerve, catching him on the shoulder instead of mowing him down. Flesh and bone had impacted with flesh and bone, destructive enough, but not lethal. Dead leaves had cushioned his fall. He was conscious of the not unpleasant smell of moulding vegetation. Scrabbling with his fingers he felt the damp layer below the dry ones on the surface.

Tentatively, he moved his right hand down his side, checking that he still had a ribcage, hip and thigh. All present. All in place.

That settled, his brain struggled to account for what had happened. He'd been upright, fit and striding through the wood to return to his place in the dragnet. It was a mystery where the bike had come from. How could it have sprung from the solid earth in front of him?

People came running. The first to reach him was one of the Wiltshire firearms officers.

'You OK?'

He released a shaky breath. 'Don't know till I get up.'

'Stay still. Don't try and move. What happened?'

'Must have been the sniper. He came from nowhere.'

Others in their body armour surrounded him. 'Call an ambulance,' someone said.

'No need for that,' Diamond told them. 'I can feel my legs.' He tried to move them and gasped as pain shot up his left thigh.

Jack Gull forced himself to the front and leaned over. No sympathy given or expected. 'What the fuck were you doing?'

'Walking through the wood, that's what. I was on my way back to the search party when this motorbike appeared from nowhere, coming straight for me.'

'What do you mean, "from nowhere"?'

'Out of the ground. Straight ahead.' He tried to point and felt a stab of pain in his shoulder.

Disbelief personified, Jack Gull stepped over to check. He thrashed around in the bracken.

'Well, fuck me.'

'What? What is it?'

'Where he came from. You wouldn't know it was here. Watch me.' Gull took a step forward and dropped out of sight. 'Impressive?' His head and shoulders reappeared. 'It's a bloody great hole in the ground.'

'I saw nothing.'

'It's overgrown, isn't it?' Now that he'd made this discovery, Gull wanted all the credit he could extract. 'Looks to me like part of the quarry workings, squared off neatly inside.'

Some of the others moved closer to take a look. The injured Diamond was only a sideshow now.

Gull said from inside the hole, 'A bloody great chunk of limestone has been taken out of the ground. He'd get a motorcycle in here, no problem, and it's got a natural ramp with some purchase where they cut into the open face. He'd found his own hidden parking spot. The scumbag was in here waiting for the right moment to get the hell out.'

'Neat,' someone said.

'No question. He planned it for an emergency getaway.'

'Will he get stopped?' Diamond said.

'He'd better.' From his sunken position Gull swept some bracken aside and addressed the man in charge. 'You sealed the area, right?'

'The roads, yes, but—'

'But what?'

'On a bike he can use the footpaths and this whole area is riddled with them.'

'Give me strength. He'll be clean away. Did you radio all units?'

'We're not total idiots.' There was some cross-border rivalry here. Wiltshire wasn't part of Gull's empire.

Gull climbed out of the dugout and went over to Diamond. 'What did this dickhead look like?'

'Helmet and visor. Leathers. That's as much as I saw.'

'Come on. You saw the bike.'

'Black, with a windshield. I'm not into motorbikes.'

'Fat lot of use that is. This is the fucking sniper. He comes so close he knocks you down and that's all you remember.'

The chief inspector said, 'I think we should lay off. The man's obviously in pain.'

'He's in pain?' Gull said. 'I'm in bloody torment. The tosser was under our fucking noses and he escaped.'

* * *

The ambulance arrived and got as close as it could. Diamond insisted on trying to walk and had to admit he needed the stretcher. They removed the protective jacket and he was made sharply aware how much his ribs hurt. He was hauled inside and driven to the Royal United Hospital.

In Accident and Emergency, he was checked by a doctor, put in a wheelchair and taken away for X-rays to his left leg, shoulder and ribcage.

'What happens now?' he asked the staff nurse in the radiography department.

'You wait your turn.'

'I don't have time to wait. I'm a police officer on a manhunt.'

The nurse gave a smile that said she'd heard every story going and this was a nice try. 'You won't be hunting anyone today. We take patients strictly in order. It shouldn't take long.'

'Nothing is broken. It's bruising or a sprain. Find me a pair of crutches and I'll save you the trouble.'

'This is radiography, Mr Diamond. We don't supply crutches.'

'There's a man over there with them.'

'He'll have a good reason.'

'And you think I don't? I tried standing up and it's obvious what's wrong. My ankle can't take my weight. If that doesn't justify crutches, I don't know what does.' He knew as he spoke the words that he'd just undermined two of his arguments: that no X-ray was necessary and that he was essential to the manhunt.

The staff were too busy to listen any more. He was left to see out time in the wheelchair, more at risk from soaring blood pressure than recent injuries.

Patients were being taken in for X-ray, not at the speed Diamond would have liked. He took out his mobile to check what was happening at the murder scene in Walcot Street.

'Can't you read?' the man with the crutches said. He pointed to the poster on the wall showing mobiles were prohibited.

Even Diamond knew there were practical reasons for the ban. He sighed and put the phone back in his pocket.

His thoughts turned to what was happening in Becky Addy Wood. The place where the motorcycle had been hidden ought to be taped off by now and the scene of crime team collecting evidence. The searchers would be combing the area in hope that the murder weapon was hidden there. What an anticlimax. Through his own failure to think ahead, a marvellous chance of an arrest had gone begging. If he'd had the wit to visualise the killer using a bike, they might have focused the hunt and got a result.

Instead, it was back to the tedious step-by-step search. Those lads had every right to curse him.

He'd spent the morning reacting to events instead of anticipating the gunman's next move. This wasn't the sort of case where you follow up clues and piece together what happened. Three police officers had been murdered and there was no reason to believe it had stopped there. Someone needed to look ahead. He hadn't much confidence in Jack Gull's foresight.

'Clarence Perkins,' the voice came over the tannoy. Once it would have been Mr Perkins, Diamond reflected. We're all overgrown children in the modern health service.

'That's me.' Clarence was the possessor of the crutches. They'd been resting against his wheelchair while he waited.

A nurse came over to collect him. 'You won't need these inside,' she told him. Watched particularly by Diamond, she placed the crutches along three of the steel chairs reserved for the walking wounded and wheeled Clarence around a partition and into the X-ray room.

Diamond looked at the clock on the wall. Twenty minutes of precious time had gone by. The temptation to leave was overwhelming. His wheelchair was parked at the end of the row of linked chairs. He tugged at the wheels. The brake was on. He was no expert at manoeuvring one of these things. No use trying to get it moving without help. He shifted his legs and got his good foot to the floor. Rising from the chair was going to hurt, but it was the only way. By twisting and shuffling he managed to get half of his backside clear of the seat and this enabled him to put the other foot to the floor.

At great discomfort.

'What are you trying to do?' one of the other patients asked.

'I need a leak,' he lied.

'Call the nurse. That's what they're here for.'

'A nurse taking me for a jimmy? I don't think so,' he said. By force of will he heaved himself upright, taking the weight on the right leg. The left one was far too sore. He was thinking maybe his own diagnosis was wrong and he really had broken it.

With his left hand as support, he started hopping towards the crutches, holding on to the next chair. And the next.

'I'm borrowing these,' he said to the man who had spoken. He grabbed one of the crutches and attached the support to his upper arm. The second was more of a challenge while standing on one leg. He got it at the third attempt, slotted in his arm and took his first step.

'The Gents isn't that way,' his well-meaning adviser called out. 'It's the other direction.'

Diamond didn't answer. He was back on the sniper's trail.

* * *

By the time he'd made it through the corridors to the main exit, his conscience had been touched by small examples of members of the public behaving as one should do in hospitals, disinfecting their hands before entering the wards, sitting in waiting areas without complaining and holding doors open for a man on crutches. Before phoning for a taxi, he called at the reception desk and asked them to inform the radiology unit that Peter Diamond would not, after all, require X-rays. Then he was off before anyone tried to stop him.

* * *

Keith Halliwell was open-mouthed. 'Guv, what on earth?'

The taxi had put Diamond down at the foot of the eighteenth-century flight of steps in Walcot Street. He made quite a performance of positioning the crutches and getting himself out of the back seat. 'Have you got a tenner on you? I can't manage these and reach my wallet at the same time.'

Halliwell shared a long-suffering look with the driver and settled the fare.

Diamond said, 'Don't let me forget.'

Halliwell let that pass. 'What happened?'

'Tell you later. This is urgent. Have any of the people in the Paragon house been allowed out yet?'

Halliwell nodded. 'We'd already detained them for a couple of hours. They weren't best pleased.'

'They wanted to leave?'

'It's natural. When you're treated like a caged beast you want your freedom.'

'Did they all go out?'

'Not together, but yes.'

'The blonde, the old couple and the civil servant? Anyone check where they were going?'

'Not our business. Actually, the old people said something about going for a coffee.'

'When was this?'

'While you were breaking the news to Mrs Tasker. We'd already questioned them all and turned their flats upside down. Is there a problem?'

'Tell me this, Keith: is there anything to suggest that Willis, the civil servant, rides a motorbike? While we were inside his place, did you notice leathers anywhere, or a helmet?'

'He's a car owner.'

'Doesn't stop him having a bike as well.'

Halliwell frowned as he cast his mind back. 'I didn't see any of the gear, but then I wasn't looking for it. I was interested in a gun.'

'Is he back yet?'

'Don't know. I can check with the guy on the door.' Halliwell had a personal radio attached to his belt. 'Still out somewhere,' he presently reported.

'I want to know the minute he gets back.'

Diamond demanded and was given an update on the investigation. It was now beyond dispute that the sniper had fired the fatal shot from the overgrown garden in the Paragon. Every resident living close enough to have witnessed the shooting had been questioned. The bullet found in the drain and the single cartridge case from the garden had gone to be ballistically tested and compared with the ammunition used in the previous shootings. Although damaged and compressed, the fragments were believed by firearms officers to be from a .45 round used with the Heckler and Koch G36 rifle, the type of weapon they carried themselves.

'Which tells us something, if true,' Halliwell added. 'But are we any closer to catching this guy?'

'Only an hour ago we were as close as it gets. He ran me down and left me like this,' Diamond said, and told his story.

Halliwell made the right sympathetic sounds. 'Nothing else you could have done, guv.'

'That isn't the view of Supergull. He reckons if he'd been there he'd have spotted the make of the bike, got the licence number and a detailed description of the suspect.'

'Yeah, the colour of his eyes, size of his collar.'

'And which aftershave he uses. Then he'd have stretched his arms, got airborne and chased the sniper all the way down the valley and wrestled him off the bike and pinched him.'

'Why wasn't Gull with you?'

'He stayed in line, obeying orders.'

'Orders from a chief inspector?'

'He's more of a team player than I am. I wanted to see the tree the sniper used for target practice. This guy is good, Keith. He knows what he's doing.'

'They have these holographic sights, guv. You see a little red spot instead of crosshairs. You can't miss.'

'Three parallel lines. That's class, holograph or not.'

'The shooting of Harry Tasker told us that. A moving target, side on.'

The crutches were getting uncomfortable. Diamond perched himself on the bowl of the Ladymead fountain and propped them against one of the pink granite columns. 'Sitting in the hospital I was going over stuff in my mind. Are we a hundred per cent sure that Willis is in the clear?'

'This guy has really got to you,' Halliwell said. 'His guns are locked up at Devizes.'

'Never mind the guns. What about the man himself? Does he have an alibi? No. He lives above the garden the shot was fired from.'

'None of them in the house have an alibi. They were all at home overnight. Any one of them could have gone down to the end of the garden and pulled the trigger.'

'I may be wrong, but I don't see the old couple or the dizzy blonde knowing which end of a gun to hold. Willis does.'

'If it's him, he's got front,' Halliwell said. 'He didn't exactly go out of his way to please us.'

'He's smart enough to know where to hide a rifle from a search party. Who's to say he doesn't have one he keeps at home?'

'Unlicensed?'

A nod.

'The sniper used a military assault rifle for the killings in Wells and Radstock.'

'Does that make any difference?'

'It's not the sort of weapon they use in rifle clubs. It's illegal.'

'We're not dealing with an amateur, Keith. If he wanted to get hold of a military weapon, he'd find a dealer.'

'Is this a hunch, guv, or something stronger?'

'Call it an informed guess. Check with the DVLC to see if he owns a motorbike.'

'As well as the car, you mean? Now?'

Halliwell was treated to one of Diamond's looks.

But the call to Swansea proved negative.

Diamond swore, sighed and shook his head.

'I know we've got Willis in the frame,' Halliwell said, 'but shouldn't we widen this?'

'Meaning?'

'What if the killer wasn't living in the house. He sneaks in the evening before, breaks into the basement and passes the night there.'

'Sneaks in through the front door?'

'When someone else is coming or going, using the entry system. If, say, the Murphys had a visitor who was leaving, all it needs is for the killer to choose his moment and slip through the open door.'

'Okay, an outsider is a possibility. Is there any evidence of someone having hidden in the basement flat?'

'Nothing obvious.'

'I wasn't expecting an overnight bag and a toothbrush. It's a dusty flat that's been empty some time. Forensics can tell if someone went through.'

'Most of Manvers Street went through this morning, guv. Well, that's an exaggeration. Ken Lockton and Sergeant Stillman and the armed response team. That's a lot of disturbance. The scene of crime team spent a couple of hours taking samples. They promised to let us know.'

'Forensics.' Diamond rolled his eyes. 'Don't call us, we'll call you. Did they manage to work out the sequence of events in the garden?'

'Before the shooting?'

'After.'

'We all assume the sniper was still in the garden when Lockton and Stillman turned up.'

'How soon did they get there?'

'Around 4.40 a.m.'

'The 999 call was 4.09. Heck of a long time for the killer to be still at the scene.'

'The theory is that he meant to leave immediately after firing the shot and something went wrong.'

'Like what?'

'Like his escape plan. Maybe he hadn't bargained for the shop alarm going off and waking people. Or it could be as simple as the basement door shutting behind him. He'd be stuck there until someone came.'

'He'd break a window or go over the wall. None of this chimes with what we know about the sniper. He's a planner. He leaves nothing to chance.'

'Chance can bugger up the best of plans, guv.'

'Agreed.' Diamond looked down at his injured

leg. 'Go on, then. He remains in the garden for some reason yet to be revealed. What happens next?'

'He hears Lockton and Stillman coming and decides to hide.'

'Leaving his rifle propped against the railing? That's another eccentric action. Wouldn't he hide the gun as well?'

'I would.'

'Me, too. Is it left there deliberately as a distraction? They spot the gun and go towards it, thinking he's long gone.'

'That's what they thought according to Sergeant Stillman.'

'But in reality he's still in the garden.'

'Or the house.'

'And after Stillman has left, the sniper picks up the gun and clobbers Ken Lockton from behind with the butt and makes his escape. Presumably the motorbike was parked somewhere near. What's that side street opposite the Paragon?'

'Hay Hill.'

'That's where I'd keep the bike for a swift getaway. Up the top to Lansdown Road and you're laughing. You wouldn't meet any of the response vehicles coming to the scene. We need to know, regardless of whether it belonged to Willis. Check the houses in Hay Hill and see if anyone saw a bike parked there overnight.'

While Halliwell went off, Diamond fingered his leg. There was swelling around the ankle and soreness, if not acute pain. His ribs hurt, too. Maybe he should have waited for those X-rays.

He spotted a familiar, lanky figure folding and unfolding his arms, trying to appear important.

'Mr Polehampton.'

The early bird of the Serial Crimes Unit turned, saw who had spoken and came over. He eyed the crutches and made no comment.

'You've been here a few hours now,' Diamond said. 'Is the crime scene still under your control?'

Polehampton gave a cautious nod.

'I expect you've got to know the area pretty well.'

Another nod.

'Have you sussed out the shops?'

'I know what's there, if that's what you're asking,' Polehampton said.

'Good. All I can see from here are places that sell sofas, sewing machines and bikes. There's a charity shop and a couple of eating places. What's up the street beyond the nightclub?'

'A stationer's, more eating places, a fancy-dress shop.'

'Nothing so useful as a pharmacy?'

'Further along, maybe.'

'You're not certain?'

'Not entirely.'

'Better ask one of the locals, hadn't you? Then nip along there and get me some extra-strong painkillers. I'll take over your job.'

CHAPTER SEVEN

Call me Ishtar.

Why? It's as good a way of starting a blog as I can think of. Shades of *Moby Dick*. But this isn't about whaling, or seafaring, or moby, or dick. Correction. I guess a moby is sure to come into it if that's what you call your mobile phone. As for a dick, just wait and see.

Ishtar is the name I've chosen for myself, not wanting the world to know who I really am. She is the Babylonian goddess of love and war. A weird combination, you're thinking, but everyone needs to be loved and most of us are willing to fight for it.

This is the start of something that may soon develop into a story of scandal, fraud and possibly more. Can't say where it will lead because the action has only just started. Three of us are going undercover. We're well placed to get at the truth, better placed than the police.

If we're right in our suspicions, the story needs exposure, which is why I've chosen to post my blog this way, through a worldwide network that reveals sensitive information while protecting the identities of the main players, not least myself. Whistleblowers and human rights activists use this facility in confidence of remaining anonymous. The thing I find funniest is that the system is so brilliant that it's also used by so-called intelligence agencies across the world to give out information while covering their sources, yet they can't unravel it to unmask other users. How is this done? As I understand it, everything I write will be bounced around such a network of relays run by volunteers that it will be totally impossible for you or anyone else to track me down to my steamy little lair, so don't even think about trying.

Got that?

Let's go.

<u>My profile</u>

Whoops—I have to be careful here or my mask will be ripped off even before I begin. I can tell you safely and truly I'm female and between twenty and thirty and passably good looking, enough to have had the lovers I've wanted, three when I was still at school, starting with the French *assistant*, the seriously yummy Monsieur F, who set the bar high for those who came after. Coming up to my exams, just turned fifteen, I was seriously poor at languages, piss-poor, my father said at a parents' evening, and it takes a lot for him to use words like that, so my form teacher arranged extra tuition and the extra wasn't what she or Daddy (who was paying) intended. I learned a lot I didn't know about masculine and feminine. It included French oral, but without words, and, believe me, I experienced the present perfect, but still failed my GCSE. Monsieur F left suddenly after only one term and after that I had to be content with spotty sixth formers who had none of his finesse and knew nothing about irregular verbs or irregular anything.

What else? I did pass enough exams to scrape into a university in the west of England—got to be mysterious about which one—and ended up wiser and poorer, twenty grand in debt and with a respectable degree that got me no job at all. The best thing I did at uni was learn to drive because after a few months attending the job centre I took over Daddy's old Renault Clio (we're all Francophiles, my family, in different ways) and started work with a florist, delivering flower arrangements, and that's what I do. BA (Hons), flower deliverer. Sally, my boss, the owner of the shop, says we cater for every occasion from the cradle to the grave. Cradle to the grave, womb to the tomb, erection to the resurrection, depend on me to arrive smiling with your red carnations.

The job leaves me plenty of scope for other diversions, if only I had the funds to enjoy them. I earn a little extra cash in hand from teaching the piano, a skill I didn't mention that comes easily to me. I've got my own flat in a part of town where I'm unlikely to bump into a rich stockbroker. Living room, bathroom, kitchen and bedroom. Just enough, until I find a way to break into the Pimm's and polo set and meet the multi-millionaire.

Enough of daydreaming. I'm going to tell you about the real stars of this blog, my co-conspirators, Anita and Vicky. They couldn't be more different.

Anita

She's the funny one, terrific company, with her own quirky way of looking at the world. I wish I could remember one-tenth of the things she comes out with. Only last night she was, like, 'If at first you don't succeed, sky-diving is not for you.' And after a few drinks, 'I think my head is hosting the Olympic Games.' Anita is seriously overweight and has no colour sense, but she's a beautiful mover. Everyone watches her on the dance floor. Oh, and she does amazing things with her eye make-up, like the Egyptian look she's currently into, using the liner to create black outlines meeting in curves that sweep high up her face. I first met her in the flower shop. She came in for a single freesia stem because she said it was cheaper to have in the bathroom than a can of air-freshener. Like me, she's single ('If you ever see me walking up the aisle, stick your foot out') and has a well-paid, useful job as the manager of a travel agency. Useful because thanks to Anita the three of us have taken a few cut-price trips to sunny places.

Now for Vicky.

She's the one with a husband. We'll call him Tim (I have to be careful over names) and she's always been mysterious about him. I think he's currently out of work. Whatever, he's out of the house a lot and seems to prefer his own company, which is why Vicky is able to spend so much time with Anita and me. She's a true friend, I'm sure of that, but there are no-go areas of her life and Tim is one of them. We don't ask. Even Anita knows better than to draw her out. Vicky is sweet-natured, a little old-fashioned from her upbringing (her parents were into their forties when they had her), generous, starry-eyed, never been known to tint her hair, but why should she when it's natural raven-black, straight out of a romantic novel? Yes, she's a beauty. More than once on our nights out Anita and I have had to rescue Vicky from testosterone-fuelled males. None of us minds being chatted up by the poor hopeful darlings, but as Anita says, you soon get to spot the ones with three pairs of hands. You can be wearing a wedding ring and a crucifix pendant and they still think you're up for it.

Vicky has never said so, and I wouldn't ask, but I know she'd dearly like to have a child. I've seen the way she looks at little kids. Why she hasn't fallen pregnant I don't know. I hope it isn't because she or Tim are infertile. Of course it could be that they don't want to start a family until Tim finds work. Vicky is a school meals assistant and I doubt if it pays much. You wouldn't know it, but a lot of her clothes are out of the charity shops. Here in this well-heeled city, people's cast-offs are sometimes as good as you'd find in the best dress shops.

That's the three of us, then. We meet a few evenings each week and again at weekends, Friday and Saturday evenings and sometimes Sunday afternoons. Often it's for nothing more exciting than a couple of drinks, cider mostly, but with Anita in the party we always have a giggle. Last night she was telling us about this customer of hers, a woman obviously in her sixties, all blonde curls and blusher, wanting to book two weeks somewhere in the sun and she'd heard about Ibiza and twenties to thirties holidays. *Twenties to thirties?* Anita, trying to be tactful, goes, 'Are you sure you want that sort of holiday? It can be rather demanding.' The woman answers, 'That's up to me, isn't it? I know what I'm looking for.' So Anita, being Anita, thinks toy boy. 'I feel bound to mention that there's a lot of drinking in Ibiza.' And the woman goes, 'I'm all for that. I carry a bottle of water at all times in case of dehydration.' Which of course makes us scream with laughter. Anita goes, 'Actually I meant drinking in bars.' And the woman is like, 'I wouldn't be going all the way to Ibiza to waste time in a bar all evening.' So Anita feels duty-bound to explain, 'That's what happens on twenties to thirties holidays. It's all about making friends, and that's where it gets done.' The woman goes, 'I'm sorry, whatever it is that gets done, I'm not doing it in a public bar. I prefer somewhere more quiet.' More hoots from Vicky and me. Anita goes, 'I'm wondering if you'd be better off on a cruise. We have some wonderful cruise brochures.' The woman is like, 'God no, I did one of those and it was up the coast of Norway and we froze. The temperature never got into double figures. All the men had cold hands. That's why this time I definitely want a place in the twenties to thirties.' Twenty Celsius, geddit?

I'm glad we had a good laugh. I could see Vicky was a bit down when we started, but by the end of that story she was fine.

Now you know the good guys in this blog, Vicky, Anita and me, and you'll be wanting to find out who the baddies are. There's only one so far and, natch, he's a bloke. Maybe it's jumping the gun to call him an out-and-out baddie. We need to know more about his shady activities before hanging him out to dry. That's our mission, to uncover the truth.

And hang him out to dry.

We first got onto him through Anita. 'I shouldn't be telling you this,' she goes with a giggle, 'but there's a client—head office insists we don't call them customers any more—who's a real puzzle to me. I call him my city break man. He's always making short trips, mostly to Europe, and sometimes to America. When I say always, that's an exaggeration. I mean about five times altogether. I shouldn't complain. It's good business for us. He pays cash, which is unusual, and the banknotes all pass the test. He buys some of the local currency from our foreign exchange, not a huge amount, about two hundred pounds' worth, and he stays in middle bracket hotels for a couple of nights. He doesn't want to be friendly with any of my staff. They're company-trained to remember clients and greet them by name, but I can tell he doesn't like that at all so I told them to ease up. I've never seen him smile. He's usually wearing a dark suit and boring tie. He's about forty, I would guess. We're supposed to have a contact address and phone number and all he's willing to give is a box number and a mobile number.'

'He must have given you a name.'

She shrugs and smiles. 'Smith. John Smith. That's the name we use for the bookings. I don't believe it.'

Vicky makes one of her solemn remarks. 'There are plenty of John Smiths. On the law of averages, he's more likely to be John Smith than William Shakespeare or Albert Einstein. Perhaps it's true.'

'Darling, it's precisely because there are so many that he chose it.'

'Doesn't it need to match his passport?'

'It's not difficult getting a false passport.'

Vicky nods. 'He's into something dodgy, that's for sure.'

I'm like, 'Drugs?'

Anita goes, 'I hope not. My company wouldn't want to get involved with anything like that.'

And Vicky is like, 'Two hundred quid wouldn't buy much hard stuff. It's not even worth the trip.'

How does she know about such things? I wonder.

'Trafficking?'

'He's not the sort. The guys who go in for that are sexy foreign brutes, and they're not going to use a travel agency.'

'A spy? Using an agency would be a good cover.'

Anita pipes up, 'You girls are getting carried away and I haven't told you the strangest bit. At lunchtime when it's nice I sometimes buy a sandwich and go for a walk in the park. Just across the street from the sandwich shop is the job centre and a couple of weeks ago I saw some guy in tattered old jeans and a hoodie coming out of there obviously having just collected his social and—get this, darlings—it was city break man. I swear it was him. I know the walk. Two days later he's in my shop wearing his suit and tie and booking two nights in Rome and buying his two hundred pounds' worth of Euros. Unemployed, funded by the taxpayer, and off on another trip.'

Vicky tut-tuts at such behaviour. 'He's a benefits cheat.'

And I'm like, 'Are you sure it was him, Anita? Hundred per cent?'

'Positive.'

'Does he know you saw him?'

'He wouldn't have used my agency again if he did. The way I see it, cheating the taxpayer is one thing, and someone ought to report him, but all these trips abroad make me think he's up to something bigger.'

'Such as what?'

'I don't know, but I sure as hell want to find out.'

Then I hear myself saying, 'The three of us ought to be up to it.'

'Finding out, you mean?'

'Combining our skills and talents to discover the truth.'

'The three snoops.'

'Please,' I say. 'Sleuths.'

Suddenly it sounds like an adventure. We've been friends up to now, giggly, on the same wave-length, whiling away our spare time, but aimless. This is something more, a project, a bonding exercise. I can tell we all fancy it.

Vicky claps her hands. 'I've got it. Next time he books a trip, you can book places for all of us to tail him and find out what he does.'

'Too expensive,' Anita says. 'The company runs a tight ship.'

'Send one of us, then: Ishtar.'

And I'm, 'What do you take me for? I can't go jetting off to foreign places like James Bond. I've got my job to do, delivering flowers.'

Anita shies away, too. 'And I couldn't fund it. That's not on. But I tell you what, Ish. We could do some sleuthing at a local level. Next time he comes in, why don't I give you a call and get you to follow him in your van, see where he goes, and at least we'll find out where he lives.'

'How would that help?' I'm backtracking fast, wishing I hadn't suggested this sleuthing game.

'We'd get to know more about him, wouldn't we?'

'Going to the police might be a better idea.'

So Anita does some backtracking of her own.

'And you know what they'll say? It's all suspicion so far. Besides, I don't want it known that I'm snitching on my own customers.'

I'm happy to agree. 'You'd lose most of your business. Anyone who can afford a foreign holiday these days must be on the take.'

'Oh, come on.'

We bang on for some time like this, but deep down I'm hooked. I want to find out what city break man's game is. After we've caught him out, who knows, we could go on to bigger things and get on the trail of the Somerset Sniper. Just joking.

The truth is we're all turned on by this adventure. Vicky's eyes are shining. Anita is practically purring. The three snoops. Sorry, sleuths. And guess who's standing by, waiting for that call from the travel agency?

I'll report what happens in my next blog—if I'm not dead meat already.

CHAPTER EIGHT

Jack Gull said without a scrap of sympathy, 'Shouldn't you be at home?'

Diamond widened his eyes. 'With one of our guys dead and the other fighting for life? I'll see the day out.'

They were back in Manvers Street police station in the incident room freshly created by DI John Leaman as office manager. Give Leaman a job and he delivered. Display boards were in place with photos from the scene and details of principal witnesses, the morning's statements already on computer, civilian support staff installed as receiver, indexer, action allocator and statement readers.

Calls were coming in steadily from the public. The standard request for information had already been broadcast. A team of trained staff were noting everything. Ninety per cent of what came in would be of no use, but every snippet of information had to be recorded and prioritised. Later Diamond would make a personal TV appeal for assistance.

Gull was forced to admit that everything was in place. His only grudging comment—in case his own empire should be undermined—was that this had to be a temporary arrangement, which prompted Diamond to say that if an incident room ever got to be permanent they'd better resign, all of them.

Photos of Harry Tasker's corpse and the wound to Ken Lockton's head dominated one end of the room, a reproach to everyone who entered. On another board were grim close-ups of the two previous victims of the sniper. In each case shots to the head had caused death.

Leaving Gull to check the displays, Diamond went across to Leaman and asked what news there was from the hospital.

'No change, guv. He's in a coma and they say it could be for weeks.'

'Are his people with him?'

'His wife and son.'

'Someone is with them, I hope.'

'Christina, one of the PCSOs, drove them in. She has a good way with people.'

'Good choice, then. And who have we got supporting Harry Tasker's widow?'

'PC Dawn Reed volunteered. She worked with Harry.'

'I know Dawn. She'll cope if anyone can. Emma Tasker isn't easy to help. So what do we have that's new?'

Leaman produced the preliminary report from ballistics. The misshapen bullet and the cartridge case were now confirmed as from a .45 round.

'Same fucking gun as he used in Wells and Radstock, as if we hadn't twigged,' Jack Gull's voice boomed from the other side of the room.

'We'd better wait for their final report before we say that for sure, sir. It may be a G36 like the others, but we can't say for certain it was the same G36,' Leaman said in his matter-of-fact manner. He yielded to no one in the pursuit of accuracy.

'I said it, chum, and you heard me,' Gull responded. 'I'm the CIO here and we're proceeding on the basis that these killings are the work of one individual with one gun.'

Even John Leaman appreciated that you don't argue with a chief superintendent who skews a point of information into a test of authority.

Typical of Gull, Diamond thought, shouting over the heads of civilian staff as if they didn't exist. Curbing himself from making something of it, he fixed his mind on the investigation.

'What I want to know is whether today's events have told us any more about the suspect.'

'Plenty,' Gull said, turning away from the display board. 'He's familiar with your routines here in Bath. He must be, to have known PC Tasker was walking that beat in the small hours of Sunday morning. He got into the garden in the Paragon, so either he lived there or knew the place well enough to con his way in. And obviously he'd sussed it out as a perfect place to shoot from. That's one of his hallmarks, doing his homework before he carries out the killing.'

'Are you thinking he's a local?' Diamond said.

'Got to be.'

'Local to Wells and Radstock, too?' Leaman got in, still smarting from the putdown.

'And Becky Addy Wood,' Diamond said. 'Unless we're mistaken about the motorcyclist and it was someone else.'

'No chance,' Gull said. 'That was our man. The practice shots in the tree. The hideout. The way he hightailed it when we got near. Obviously he used the wood as his base.'

'If he's local,' Leaman said, 'why hide in a wood? Why not work from home?' His dogged logic was starting to sound insubordinate.

Diamond headed off another dust-up. 'Because he doesn't want to appear suspicious. He may be living with someone else who doesn't know he owns a gun.'

Gull nodded. 'Fair point.'

'Tell me,' Diamond said. 'Do we have any fingerprints from the previous shootings?'

'No fingerprints,' Gull said. 'He's too smart to leave any. Shoeprints. A nice clean set from the tree house he used as a hide in Wells.'

'But they're on file here, are they?' Diamond's thoughts were still with Willis, the clever-dick civil servant. 'So at least we have something to compare with, if we come up with a suspect?'

'If he always wears the same pair of trainers, yes.'

Moving on, Diamond asked, 'Did you find anything more after I was taken to hospital?'

'In the woods, you mean? Less than I hoped for. Some boot prints, a few tyre prints, no use until we find the boots and a bike that match them. I'm assuming he buried the rifle somewhere in the wood, but you saw what the ground is like. We could have fingertip searches for a month and still not find it.'

'He may be back to collect the gun.'

'I thought of that,' Gull said. 'Told the Wiltshire guys to keep a twenty-four watch for the whole of next week. They're not happy. The chief inspector talks about resources and calls it an Avon and Somerset crime, as if his county has no stake in it. The point is that the sniper isn't fucking interested in who polices what. He's as likely to strike next in Wilts as he is here.'

'That's if he spots a copper on the beat at night,' Diamond said. 'What are we going to do about that?'

'What do you mean?'

'Are we going to send out more guys to be shot at?'

Gull frowned. 'We can't abandon the streets. The public wouldn't stand for it.'

'The public isn't risking its life. The public can lock its doors and go to bed in safety.'

This flew in the face of modern police procedure. After a pause, Gull said, 'I don't know if I'm hearing right. It's your job and mine to keep the streets safe at night.'

'We can do that in patrol cars,' Diamond said. 'Personally, I've never been all that impressed by foot patrols.'

'You're on a loser there. Community policing. It's government policy. Every politician who gets elected calls for a bigger police presence on the streets. The papers scream for it. The public wants it. That's democracy.'

'This argument was going on when I first joined the police. Joe Public may feel comforted by the sight of a bobby walking up the high street, but what happens when a crime is committed? They call 999 and expect quick action. That guy on the beat isn't there before a response car.'

'Yes, but we can't measure the deterrent effect. You can't say how many villains were put off robbing old ladies by the sight of bobbies on the streets.'

'Not many,' Diamond said. 'When old ladies are robbed, it's in their homes mostly, not outside.'

'You're missing the point,' Gull said. 'The public sleeps easier at nights knowing we're out there.'

'And up and down this country a police officer is assaulted on the streets every twenty minutes.'

'Don't quote stats at me, Diamond. Up and down this country includes the West Midlands, Strathclyde and the Met. We're Avon and Somerset, remember.'

'Peaceful old Avon and Somerset where upwards of a hundred and fifty officers have been victims of assault over the last year. And what is more—'

'A hundred and fifty-one.'

Diamond was halted in mid-flow, but not by Gull. John Leaman had spoken again.

'What?'

'A hundred and fifty-one, guv. We've got to add you to the list.'

Without intending to, Leaman had defused the argument.

Gull gave a rare smile. 'He's right. Some people

will do anything to prove a point, even flinging themselves under fucking motorbikes.'

'In point of fact, gentlemen,' Diamond said with all the dignity he could muster, 'I wasn't in Avon and Somerset at the time. I was in Wiltshire.'

The neighbourhood policing debate stopped there. Fortunately the adrenalin rush of clashing with Gull had stopped Diamond thinking about his injuries. His brain was functioning again.

'Look at this from the sniper's point of view,' he said, getting back to the issue that mattered. 'The first two shootings, in Wells and Radstock, appear to have been carried out without a hitch. He gave nothing away except a few shoeprints and the inevitable, the calibre of the bullets he used. Today was different. He managed the killing okay, except for losing a cartridge case in the undergrowth, but after that things went belly up. For some reason he got trapped in that garden and could have been caught by Lockton and Stillman. He got lucky when Lockton thought he could act alone, but he was forced to clobber Lockton, which was never in the plan.'

Gull took up the narrative. 'Yes, and after that, he gets on his bike and drives off to the woods and has another close call. He didn't reckon on us getting on to him so soon.'

'By his high standards, today was a mess,' Diamond summed up. 'He won't be feeling so chipper. If, as we believe, he hid the gun in Becky Addy Wood, he'll be worried that we'll make a search and find it. He knows that's difficult, but not impossible. With metal detectors we may locate it. And if he intends to carry out more shootings, he'll need that gun.'

Gull wasn't comfortable when Diamond was doing the talking. 'He's an expert marksman. He may well have other guns. If so, he could afford to leave it buried, rather than risk going back.'

'I'm not so sure, Jack. That rifle has served him well. Gunmen get attached to their weapons like snooker players with their cues. Bearing in mind that it's a tell-tale piece of evidence with his prints and his DNA and maybe some of Ken Lockton's blood and hair adhering to the stock, plus the fact that he wants to use it again, I'm sure he'll run the risk of going back for it.'

'If he does, we'll collar him.'

'You're talking about the stake-out?'

'Right.'

'Which we're asking Wiltshire to provide, but with their limited resources. It's a bigger area than it first appears, that wood, and he seems to know it well. He'll back himself to outwit a few coppers on a twenty-four hour watch. The question is when does he return? He'll go by night, when he has the advantage of knowing the terrain. But does he play the long game and leave it until he's ready to stage another murder, or will he want to collect his gun before then?'

'He's cool. He'll play the long game,' Gull said.

'Can't agree. Every hour that gun is in the wood it will prey on his mind that we'll find it.'

'In his shoes, what would you do, then?' Gull clearly resented having to ask.

'Go back tonight or tomorrow. I'd approach the wood on foot and be armed, maybe with a handgun, in case I was spotted.'

'You'd need a torch.'

'That goes without saying. And a backpack.'

'What time would you go?'

'Well after midnight. All of the shootings have occurred not long before dawn. He'll need some shut-eye after last night. I expect he's catching up right now, while we agonise over what he does next.'

Reluctantly, Gull was persuaded. He chewed at his thumbnail. 'Are you recommending we step up the numbers on watch in Becky Addy tonight?'

Diamond shrugged. 'Put out as many men as we can spare. The odds are still stacked in his favour.'

John Leaman made a point of his own. 'Especially with local knowledge.'

'We'll stake out all the footpaths leading up to the wood,' Gull said.

'He'll have thought of that,' Leaman said.

'What's he going to do, then, smart-arse? Parachute in?'

'He'll avoid the footpaths,' Diamond said before Leaman got into a slanging match. 'He'll cut across country. We'd do better looking at the map and deciding where he might leave the motorbike. I'm assuming he'll arrive on wheels and park it somewhere out of earshot. That's the biggest risk he takes. Does he leave it along a country lane where it would stand out or in a street with other vehicles?'

'The street option sounds more likely.'

'Agreed. Shall we look?'

The map of Becky Addy Wood was already pinned on the incident board. 'You've got Avoncliff down in the valley with the canal, the river and the railway acting as barriers,' Leaman said, spreading his hand across the features he mentioned. 'Above the wood you've got the village of Westwood and quite a few small streets.'

Diamond weighed the options. 'This morning he escaped down the hill and presumably along the towpath. He'll figure that we'll have that route covered. I doubt if he'll come by way of Avoncliff.'

'Westwood, then?'

'It's more likely.'

'What's this?' Gull asked. He traced his finger along the fine double line that snaked from Westwood eastwards to the edge of the town of Bradford on Avon, about a mile off. At the top end it passed close to Becky Addy Wood.

'Jones Hill.'

'We should stake that out.'

'Fine, but I don't think he'll come that way,' Diamond said. 'There's no obvious point where he can change route if he's seen. You know what local lanes are like, with high sides. He's got better options through Westwood.'

'You're really getting into this guy's head,' Gull said.

'He almost got into mine, literally.'

'Right, then.' Needing to assert himself, Gull inflated his chest and jutted his chin in a posture reminiscent of Mussolini. 'We warn Wiltshire Police Authority that we expect the sniper to return to Becky Addy tonight or tomorrow, so they can get a strong presence there, and we tell them we're blanketing Westwood with our own people. Cross-border co-operation. Will you take care of that?'

'I was thinking in view of these . . .' Diamond lifted one of his crutches a few inches off the floor.

'Are you in pain?'

'Not acute pain. I took something for it.'

'My role as head of serial crimes is to decide the strategy,' Gull said, regardless that Diamond had been deciding it for the past ten minutes. 'It's up to you to implement the action. If you're unfit, you'd better say so and we'll appoint a deputy.'

'I'm okay.'

'Good. I've been on the go some hours and I'm going to leave you in charge for the time being.' He noticed Leaman checking the clock. 'No need to log my comings and goings, by the way. The SCU is free ranging.' He stalked out.

'Free range, as distinct from battery birds, like you and me,' Diamond said to Leaman.

'If you want a rest, guv, I can set things up for tonight.'

'You heard me say I'm okay,' Diamond said. 'Would I lie to Jack Gull?'

No response.

Diamond eased the crutch from his right arm and let it fall to the floor. 'I don't need both of these any longer. I can manage with one.' He hobbled a few steps to the board plastered with photos of all three shootings. 'Gull and his people are convinced these attacks are random. They say they researched the murdered officers and there's no reason anyone would want to shoot them for who they were.'

A frown from Leaman suggested he, too, had taken this as gospel.

Diamond continued, 'They made up their minds before Harry Tasker was killed.'

Leaman scratched the back of his head, unsure where this was leading. 'They must have gone into it carefully.'

'I'm sure.'

'But you think they could be mistaken?'

'Put it this way, John. They're the Serial Crimes Unit. Serial killing is their business and serial killing is usually random. After two shootings they look at the history of the victims and can't see any link between PC Hart, the Wells guy, and Richmond, the Radstock guy. So it's random. And when shooting number three occurs—same weapon, same time of day, same MO—their suspicion hardens into certainty. They're so sure that they don't even consider checking whether victim three has anything in common with victim one or victim two—apart from being a cop.'

Leaman's eyes widened. 'Is that possible?'

'It ought to be looked at. We have Harry Tasker's file here and more importantly we have people who knew him. Personally I know sweet FA about Hart and Richmond.'

'Their records will be at Headquarters. Must be, if Jack Gull and his team were studying them. I can ask them to share them.'

Diamond shook his head. Some craft was wanted here. He didn't want Headquarters thinking he'd pulled the rug from under Gull. 'Rather than dealing with Portishead, I'll speak to Wells and Radstock, where these guys were based. Their personnel units must have supplied the profiles. They can supply us as well. I'll tell them we have an incident room here and we need everything in our system. We're not dealing with one case in isolation.'

* * *

In twenty minutes, he had the information he

wanted. Leaman brought it up on the screen. Diamond wheeled his office chair closer.

PC Hart, Martin, aged 31 at death, had joined the police only four years before, after a short career teaching physical education. Born in a village near Wells, he had attended a local comprehensive where he had excelled at sport, notably basketball and fencing. As a fencer, he'd been on the fringe of international selection and this had helped him to a sports course at Bridgwater in spite of mediocre exam results. He'd trained as a teacher and taken up water sports. While still at college he'd met Juliet Strang, from Portsmouth, a swimmer, and they lived together until after obtaining their degrees, when they married. He was appointed teacher of PE at a state school in Minehead. His wife gave birth to twin daughters in the first year. School teaching hadn't suited Martin Hart's temperament. He found working to a timetable restrictive, preferring games and leading school teams to the daily routine of lessons. But there had been no problems over discipline. If anything, he was too demanding of the students and expected standards they were unable to match. After six years of teaching, he decided on a change of career and applied to join the police. He was regarded as a good candidate, physically fit and with satisfactory references from the school. He'd completed the training and joined Wells as a probationer and impressed everyone with his communication skills and confidence dealing with a variety of situations. Confirmed as a fully fledged constable, he was tipped to get promotion to sergeant within another year. His home life appeared good. After the twins, another child, a son, had been born, and the family lived in a rented house in a well-regarded estate north of the city. His wife Juliet worked part-time as a lifeguard at the local sports centre and coached the swim team.

'A sheltered life, really,' Leaman said in summary.

Diamond nodded. 'Family man, lived in Somerset all his life. How would a country boy like this give offence to a gunman?'

'Are we assuming it wasn't a random killing?'

'That's the point of this exercise,' Diamond reminded him.

'Maybe the gunman happened to have been a kid at the school where he taught.'

'Not bad, John. Not bad. And had a grudge about the way he was treated? Compulsory games?'

Leaman smiled. 'It would have to be worse than that. Some of these PE teachers are sadistic bastards.'

'Tell me about it.' Memories of school cross-country runs stirred in Diamond's brain. Those formative experiences went deep, himself with the stragglers, smokers and fat boys at the back of the pack, too breathless to run, shivering in shorts and singlet, and being threatened with an extra round of the course by a bully in a tracksuit. 'There were times when I would gladly have shot mine, but I hope I've got over it.'

'They say it's self-perpetuating.'

'What is?'

'You get bullied and in due course you become a bully.'

'Get away.'

It was a rare moment of triumph for Leaman. He'd got one over his assertive boss.

'We're guessing here,' Diamond said testily. 'Move this on. Let's look at the other victim.'

PC Richmond, Stanley, had been older than Hart. Aged 41 at death, a career policeman, he had joined Bristol Central after leaving school. His file showed he'd moved around more than most in his first few years: Crewkerne, Minehead, Glastonbury, Somerton, Ilminster, Wincanton.

'Why so many moves?' Diamond said.

'Sometimes you get a bloke who doesn't fit in.'

'An awkward bugger? I've met a few.'

Leaman reddened.

'Nothing personal. Then there are restless guys who are always putting in for transfers. Was he married?'

'No. Ah, this could explain why he was often on the move,' Leaman said, and read aloud. '"Has an interest in folklore and writes articles for *Somerset Life* and other magazines." I expect he was gathering material for his writings.'

'He was supposed to be keeping law and order.'

'He could still have combined it with his hobby.'

'Which must be why he never made it to sergeant.'

'Just look at the list of postings. Glastonbury, famous for its mystical connections. Somerton, supposedly the meeting place of various ley lines. Wincanton had its witch trials. He did his research, wrote it up and then asked for another transfer.'

'He ended up at Radstock. What's there, apart from disused coal mines?'

'Bronze age stuff. Saxon burials.'

Diamond was impressed. 'You're well up on all this. Are you a rucksack and shorts man on your days off?'

Leaman hesitated. 'I take an interest, but I wouldn't say I'm well up on it, not like Stan Richmond.'

'Ever met him on a dig?'

Leaman shook his head. 'I can see I'm going to regret this.'

Diamond revolved his chair to turn his back on the screen. 'So we have a sporting ex-teacher and a folklore buff. A muscleman and a hippie. Not a lot in common except they both joined the police.'

'Both lived in Minehead at one time.'

'Did they?' Something he'd missed. Once more he was forced to respect Leaman's attention to detail.

'Hart taught there and Richmond was on the strength, but not at the same time.'

'May be of interest, maybe not. Personal files only tell you so much. Christ only knows what mine says. They miss out the really interesting bits. For that, we need to talk to family and friends. I read in one of the tabloids that Martin Hart was known to his friends as Ossy. Why was that, I wonder?'

'Aussie, like Down Under?'

'Ossy. With a double s.'

'Short for Oscar?'

'Search me. His name wasn't Oscar. That's what it said in the press. Reporters are good at finding out personal stuff like that. Brings them to life. It's what people like to read. But Why Ossy? Ozzy Osbourne I can understand, but Ossy Hart? Am I missing something?'

Leaman gave a shrug.

'I'm not saying it's important,' Diamond went on, 'but this is the kind of detail you don't get from reading official files on a bloody computer.'

'Most of the newspapers are on computer,' Leaman said, as a true apostle of the world wide web.

'Check them out, then,' Diamond countered, never one to miss an opening. 'See if they teased out anything we don't know. But I'm going to send Ingeborg to Wells and Radstock to get the real dope on the victims.'

DC Ingeborg Smith had once been a crime reporter who had more than once put Diamond through the wringer.

'Is that wise? Jack Gull won't like us going it alone,' Leaman said.

'Gull is too busy to notice. I wish we could find a connection between these two and Harry Tasker,' Diamond said. 'All I got from Tasker's wife is that he fished and watched TV in his time off. Was that really all he did? Does anyone here know any more about him?'

'He wasn't much of a communicator.'

'She mentioned that, too. And he griped about Freemasonry in the police.'

'Why was that?' Leaman said in a challenging tone. A muscle twitched at the side of his mouth.

Diamond raised his hand as if to concede that he'd bowled one bouncer too many. 'You're one of them. I forgot.'

Leaman twitched again. 'There's nothing in our conditions of service to say I shouldn't be one of them, as you put it. Plenty of us are, and proud to be. What was Harry Tasker's problem with it?'

'Favours, I expect.'

Leaman simply clicked his tongue.

'Isn't that what persuaded you to join?'

Leaman sighed and rolled his eyes upwards.

Diamond grinned. 'No need to get shirty, John. You're a secretive bunch, up to all kinds of weird practices, but I don't think you take shots at non-members, even stroppy non-members like Harry Tasker.'

* * *

Ingeborg was delighted to be asked.

'It's not exactly undercover,' Diamond told her, 'but you don't need to go through official channels. I'd rather you shared a drink with the Wells CID lads than knocked on the chief superintendent's door.'

'Do I get expenses?'

'You can claim for your travel. You'll drive, I expect?'

'Will it also go to a round of drinks?'

'You're a girl,' he said, frowning. 'You get drinks put in front of you.'

There was a pause while Ingeborg composed herself. 'Not necessarily, guv.'

'If all else fails, then.'

'And what am I meant to find out?'

'All you can on Ossy Hart. His friends, contacts, the things he talked about, particularly his life outside the police. Family, sports. Was he one of these hearty types who make themselves unpopular? Why was he known as Ossy when his name was Martin? You're going to seem nosy and they may resent it from a stranger, but if anyone can charm it out of them, you will, and we're doing this for professional reasons. Let them know you're CID and from Bath. They'll know all about the shooting.'

'And you want me to do the same in Radstock?'

'Tomorrow morning. Stanley Richmond.'

'Even if you catch the sniper tonight?'

'If we catch him, we'll want to know why he did it.'

'Wasn't it random?'

She didn't get an answer.

CHAPTER NINE

Diamond was never sure whether sleeping in the day helped. Generally he would wake feeling worse than when he closed his eyes. Today he had no choice. He was dog tired and the painkillers acted as sedatives. After getting home at five, he made short work of a stack of cheese and pickle sandwiches, opened a pouch of tuna for the cat and fell into bed. Good thing he had enough of his wits about him to set the alarm for eleven—p.m., not a.m., as he felt he deserved.

* * *

The sleep must have helped, but it didn't feel like that when the beep-beep broke into his dream of cruising the shallows of a slow-moving river in a flat-bottomed boat with Steph miraculously alive again, lightly holding his arm. When he flexed he found he'd been stroking his right bicep with his left hand. With an anguished groan, he reached out to stop the alarm repeating. Darkness had set in. He heaved himself off the pillow, groped for the light switch and stared at the clock. Stark reality replaced the dream: three brother officers murdered and their killer out there somewhere. Under an hour to get to Westwood.

He put his feet to the floor and was sharply reminded to reach for the crutch.

Curled up at the end of the bed on the softest part of the duvet, Raffles must have heard the yelp of pain. The ears pricked, but that was the only move.

The temptation to prod that cat was strong. Instead Diamond phoned John Leaman to check what had happened in the last few hours.

Nothing of note. The search for the weapon in Becky Addy Wood had been abandoned at dusk. Ken Lockton remained comatose in the Royal United. No significant finds were reported from the Walcot Street murder scene.

The route took Diamond through the city, so quiet on a Sunday night you could have heard the wheeze of sleeping pigeons. He went over Claverton Down and linked up with the Warminster Road, the A36, where the only other vehicle he saw was a huge articulated truck parked in a lay-by, the driver dozing in his cab. Was everyone asleep? The people of Westwood would be. In all the outlying villages they kept country hours.

He opened a window to let in some reviving air.

He could be certain John Leaman was awake. The call to his mobile had found the reliable DI already in Westwood. If their estimate of the sniper's intention was right, there wouldn't be anything happening for some hours yet, but the men had to be strategically posted and the village streets checked for parked vehicles, especially motorcycles. Leaman was seeing to this. There could be no better choice for the job. He was a biker himself and bored everyone rigid with his talk of Suzuki Bandits.

A winding minor road brought Diamond on a steep descent through the village of Freshford, a place he regarded with some respect, and not only for its well-stocked inn. In 1974 when North Somerset was redesignated as Avon, the defiant inhabitants held a mock funeral in protest.

Passing through that hotbed of insurrection, he crossed the sixteenth-century bridge over the Frome and his headlights picked out a rare stretch of level road, the floor of the Limpley Stoke valley. This didn't last long. He was soon climbing Staples Hill and entering another county. Wiltshire was outside his jurisdiction.

But he hadn't been expecting a border control.

Lights. Cones. A figure in a reflective jacket waved him down.

He lowered the window. 'What's up?'

The young police officer had to be a Wiltshire man. Not a glimmer of recognition. 'Do you mind telling me where you're going, sir?'

'No, but I'll tell you who I am.' Diamond brandished his warrant card. 'Is there a lion on the loose?'

There was no answer.

'Why are you stopping the traffic?'

A sharp change of tone. 'Sorry, sir. Orders, sir.'

'Who from?'

'DI Polehampton, sir, Serial Crimes Unit.'

Polehampton. The blood pressure rocketed. What was the point of a stake-out if everyone coming into the area was alerted?

'You can stop this nonsense right now, clear the road and get out of sight, do you understand? Those are my orders. Do it.'

Chuntering, gripping the wheel, Diamond almost missed the narrow lane leading to the village.

Westwood is large enough to be divided into Upper and Lower. The part he had reached, on the edge of the ridge above the Avon valley, was the Upper. He drove past a mix of cottages and modern houses to a clearing where upwards of thirty uniformed police had gathered. These were Avon and Somerset men he recognised. John Leaman was among them.

How ridiculous.

At boiling point by now, Diamond flung open the door, put his crutch to the ground and emerged with a limp almost as menacing as Anthony Sher playing Richard III.

He had their complete attention.

'This is supposed to be an undercover operation,' he said. 'What are you doing here?'

Leaman cleared his throat. 'Guv, this is me, John Leaman.'

'I can see who you are. In fact, I can see all of you. I could see the chequered caps from two hundred yards off in the moonlight.' To be truthful he'd seen them in his headlamps, but the point was the same. 'We're supposed to be staging an ambush, not a passing-out parade. I suggest you remove them now.'

They did so.

Leaman said, 'I'm responsible, guv. I picked this as the quietest place to meet.'

They had to assemble somewhere to get orders, even Diamond had to concede, and this was away from most of the houses, with only a farmyard across the street. He asked Leaman for a progress report. All the streets in Upper and Lower Westwood had been checked for parked vehicles. Registration numbers had been noted. Four motorcycles had been located, three in the lower part of the village. Leaman reeled off the makes and details. All were registered to local residents and now under surveillance.

'Was this done without waking half the village?' he asked. 'We don't want an audience tonight.'

'Those were their orders, guv.'

'Get them dispersed, then, and out of sight. Do they know what to do? No heroics. Leave that to the armed officers. Simply observe and report. I don't want to see another bobby until the sniper is dead or disarmed.'

'They've all been told.'

Actually Leaman had done a good job. The hat-bands could be forgiven. The men moved off in different directions.

'Where's Polehampton?' Diamond asked, switching his anger to the main offender.

'With Jack Gull, I believe. They went to the woods to liaise with the Wiltshire team.'

'Did you know he ordered a stop on vehicles approaching Westwood?'

Leaman put his hand to his head. 'He said something about surveillance.'

'Since when was surveillance Mr Plod with a torch in the middle of the road? I'm wondering if he's sealed off all the other approaches. Can you reach him on your radio?'

All Leaman got was static.

'Try Jack Gull, then.'

Supergull's abrasive voice came on the line. 'That you, Diamond, on the fucking scene at last?'

'Yes, but no thanks to your deputy,' Diamond said, and told him about the roadblock. 'If he's sealed off the village, we're all wasting our time here.'

'Sounds like a slight balls-up. Hold on.'

Good as it would have been to hear the exchange between Gull and Polehampton, Diamond had to imagine it.

Finally Gull came back on line. 'No problem. All the stops have now been called off. A temporary measure to make sure we bussed all our men in without being overlooked. We've staked out the woods down here. No chance anyone can come or go without being observed. That's if you and your men have control of the fucking village.'

'Control is a strong word. We're in place,' Diamond said.

'Where are you going to be?'

'Me personally? Free range.' He winked at John Leaman.

'Keep in touch, then.'

'Until I ask for radio silence,' Diamond said, begging the question who was running this. 'That'll be necessary later.' He switched off. No 'over and out' in case Gull wanted the last word.

He was starting to feel restored. Next, he wanted a look at the parked motorcycles. 'Are they far off?'

'Too far for you to walk,' Leaman said.

'Hop in the car, then.'

Guided by Leaman, he drove down to Lower Westwood. The two levels of the village had once been separated by fields, Leaman told him, but during World War Two a small business called

Royal Enfield manufacturing—of all things—motorcycles had been acquired for secret war work and almost a hundred extra bungalows were built for workers drafted in from the Midlands. More infill had taken place since and Upper and Lower were defined only by the two through roads north and south.

They toured the small streets in Diamond's car. He decided the chance of the sniper owning any of the three bikes parked in Lower Westwood was small. It would be too much of a trek from Becky Addy Wood.

'Do you think he's in the area already?' Leaman asked.

'Could be, if he got in before Polehampton closed it down. My sense is that he'll come early. He'll want to do a recce before entering the wood.'

'But you don't think he'll park the bike at this end?'

'Unlikely. Now that I've seen the set-up, John, Upper Westwood definitely gives him the most options.'

'He could be using a car this time.'

Diamond gazed at the long line of parked cars in a street called The Pastures. 'Thanks for that. Cheers me up no end.'

'A car would be less obvious, when we all know he used the bike before.'

'I get the point. You don't have to hammer it home.'

'Let's hope Jack Gull nabs him in the wood, eh?'

'We can hope. How many men does Gull have?'

'Fifty or more, plus the armed response team. They're covering all the routes in.'

'All the obvious routes in. I still think Westwood

is the most likely.'

'I don't want to be pessimistic,' Leaman said, 'but this is a guy who surprised us once already.'

'One thing is certain. He knows the wood.'

'And you still think he'll come for the gun?'

'I do. It's a balance of risks. In another full day of searching we'd probably find it. Forensics would extract enough information from that gun to lead us straight to him. He has to recover it fast, so he'll take his chance tonight.'

They returned to Upper Westwood and Leaman showed him the fourth bike, a black Yamaha, parked off the road in a lane between two stone walls.

'This is the best bet yet,' Diamond said, trying to visualise the bike that had run him down. 'Have you checked the registered owner?' The Police National Computer came in useful sometimes, even he would admit.

'Someone called Jones.'

'Has it been used in the last hour?'

Leaman got out and put his hand tentatively close to the exhaust pipes. He shook his head.

'We need a man observing.'

On cue, a constable bobbed his head above a drystone wall. He'd been crouching in somebody's garden.

Diamond grinned. 'Magic. But don't do that if the sniper comes for the bike. He'll blow your brains out.'

'Very good, sir.'

'It wouldn't be. Down again, lad.'

They parked the car in Chestnut Grove, a side street of bungalows. A cloud passed in front of the moon and darkness took over. 'What do you make the time?' he asked Leaman.

'Just after one-fifteen.'

'Hours yet. Where are you posting yourself?'

'Opposite where you first saw us, near Upper Farm. There's a place that gives some cover.'

'I didn't notice.' He grinned. 'No bad thing.'

'It's the way down to the stone quarry.'

'Where we were in the wood today?'

'Not the open-cast bit. The underground workings.'

Diamond's insides clenched. He should have remembered Westwood was well known for its stone mine.

'It's huge, I was told,' Leaman said, heaping on the embarrassment without realising how personally Diamond was taking it. 'It stretches right under where we're standing and a long way beyond.'

'I know.'

But he was unstoppable now he'd started. 'The war work I told you about was done in the mine. The employees were on twelve-hour shifts and never saw daylight for days on end in the winter months. The government installed a room for sun-ray treatment so they could get their vitamin D.'

Diamond wasn't listening.

'Or is it E?'

No response.

'I don't think you heard a word I was saying,' Leaman said in an injured tone.

'I did. You're on about the mine.'

Only a couple of years ago Diamond had pursued a suspect through the disused underground quarry at Combe Down. The workings had been a honeycomb. Leaman knew about this and still didn't seem to appreciate the potential a mine had as a secret means of approach and escape.

Diamond said, more to himself than Leaman, 'Why didn't we notice this on the map in the incident room?'

'Because maps only show you what's on the surface.'

True. Prosaically, maddeningly true.

'Is it secure?'

'Metal doors, padlocks. You wouldn't get in without a crowbar.'

'I want to be sure of that. Come on.'

Leaman raked a hand through his hair. 'Do you really want to go there, guv? It's steep.'

'Show me now.'

Leaman produced a small hand torch. 'The mine is one of the last still in use as an underground stone quarry,' he said, keeping up his tour-guide mode in a too obvious try to cover the unease between them. 'They dig out huge blocks and leave them to dry out for a while, so they're firmer. Then they load them on to flatbed trucks.'

Diamond was silent.

The going down wasn't so bad as all that for a limping man. Only the ramp down to the entrance was tricky.

Several of the massive limestone blocks were stacked nearby, pallid in the moonlight, each stencilled with a number. Diamond asked for the torch and made a close inspection of the doors and satisfied himself that they were, after all, secured with strong metal fastenings. Nothing had been forced as far as he could tell.

'Looks solid enough.'

'It needed to be,' Leaman said. 'They hid the Crown Jewels here during the war.'

'Pull the other one, John.'

'It's true. The mine had to be air-conditioned and kept at a special temperature. It's amazing what was stored here, all crated up, of course. They built a narrow-gauge railway underground to transport the stuff. The Elgin Marbles, the statue of Charles I and the Banqueting Hall ceiling from Whitehall, the bronze screen from the Henry VII Chapel in Westminster Abbey.'

The level of detail was persuasive, but Diamond remained sceptical. 'Who told you this?'

'One of the Wiltshire sergeants who knows the village. He'll be hunkered down in Becky Addy Wood by now. He said the local police helped to guard the place. The British Museum supplied most of the security and our people had to help at night.'

'I thought they used the London tube to store the treasures.'

'They did until 1942. Then they decided it was safer to move them here. Twenty-five thousand square feet of storage, all secured with strong-room doors brought from Bloomsbury.'

'I'm starting to believe this—as if it matters now.' Diamond stepped back from the main door to the mine.

'All right, then?' Leaman asked.

Plainly it wasn't. 'All these mines have ventilation shafts,' Diamond said. 'I'd like to know where they come out.'

'We'd have to ask the locals.'

He checked the time again. Approaching 2 a.m.

'I'd better get a move on. If I head down the track, I come to the quarry first and then the wood, right?'

'I don't advise it, guv. It's bloody dangerous. If you don't fall over and break the other leg you'll get shot by the firearms team, like as not.'

'Radio ahead and tell them I'm on my way.'

'I can't come with you,' Leaman said. 'The men expect to find me here.'

'I don't need a bloody attendant, John.'

He didn't tell Leaman he was confident of this end of the operation. Gull was the weak point.

Without more argument he started picking his way down the escarpment, gripping the crutch with one hand, the torch with the other. Necessarily slow, he was unlikely to trip, he told himself. The moon was fully visible again, allowing him to choose the best footing. He heard from behind him the faint sound of Leaman making contact on his personal radio, occasional snatches of words raised in emphasis: 'insisted . . . couldn't possibly . . . with a crutch, yes . . . I should think in the next three-quarters of an hour.'

Sooner than that if I'm any judge, Diamond thought. He was moving better than he expected. The going was easier down the slope than over flat ground, and when his injured leg made contact it didn't feel as painful as earlier in the day. Severe bruising, probably, and nothing worse. His self-diagnosis in the X-ray department was paying off. He'd saved the National Health Service some funds and saved himself from a dose of radiation.

A voice of reason broke in and told him he was a raving idiot to be doing this alone. If the sniper was about and wanted another kill, he couldn't have an easier target. And if the sniper didn't get him, some trigger-happy firearms officer would.

Friendly fire, they termed it. A classic oxymoron, and not a good way to go.

Better not stop for a rest.

He picked up a little speed instead. Ahead he could see the road down to Avoncliff and the dark patch that was Becky Addy. This was where the search teams had been unloaded yesterday (it was safe to call it yesterday now—and, hell's bells, it felt like two days ago instead of less than twenty-four hours). Back then, the minibuses had parked beside the road. Tonight they must have delivered the men and moved off to some place less conspicuous. Give Jack Gull some credit. He'd got this right.

Even so, the sniper would be expecting a trap.

Increasingly, the crutch was striking chunks of stone half-buried in the ground, an indication that he was close to the site of the old quarry.

He stopped.

From the thicket to his right came the snap of a twig, a sharp, strong sound that could only have been made by foot pressure.

He flung himself face down and lay still. He was on open ground in clear moonlight, an easy target. Go on, you bastard. Pull the trigger and let me have it. You can kill me, but the others will know you're here.

Another sound came from the same bush, the crunch of dead leaves, too forceful to have been caused by the wind.

Only fifteen to twenty yards off.

His heart pounded his ribs.

He pictured the sniper taking aim, prone, propped on elbows to secure the gun. Professional pride dictated that the bullet should enter the temple just above the ear. A clean kill.

I can deny you that, matey. He brought up his arm and wrapped it around his head. The shot would still penetrate his arm and smash into his skull, but clean it would not be.

Still more delay. Seemed he'd bought a little time. He tilted his head a fraction for a sight of the bushes where the sounds were coming from.

Something moved low to the ground.

A silvery figure shuffled towards him in the moonlight, smaller than he expected, and—surprisingly—with a black and white muzzle.

A badger.

Suddenly the animal sensed where Diamond was and veered off left. The last he saw of it was the sway of the rump disappearing into a hole in the ground.

He might have laughed if he hadn't had the shakes. The sense of imminent death had not been funny. He waited a couple more minutes to get a grip on his nerves, then hauled himself to his feet and hobbled on. He wouldn't be telling anyone about the experience except, perhaps, Paloma after a few drinks.

Becky Addy beckoned. He'd reached the curve of the road down to Avoncliff where you plunged into the heart of the wood. Here he was certain to be in someone's gunsights. He'd have regarded it as dereliction of duty if he wasn't.

When the challenge came, it wasn't, 'Who goes there?'

It was a shout of, 'Armed police,' followed by a respectful, 'Mr Diamond, sir?'

Reasonable. He'd warned them he was on his way. 'Yes.' He held up his hands—torch in one and crutch in the other—and limped towards the source of the voice.

The black body armour of the policeman merged so well with the bush he appeared from that he got within twenty yards of Diamond before he was obvious. Hooded and gloved, and in night-vision goggles, he kept his MP5 sub-machine gun up to his shoulder and trained on Diamond. He was following firearms unit protocol.

For his part, Diamond was doing his best to send a telepathic message: careful with that trigger.

'You're welcome to use the crutch, sir.'

'Thanks, and you're welcome to lower the gun.'

Protocol was satisfied. The officer relaxed his stance. 'Superintendent Gull is expecting you. Would you follow me?'

'Point me in the direction. I'd rather you stayed at your post.'

'No need, sir. Two other guys are with me.'

He hadn't spotted them until now. Hooded and in black like the first man, they were almost close enough to shake hands except that they were gripping their Heckler and Koch carbines. Both nodded as he went past.

Jack Gull was even better hidden. He'd taken position between a tall holly bush and an enclosing mass of laurel that effectively formed a natural shelter. Inside, he was seated on a folding canvas chair with his feet up on a low branch. In his hand was a hip flask, presumably of liquor. 'Welcome to HQ.'

Diamond was not impressed, surprised or envious. 'What's happening, then?'

'Not much. Any action in the village?'

'Plenty of time for that.'

No offer of a seat. Gull didn't even remove his

feet from the branch. Although he was wearing combat trousers and body armour, he didn't look as if he had any intention of putting himself in the line of fire.

'I hope you haven't made the wrong call here,' he said, taking a swig from the flask.

'What do you mean?' Diamond said.

'About the sniper burying the gun in the woods and coming back to collect it. We've committed a lot of resources.'

'Losing confidence, are you?' Diamond said. 'Back in the incident room you were with me a hundred per cent. In fact, you were the first to come up with the theory.'

'Was I?'

'That's my recollection. You talked about the bullets in the tree and the signs that he camped here.'

'If you say so.'

'But I don't mind taking the credit when we reel him in,' Diamond said.

'Get stuffed.'

'Where's Polehampton?'

Gull shrugged. 'Somewhere out there, checking the frontline.'

'I'd feel a lot safer if he was here. How did he come to join your outfit?'

'Influence. His father-in-law is in the government.'

'Can't you find him a desk job?'

Gull shook his head. 'I want him where I can keep an eye on him.'

'Like out in the woods?'

No answer.

Diamond asked, 'So what do you reckon is the

sniper's motive in shooting policemen?'

'Obviously revenge. Some arsehole with a grudge against us. There's no shortage of cop-haters.'

'Someone with form, then? A professional?'

'You bet. Anyone who can handle a G36 like this guy is no beginner.'

'And you're an expert, of course?'

'Anyone joining the SCU has to go through the assault weapons courses with CO19 at Milton Keynes. The initial firearms course alone is thirty-five days and then there are the rifle courses. If they ever took you on, which isn't likely, you'd learn that H&K are the tops for reliability. The G36 works with a spring-buffered short-stroke gas piston system that is self-regulating. Mind, they're expensive. I'd say the sniper's weapon is worth as much as your car on the black market.'

All of the jargon was putting a glaze over Diamond's eyes, but he still had an interest in the gun. 'Worth coming back for, then?'

'Would you come back for your car?'

'I wouldn't bury it in a wood.'

'I haven't told you the beauty part,' Gull said. 'You can fill your H&K with dirt, chuck it in a lake, drop it off a cliff, drag it through the jungle and it will still operate.'

'I expect he wrapped it in something.'

'Naturally. He wouldn't want the job of cleaning the fucker. But if he did, they're dead easy to break down and clean. I've done it.'

'On the firearms course?'

'Well, yes, I don't own one. They're illegal. Paramilitary. Even in the States, they're banned. At one time H&K tried marketing them as semi-automatic sporting rifles. Legislation put a stop to that.'

'But illegal arms dealers still supply them?'

'To the right customer.'

'The wrong customer.'

'Depends on your point of view.'

'How many of these guns are in circulation?'

'How long is a piece of string? Put it this way: we're not going to trace the murder weapon by going to the manufacturers and asking.'

'Could it be police-issue?'

'Easily. They told me on the course how many go missing. Hair-raising. And even more are knocked off from the armies across the world. A bent NCO in a regimental armoury can make a fortune. They simply fiddle the inventory.'

A rustle from the laurel bush interrupted him.

'What's that?' Diamond said, thinking wildlife, anything from a snake to a deer.

It was static from a walkie-talkie. Jack Gull put out a hand and withdrew his personal radio from where it was hanging from a branch. Over the rustling came a voice: 'Oscar One to Bravo. Stand by. Something happening here. Sounds up ahead.' The speaker was a moonraker, Wiltshire through and through.

'Report your position,' Gull said.

'The bushes are moving.'

'Your fucking position, Oscar One.'

'590811. He's coming this way.'

'Let him come,' Gull said. 'Stay where you are and let him come. Calling all armed units, we have a sighting at map reference 590811.'

'There are badgers in this wood,' Diamond said as if he was a nature study expert. He thought of the hapless copper out there in the darkness practically pissing himself with tension. A mistake now could compromise everything.

'Can you see anything?' Gull said into his radio.

A crackle of static followed by a hiss, but no voice.

'If he's as close as all that, he won't speak,' Diamond said.

'Speak up, Oscar One,' Gull demanded into the radio.

Silence.

'Disconnected,' Diamond said.

'Will anyone out there tell me what's happening?'

'Bravo?' the radio spoke. A different voice.

'Yeah?'

'Unit Two. Reference Oscar One, we're moving in.'

'Thank Christ for that,' Gull said. To Diamond, he said, 'That's the gun team.'

CHAPTER TEN

Being at HQ, as he called it, evidently gave Jack Gull a sense of power. It did nothing for Peter Diamond. He felt marginalised. All the action was happening at the far end of the wood and he could do nothing to influence it. While he was holed up behind a holly bush, young police officers with no experience of this kind of skirmish were risking their lives against an armed killer. His main impulse was to get out and give support. If he hadn't been handicapped by the leg injury he would have been there. He felt wasted here, listening to Gull swearing into the radio, increasingly infuriated.

The speaking was all one-way.

There hadn't been anything back from the armed police or the bobby known as Oscar One for two or three minutes. In this situation two or three minutes seemed like an hour of normal time.

'Nobody's fucking listening to me.'

'It's not about you,' Diamond told Gull. 'If they switch off, it's for their own safety.'

'Just as long as they got the tosser this time.'

'Just as long as no more of ours are killed.'

'You think he's on a spree?'

'He'll be armed for sure.'

'Our lads are trained. They'll take him.'

But at what cost? Diamond feared for the copper who had radioed the first sighting. He wouldn't be armed or trained. Neither would the other Wiltshire lads drafted in to keep watch. The last words heard from Oscar One had been, 'He's coming this way.'

'Did you make a note of that grid reference?'

'Of course I fucking did. We know who was on the spot and we know the gun team went in,' said Gull. 'I'm trained for the job.'

'Where was it in relation to here?'

'I get you.' He produced a map from the side pocket of the combat trousers, unfolded it and flicked on a torch. 'Oscar One was speaking from the north-east edge of the wood, which means the sniper will have come from the Jones Hill side.' He looked up from the map, and it was not a friendly look. 'If I remember right, you dismissed Jones Hill and said he'd come through Westwood.'

'We don't need to know where he came from,' Diamond said. 'All we need is where he is right now.'

Gull hadn't listened. 'He wouldn't flog his way through half a mile of sodding wood to get where he is. He'd come from the north.'

'It's history, Jack.'

'He knows where he hid his rifle and he picked the quickest route.'

'Or the smartest.'

They slipped into silence, with never a chance of agreeing. Gull was chewing his thumbnail again. Diamond's thoughts were with Oscar One, the luckless copper who had called in. This operation had been rushed. Ideally only armed officers should have been posted in the wood.

'Don't you think you should move more of your marksmen to the scene?'

Gull shook his head. 'The gun team make their own tactical decisions. I can speak to them, but they judge when and where to move. Makes sense.'

'A law unto themselves.'

A shrug. 'SOP.'

'And what's that when it's at home?'

'Standard operating procedure. I'm in overall charge, of course.'

This came across as a hollow claim. Right now Gull didn't look like the man in charge. He'd got up from the canvas seat and was pacing the small area like an expectant father outside the delivery room.

Diamond had to step aside for him to pass. 'Mind if I sit down?'

'Be my guest.'

'It's turned on, is it?' Diamond asked when he'd lowered himself into the chair.

'What?'

'Your radio. I can't see a light.'

Gull looked down, swore again, fiddled with the controls and got the static sound back. Immediately a voice asked, 'Anything happened yet? This is Delta Three. All quiet here.'

'Then get off the fucking line.'

A faint 'Charming' could be heard before Delta Three signed off.

Gull tried once more to raise Oscar One and got nothing.

'Here's a suggestion,' Diamond said. 'Why don't you leave me here in charge while you go out and check what's really going on? I can't move fast, but you can, and you've done the training. Are you armed?'

'I've got my Glock, that's all.'

'Handgun?'

'Yeah.'

'More than most of those poor beggars have got. They're armed with batons at best.'

'They'll have protective jackets.' Even Gull appeared to realise this was a callous remark. 'They know better than to get involved. We laid it on the line.'

'No use laying it anywhere if an armed sniper gets a sight of you.'

A long pause.

'So you think I could be more useful out there,' Gull said. He replaced the stopper on his hip flask and pocketed it.

'Sure of it. Have we got a spare radio? I can take any calls that come in, but I reckon the guys close to the action have switched off. You're wasted here.'

'Okay, I'll go.' Whatever Jack Gull's limitations, he wasn't a coward. He'd wanted to oversee the mission from the hub, and this hideout had ceased being that. He handed the radio to Diamond saying he'd pick up a spare from one of his team. 'Keep me fully informed, Peter. Refer all decisions to me.'

'Goes without saying,' Diamond said.

He watched Gull put on night-vision goggles and a ballistic helmet and then he was gone.

The next phase would be a trial for Diamond. He hated being so passive. Better make sure the radio was working. Really it was a form of mobile phone. The police had been using them ever since he'd joined the Met. They'd called them 'bat phones' in those days, which dated him. Still, he could say he'd used a mobile a good twenty years before they became trendy.

The distinguishing feature of the police radio was the static, a grating, unmusical sound that usually meant someone was about to get in touch and alerted everyone around as well. The armed police used earpieces for covert operations like this.

He had the thing in his hand and was turning up the volume when it spluttered into life. 'Bravo, can you hear this?'

For a microsecond he had to think who Bravo was, and then: 'Right. Bravo here. Who is this?'

'Oscar One.' Said in the reassuring West Country burr.

'Christ, lad, are you okay?'

'No problem.'

'Thank God for that. What happened?'

'I saw him, sir, a guy moving through the wood who has to be the suspect. He was heading my way, darting from tree to tree. He got as close as ten yards and then beetled off to the right of me. He's away now, I think.'

'Which direction?'

'West to south-west, I reckon.'

'Deeper into the wood?'

'Yes, sir.'

'Description?'

'There wasn't much light to see by.'

'Try.'

'I only caught the outline of him. He's wearing dark clothes. Some kind of baseball hat, I reckon. He's not all that tall. Moves well, like he's fit.'

'Armed?'

'If he is, he isn't carrying a rifle.'

'Moves well, you said?'

'Bent over, like he didn't want to be seen.'

'Did he spot you?'

'I don't think so. I'm well hidden here. In fact, I got a real shock when someone put his hand on my shoulder from behind and he was one of ours. Freaked me out.'

'An armed officer?'

'That's right, sir. There were others, I think. I told him what I've just told you and they headed off after the suspect.'

'You did well, Oscar One.'

'Thank you, sir.'

'You may be in for another shock. The CIO is on his way to you now. You're still in the position you gave us before?'

'The same, sir.'

'And are you alone now?'

'Some others are hidden nearby.'

'That's good. Stay out of sight in case he's back. Over and out.'

The description of the suspect was not much help. What could you expect at night in a heavily wooded area? One good thing was that the sniper wasn't carrying his rifle. No doubt he was on his way to collect it. Diamond's guess was that it was buried somewhere close to where the motorcycle had surfaced.

That would be this end of the wood. Not far off from here.

Wanting to check the map for himself, he looked around and realised he couldn't. Gull had gone off with the only copy. How dumb was that? If someone radioed in with another sighting, there was no way of checking the position.

Presumably maps had been issued to everyone. He needed one—and fast.

He got up from the chair, leaned on the crutch and hauled himself outside. The moon had gone behind a cloud again. Amazing what a difference it made. He could have kitted a funeral out of the darkness.

'Anyone about?'

Silence.

'I need some help here.'

He'd spoken softly, assuming that the men who had shown him the way weren't far off. He didn't want to yell.

The only other option would be to radio for a map. Not the best way to encourage confidence in the ranks.

He was on the point of returning inside the hideout when a voice from his left said, 'Sir.'

One of the ninjas.

Diamond explained the problem. Map, Maglite torch, pencil and notepad were provided. 'Any signs of activity out there?' he asked.

'All quiet, sir.'

'Stay alert. He could be heading this way.' The

order was superfluous, but he felt he had to say something to reassert his dented authority.

Back in the hidey-hole, he opened the map and worked out approximately where he was and what the coordinates were.

The radio rustled and a voice he recognised said, 'Bravo, this is Jack. Over.'

Gull hadn't assigned himself a call-name. He couldn't be Bravo any more, so it was first-name terms.

'Go ahead, Jack,' Diamond said.

'Can you recall that grid reference?'

Diamond grinned. 'It's all right. Oscar One called in. He's okay. The target moved west.'

'We had a sighting?'

'Yes, but we're not much wiser.'

'I'm returning to base.'

'As you wish.'

The radio hissed as Gull signed off.

Diamond sat forward in the chair, waiting. One of the silent watchers, surely, would soon report another view of the sniper picking his way through the wood. The man was either incredibly lucky or skilful or he'd given up and gone. It was weird to be here with the radio knowing that the firearms officers were posted at strategic points through the wood waiting for the same snuffle of static that would start his own pulse racing.

Then he heard a sound that wasn't from the radio.

An explosive burst from the wood startled him so much that he tipped the chair backwards and almost fell. He couldn't tell the precise direction. It was followed by another, surely a rifle shot.

Not an echo, but a second bang.

Immediately, the radio came alive with a babble of voices. 'Jesus!'

'I heard shots.'

'That's got to be him.'

'Where did it come from?'

'Gunfire, close by the quarry end. Delta Three going in.'

Gull's voice. 'This is control calling all units. Will someone give me a fucking grid reference?'

'Delta Three again. Our best estimate is 598807. Over.'

Gull: 'Did everyone get that? 598807. All SFOs, repeat SFOs, close in on the target area. And now I'm ordering radio silence.'

His heart thumping, Diamond came to a rapid decision. If Gull was running the show, calling himself 'control' again, leave him to it. Two men in charge could lead to disaster. He didn't need to do anything in this emergency except stay tuned. The wise thing was to follow what was going on in case he needed to take over. But what *was* going on? The shots had sounded close, definitely from this end of the wood. He had to assume the first, if not both, had come from the sniper. None of the firearms officers had reported preparing to shoot.

When the sniper used his gun, he aimed to kill. Up to now, he hadn't been known to miss.

There followed a petrifying period of silence. Diamond pictured the armed police homing in on the place where the shots had been heard. They were coming from all parts of the wood. The sniper would be surrounded, but at what cost?

Three minutes went by.

No more sound.

This was becoming unbearable.

Diamond flicked on the little torch and tried to find the location on the map. A grid reference—someone's estimate of a grid reference—wasn't the number of a house or a car registration. It was an informed guess, no more. In the digital age we treat strings of numbers with all the respect accorded by ancient philosophers to the four elements. 598807 sounded like a combination that would open a vault. It was only a stab in the dark.

Tracing his finger up and across, he stopped it over nothing of interest. He estimated that the firing had come from about two hundred yards north-west of where he was now, somewhere close to the place where he'd encountered the badger. There wasn't a lot of cover there, more bushes than trees. There was no certainty which bush might be hiding the killer. Sending men in was a huge risk, even when they were in body armour. It only wanted a cloud to move away from the moon and a crack shot like the sniper could take out three or four before his fire was answered. And knowing the wood as he did, he might still have an escape plan.

Diamond released a long, shaky breath.

Then he heard a soft sound nearby. It could have been a falling twig. There was a lot of dead, dry wood outside. Or it might have been the wildlife again.

He switched off the torch and stood up.

Picked up the only weapon to hand, his crutch. Made from light alloy for ease of handling, it was no weapon at all in reality.

More sounds from outside, heavier and regular. Someone was stepping fast towards the holly bush.

Diamond raised the crutch and held it in front of him like a fencer. Instinctive, but futile. It might stop a paper bag in the wind. Not much more. Balanced on one good leg and one dodgy one, he'd fall over if anyone grabbed it.

The steps got louder. No question that they were human.

It crossed Diamond's mind that the sniper, being familiar with Becky Addy Wood, very likely knew of this hideout.

The steps stopped.

He held his breath and waited, watching the narrow space between the laurels and the holly, straining to see anything.

A metallic gleam appeared. He was certain it was a gun, a black automatic, and it was levelled at his chest.

'Take it easy,' he said. 'I'm not armed.'

'Fucking better not be,' Jack Gull said, stepping in and returning the Glock to its holster. 'Careful with that crutch. You could hurt someone. You were so quiet here I had to be careful. Could have been him, lying in wait. He's at this end of the wood.'

'And it's gone quiet again,' Diamond said.

'I don't mind that. By now we've got the rat encircled.'

'Let's hope so. What next?'

'They've all had time to get in position and find cover. I'm going on air again.' Over the radio Gull asked all SFOs—the Specialist Firearms Officers—to report their positions.

Back came a mind-numbing series of numbers. Gull got them into a notebook and said to Diamond, 'That's all units accounted for. He must have missed with his two shots.'

'We haven't checked the unarmed men.'

'We'd have heard. Be positive, for Christ's sake.' He broadcast another message to his little army. 'Hang fire, everyone. Bravo here, and I'm about to join you.' Then he stooped under the laurel branches and came up with a loudhailer and a full-length shield. 'I'm doing this the civilised way,' he told Diamond.

'Bravo, Bravo,' Diamond said, being positive.

A few minutes later, there had been no more firing. He heard Jack Gull's amplified voice say, 'Armed police. We have you surrounded. Put down your weapons, step out with your hands on your head and lie face down. It's the only way you'll survive the next two minutes.'

Silence.

Diamond was strongly tempted to watch what was happening.

Perhaps another minute passed.

'Okay,' Gull radioed, 'let's get some light working for us. Delta Three, toss in a mothball.'

The temptation was too strong now. Diamond stepped to a position partly shielded by the holly bush yet with enough view of the area brilliantly lit by the magnesium pyrotechnic. The dazzle lasted long enough for him to see every yard of the terrain, each bush, each tree, each slab of rock.

But no movement.

A single taller bush of hawthorn looked large enough to be hiding someone.

The firework fizzled and darkness returned abruptly.

'This is your last chance,' Gull said through the loudhailer. 'I'm not bluffing. Armed police. We're about to come in with our MP5s blazing.' Over the radio he ordered another mothball. 'Stand by, everyone. Delta Two, you go in first. Delta One, covering fire. Wait for the order.'

A tense few seconds.

The ground fizzed into brilliant light again.

'Go, go, go!'

Four armed policemen dashed forward and took up positions behind whatever the terrain offered in the way of cover. The nearest man was about twenty yards from the hawthorn bush.

Another magnesium ball was thrown in. There was a burst of gunfire. Smoke rose from the MP5s and the smell of cordite invaded Diamond's nostrils.

No answering shot.

'Go, go, go!' Gull yelled.

The gunmen sprinted forward and hurled themselves at the hawthorn. More gunfire.

More smoke.

But it was police gunfire and police smoke.

One of the men was crawling behind the bush. A moment of panicky silence followed before he shouted, 'Negative.'

Complete anticlimax. Everything went dark again.

'Don't anyone move,' Gull ordered through the radio. 'He's not gone away.'

How do you know, Jack? Diamond thought to himself. But he'd probably have said the same. It was basic good sense not to present the sniper with an easy target.

A good five minutes went by. The only movement was overhead, a cloud clearing away from the moon. In the improved light, a few frontline officers squirmed to different positions and one of them made a discovery.

The radio spluttered and this time the voice wasn't Gull's. 'Delta Two to Bravo. Something here. Looks like a burnt-out length of fuse and it's attached to a piece of cardboard casing. Could be the remains of a mini ground-burst.'

'There's another one here,' a second voice said. 'That'll be the two shots we heard. Ever been had, guys? He treated us to a fireworks display. A slow fuse on a banger. The tosser was out of here before we even turned up.'

A simple distraction device.

Jack Gull was lost for words.

Torches were switched on. The Delta Two officers got up from their crouching positions and stood beside the hawthorn, at a loss. Others came out of hiding and joined them. Diamond left the cover of the holly bush and limped over. Disappointments such as this were all too familiar. One thing he'd learned was not to let it show to the men who'd taken the main risk. Their bravery wasn't in any way diminished.

'Don't trample the ground,' he said. 'We're treating this as a crime scene.'

'That's a vain hope,' Gull said, cradling his loudhailer like a comforter. 'He's done us again.'

'Look on the bright side,' Diamond said. 'No one died this time. When I heard the bangs I was thinking we'd lost someone, maybe two.'

'How did he get here without being spotted? We've been here all fucking night.'

'He's smart, that's why, and he has local knowledge.'

'He's drawn all our firepower to this end of the wood and he's away.'

'We still have pockets of men observing all over,'

Diamond said. 'They could spot him yet.'

'Don't hold your breath.'

Then, as if on cue, a radio voice broke in. 'Oscar One calling. Oscar One calling. He's back and this time he's got his gun.'

CHAPTER ELEVEN

Oscar One's position was about three-quarters of a mile off. With the sniper on the move, it wasn't feasible to get the firearms officers there fast enough to stop him and it was out of the question to ask unarmed observers to tackle a killer carrying a rapid-fire assault rifle.

'Can you keep him under observation?' Diamond asked.

'From here, sir?' Oscar One said over the radio.

A small sigh from Diamond. 'Leave your present position and get after him. Take care he doesn't see you, for Christ's sake.'

'We need a fucking chopper for a job like that,' Jack Gull said.

Diamond ignored the comment. There was no way the police helicopter could be brought into use in time to make a difference. 'Where is he heading?' he asked Oscar One.

'Downhill, sir.'

'Towards Bradford?'

'Towards the canal, anyway.'

The Kennet and Avon canal ran through the bottom of the Limpley Stoke valley parallel to the river and the railway. At the town of Bradford on Avon it diverted south. The sniper had apparently escaped this way yesterday. In the planning for tonight, Diamond had predicted he would use the Westwood route.

Big mistake.

He held out his hand. 'Map.' One was provided. 'How will he do it? He'll need to cross the canal.'

'And the river,' Gull said, as if pursuit would be impossible. 'And the railway.' He was increasingly negative about the whole operation.

'Okay, let's deal with this,' Diamond said, studying the map. 'The nearest crossing point is the aqueduct at Avoncliff where the canal crosses the river and the railway. I know it. I've been there. It's a footbridge as well. Once across, he can pick up a footpath heading into Winsley and he's away if we don't stop him.' He turned to Gull. 'Let's get men down there and block it.'

'Why the fuck didn't we do this already?'

'It wasn't my call, was it?'

'You had a voice in the planning.'

'Yes, and I thought he'd come by way of Westwood and I was wrong. Slap my wrist if you want, Jack. This is spilt milk.'

Gull rolled his eyes and said nothing.

'But we've got to be careful here,' Diamond resumed. 'A small team of armed officers for the aqueduct, yes, but the main force may be needed elsewhere. Actually, it doesn't look as if he's making for Avoncliff. He's at the far end of the wood, the eastern edge. Would he trek all that way and then double back? I don't think so. He seems to be heading along the side of the canal.'

'Where there's no crossing point.'

'There is. Look here.' Diamond tapped the map. 'The swing bridge by the sewage farm.'

Gull wasn't used to being corrected. He took a brief, disbelieving glance and had to admit he was wrong. 'But that only gets him across the canal. He won't get over the river without swimming for it.'

'He doesn't need to. If he follows the towpath all the way through this green bit—the countryside park—he'll reach the Frome Road eventually. Or if he doesn't use the swing bridge and stays this side of the canal he can come through Grip Wood, rough going, no towpath, but better cover.'

Grip Wood, on the south bank, looked about as long as Becky Addy and would be just as dense. The strips of woodland must have been linked in ancient times when most of the valley was forested.

'What we do,' Diamond said, 'is transfer our main firepower to this side of the Frome Road south of Bradford. We put stops on the towpath and all points east of the country park.'

'If he's armed with his sniper rifle now, it's going to be a bloodbath.'

'AFOs are trained to deal with exactly this kind of situation.'

'All of this depends on him taking the canal route.'

'True. I'm relying on Oscar One to keep us updated.'

The downside was that Oscar One had gone silent, presumably already doing his covert surveillance.

Gull marched over to the senior firearms officer to pass on the new orders. He had virtually ceded control to Diamond. The trickery over the fireworks had deflated him. Although both men had been guilty of errors, Supergull with his loudhailer had insisted on the high profile and made a public fool of himself.

A small team was despatched down to the Avoncliff aqueduct, but the main firepower would be posted to the opposite end, where Diamond had predicted the sniper would be heading, this side of the Frome Road. The men would be driven there in their minibuses and they should have time to find cover. It would take the sniper on foot at least another twenty minutes.

Diamond thought about getting in radio contact with John Leaman and telling him to divert most of the men in Westwood to the new point of ambush. Unarmed as they were, they could be useful as observers, but their presence would complicate the operation. Best keep it simple, he decided.

'Do you want a piece of the action?' he asked Gull.

'You mean by the road?'

'You're armed.'

'It's only a sodding handgun. I'll be of more use at the aqueduct.'

'As you wish.'

So it was Diamond armed only with a crutch who joined the firearms team heading for the minibuses. He was too hyped up to care about personal safety. All this could soon be over if he got the sniper's thinking right this time. What he needed was an update from Oscar One. Frustratingly, nothing was coming through on the radio.

Two buses had been driven down from Upper Westwood to the rendezvous at the bend of the road. When the first had filled, he clambered aboard and took the single seat across from the driver. In their body armour laden with radios, tasers, plasticuffs and cutters, torches and handguns, the men needed two seats each. Tension was high. No one, however well trained and experienced, could feel confident being transported to a new, unseen location. Little was said as the wheels bumped over the rough ground and back on to the more even surface.

Getting impatient, Diamond checked that his radio was still switched on, the volume turned high. To be fair, he hadn't instructed Oscar One to make regular reports on the sniper's movements. Maybe that was another error on his part. He shouldn't have assumed it would happen. After all, who was Oscar One? Not one of these macho AFOs, but some young bobby who spent most of his duty time behind a desk. Pure chance had catapulted him into this crucial role. He couldn't be expected to know what to do in pursuit of a killer. It was enough to hope he had the savvy to remain unseen.

A voice could be heard over the heavy drone of the engine in low gear powering them up the steep incline. Not from Diamond's radio. One of the firearms officers was speaking at the back of the bus. 'He's scum. He's totalled three of our lads, doing their job.'

Diamond turned around. 'I don't know who was speaking just then. What you said is fair comment, but getting angry won't help any of us do the job. We have standards, right?'

'You don't need to tell us, guv,' another voice said. 'We've done the training.'

Someone else spoke. 'Angry or not, we're still supposed to take him out.'

'Out of action, yes,' Diamond said. 'Get this straight, all of you. The object is to take the man alive, disable him if need be, but not to kill him. A corpse full of bullets will be a failure. Do that and we'll all find ourselves on a public enquiry being ripped to shreds by some lawyer. We're police officers in pursuit of an armed suspect. Doesn't mean we shoot to kill. Too many deadly mistakes have been made by armed officers in the past. It's not our aim to add to them.'

More was probably said that he didn't hear. He understood the strength of feeling against the sniper, but he wanted an arrest, not a revenge killing. The pressure of a shoot-out, the real thing, would test these young officers to a degree no amount of training had prepared them for. Mishandled, this operation could turn into a nightmare.

They were driven fast through Upper Westwood. With his acute discomfort at any speed over forty, Diamond now regretted choosing the front seat, the more so when they swung left and started down the ultra-narrow Jones Hill. Tall hedgerows caught in the headlights accentuated the velocity. Occasionally an overgrown bramble scraped the side of the bus. He put a hand to his face as if scratching his head and peered through the slits between his fingers.

'Where do I put you down?'

'What?' he uncovered his eyes. They'd done the descent and were approaching the Frome Road, the southern route into Bradford on Avon.

The driver didn't repeat the question. It was plain enough.

Diamond unfolded the map and took a rapid decision. 'There's a place called Victory Field. Over the bridge and sharp left.'

Before they disembarked, he conferred with the

senior man. Protocol mattered now. The armed response team expected to run their own show, but the strategy, such as it was, was being decided at a higher level.

It was agreed Diamond should issue instructions to everyone. 'We can't say which side of the canal the suspect is, so we're covering both. As you get out we'll send you in pairs to various points. By the look of it, we have some open spaces here. Tough for you, but a lot tougher for him. Find whatever cover you can. Keep in radio contact and listen up. It's not impossible there are people out walking, even at this hour, so for God's sake don't shoot the first thing that moves. The suspect is wearing a baseball cap and is probably armed with a sniper rifle and will be coming from the Avoncliff direction. I'll try and let you know when we have a sighting. Let's get this job finished tonight.'

He stood outside with the sergeant in charge and despatched them as they stepped down. They looked incredibly young, some of them plainly scared. The majority fanned out across Victory Field to find points of cover. Some huge trees and the famous fourteenth-century tithe barn and a two-storey granary building offered possibilities. Other pairs looked for positions above and beneath the road bridge over the canal.

He and the sergeant moved to the second bus and repeated the instructions before everyone disembarked. He stressed what he'd said earlier to the first lot, about the need to be responsible, not vengeful.

Both buses were driven off to park in front of the railway station.

This had the making of an effective stake-out,

but would it work? He was about to find out.

He used the radio again. 'Oscar One, report your position. Over.'

Oscar One remained silent.

On the bridge over the canal Diamond watched the shadows of clouds crossing the moonlit Victory Field. His mood was uneasy. He wasn't trained for this role, making life or death decisions on the hoof. He preferred the more measured detective work.

To make sure his radio was working he called John Leaman. The response was immediate. The Avon and Somerset men were still in place in the village.

'You've been following what's happening, I expect.'

'All the way. No joy yet?'

'Not yet.'

Jack Gull came on air from his chosen position at the aqueduct. No one had been sighted there. 'Looks like he headed your way.'

'We can hope.'

'If it's a no-show, you owe me, Diamond.' Still negative and still quick to blame.

Three minutes went by.

The static alerted him again. 'Sierra Three at Barton Bridge, repeat, Barton Bridge. We have a sighting.'

Barton Bridge, another of Bradford's ancient structures, seven hundred years old, spanned the Avon only a few hundred yards from where Diamond was.

Pulses raced.

'Description?'

'Average height and build, baseball cap, holding

something, could be the gun, moving at a fast step south-east towards the barn.'

He pressed the radio close to his mouth and spoke softly. 'Stand by, everyone. Hold your fire and let him come. We'll challenge him near the barn. I repeat: hold your fire.' He'd posted enough armed men in the area to handle this. As the suspect approached the building he'd find it acted as a barrier closing off one of his escape routes and the police would surround him.

With cruel timing, a large cloud scudded across the moon and drastically reduced the light. The marksmen had night-vision glasses, Diamond told himself. This shouldn't hamper them too much. Personally he was finding it difficult to make anything out. But if his sight was impaired, then so was the suspect's. Use the dark to your advantage, he told himself. Maximise your opportunity. You have the chance to get closer in reasonable safety.

He started limping across the turf towards the barn. His heart was pounding against his ribcage, not with the exercise, but the stress. Could he rely on those young firearms officers to act responsibly?

A series of sharp sounds close at hand pulled him up sharply.

'Oscar One to Bravo. Over.'

Oscar One. Finally.

He tucked the crutch under his arm and grabbed the radio. 'I hear you. Where are you?'

'I lost him, sir. I'm sorry.'

'How? What do you mean?'

'He gave me the slip near the swing bridge. I reckon he legged it over the fields. I followed the trail into some kind of park, thinking he must have gone that way.'

Some kind of park? 'It's okay, Oscar One, you did all right. We have a sighting of him.'

'Thank Christ for that.'

'Where are you now?'

'I'm not sure, sir. It's gone dark. I must be quite close to the river, I think. I can hear it on my left.'

'If you're that close, you're not far from where we are.'

'I can just see some buildings up ahead.'

A chill crept over Diamond's flesh. 'Are you wearing a baseball cap?'

'My police issue cap.'

'Are you carrying anything?'

'Only my PR24, sir, for protection.'

'Your what?'

'My baton.'

He pictured the standard side-handle baton: two feet long, black, metal, easily mistaken for a firearm in this poor light.

'Stop where you are, Oscar One. Don't take another step. Drop the baton and stand still.'

'Sir, I think he's away out of it.'

'Do as I say.'

If he was right, Oscar One was the man at Barton Bridge, seconds away from being ambushed by armed police.

Fumbling with the radio controls, Diamond managed to get out a general message that the sighting at Barton Bridge was now believed to be of a police officer. On no account was anyone to fire a shot. He insisted on getting responses from each of the firearms teams.

In addition he got one from Jack Gull. 'Fuck you, Diamond, what are you playing at? Has the killer got clean away again?'

CHAPTER TWELVE

Oscar One was not the rookie constable Diamond had pictured. With hair turning silver at the sides, he was one of the unsung majority who see out their time without moving up the ranks. No discredit in that. In Diamond's experience the promotion system was designed to reward conformity rather than imagination and risk-taking. You found more likeable blokes, more kindred spirits, among beat officers than in senior positions.

His name was Henry Shilling and he wasn't used to finding himself in conversation with someone of superintendent rank.

'Not your fault, but we almost gunned you down,' Diamond told him. 'You could have been front-page news. The papers like a friendly-fire story.'

'Thank you, sir.'

'What for?'

'Saving my life.'

'Self-interest. Sensitive ears. I can't stand gunfire.'

PC Shilling frowned and blinked. He wasn't on the Diamond wavelength yet.

The big man was thinking the sensitive-ears quip wasn't bad for four thirty in the morning. He went on more straightforwardly, 'But I'm glad you finally used your radio. That's what saved you. Saved my career, come to that, so I owe you. Tell me something.' He paused, not wanting to make this sound like a rebuke. 'Why didn't you get in touch before?'

'Two reasons, sir.'

Diamond raised his palms. 'No one "sirs" me. "Guv", if you must. What are your two reasons?'

'At the start I didn't want him to overhear me.'

'You got as close as that?'

'You told me to go in pursuit and I did. Reason two: towards the end I lost him, so I couldn't report his position. I was hoping I'd catch up again.'

'And be able to report something positive?'

'Well, yes.'

'Understandable.' It was easy to grasp what had run through PC Shilling's mind while he was legging it along the towpath in pursuit. Diamond would have felt the same, torn between confessing to failure and trying to reverse it. 'But you're still the main player.'

'How come?'

'The only sighting of this killer. If you don't hold the ace of trumps I don't know who does. What can you tell me about him?'

A troubled look surfaced on PC Shilling's features. 'I didn't see much.'

'Even when you were so close it wasn't safe to use the radio?'

'The light wasn't good.'

'Think back. Get him in your mind's eye again. What's he wearing?' There was a touch of the hypnotist in Diamond's manner, but it was only a surface effect. He couldn't get anyone to relax if he tried.

'Like I told you. Baseball cap and dark clothes.'

'Jacket or shirt?'

'Tight-fitting jacket. He's slim. Moves like a fit man. I think he was in jeans and trainers. And he carried the gun.'

'Ah, the gun. What type?'

'Short-barrelled, chunky, like our own lads use, and with extra bits.'

'Extra bits such as?'

'I don't know much about firearms, guv.'

'I gathered that. You know what a telescopic sight is?'

'There was one of them, yes. Some kind of folding stand under the barrel. And a holder for the bullets.'

'A box magazine. How did he carry the gun?'

'In his right hand, the barrel towards the ground. But he stopped once and drew it to his chest and gripped it with both hands. He turned round. I think he heard me kick a stone.'

'Scary.'

'Very.'

'You took evasive action?'

A grin. 'Flat on my stomach in the long grass. He didn't see me, I think.'

'You wouldn't be telling the tale if he had. Where did this happen?'

'About a hundred yards after we crossed the swing bridge.'

'We'll take a look in daylight. We should be able to find where you were lying. Let's get back to him. What height would you say?'

'About the same as me. I'm five nine.'

'Anything memorable about the way he moves?'

'A bit of a stoop, but that could be the weight of the weapon. It looked heavy to me.'

'Six pounds or more, probably. You wouldn't want to carry it for a mile or two, as he did. Did you see his face at any stage?'

'Not enough to tell you anything about it.'

'Clean-shaven?'

'Hard to tell. If he had a beard it wasn't bushy.'

'And he kept the baseball cap on all the time?'

'All the time.'

'Where did he give you the slip?'

'If I knew that, I'd have called in when it happened. I went on for quite some way, thinking he was still ahead of me. What with the poor light and the bends in the path I was losing sight of him every now and then. Thinking back, it must have happened about halfway between the swing bridge and here. Maybe he did spot me following him.'

Diamond shook his head. 'You'd be dead meat if he had. It's possible he heard you and decided to go back. He knows this area, that's for sure. He was taking a calculated risk approaching the town by way of the park. For about half a mile he was on a narrow strip with the river to his left and the canal to his right. We could have trapped him there. I think he came that way thinking we hadn't had time to prepare an ambush, then lost his nerve or more likely changed his mind and doubled back. He could still be lying up somewhere.'

'Is it worth making a search?'

'Until daybreak our chance of locating him is nil. We'll organise what we can at first light, but I'm not optimistic.'

'Should I rejoin my unit in Becky Addy Wood, guv?'

'No. Take off your shoes.'

PC Shilling gave Diamond a long look. He'd gleaned that he couldn't take everything at face value from the man from Bath. 'My shoes?'

'I want forensics to look at them. Unfortunately I can't offer you a replacement pair. You'll just have to tiptoe to one of the minibuses in your socks and curl up on a seat and get some shut-eye. I'm going to need you later.'

* * *

The hour before dawn—not the time you want to be awake—was when it fully sank in with Diamond that a unique opportunity was lost. The best that could now be hoped was that forensics would pick up some traces. Helpful as Shilling had tried to be, his description of the suspect was of negligible value. People's estimates of heights were unreliable and a change of clothing would negate all the rest.

Was this the moment to hand the whole sorry case back to Jack Gull, who was still officially running the show? The Serial Crimes Unit had the firepower, all the expertise, and was better equipped for action than a middle-aged detective with a beer belly and a limp.

I don't think so, he told himself.

The latest killing was on his patch. Harry Tasker was Manvers Street family and the family cared. No one—least of all Diamond—was going to back off. And if Gull or any other jobsworth wanted to argue they would come up against the fact that the sniper had demonstrated local knowledge, set up camp in Becky Addy and dominated the terrain like a territorial jackal.

'I'll need more of your foot soldiers than we had overnight,' he told the inspector in charge of the Wiltshire contingent. 'This lot did all I could have asked and deserve their sleep, but replacements must be here before they go off duty. There's a search to get under way. And in case you're about to ask, I'm bussing in more from Avon and Somerset.'

'What I was about to ask is who is funding this,' the inspector said. 'It seems to be your operation with our manpower. I'm seriously overrunning my budget.'

'In the interests of cross-border harmony, I won't tell you where to stuff your budget. Don't push me, chum. It's been a long night.'

Various duty officers, at Forensics, Headquarters and Manvers Street, had to be called. There was a certain satisfaction in reminding them that even at this hour he was on the case and requiring back-up and expecting results. Finally he called Supergull and updated him.

'You seem to have a lot of energy,' the head of the SCU commented.

'I grabbed some shut-eye earlier, quality shut-eye. How about you?'

'Knackered.' So utterly knackered that Gull had forgotten to preface it with a strong adjective.

'Better get your head down, Jack. It's under control.'

'Right, I'll do just that.'

Without even a murmur of protest.

Actually Diamond was feeling chipper. The sleep he'd fitted in before midnight had set him up nicely. He'd probably experience something akin to jet lag later. For the present he was Mr Motivator.

Soon after the first flush of daylight, he took a walk with PC Shilling (in borrowed shoes) and a scene of crime team through the countryside park to look for the place where Shilling had lain prone in long grass. The dawn chorus was exhilarating and the sudden shafts of light through the trees made a show better than anything Walt Disney had ever put on film. For one fleeting moment he persuaded himself he should rise earlier more often. Then he remembered why he was here.

Distances can be difficult to judge in stress situations and Shilling's first estimate of where he'd hit the ground was wrong by almost fifty yards. One of the team walked on and found the place eventually, enough grass still flattened to leave no doubt.

'Do you want this taped off, sir?'

'No need. I'm more interested in where the suspect was.'

Henry Shilling pointed. 'Twenty to twenty-five yards in that direction, no more.'

'Let's see.' Diamond's faith in Shilling's judgement of distances was draining away. However, the ground conditions gave rise to hope that the search was worthwhile. This stretch was close enough to the Avon to get flooded from time to time. Marsh flowers like the creeping buttercup thrived here and so did riverside trees such as sallow, willow and alder. The ground dried hard in warm weather, but a stretch of the path was still moist from recent high water.

He started forward.

'Watch how you go, Mr Diamond.' This urgent shout came from one of the forensic team and it wasn't Diamond's limping gait that concerned him, but the possibility of shoeprints being stepped over and ruined.

He stopped. 'One of you lot had better go ahead.'

The process took fifteen minutes longer than it would have with Diamond leading the way, but it produced a result: a number of clean prints in an area of light mud. The marks showed the sort of intricate patterning typical of rubber-soled running shoes. And yes, they were measured at twenty-three yards from where PC Shilling had hidden in the grass. The direction and positioning suggested that the wearer of the shoes had stood there and half turned before moving on.

'These are stunning. I couldn't ask for better,' the forensics team leader said as if he was judging a flower show. 'Tape off this area and we'll get some photos first and then do the casts.'

'You'll be able to identify the make of shoe?' Diamond asked.

'No question. We keep a database of all the makes. Better still, there's evidence of wear noticeable even to the naked eye, so we should be able to match them to the actual pair of shoes. You get little cuts, nicks and scratches that can be just as helpful as fingerprint ridge patterns.'

'We still have to find the shoes.'

'True, but you can also look for matching prints elsewhere. Were any found at the crime scenes?'

'I believe they were.'

'A word of warning. I wouldn't get too excited,' the man from forensics added, having stoked up a heap of excitement himself. 'Prints found on a public pathway won't stand up in court, even with your police witness. A competent defence lawyer will eat you alive on what we have so far.'

'It's a beginning,' Diamond said. 'Up to now all we have is a worthless sighting of the suspect on a motorbike.'

'Why worthless?'

'Because the witness is a dumb cluck who can't

tell one bike from another.'

He and PC Shilling left them to it.

* * *

The systematic search of the area had been under way almost two hours with no new finds when Diamond took a call on his mobile from Keith Halliwell.

'How are you holding up, guv?'

'Okay.'

'And how is the pain in the—'

'Jack Gull? He's gone to bed.'

'I meant *your* pain in *your* leg.'

'Not a problem. Hasn't hampered me one bit. Where are you?'

'The incident room. Remember you asked me to look for fingerprints for Willis, the guy living on the top floor in the Paragon house?'

'From his car, yes. And you got a good set. Any news yet?'

'He isn't in the system. Seems he's a law-abiding citizen.'

'Pity.'

'Also a call came in from Harry Tasker's widow. She'd like to see you as soon as possible.'

'See *me*?' Yesterday's meeting flashed up in his memory: the next-of-kin interview he'd rather forget. 'Something wrong?'

'She wouldn't say. Wouldn't leave a message. Wouldn't want anyone else to go there. She had a female officer with her yesterday, but she soon sent her packing. I didn't press her for information, in view of her sad loss. I promised you'd try and get there later today.'

'I'd better. Did it sound urgent?'

'Hard to tell. The voice is kind of flat. The shock has kicked in, I guess.'

'It kicked in with a vengeance while I was with her. If she's calmed down, that's a help. Maybe it's about getting the body released for the funeral. When's the autopsy?'

'This afternoon.' A pause from Halliwell. 'You'd like me to be there?'

Diamond disliked being predictable. 'Who else is about?'

'Nobody much. Half the station are up at Westwood on a door-to-door round in case anyone witnessed the suspect in the last few days. John Leaman is catching up on sleep. Ingeborg is in Radstock.'

'Radstock?'

'You may remember sending her there to get the dope on their murdered officer.'

'So I did.' It seemed a month ago.

'Looks as if it's me for the post-mortem, then.' Halliwell refrained from adding 'as usual'.

'You're a tower of strength, Keith. If it weren't for my dodgy leg . . .'

'. . . which you said hasn't hampered you one bit.'

'Ouch.'

'Okay, guv. I'll head off to the mortuary. No one is better placed than you to handle Mrs Tasker.'

Open to debate, Diamond thought.

* * *

More shoeprints were found matching the set discovered earlier. They were in a stand of larch at the eastern edge of Becky Addy Wood, where

PC Shilling had first seen the suspect. The finds might not impress a court of law, but they were encouraging to Diamond. He was satisfied they had been made by the suspect. They could be compared with any shoeprints found at the murder scenes in Wells and Radstock. Photos and fresh casts were taken.

Towards midday John Leaman returned to duty and took over. 'You deserve a siesta, guv,' he said.

'A black coffee will have to do,' Diamond said. 'I'll go home and feed the cat and then visit Emma Tasker. She's asking to see me. God knows why.'

* * *

The gasholder at the Windsor Bridge works loomed and he stopped the car as close as he could to Onega Terrace, opposite a row of houses called Park View. Grimly appropriate, he thought. In theory, there was a park across the street, but any view was masked by a solid mass of tall conifers, so the residents had to settle for parked cars.

A large woman, much larger than the widow, opened the door. Diamond explained who he was.

The woman looked him up and down with suspicion, probably taking him for a pressman, in spite of who he claimed to be. She was evidently a neighbour doing her best to shield Emma from unwanted callers.

He told her he'd been invited to call.

'What did you say your name is?'

He heard Emma's voice from deeper inside the house. 'If he's the big thug who was here yesterday, send him in.'

Not the best testimonial I've been given, he

thought.

He was shown into the room where Emma Tasker sat in an armchair, wrapped in a blanket made of hand-knitted coloured squares. 'What caused that?' she said, eyeing his crutch.

'Fell over.'

'Drunk?'

He shook his head. 'Man drove at me on a motorbike.'

'So it isn't just a try for sympathy in case I lose my rag again and start throwing things at you?'

He chanced a quick smile and failed to get one in return.

'What man? One of your own?' Again, the remark sounded flip, the sort of bitter humour he was used to at work. But still her face showed not a flicker of amusement.

'No, a suspect. He was hiding in the woods near Bradford on Avon.'

'Did he get away?'

'Up to now, yes.'

'Is he Harry's killer—Harry and the other two who were shot?'

'It's likely.'

'Bastard. And you let him get away?'

'Unfortunately, yes.'

'He'll shoot someone else now.' She was unrelenting.

'I hope not.' The words sounded feeble as he spoke them and he tried for a stronger response and did no better. 'We'll not rest until he's caught.'

'He's got nothing to lose,' she said. 'He'll go on picking off good men while you lot fail to catch him.'

'Believe me, ma'am, we're doing everything in

our power to stop him.' Quickly, he changed tack. 'And how are you coping?'

'It's no picnic.'

'I'm sure.'

'I haven't had any sleep yet.'

'Get your doctor to prescribe something.'

Her voice took on the hard edge of the previous day. 'You've done this before, haven't you? You're the duty comforter, the guy they send to all the police widows. Couldn't they rake up anyone better than you?'

'If you'd prefer me to leave . . .'

She shook her head. 'You're all as bad as each other. I had to identify Harry this morning at the mortuary. They sent a car and two officers, male and female. They treated me as if I was ninety, calling me dear and trying to hold my arm. I didn't take kindly to it and I told them.'

He had no difficulty picturing it.

She was able to talk openly about the experience. 'The sight of him wasn't as bad as I expected. His face was hardly damaged at all. Of course they were careful to cover the sides of his head where the bullet went through. He looked fairly normal.'

He gave a nod, rather than chancing any comment.

Her account moved on. 'They told me they're releasing the body later today. I don't want one of those big police funerals with hundreds of bobbies who never knew him lining the street and all the top brass showing off their medals in the church. Harry's send-off is going to be low key. Just a few family and friends.'

This time he had to respond. 'Whatever you say. We'll respect your wishes. Some of his close colleagues will want to be there, I'm sure, but it doesn't have to be too formal. You won't be able to keep the press away, unfortunately.'

'I've got used to them already. It's ghoulish, all this interest in photographing the widow.'

'If you'd like some of our lads to keep them from troubling you, I can arrange it.'

'No need.'

A pause in the outflow of words made him think this was the opportunity to leave. 'I'll pass on what you said about the funeral, just in case the high-ups were planning anything. Is that why asked me to come?'

'No.' She pointed across the room. 'On the table there's a small piece of paper, folded. Bring it over.'

The square dining table had various things on it: a heap of coins, some credit cards in a small leather case, keys on a ring and the paper, white, small and folded once. He handed it to her.

'The contents of his pockets,' she said. 'They returned them to me at the mortuary. This was tucked in among the credit cards.' She unfolded the paper and handed it to Diamond. 'What do you make of that?'

CHAPTER THIRTEEN

The limp remained, but Diamond had progressed to a walking stick. In truth the soreness in the leg felt about the same. Knowing how appearances influence people's opinion of you, he'd discarded the crutches for good and arranged for them to be returned to the Royal United Hospital.

The team noted a change in his looks when he stood to update them on the morning's discoveries. The unhealthy pallor was gone, replaced by unhealthy ruddiness from high blood pressure.

The guv'nor restored.

The improvement was largely due to a rise in confidence. He'd floated the idea with John Leaman that the killings might not, after all, be random, as Jack Gull and everyone else assumed. The latest discovery appeared to support his thinking.

'Some of you know Harry Tasker's widow Emma asked to see me this morning,' he said. 'Between ourselves, I was surprised to hear from her. She'd already given me a hard time—and I don't blame her in the least—when I first broke the news of Harry's murder. You never know how anyone will react to a shock like that. She's bitter that Harry was on beat duty the night he was shot and she blames us almost as much as his killer. I did a poor job of comforting her. So today I was expecting more aggravation. I won't say it was all sweetness and light, but we discussed a few things. She wants Harry to have a low-key funeral.'

'Is that possible?' Halliwell asked.

'No uniforms, no guard of honour. A simple service for close friends and family.'

'No police?'

'A few of his closest mates from uniform. If we want to honour him ourselves we'll have to find some other way.'

'She won't stop the media being there.'

'We make damn sure they behave.' He turned to the main matter. 'But the reason Mrs Tasker wanted to see me was something I wasn't expecting.

Harry's personal possessions—the contents of his pockets when he was shot—were returned to her this morning. Among them was this.'

He raised it for all to see, a strip of white now enclosed in a transparent evidence bag. 'Found in the little case he kept his credit cards in. A scrap of paper with two words on it obviously produced on a computer printer.' He passed the bag to the youngest member of the team. 'Read them out, would you?'

'Me?' DC Paul Gilbert did as he was asked, but in a throwaway tone that meant nothing. '"You're next".'

A moment of bemused silence followed.

'*You're next*,' Diamond repeated, spacing the words to give them their full sinister meaning. 'Do I need to say more?'

No one was willing to commit.

'Come on. Liven up.'

Finally John Leaman said, 'A note from the killer?'

'That's the obvious interpretation, and we can't ignore it. However Harry came by the note, he must have thought it was worth keeping. Whether he took it as a death threat, we can't say. He didn't behave as if he was going in fear of his life.'

'Some kind of practical joke,' Keith Halliwell said. 'That's what I would think if it was sent to me.'

'Joke?' John Leaman said. '"You're next"—what kind of joke is that when some madman is targeting us?'

'Black humour.'

'If that's humour, I don't get it.'

Diamond was listening keenly. To get his own thoughts straight, he had earlier run through a raft of similar possibilities. He wanted the team to reach its own consensus that the note was fundamental to the investigation.

Halliwell was sticking with his joke theory. 'Well, it may have nothing to do with the shootings. Suppose Harry was one of those guys who never buy a round of drinks? A note like that would amuse his mates.'

'Was he a tightwad?' someone asked.

'Now you're speaking ill of the dead,' Leaman said.

'Why would he keep the note, anyway?' another voice said.

Then Ingeborg spoke up. She'd driven back from Radstock in the last hour. 'We've got a duty to take it seriously. Unless we can prove it's unimportant we have to assume it's evidence.'

'I'm not dismissing it,' Halliwell said. 'I'm keeping an open mind. We don't know how long he's had it in his pocket.'

'May I see?' Ingeborg said. 'I did the forensics course a few weeks ago.'

Smiles all round at this naked self-promotion. Even Diamond grinned.

'No need to remind us,' one of the older DCs said. 'We filled in for you.'

She ignored him, well used to backchat from colleagues.

Gilbert handed her the evidence bag.

Ingeborg inspected it from several angles and then turned it over. 'Printed on an A4 sheet in Times New Roman, font size 14. It looks very much as if the person who wrote it didn't want to be detected. The sheet was trimmed with scissors. The top is even, but the lower cut isn't a perfect match.

A document examiner might get more information.'

Looks were exchanged. The team were more amused than annoyed by the Sherlock Holmes impersonation. Ingeborg was popular, for all her striving.

She hadn't finished. 'Latent fingerprints may be the best hope, but we must allow that at least five different people have handled it since it was printed.'

'Five?' Halliwell's eyebrows arched in surprise.

'The person who printed it, Harry himself, the mortuary person who removed it from his pocket, Emma and our esteemed leader.'

The spotlight was back on Diamond, not renowned for handling evidence to the highest forensic standards.

'How do you know I didn't use tweezers?' he said. No one gave this a moment's credence, so he continued, 'To be truthful, I didn't. Inge is right. If there are prints, they'll include a bunch of extras on top of the ones that interest us. I don't expect any miracles from forensics. However, Inge is also correct in saying we can't ignore this as a likely death threat.'

'Meaning the random-killer theory could be wrong,' Leaman said. 'Jack Gull could be barking up the wrong tree.'

'And the media and most of the public,' Ingeborg said.

'Right.' Diamond folded his arms. 'That was hard going. Are you lot still half asleep, or what?'

'Are you going to tell him, guv?' Halliwell asked.

'Tell Gull? When I do, I know what he'll say.'

'It's a red herring.'

'Except Jack will put it a touch more forcefully.'

He took a look around the room and made sure he missed no one on the team. 'Are you with me now, all of you? The note appears to show that the killer knew Harry. If the other two victims received similar notes, he knew them as well. If so, our job has just got a whole lot simpler.'

'Simpler?' Halliwell said.

'We've narrowed the search.'

'Someone with a grudge against all the victims?'

'Who knew each of them, tracked them down and murdered them.'

'In three different towns?'

The last comment was supposed to sound a sceptical note, but Diamond treated it as support. 'Right. And there's another factor. It wasn't just a matter of shooting at any cop who walked by. The sniper knew when these individuals were going on duty.'

'That begs some tough questions,' Ingeborg said. 'He'd need inside knowledge.'

'One of our own?' Halliwell said in rampant disbelief. 'A cop?'

Murmurs of dissent rumbled around the incident room. Suddenly the looks Diamond was getting weren't complimentary. They weren't just disbelieving. They were unfriendly. One cop killing another was too much to swallow.

'It has to be faced,' he said, and he'd had an hour or so longer to come to terms with it. 'Cop, PCSO or civilian support staff. Who else sees the duty rosters?'

The murmurs turned to a buzz of angry voices talking among themselves. Diamond became anxious. He was in serious danger of losing control. In his long years of service here, he'd not had many run-ins with the team. This hostile reception was ominous.

He believed they would agree with him when they were over the first shock. All they needed was longer to think this through, as he had. Better move on, he decided.

He had to shout to be heard. 'Ingeborg.'

The noise reduced, giving way to interest in whether Diamond's blue-eyed girl had just said something really over the top and the old ogre had picked it up.

Ingeborg glared back at him as if he was recruiting for the devil.

He made an effort to sound reasonable. 'We haven't heard from you about your visits to Wells and Radstock. How did you get on?'

Her intake of breath sounded like a blowtorch. 'I'm trying to get over what I just heard. It's beyond belief that any police officer would gun down three of our own. If this is the price of taking that scrap of paper seriously, I'm not sure I'm with you any more.'

'You don't like it, I don't either,' he said, appealing to everyone in the room. 'I could be out on a limb here, but as you said a moment ago we have a duty to investigate. Now, Inge, do us the favour of reporting back, as I asked.'

She tossed her head, more to suppress the outrage she felt than in defiance. 'There's not much to add to what we have on file. I spent last evening with some of the lads from Wells CID. They've had longer to come to terms with all this than we have and they're in no doubt that it was a random shooting.'

Nudge, nudge, he thought. He could hear

murmurs of approval for the Wells lads.

'You've made your point. Now what did you pick up?'

'Only snippets. Ossy Hart came to Wells as a probationer and had just four years of service there.'

'Where did he train?'

'Foundation training at Portishead. Before that he was a PE teacher.'

'In Minehead. We know this already.'

'Sorry I spoke,' Ingeborg said, still fractious.

'Go on. I'm impatient—as if that wasn't bloody obvious.'

'I was going to say that the Wells bunch liked Ossy. He ticked most of the boxes. Reliable, good timekeeper, very fit, so hardly a day off duty, good at dealing with the public, always well turned out.'

'Which are the boxes he didn't tick?'

She reflected on that for a moment. 'He was a tad too ambitious for some of them. It showed. He was looking to get promoted as soon as he could.'

'Promoted? He'd only just completed his probation.'

'Two years, guv.' There was more than a hint of protest in the remark. Ingeborg was a high-flyer herself, looking to get a sergeant's stripes soon.

'Okay,' Diamond said. 'I can see it would rankle with the others. What else?'

'He didn't like paperwork.'

'He's not alone there.'

'Yes, but he skimped and got caught out a few times.'

'Hardly a capital offence if it didn't upset the running of the place too much. Anything else?'

'They said he was a bit physical.'

'Meaning what?'

'Being strong, he'd grab people by the arm to make a point and let them know he had a firm grip. I'm talking about his colleagues, not just villains. A couple of the girls said he'd left bruises and they told him to be more considerate, but he never seemed to learn.'

'Annoying, but not enough to make anyone want to murder him. Did he make any real enemies at Wells?'

She gave an impatient sigh. 'If he did, no one was saying.'

'I can understand why. And what about the nickname? Where did that come from?'

'The "Ossy"? I didn't find out. They said he was given it before he joined the police. He didn't seem to mind. When he started at Wells he said he preferred Ossy to his real name of Martin.'

'Nobody asked where it came from?'

'If they did, they didn't get an answer. No one could tell me. Does it matter?'

'Maybe, maybe not. Nicknames are usually given to people for a reason, some quirk of character they have, or an incident that happened to them. I was hoping we might learn something we don't know already.'

'If you really want to find out, his widow would know.'

He snapped his fingers. 'Good thought. And she might tell us a whole lot more that could be useful.' Then he hesitated. 'No, I'd prefer not to approach her at this stage. I'm assuming she's been interviewed already by Jack Gull or one of his team.'

'A widow too far?' Ingeborg said.

He frowned. 'What do you mean by that?'

'I'm wondering if Emma Tasker has put you off interviewing widows. I don't mind going to see this lady if you want.'

He wasn't amused. 'It's not that. I don't intend to give Gull any grounds for complaint. He could close us down if he gets the idea we're running a rival show.'

'Which we are,' John Leaman said.

'In the interest of the truth. But let's face it, Gull is the headquarters man and his remit is to investigate serial crimes. Ours is to assist him over the murder of Harry Tasker. We need to tread carefully.'

'That'll be a first,' a voice said from the back, and got a laugh. The mood of Bath CID was still bordering on rebellion.

Diamond had the sense not to jump down the joker's throat. 'Inge, did you learn anything else from Wells?'

'Not really.'

'And you went on to Radstock and made enquiries about PC Richmond. Did he have a nickname?'

'None that I heard about. He was Stan to everyone there. A loner, wrapped up in his folklore hobby. Always willing to talk about ancient fairs and stone circles, but clueless about the things the others were into, like football and last night's television. He often had his head in a book.'

'A good copper?'

'No one had any complaints. He did the job and evidently knew the law better than most. Unlike Ossy Hart, he had no desire to be promoted. He worked his shift and overtime when required, and that was all he seemed to want. They used to joke that he was away with the fairies the rest of the time.'

'How did he take that?'

'In good humour. He didn't seem to mind.'

'He wasn't gay?'

She rolled her eyes. 'The fairies they meant were the little people.'

'He didn't make enemies?'

'No. It was a massive shock to everyone when he was shot. There's no question Stan Richmond was well liked. They were genuinely sad that he was killed.' She paused. 'They'd be amazed to hear it suggested he was shot by someone who worked with him.'

Another nudge. More like a dig in the ribs.

He was trying to stay calm. 'Stan Richmond moved around a lot in his career. Is it possible he overlapped with either Ossy Hart or Harry Tasker?'

'Certainly not Ossy. He only ever served at Wells.'

'He trained at Portishead.'

'Yes, but almost twenty years after Stan Richmond went through. As for Harry, I wouldn't know about his service record before he came to Bath.'

Halliwell was shaking his head. 'I've looked at his postings. There's no overlap.'

'Okay,' Diamond said, needing to lay out the realities. 'Let's deal with what we know so far. The sniper uses a G36 rifle—and that's also a police-issue weapon—with deadly accuracy. He's well informed about foot patrols. He's good at hiding up and escaping stake-outs. He seems to anticipate our moves and know our routines. I'm going to need a list of all personnel who served with the three victims—and I mean everyone, top brass, CID, uniform, PCSOs and civilian staff.'

Total silence.

Ingeborg was the first to speak. 'That sounds to me like a witch-hunt.'

'And that's a comment that does you no credit, Inge,' he said. 'This is a murder enquiry, remember? "You're next"—right? If we take it seriously—and I'm telling you that's our duty—Harry was picked out to be shot. We must assume the others were picked, too, all serving policemen. If they were lorry drivers or construction workers, you wouldn't think twice about checking the career records of people who served with them. I've been around long enough to know that not all police officers are angels. In fact, I could name several who committed murder. This may go against the grain, but it has to be done.'

Ingeborg shook her head and went silent.

You could have built a wall from the antagonism in the room. Still, he wasn't backing off.

'Keith, you can take this on,' he told Halliwell.

'Do I have to?'

'What?' This time the shock was on Diamond's side and it was like being hit by a demolition ball. For his oldest colleague to question an order, this had to be a full-blown revolt. 'It's a routine job, for pity's sake. Someone in personnel will press a computer key and the names will roll out at your end.'

Halliwell had turned crimson. 'I'm not happy with it, guv. It seems disloyal.'

'Not to me, it isn't.'

'You're putting me in an impossible position.

We're being asked to investigate hundreds of brother officers for murder. I've never done that before.'

'If we had a union,' Ingeborg started up again, 'it would be a strike issue.'

She earned sounds of support for saying that.

'But we don't,' Diamond said, 'and our job is to uncover the truth. I don't like what I'm hearing. All I want at this stage is that list of names. No one is being fingered. We'll eliminate most of them straight away.'

'And finger the ones who are left,' Ingeborg said.

He was incensed. 'That's out of order.'

Flushing all over her blonde skin, Ingeborg paused before saying, 'Guv, have you any idea what this kind of shake-out is going to do for everyone's confidence, morale, team spirit—all those things we pay lip service to.'

He hadn't expected this degree of opposition. No one was siding with him and neither could he expect them to now that Keith Halliwell had dug his heels in. Ingeborg sounding off was one thing, but Keith wasn't a hothead. He carried the respect of the entire team.

It came down to a test of Diamond's own self-belief. He'd been arguing that the killer's knowledge of police duty rosters made it inevitable that the crimes were internal. Was there a flaw in his logic?

There was. He had been expecting someone on the team to nail him.

In their stroppy mood they had failed to see that if the sniper was a policeman targeting specific victims he had to know the beat rosters at three different stations over a period of twelve weeks.

Just about impossible.

So there was still a chance that the 'You're next' note was a joke, as Halliwell had first suggested, unrelated to Harry Tasker's shooting and not connected to the crime. If so, then Gull, blast him, could be right in his assumption that the choice of victims was random.

I'm losing my authority here, he thought, and my case isn't watertight. I've failed to convince my team. Usually I have a sense of what is solid evidence, but have I been too hasty?

He had a nagging suspicion that he was motivated by the rivalry with Jack Gull. Had he let the man get under his skin to that degree?

Uncharacteristically, he backed down.

'I'm not going to make an insubordination issue out of this,' he told them, making it sound as much like a smooth transition as he could. 'We've been together too long to allow a difference of opinion to stop us from functioning. I don't mind admitting that what I suggested takes some swallowing. I've had longer than you to think it over. Keith . . .'

Halliwell did a fair impersonation of a rabbit in headlights. 'Guv?'

'You can disregard that order I just gave you. I'll re-examine everything I just said. In return I'm asking you—all of you—to reflect further. If you have any better ideas, then for God's sake make them known to me.'

This, from their shit-or-bust leader, created as big a sensation as the issue itself.

* * *

In the Wife of Bath (a Pierrepont Street restaurant

renowned for its generous portions) that evening with Paloma Kean, his friend and occasional partner, the shit-or-bust leader confessed to bust. 'I boxed myself in. Messed up totally. I could feel the ground crumbling under me and there was nothing I could do. Even as I was speaking I knew if I were one of them I'd feel just as angry.'

'But if you believe a policeman is involved in the crimes, it has to be faced,' she said.

'Only if it's true. The question is whether the evidence stacks up, and it does—but not enough.'

'Go on.'

'I can't work out how he knew so much about the day-to-day running of three different police stations.'

'Was he transferred? That happens, doesn't it?'

'Not twice in three months.'

'Are the beat duties notified to your headquarters?'

'Good thinking, but no. It's decided at the local level. There's enough form-filling without that.'

'I've run out of ideas, then.'

'Me, too, more's the pity.'

'There's another thing I can't understand,' Paloma said. 'Why would the sniper send a note like that? What's the point?'

His eyes widened. This was a different angle. 'Bragging, I suppose.'

'It conflicts with everything else he does. He's secretive, stealthy, keeps his distance. Why risk sending a note and potentially revealing information about himself?'

He started thinking aloud. 'Maybe all the secrecy doesn't satisfy him. He wanted Harry Tasker to know he was next for execution.' He leaned back in his chair and rested the knife and fork on the plate. 'You're on to something here. The note doesn't have much point unless there's some history behind it. I wonder if Harry himself knew why the others had been murdered. There could have been bad blood that involved all three—and the killer. Then the note makes sense. It was sent out of malice. Harry received it and knew his turn had come. For the sniper, that brought satisfaction.'

'Sadistic.'

'That's my reading, anyway.'

'If I received a note like that and knew what it meant, I wouldn't agree to walk the beat at night,' Paloma said. 'I'd find any excuse to save my skin.'

'Fair point, but where would you be safe? This is a clinical killer. You'd have to resign your job and never leave your home. And would you feel any safer in there? I doubt it.'

'So you're saying each of the victims knew who their killer was?'

'It's possible.'

'Couldn't they have informed on him?'

'If they all got death notes, you mean? It depends what motivated the murders. I'm speculating now, but it could have been some bad business they didn't want made public at any cost.'

'Bad business?'

'Some kind of scam.'

'But they were police officers.'

'We're not all angels, as I had to remind the team. Corruption gets exposed once in a while, and some goes undetected.'

'I thought you said the three victims never served together.'

'Yes, but the sniper could have served with

all three at different times. That's why I'm so committed to getting staff lists and going through the names.'

'You're sticking with that?'

'Definitely, but as a solo effort. My team are dead against it.'

'They'll find out,' she told him.

He nodded. 'They know me, anyway. Obstinate old bugger.'

'I'll second that. You should have gone for that X-ray.'

'I went. Just didn't stay.'

'Is it still painful? You seemed to be limping on the way here.'

'Trying for sympathy. I can't get enough.'

'Well, you look tired.'

'Lady, that's not sympathy. That's a taunt. You don't tell your date he looks tired.'

She smiled. 'I wasn't thinking of this as a date. If it's sympathy you want, I'll offer some, but forget the date bit. Men feeling sorry for themselves aren't much of a turn-on.'

All in all, this hadn't been his day. He regrouped rapidly. 'Okay, here's the deal. Leave out the sympathy, come home with me and we'll crack open another bottle of wine. Does that sound more like a turn-on?'

Paloma laughed. 'Kind of.'

CHAPTER FOURTEEN

Yes, it's another blog from me. The call from Anita couldn't have come at a worse time.

Monday morning and I was driving to the undertaker's to deliver a vanload of floral tributes for the funeral of an ex-mayor of the city, sprays, wreaths, basket arrangements, the works, including his name spelt out in two-foot high letters in white carnations. The name was Bartholomew, so you'll understand the struggle I had getting a thing that size into my dinky little van. I was driving with the B resting on my shoulder, the flowers tickling my ear. Anita's hushed, excited voice on the mobile was like, 'Babe, it's me. He's just walked in, city break man. Can you get here really fast, like in the next five minutes?'

'Sorry, sweetie,' I told her. 'I'm on a job the other side of town.'

'Ten minutes, then?'

'No chance. I'm making a delivery.'

'A delivery? Oh my God! Tell me it's only flowers.'

What did she think—that I did midwifery as a sideline?

'You haven't seen how many. This will take forty minutes, easily, and I have to be respectful. I can't just dump them and run.'

So the chance went begging.

Later, when all was explained and forgiven, Anita was like, 'I would have kept him talking if I could. The trouble is, most men aren't talkers and he's an extreme example.'

'They keep it bottled up,' Vicky added from the bottom of her heart. I knew, I just knew, she was speaking from experience.

The three of us had met for a late cuppa in our city department store. The restaurant on the first floor stays open until five-thirty and we get in there at five and sit in comfy leather armchairs at a low round table and order pots of tea. I don't think we're too popular with the waiters. By then they're thinking about going home. We're not much trouble. We don't order cream teas, or anything. Once Anita was tempted to ask for a scone and the waiter goes, 'Just the one scone?' and Anita goes, 'Lordy, yes, I've got a figure to think about.' The waiter goes, 'No cream? No jam?' And we're creased up laughing. But when the scone came it was so small you could have eaten it in one bite. You should have seen Anita's face. I think they usually serve these mini-scones to the tourists in twos or threes with jam and cream. Ever since then we settle for the tea and nothing else, but we never tire of reminding Anita and asking if she wants a scone. Often we have the restaurant to ourselves. The town is dead between five and ten, when the clubs open.

Getting back to our usual topic of men and are they necessary, Anita is still on about city break man. 'All blokes can talk about football, in my experience,' she says. 'They all have a theory why England will never win the World Cup again. I've heard it so often that I'm an expert myself. But I had the feeling city break man would have got suspicious if I'd started cold on do you favour a four four two formation.'

Vicky went, 'He might have thought you were proposing group sex.'

'On a Monday morning?'

'You never know your luck.' Then Vicky gave me a sly nudge under the table. She was quite skittish for once. 'Maybe that's the way we should be handling this, instead of trying to follow him home.'

'Group sex?'

'No, you daft ha'p'orth. One of us chatting him up.'

'I'm not his type,' Anita goes. 'I'd get nowhere. Ishy might appeal to him.'

'Hold on,' I put a stop to this before it could take flight. 'No way am I offering my hidden treasures to a perfect stranger who sounds like a weirdo. It's your suggestion, Vicky. You're the one with the looks. How about you making the first move?'

She turned beetroot red. 'I couldn't possibly. My situation is different.'

I'd forgotten about her guy Tim. Most of the time he's best forgotten.

'Summing up,' she added swiftly, trying to cover her embarrassment, 'we're none of us willing to sacrifice ourselves for the cause.'

'Come on, girls,' Anita went. 'One of you talks about sacrificing herself and the other's on about her hidden treasures. This doesn't have to end in bed. Surely we can charm a few truths out of a guy without lying back and thinking of England?'

Vicky turned pink again. 'Don't look at me.'

But that's exactly what Anita continued to do. 'Vicky, my petal, I don't see what stops you being part of this. It's only jaw-jaw and not paw-paw. We know you're in a relationship, but your man can't object to a bit of harmless chat.'

'To be honest, I don't do harmless chat.'

'Really? Do you always end up in the sack?'

'Per-lease.'

Anita gave a sigh like a punctured tyre. 'I'm starting to have second thoughts about this adventure. Are we, or are we not, the three sleuths? Seems to me we're turning out to be the three stooges. Are you two fully committed to finding the truth about city break man?'

'It's easy to say yes when we're all in it together,' Vicky goes. 'Safety in numbers. The fun goes out of it when we think about being alone with him.'

I chipped in here with: 'Let's face it, Anita, you haven't done a very good job of selling him to us.'

'He's not nice. That's the whole point of finding out what grubby little game he's playing. We know he's a benefits cheat. What else is he up to? If we can find out where he lives, it's a start.'

Trying to be positive, I'm like, 'All right, let's give it another try. Next time he's in your shop give me a call and I'll do my very best to get there.'

Vicky goes, 'What did he want this morning? Did he book another city break?'

'To Amsterdam.'

'Then it's got to be drugs or girls.'

'Do you think so?'

'He's not going to Amsterdam to buy tulips. He can get them from Ishy's shop.'

'My guess is it's boring old football,' I threw in. 'All these European cities have big teams. Instead of going to Chelsea or Arsenal every week he saves up some cash and goes to watch Real Madrid or some such. What's the Dutch team called?'

'Ajax.'

'Are they playing this time of year?'

'Football is all the year round, isn't it? The back pages are always full of it.'

Anita pulled a long face. 'Football. If that's all it is I'm through with spying. I'm going to bake cupcakes instead.' Then without warning she put both hands over her face and in a strangled voice announced, 'There he is, there he is, there he is.'

'Who?'

'City break man. Don't look. Stay normal. He just walked in. He mustn't see us together.'

There's a counter quite close to our favourite table where they have the cakes and things on display as well as wine to go with the lunches. Actually I think they call it a bar, but it's neither one thing nor the other. I glanced across to where this guy was standing with his back to us talking to the waiter. He was in a grey top with the hood pulled down and scruffy black jeans (city break man, I mean, not the waiter). From what I'd heard, this was the downmarket look he favoured for his job centre visits.

'Are you certain it's him?'

'Hundred per cent. I'm about to make my escape,' Anita went, rising from her seat, as if the word adventure had never crossed her lips. 'It's over to you, Ishy.'

'Me? I don't have my van,' I went.

Then my one-time ally, Vicky, really landed me in it. She stood up and went, 'I'm coming with you, Anita, to give you some cover. This'll work better if Ishy follows him alone.'

Those two scaredy-cats then made a beeline for the exit, slim Vicky doing a poor job of shielding the more ample Anita. Fortunately city break man was too busy ordering his coffee to notice.

I was left high and dry. The place was empty of customers apart from him and me. How ghastly, I thought, if he brings his coffee to my table and wants to get friendly.

Who was I kidding? He chose a table across the room, about as far from mine as he could get and half hidden by a palm tree in a pot. Thinking he was unseen, he pushed back his hood. I noticed that his dark hair was cut fashionably, unless the hood had caused the bit on top to spring up.

Ten minutes passed, time for me to dwell on the hole I was in and consider my options. If I wanted to stay friends with Vicky and Anita I had to make a show of following this guy home—always assuming he would go home after finishing the coffee. I wasn't used to cloak and dagger stuff. Tagging after him on foot was a different thing to doing it from the safety of my van. What if he spotted me?

Don't be such a wimp, I told myself. This is supposed to be an adventure.

Then he got up from the table, looked around, returned to the counter and spoke to one of the staff. She pointed to the door across the room and I knew what was going on. He wanted the gents. The loos are on the top floor next to the hairdressing salon. He made straight for the stairs. It made me think I needed to go up there as well. Autosuggestion. No way could

I take the risk. I had to be watching when he came down. I'd just have to think of other things and hope his journey home was quick.

I got up from the armchair and settled our bill (my two soul sisters had left without paying) stepped over to a better vantage point and stood refreshing my lipstick. From there I'd see him come downstairs—assuming he hadn't made his escape through a toilet window.

Cool it, Ishy, I told myself. The poor guy hasn't the faintest idea he's being followed.

Out he came in a couple of minutes and the game was afoot. Through the restaurant he headed and into the electrical department, making for the escalator to the ground floor. I followed thirty yards behind, ready at any time to take a close interest in toasters and steam-irons if he looked round. Actually tailing him was easier here than in the restaurant, because there were a few other shoppers as distractions.

His movement was purposeful, as if he'd spent too long over the coffee and needed to make up time. He kept moving on the escalator and I realised I'd have to go some to keep up with him. So it was bad luck for me when a woman and child got on the moving stairs ahead of me and blocked my way. I couldn't squeeze past without risking an accident. All I could do was watch which direction city break man was taking.

Straight past perfumery to the main exit and out of sight.

On ground level I zigzagged past the mother and daughter, declined the offer of a squirt of perfume and dashed for the swing doors.

In the street, I looked right and left.

Vanished.

I'd failed at the first fence.

How the heck did he do it? I asked myself. There were no buses in sight. Perhaps he'd hailed a taxi. He couldn't have walked.

I believe I sighed heavily. Didn't stamp my foot, but made my frustration clear, shaking my head.

Which was when a voice behind me went, 'Something the matter?'

I swung around and found myself eye to eye with city break man. He must have been standing against the wall to the right of the exit. He had a mobile in his hand that he closed and put in his pocket.

'No, no,' I went, immediately on the defensive. 'No problem.'

He shrugged. Hollow-cheeked and red-eyed, he fitted the druggie explanation better than the sex-tourist or the football fan, but at the time I was too confused to make such subtle distinctions. I'm only remembering later. The face had a faint echo of good looks, pitted smile lines that made it hard to dismiss.

He was like, 'I'd say you were looking for someone.'

'In a way, yes.' I was at my wits' end to concoct something. 'I thought I recognized an old friend in the shop. She came out here and seems to have gone.'

'What's she wearing?'

What was she wearing? Put on the spot, all I could think to say was what Anita was dressed in. 'Blue. A short blue jacket and black skirt.'

'Can't say I noticed her,' he went. 'Weren't you up in the restaurant just now?'

'The restaurant? Oh, yes.'

'Saw you then.' He didn't say he'd seen my two companions, which was some relief. Almost everything he'd uttered up to now could have been construed as a chat-up line. He'd noticed me. He might even have fancied me. The others would say I was letting a major opportunity slip through my fingers.

I can't plead inexperience. I knew what I ought to be saying. Normally I'm the equal of any smooth-talking bloke.

Instead I came out with a feeble 'Thanks, anyway,' that drew a line under the conversation. I wasn't the alpha female I'd always promised myself I would be, given the chance. Instead of reeling him in, all I did was put space between us.

'No sweat,' he went, and walked off.

What now? I thought. I follow the guy and he turns round and thinks I'm attracted to him. Is that the impression I want to give? That's certainly what my sister sleuths would want. My own instincts were all against it. When the chemistry is right I'll happily start up with a guy, or so I tell myself.

Bollocks.

Let's be truthful. I funked it.

I started rationalising like fury. The others hadn't remotely expected me to get friendly with him. They'd be content if I followed him home and noted his address. That's what I settled for. I'd go into Indian scout mode, taking cover at every opportunity. Shop doorways would be useful along the high street. The task would be harder in a residential road.

He'd already got some way ahead, marching up the hill at the brisk rate he'd started with. I was a good sixty yards in the rear. I crossed the street, thinking I'd be less obvious on the other side, and stepped out, keeping him in my sight. The grey hooded top didn't show up too well at a distance. I simply had to get closer or I'd lose him. In the heels I was wearing it wasn't easy. He was in trainers. He could step out, no problem.

Ours isn't a huge city, and I'm reasonably well known to customers from the flower shop as well as lots of friends and neighbours. In the first two hundred yards I saw two people I would usually have stopped to speak to. They had to be content with a wave and, 'in a hurry' from me. There may have been others I didn't even spot.

At the end of the street he turned right and was temporarily lost to view.

Panic. I broke into a run.

I was just in time to reach the corner and see him step into a pub whose name I'm not going to divulge. This was something I hadn't bargained for. What now? Should I go in and risk being seen? I had no idea how crowded it was inside.

At this time of evening, I reasoned, there ought to be other drinkers. Presumably city break man would step up to the bar and order a drink. Going in immediately after him gave me the best chance of getting inside unnoticed.

Then what?

If I approached the bar he was sure to notice me. If I stood aimlessly or even found a seat I'd get some funny looks. A lone woman in a pub who isn't there to buy herself a drink is open to misinterpretation. It wasn't as if I had a Salvation Army tin to rattle.

On the other hand, I didn't fancy waiting outside.

In the end it wasn't a decision out of Modesty Blaize. A basic need settled it. All pubs have loos. I'd been wanting one ever since missing my chance in the department store.

I pushed the door and stepped inside, rapidly noting that the place was reasonably busy and that city break man was at the bar with his back to me waiting to be served. The door for the Ladies was to the left, discreetly recessed. I was in there like a homing pigeon.

When I emerged, I had a plan. As I anticipated, he had moved away from the bar. I sidled up to it and ordered a glass of house white and asked for the hot food menu. There was a long mirror behind the barman and I used it to check where my man had parked himself. He was at a table to the left of the entrance and facing across the room. In front of him was a pint glass of beer. I was out of his sight-line.

I took my wine to a table behind him. The folding menu came in useful to duck behind in case he turned round. I was feeling more comfortable about this caper now. It was just a matter of making the wine last and keeping up the observation, or 'obbo' as we sleuths call it in the trade.

Ten minutes passed agreeably enough. I

rather wished Anita and Vicky could have seen me now, much more calm, in control, shadowing my unsuspecting suspect. The wine wasn't the worst I'd tasted, either.

Then he was joined by a woman.

She was dark-haired, elegantly dressed in a businesslike slate-grey pinstripe suit softened by a pale blue scarf worn over the shoulder. Thirtyish, I estimated.

He didn't stand to greet her and there was no embrace, nor even a token kiss. She took the chair opposite. He didn't have the grace to buy her a drink. There was a short exchange of words and then he produced what looked like an envelope and handed it to her. She opened it, checked the contents, tucked it in her bag, got up and walked to the exit.

I was in two minds whether to follow. Something of interest had been handed across and I strongly suspected it had a bearing on our investigation. But you can't be in two places at once and my main quarry was still here.

City break man didn't remain long. Perhaps a minute after the woman had left, he got up. He hadn't finished his beer, but he was off. Mission accomplished, it appeared.

I shielded my face with the menu. I'm sure he didn't see who I was.

And just for a moment I was tempted to let him walk away to God knows where, just as the woman had. Inside I was as twitchy as a daddy-long-legs at a window.

Somehow, I found the courage to take up the pursuit.

Outside, it was getting darker. The cars had

their headlights on. Hardly anyone was about. Sensible people were at home, getting supper. We were coming to a section of town where the shops had metal grilles in front of the windows. All my new-found confidence drained. I was your typical nervous woman thinking each shop doorway concealed a rapist or a mugger. Cursing the giveaway clicking of my heels, I stayed close to the kerb feeling less and less committed to this crazy quest.

But it was soon over. City break man turned right, crossed a kids' play area and entered what looked like a council tower block. I looked to see how many floors there were. There must have been at least two hundred flats in the building.

I needed to know where he was going.

I pushed at the swing door and followed him.

He'd already started up a foul-smelling staircase covered in graffiti. I could hear his steps, so I followed him, counting the floors. At the fifth, I hesitated at the swing door he'd just gone through. It was still moving back and forth. Fortunately it had a square of glass and I spotted him halfway along the corridor using a key to let himself into one of the flats. I waited for him to close the door before I crept forward and checked the number.

With that, I don't mind telling you, I'd reached the limit of my sleuthing for one evening.

CHAPTER FIFTEEN

When I got home there were anxious messages on the answerphone from my two so-called sleuthing buddies. I was to call Anita however late it was ('Wake me up if necessary and give me a rollicking'). But Vicky's message was more of an apology. She said she'd felt terrible about leaving me to cope on my own, and she hoped I understood that Anita had been in such a state that she needed shepherding out of the shop.

I called Vicky first. Actually I was home before ten, which I thought was a reasonable hour to touch base.

Her voice was strained. No joy that I survived. No curiosity about what happened. Just: 'It's not the best time. May I call you back?'

'Any time,' I told her, 'I'll speak to Anita.'

She's a puzzle, that Vicky.

Anita was totally different, firing at least six questions at me before I could get a word in.

I gave her the gist of what my mission had uncovered: the council flat in the ugly tower block off the main road out of the city.

She asked me, 'Was his name on the door?'

'God, no. Just rusty old numbers. 513.'

'Do you think he really lives there? Could he be leading a double life?' The council flat existence conflicted with Anita's image of city break man as a big-time villain.

'How would I know? All I did was follow him there.'

'And the woman he met in the pub? What was

all that about?'

'You tell me.'

'She was a classy dame, you said?'

'Smartly dressed, for sure.'

'But they didn't act like lovers?'

'No, it looked strictly business. They obviously knew each other, but there was no embrace, no smiles even. He handed her something in an envelope and she left immediately.'

'What size envelope?'

'Standard A4, I think.'

'Not large enough for drugs?'

'Probably not. It wasn't padded.'

Anita went, 'She's in on the scam. We've got to investigate her as well.'

I was firm with her. 'One's enough to be going on with. Let's concentrate on him.'

'All right. Now we know he lives in council property we can find out his real name. There must be lists of tenants.'

'I expect he told the council he's John Smith, like he told you. Maybe he really is John Smith.'

'So? The name may not be so important, but we can check. One of my clients works in the council offices. She'll help.'

Her enthusiasm lifted my spirits, weary as my legs were from trailing after city break man, or John Smith, or whoever he might be. 'I'm wondering what he handed the woman in the pub.'

'Blackmail money?'

'I doubt it. Where would he get enough to pay her off as well as funding all his trips abroad?'

And she was like, 'What's your theory, then,

wiseguy?'

'He's a private detective and she's hired him to find out about her husband's trips abroad. The envelope contained his latest report.'

'That's good, that's very good, but wouldn't she want to hear it from him rather than reading it later? I know I would.'

'Maybe she's just the messenger and the report is for someone else.'

'That's better, but if he's in work as a detective what's he doing drawing benefits and living in a council flat?'

'Amateur detective.'

She screamed with laughter. 'What—Lord Peter Wimsey? Miss Marple? You've got to be joking.'

'Actually, I was—I think.'

'Listen, my flower. Let's sleep on this and meet up tomorrow and plan our next move. Have you spoken to Vicky yet?'

'She said she'd call me back.'

'She's pleased you're okay, I bet.'

'She didn't actually say. I caught her at a bad moment, I think.'

'Poor lamb. It's that husband. He's a drag.'

'Really? Have you met him?'

'No, but I pick up on things she says. I think he's out of work and he takes it out on her.'

'Knocks her around, you mean?'

'Hard to tell. She's not going to boast about it, is she? Sometimes living with a deadbeat is punishment enough. You and I should count our blessings.'

'Being single?'

'Give me a world without men. No beer, no

football, just fat, cheerful women.'

We ended the call. Tired as I was after traipsing round the streets, I didn't like to go to sleep in case Vicky called. I spent the next hour writing this blog, getting up to date, which is where you are now. It's almost midnight and she hasn't called. I know if I go to bed I'll lie awake thinking about this quest of ours and whether deep down I really want to go on with it.

* * *

Good thing I have a hands-free phone in my van because the others always seem to ring me when I'm on the road. This morning I was halfway to the shop when Vicky called.

'So sorry about last night. I was waiting for a call from Tim. He'd be suspicious if I was talking to someone else. He was out until late. By the time he got through, it was too late to call you.'

Another piece of the jigsaw that is Vicky's marriage.

'But I'm dying to know how you got on.' Her voice was more chirpy now.

Without enquiring any more into Tim's night life, I gave her my story, adding Anita's take on it all.

'You did brilliantly,' she went. 'I'm sorry you were left to go it alone. We're not very professional as investigators, are we?'

'We couldn't all three of us have gone trailing after him. You were right to spirit Anita away. He would have recognized her from the travel agency and we'd have had awkward questions to answer.'

'He'll recognize you now as the bird he met outside the store.'

'The jumpy bird who nearly had a fit when he spoke.'

'Who can blame you? I'd have died of shock.'

'You realize what this means?' I went. 'He knows Anita and he knows me now. If there's any more tailing to be done, it's got to be you.'

'I'm up for it,' she went at once. 'Tell you something, Ishy. This has really given me a fantastic boost. When I'm feeling down at work or at home I only have to think about the sleuthing sisters and I'm raring to go again.'

After that, how could I say I was having second thoughts about the whole shenanigans?

* * *

Mid-morning came a call from Anita. Yes, I was in the van again, on my way back from delivering a dozen red roses to a house in the Royal Crescent. The old lady who opened the door had got quite chirpy, clearly thinking they were from an admirer. Then she looked at the card and found her daughter was the sender. She'd forgotten it was her birthday. I'm glad the daughter wasn't there to hear what she said, ungrateful old bat.

Back to Anita. 'Guess where I am, poppet.'

'Obviously not where you ought to be.'

'Too true. London Airport.'

'Heathrow? Are you off somewhere nice?'

'No such luck. I'm on patrol.'

'On what?'

'Sleuthing—for us, the sisters.'

'At the airport?'

'The BA check-in. City break man should be here any minute for his flight to Amsterdam. After what you saw last night I put two and two together and here I am.'

'I don't understand why.'

'Tell you later. I've made an arrangement with the check-in staff. Told them who I am and who I work for and said we made a boo-boo and forgot to include the hotel voucher in his travel-pack. When Mr John Smith, bound for Amsterdam, turns up, they'll give me a wave and I'll go over.'

'What will that achieve?'

'At the very least, I'll know he really is making these trips to Europe.'

'Is there any doubt?'

'In my suspicious mind, yes.'

'Isn't there a flaw here? If he's travelling light he doesn't need to check in. He can get his boarding pass from one of those self check-in machines and go straight to the departure gate.'

'That's where I'm smart. I asked the BA girls to put a stop on his ticket so he has to report to the desk and I don't miss him.'

'Did you really forget the hotel voucher?'

'No, he's got it, but you know what people are like when they're travelling, all luggage and loose bowels. He'll have no difficulty believing something is missing. I've got a duplicate voucher I can hand over.'

'I must be dense, Anita. I still don't understand why you're doing this.'

'All will shortly become clear, darling, as the parachute instructor said when he pushed the first-timer out of the plane.' And with that she rang off.

She sounded hyper, I was thinking as I continued my journey. Is she really a good person to link up with? Up to now our little game hasn't inconvenienced anyone else. From now on it's less of a game. She's fun to be with while it stays like that, but do I want her involving me in the serious stuff?

I felt like the first-time parachutist.

* * *

We met later for a cheap pizza. Food has to come first—for two of us, anyway. Anita had returned from Heathrow and was practically hopping up and down, so eager to tell her tale. We didn't exactly gag her, but Vicky insisted we ordered before chatting and I agreed.

It was nice to see Vicky smiling, blissfully unaware of the lads at the next table giving her the eye.

We placed our order and handed over to Anita.

By now she was bursting to tell us. 'After last night, when Ishy saw city break man meet in the pub with the smart bird and hand her something in an envelope, I got to thinking was it drugs, blackmail, or what? Ish had a thought he might be a detective handing over his report on the lady's cheating husband.'

'Nice one,' Vicky went, with a nod to me.

Anita raised her finger. 'But listen to this. When I thought about it later in bed I came up with an even better theory. What if the envelope contained the ticket to Amsterdam he'd bought from my agency?'

I was like, 'Why would he give the ticket away?'

'It was never meant for him. Someone else was going to fly out in John Smith's place.'

'The woman?'

'No. She was only the go-between, his PA or something. She couldn't pose as John Smith, but a guy with a forged passport might.'

'Why?' Vicky asked.

'Because he's up to something.'

Vicky gasped. 'Terrorism?'

Anita shrugged. 'Could be. Definitely something illegal.'

I exchanged a look with Vicky. Both of us were shocked. The game is turning far too serious.

Anita steamed on, 'So I'm keyed up, ready for anything. Time goes by and most of the Amsterdam passengers have checked in. Finally one of the BA girls gives me a wave. I can see the back of the man at her desk and sure enough he's got a carry-on case and nothing to check, so he must have tried to use the machine. But get this, girls. He isn't the guy we know as city break man.'

'Are you certain?'

'Of course.'

'What did you do?'

'You're going to be so proud of me. I took a couple of photos of him with my mobile while he was busy demanding his boarding pass. He had no idea I was doing it. Is that cool?'

'Polar cool.'

'Then I went up to the desk and spoke to him. I had a choice, didn't I? Challenge him and say he wasn't the geezer I knew from the travel agency or play along as if I didn't know, like someone had sent me. That's what I did. I asked if he was John Smith and he nodded, bloody liar.'

'What did he look like?'

'Better looking for a start. About the same age and build, but definitely a cut above our guy. Brown, intelligent eyes, whitened teeth, dark hair smoothed back. He was wearing casual clothes anyone could tell were expensive. Well, you can see the pictures I took.'

She showed us her mobile. The image was tiny, of course, but sharp considering how it had been taken. Her summing-up of his appearance was spot on. I gave it a close look.

And Vicky was like, 'Did he speak?'

'Sure. He glanced at the voucher and thanked me, smooth as you like.'

'Any accent?'

'Plummy, like the voiceovers for Famous Grouse. It was all over very fast. He pocketed the voucher, took his boarding pass from the BA girl and was away. I gave him a few seconds and then followed him up to the departure gate. I watched him go through. He'll be in Amsterdam by now.'

'If he didn't hijack the plane,' Vicky went.

'We'd have heard.'

'What's he up to, then?'

'Don't know, but I doubt if it's sightseeing. There must be plenty of reasons why someone travels incognito.'

'Most of them illegal,' I went. 'But it's high risk these days. Whatever he's up to, it's got to pay well.'

'Perhaps he's a spy.'

'You're scaring me.'

'If he is, we'll be under surveillance ourselves.' Vicky leaned forward and lowered her voice. 'Don't look now, but I just noticed the guys on the next table are taking an interest in us.'

Anita and I laughed. 'It's you, sweetie,' Anita went. 'They're watching you. If they're MI5, I'm a prima ballerina. It's the usual story. Can't take you anywhere.'

Vicky's face looked as if one of us had slapped both cheeks.

'The question is—what next?' Anita went. She was going to push this as hard as she could.

'Not much we can do if he's in Amsterdam,' I went, more in hope than expectation.

'He's back tomorrow, darling. It's only one night in the hotel. I'm thinking one of us should be at the airport when he arrives and follow him home, find out where he lives.'

'Difficult.'

'Why?'

'Think it through. Ten to one he's left his car at the airport. He'll get into it and drive off. How are we expected to follow him? If you're looking at me, you've got to remember my van isn't built for speed. By the sound of him, he drives a Porsche, at the least.'

Vicky lifted her shoulders a fraction. 'And I don't have wheels at all.'

'Great,' Anita went. She's about to tell us what wimps we both are, but we're saved by our waitress arriving with the pizzas. Vicky and I make a big deal out of deciding whose is which and if there are extra sauces. By the time it's settled and the waitress has gone, Anita has calmed down. I wouldn't say she's run out of steam because I'm sure she never will.

'I don't want us to become a one-woman team,' she went.

'Now let's be fair,' Vicky went. 'Ishy was out on the streets alone last night. If you want to have a go at someone, pick on me.'

'I'm not knocking you or anyone,' Anita went. 'Let's not fall out over this. Are we agreed something dodgy is going on?'

We each gave a cautious nod.

'The thing is, we don't know what. The Heathrow man is travelling on a ticket someone else bought. I doubt if it's for terrorism. Terrorists don't go to travel agencies to have their flights fixed. Neither do MI5. This is more likely to be a small-time crook who wants to pass himself off as a tourist.'

She was talking sense now and we listened.

'We can't even be certain he's a crook. He could be up to naughties of some description he doesn't want his wife to know about.'

'In all the European cities?' Vicky went.

'Meeting up with his mistress, who lives abroad.'

'Would he go to all that trouble to cover up the trips?'

'He might, if his wife is already suspicious.'

'He doesn't take much spending money.'

'Credit cards. But I think the petty crook is the best bet. He's up to some racket that entails travelling around Europe. It can't be beyond the wit of three intelligent women to find out what.'

'But how?'

'Let's find his real identity. Next time city break man comes to the agency and makes a booking, we know the pattern.'

'The MO,' Vicky went.

'Come again.'

'The MO. It's a police expression. Means the same thing you said.'

'Why bother to mention it, then? He's going to meet the woman and hand over the tickets. This time we follow the woman. She should lead us to Heathrow man. Then we find out who we're dealing with.'

Vicky smiled and clapped her hands. 'Neat. I'll volunteer to be the tail.'

Anita grinned. 'The best tail in town, as the guys on the next table will testify.'

Harmony was restored among the sleuthing sisters. We laid into those pizzas and had the key lime pie as well.

Over coffee, I asked Anita for another look at her mobile.

'Heathrow man? D'you fancy him?' She turned to Vicky. 'I think she does.' She brought up the picture and handed the phone to me.

I checked the little image. 'Not really. But I can tell you who he is.'

One good thing about my job is that you meet people. Flowers are wanted for most of life's special occasions and almost everyone buys them. This is a blog, not a commercial, so I'll simply ask you to recall the times when you've been into a florist's, or phoned, or ordered online. See what I mean?

Our shop has a central location and we have a

monopoly in our part of the city (the location of which still has to remain a mystery). It's quite a fashionable location actually. Without giving too much away I can reveal that we have more than our share of the rich and famous. As the delivery girl I get to meet some starry people, and I mean internationally starry. Celebs aren't worthy of the name unless they are forever taking delivery of orchids, lilies and roses. Some see me so regularly that they know me personally and if I were indiscreet I'd tell you which of them are nice to deal with and which are plain rude. As well as film stars, TV presenters, models and footballers, I visit titled people, captains of industry, admirals, brigadiers and lottery winners. At least two of our clients are on the wrong side of the tracks. I often deliver red roses to a house known to be a brothel. And we have a regular who made his money out of gang warfare and protection. He treats me okay. He buys in bulk, a vanload at a time of whatever we have in stock, leaving the choice to us. He'll give a party and want flowers all over the house—which is big, believe me.

You may be thinking I was bluffing when I told my two fellow sleuths I recognized Heathrow man. Was it a clever way of putting a stop to our investigations? I've already told you I was having second thoughts about trailing around after strange men and Vicky seemed to share my opinion, but neither of us wanted to fall out with our bubbly friend, Anita. What better way could there be of bringing the project to a grinding halt than pretending to identify Heathrow man and dreaming up a logical reason for his strange behaviour?

For example, I could say I happened to know he was an executive director of TAI, the Travel Agents' Inspectorate, who from time to time check on the efficiency of high street agencies. He didn't visit Anita's branch in person, but hired a member of the public (city break man) to buy the tickets and report on the treatment he was given. City break man handed his report and the tickets to the bigwig's PA, who in turn delivered them to Heathrow man, who made the trips and checked the quality of the flight service and the foreign hotels.

An explanation like that would put the wind up Anita for sure and stop our sleuthing stone dead. We could all go back to our comfortable girlie chat. I'm sure there are different scenarios one could think up.

But hand on heart, I didn't make anything up. I really had recognized Heathrow man as one of my clients. I've been to his house a number of times. It's not a palace and he's not a household name. I deliver buttonholes there, a carnation for him and a corsage for his lady, generally a rose in bud with some kind of surround like maidenhair fern. I assume they go to formal dinners or receptions quite often. I haven't met the lady, but the guy comes to the door and he's definitely the fellow Anita snapped at Heathrow. I'd stake my life on it.

'Brilliant,' she went, palms in the air, eyes like searchlights. 'Who is he?'

'Like I just said, someone I deliver flowers to.'

'Don't keep us in suspense, you tease. You can do better than that.'

'I'm trying. I can't recall his name just now. I know the face, for sure.' And I meant it. My memory had gone into sleep mode.

'For crying out loud, Ish. The name must be written on the order.'

'But I don't have an order with me, do I? I'm calling on people all day long. Some of them I remember by where they live. He's at the top end of Blahblah Avenue.' (made-up name)

'Nice neighbourhood. What does he do?'

'Apart from opening the door and taking in buttonholes? I can't tell you. I don't question the clients. If he had a brass plate on his door I'd know, but he hasn't.'

She gave up trying to dig the name out of me. 'Well, it's not beyond the power of three intelligent women to find out. It's so much easier when he's local.'

'We know he's in a relationship,' Vicky added.

'And they go to functions together.' Anita clicked her fingers. 'I reckon we've identified the go-between, the woman who meets city break man and collects the tickets.'

'Could be. Could well be,' I went. 'I don't think I've ever seen her.'

'You can get his name from the shop. They'll have copies of receipts. They must have.'

'I'll try and get it tomorrow.'

'We may still need to do surveillance to find his line of work. Don't you chat him up when you go to the house?'

'We're not all as chummy as you,' Vicky went, smiling at Anita.

'I can't let clients think I'm nosy,' I explained.

Anita gave me a pained look with her Nefertiti

eyes. 'Friendly isn't nosy. You learn a lot by being friendly.'

There was a second or so of thoughtful silence while I'm certain each of us was wondering how many of our innermost secrets we'd revealed to the others.

Then I was like, 'All right, leave it with me and I'll definitely find out who he is, or who he claims to be. Then we can decide what to do next.'

I was already wishing I hadn't opened my big mouth. I was putting my job at risk here, giving out information about clients. You may not think a flower deliverer is in a position of trust, but she is. She knows about the passions and desires of half the town. I didn't take an oath when I started the job, or sign the Official Secrets Act, but it gets home to you day by day that you'd better keep certain things to yourself. Once you break a confidence, where do you stop?

Maybe I do know the true identity of Heathrow man and something in my brain is blocking it out.

CHAPTER SIXTEEN

In sunshine early next morning Diamond drove down to the cathedral city of Wells, through a series of places that sounded as if they had been dreamed up by Agatha Christie: Peasedown St John, Midsomer Norton and Farrington Gurney. In reality much of this was former mining land rather than the English countryside at its most picturesque.

When the Somerset coal industry withered and died in the fifties and sixties, these little communities, much extended by affordable housing, became dormitory outposts for Bath.

The journey was not much over twenty miles, and he took it sedately in his Honda using most of the hour to get there, thinking not about social change in rural England, but where he would get breakfast.

In Wells, he found a privately owned café open before eight thirty, so rare a discovery in the West Country that he was tempted to believe this would be his lucky day. Over a plate of fried bacon, two eggs, mushrooms, tomatoes and baked beans, he studied the file he'd brought with him. He was in Ossy Hart territory now, but with a different agenda from the one he had given Ingeborg. First he was going to find the spot where Ossy had been gunned down. Then he would call on Mrs Hart. *A widow too far*: get away.

He marked both locations on the street map, checked his watch, drained his cup, paid up and moved on. The city was barely awake. Window-cleaners were at work on the shop fronts. How they got clean results with so little water he couldn't fathom. His own efforts at home always left smears that he rubbed with paper tissue and usually made worse.

He had no difficulty finding the scene of the shooting. The tree house the sniper had used as a firing position was in a private garden west of the town. A walnut tree with a massive trunk towered over the street from behind an eight-foot brick wall. Where the first great limbs thrust out from the bole, a platform had been erected twelve feet above ground and stabilised with struts bolted into the trunk. A child-size wooden cabin was built on it and a ladder of split logs gave access. You could just see the top rungs above the wall.

It could have been purpose-built for murder.

Across the road and a short way to the right, between twenty and thirty yards off, was a street lamp. Anyone walking under there by night was an easy target. Enclosed, crouched in this snug hideout built for play by some loving father, Ossy Hart's killer had pointed his assault rifle from an open window. With a secure position and a ledge to prop his elbows on, he'd taken aim across an unimpeded view. When his victim had stepped in front of the crosshairs or been pinpointed by the red spot, the sniper had released the bullets. Then he'd climbed down the ladder and escaped unseen, sheltered by the wall. A convenient garden gate was only thirty yards off.

Diamond didn't cross the road to examine the spot where Ossy had died. The police tape had long since been removed, any blood washed away. Forensics had scoured the street for traces twelve weeks ago. Nothing would have escaped their attention. Instead he stood below the tree in empathy with the dead constable. Up to now, his prime concern had been the shooting of Harry Tasker and the attack on Ken Lockton. Today he felt kinship with PC Hart, the ex-teacher. Was it sheer bad luck that you happened to be the copper walking by, Ossy, or was your name on the bullet? Did you know your killer? Either way, a young married father had been picked off with one impassive squeeze of the trigger.

The murder of a police officer on duty is a rare

event, rightly rated among the worst of crimes, sure to produce an eruption of outrage. SIOs will always say they treat every homicide with the same investigative zeal, yet the pressure to make an arrest for a police killing is unrelenting. Getting it done is a petrifying responsibility. Getting it right is no certainty.

He returned to his car and sat for a long time in silence, feeling that burden, an ordinary man doing his best to deal with the extraordinary. The tree house was still in sight through his windscreen. On this bright morning, yesterday's theory that the sniper must have been a brother officer felt less tenable. The notion of a policeman sneaking into that hide and waiting for one of his own kind to come within firing distance was hard to accept. If Bath CID refused to swallow the new scenario for the shooting of Harry Tasker, what would they have made of Ossy Hart's murder? Diamond knew the answer. And now he, too, was at risk of being swayed into disbelief.

Better do what I came here to do, he decided. He started the car and drove north to the estate where Ossy had lived. A small end-terrace house with a door painted red.

9.43 a.m. He'd spent longer contemplating the crime scene than he realised. He hadn't made an appointment. He'd fixed 9.30 in his own mind as a reasonable time to call, after the kids had been taken to school.

Sounds from inside came as a relief. Juliet Hart opened the door and she was not the red-eyed widow he expected. Flushed with health, lean as a streak, bright-eyed and welcoming. Natural red hair combed back and fastened with a green ribbon.

Silver jumpsuit, matching Nike trainers.

'Hi.'

His hand went to raise a non-existent hat before he remembered his trilby was on the back seat of the car. He tried a polite smile. 'Mrs Hart? Sorry to bother you so early in the day. Sorry to bother you at all.' He felt in his pocket for the ID. 'But it's necessary.'

'Are you collecting for something?' she asked, not unfriendly. She must have seen his stick and decided he was disabled.

'No, ma'am. Surprising as it may seem, I'm a police officer.'

'You're on the investigation. Good for you,' she said without looking at his warrant card. 'But I doubt if there's anything more I can tell you.'

'I'm not from Wells Police. I expect you heard about the shooting in Bath at the weekend. That's why I'm here.'

'You're over from Bath? Did you know the man who was killed there?'

'Not all that well. I'm CID. He was uniform.'

'Same as my Ossy.' Said in as measured a tone as if she was talking about matching hats.

She's over-compensating, he thought, remembering the sudden avalanche of anger from Emma Tasker. He prepared for something similar, or tears, at the very least.

But she added as if discussing last night's TV, 'Do you think it was the same gunman who shot Ossy?'

This wasn't the way it was supposed to be, the interviewee asking the questions. 'Everything points to it.'

'They don't seem to have made much progress.'

She glanced at his stick again. 'You'd better come in and sit down. I was exercising, skipping in the garden. It's my chance, when the children are in school.' She led him into an open-plan kitchen-diner and cleared newspapers from a chair. 'Do you drink juice? I have beetroot, cranberry or pomegranate.'

'I'll pass, thanks. You carry on. You must be thirsty.'

'Am I in a sweat, then? Is it so obvious?'

'Glowing.' Steph had taught him that refinement.

She smiled, took a jug from the fridge and filled a glass with pink liquid that could have been any of the three on offer.

He took note of his surroundings. Mainly wood. Pine in the kitchen, beech slats along one wall. A wood-framed sofa and low tables. Parquet floor. Even the pictures on the wall were of forest scenes.

'In case you're wondering, I had a lot of sympathy cards, getting on for two hundred, but I don't display them,' she said. 'Ossy had so many friends. However, I don't need to be reminded that he's gone, and I'm trying to get the children back to some kind of normality.'

'I understand,' he said. And he did. On the day after Steph's funeral, he'd stuffed all the cards into a carrier bag and stowed them in the loft.

'I'm not ungrateful for all the support. They gave him a mega send-off.' There was pride in her voice. 'When it comes to something like this, the police are brilliant. They offered to take over, and I'm so glad I let them. The funeral was in the cathedral. The chief constable came, and the lord lieutenant and lots of local people we didn't know who just wanted to show respect, I suppose. Well, after that,

I spent a week dealing with everything, writing letters and filling in forms. You wouldn't believe all the paperwork there is when someone dies. But it stopped me feeling sorry for myself. And then I started my life again. That's what Ossy would have wanted. He always believed in moving on, whatever problems cropped up.'

'Sensible,' Diamond said, thinking sensible if you can be like that. Grief makes its own agenda. For Emma Tasker, anger. For this woman, refusal to be downed. With three children to care for, she was forced to be forward-looking, but there would be an undercurrent of pain.

And in a strange way, he found the steely exclusion of grief just as difficult to deal with as the anger.

She brought the drink over to the armchair opposite him and sat with her legs curled under her.

This time he got a question in first. 'Do you mind going over some things you may have been asked before?'

'Not at all, if they lead to a result.'

'Let's hope so. Did Ossy ever speak of Stan Richmond, or Harry Tasker?'

She shook her head. 'Not to me.'

'Stan Richmond was the Radstock victim. Did Ossy visit Radstock?'

'On the odd occasion. It's not one of our favourite places.'

'Bath?'

'Rather more often. We'd go there for the sports facilities sometimes. The theatre, around Christmas, for the pantomime, but Wells has most of what we want.'

'I'm wondering if he went there alone.'

'To Bath? Hardly ever. Days off were precious, what with all the overtime and shift work, so we did things as a family.'

'I heard he was keen on his job.'

'That's for sure. He was studying for the sergeants' exam, hoping to get his stripes next year.'

'He got along with the Wells lads, did he?'

'Lasses, too. Yes, they're a friendly lot.'

'Nobody got up his nose?'

She shook her head. 'He never mentioned anyone.'

'And in his dealings with the public, did he make any enemies?'

'A few, I expect. You're bound to, if you're doing your job and nicking people.'

'Did anyone threaten him?'

'I was asked this before. It's obvious they could have, some of the hard lads he dealt with. If so, he didn't tell me and he didn't let it bother him. His years as a teacher helped him deal with troublemakers. He was quite a disciplinarian. Too much so, for schooling in the twenty-first century.'

'Were there any feuds hanging over from his time as a teacher? Former pupils who still bore a grudge?'

'I doubt that. Ossy always dealt with misbehaviour on the spot, twenty press-ups or whatever. Then it was over and forgotten. The Minehead kids respected him.' She glanced down at her polished fingernails. 'I understand where you're coming from. I just think it's not a profitable line of enquiry.'

'Do you have a theory of your own?'

'As to why he was shot? It was the uniform, wasn't it? Someone hated the police and Ossy happened to be on duty that night. Simple as that.'

The standard line. Diamond didn't want to dent her confidence with his disturbing theory of the killer targeting certain individuals. He was warming to this upbeat young woman and her positive way of dealing with her loss. 'I'm curious to know where his nickname came from. He was Martin by birth, wasn't he?'

She laughed. 'The "Ossy"? The kids he taught called him that and it stuck. He quite liked it and so did I. It seemed to suit him.'

'But how did it start? These names generally mean something in the first place.'

'Don't they just? It was a very big deal at the time.' She paused and looked away, clutching the back of her hair in the first suggestion of nervousness she'd shown. 'After he came here and joined the force he played it down. I doubt if he told anyone.'

He waited while she composed herself. This wouldn't be easy for her if Ossy himself had been guarded about the name.

'No harm in talking about it now he's gone,' she said finally. She'd reached her decision and recovered her equilibrium. 'Minehead, where he was teaching, has a rather special May Day celebration. Actually it goes on for several days. The first we knew of it was when one of our neighbours knocked on our door and said he was on the organising committee and he'd like to propose my husband for the Sailor's Horse.'

'What on earth . . .?'

This relaxed her again and she smiled. 'That was exactly our reaction. It's an honour, actually, but you have to be fit to do it. They have this age-old ritual involving people dressed as hobby horses, or 'obby 'osses, in the good old Zummerzet dialect.'

Diamond raised his thumb. 'Got you.'

'Have you heard of it?'

'Vaguely. Tell me more.'

'The Sailor's Horse is the main one. He wears a brightly coloured headpiece with an ostrich feather plume. It's supposed to be a horse's head but actually is more like a clown's face. Then he has a large wooden frame strapped to his shoulders supporting something that's a cross between a boat, a horse and a party frock. The best you can say for it is that it's colourful. It's made up of thousands of ribbons and a fabric skirt with the words "Sailor's Horse" written on it in big letters, in case anyone misses the point—which is quite possible.'

'He agreed to do it?'

'He had to parade around the town for several days dancing to a special tune played on drums and a squeeze box. What's the proper name for those things?'

'Accordion?'

'That's it. The men are dressed as sailors. They're collecting for charity—the lifeboats, I think—and if people don't pay up they'd better look out, because they're likely to be harassed by the 'oss.'

'Strictly speaking, that breaks all the rules about collecting,' he said, tongue in cheek.

'Yes, and it gets worse. Any man refusing to pay up is liable to get a few lashes from the 'oss's long tail. And just to add to the mayhem, the horse is supposed to chase the women and children.'

'He's a threatening figure, then?'

'Certainly was in times past. He was backed up by men known as gullivers, armed with whips and huge pincers. They put a stop to that after one of the local townspeople was killed.'

'Killed? When was this?'

She laughed and flapped her hand. 'Not what you're thinking. Way back in the eighteen hundreds.'

'Even so, if someone died I'm surprised it was allowed to continue.'

'They changed the way it was done. Nowadays the Sailor's Horse just has some jolly jack tars in tow. I think the two rival horses are allowed to have their gullivers, but they dress in fancy costume and don't threaten people. It's pure carnival these days and stage-managed.'

'What part do these rivals play?'

'The Traditional Sailor's Horse and the Town Horse? They appear from time to time and have ritual fights with the Original Sailor's Horse, the one Ossy played.'

'I can see why a PE teacher was picked for the job.'

'Yes, it's quite demanding physically, but Ossy didn't mind. The worst bit was getting up really early on May Day to greet the sun at five a.m. Nobody seems to know for sure how far back the whole thing goes or what it represents, except that it ushers in the start of spring.' She took a sip of her juice. 'Do you really want to know about this? I doubt if it has anything to do with the shooting.'

'Everything you can recall about it,' Diamond said, trying to contain his excitement. He'd already made a link with Stan Richmond, the folklore enthusiast. The weird ceremonies in Minehead must have been followed with interest by the loner from Radstock.

'Well, they'd start off at the Old Ship Aground on April the thirtieth, known as Show Night, or Warning Eve, doing the rounds of the pubs, rattling the tins. Then, like I just said, he had to be up early next morning and in costume bowing three times to salute the sunrise at a crossroads. May Day was really quite a marathon. He'd dance all around Minehead seeing off the other horses and chasing the kids and scaring me silly by dancing ever so close to the water's edge at the harbour. The whole thing would go on like that each evening until May the third, visiting all the outlying places, including Dunster Castle, except if he was lucky and there was a Sunday in between, when the Sabbath had to be observed.'

'Hard work.'

'He was knackered by the end.'

'From what you say, it sounds as if he did it more than once.'

'He became the regular Sailor's Horse for two or three years before we left Minehead and they would have had him back even after we moved here, but he decided it wouldn't be the thing for a policeman to be demanding money with menaces and chasing women and children, even for a good cause.'

Diamond smiled. 'He had a point.'

'People were sorry when he gave it up.'

'I expect you've got photos.'

'You can find them on the internet if you want.'

'Don't you have any yourself?'

'Ossy had a scrapbook with lots of pictures and cuttings, but it was borrowed a couple of months ago and I haven't got it back.'

'Why not?'

'Some American wanted it. He was talking big about filming the whole thing for a scene in a Hollywood action movie.'

He leaned forward. 'Who was this?'

'I don't think I discovered his real name. Ossy called him Cubby.'

'Not *that* Cubby?'

A giggle. 'No, he's dead, isn't he? That was Ossy's sense of humour. We took everything this man said with a large pinch of salt. I mean he was offering silly money, thousands of dollars, if Ossy would go back to Minehead and wear the costume and do the dance.'

'Wasn't he tempted?'

'He didn't believe it would happen. He said—pardon my language—these film people are bullshit artists. And he wouldn't risk losing his stripes through becoming a laughing stock.'

'So he turned it down?'

She paused as if choosing her words. 'He didn't sign anything or get paid any money for sure, but the door wasn't entirely closed. Cubby suggested using a stage name to protect his identity. They were really keen to get Ossy. He was the best Sailor's Horse for years, everyone said.'

'And this all happened recently, you said?'

'Just a few weeks before Ossy died.'

'Did Cubby say if he was talking to other people?'

'I got the impression he'd already been to Minehead to look at the location, as he called it.'

'Presumably the Minehead people put him in touch with Ossy?'

'Must have.'

'Ossy obviously had some faith in the man or he wouldn't have trusted him with his scrapbook.'

'He was like that, generous.' For the first time, her face betrayed a hint of emotion, a faint watering of the eyes. She took a sharp breath and said, 'I expect I'll get his book back. It will be nice for the children to have as they get older.'

'You didn't meet this Cubby yourself?'

'No, I simply heard Ossy's stories of him. We had a good laugh about it. What we'd wear for the premiere and the Oscars night. That kind of thing.'

'Would you have his address anywhere? People like that usually give out business cards.'

She shook her head. 'I went through his papers looking. I'd like to get the scrapbook back. There was nothing.' Then she said, 'I don't see how any of this affects the investigation.'

In his eagerness he'd failed to keep in mind her belief that the shootings were random killings of the first policemen who came within range. He didn't wish to cause more distress. He suspected her bravery was wafer thin. 'We look at everything, however remote.'

How feeble was that?

'Clutching at straws?' she said.

'It's a matter of being thorough. We owe it to Ossy and the others to look at every possibility.' His words struck home with himself as he spoke them. This was pussyfooting and it wasn't going to succeed. He had a duty to press her for more information, even if it pained her. 'Do you happen to remember if he had any kind of warning that something bad was going to happen to him?'

Her eyes widened. 'Why?'

After wavering too long between honesty and

altruism, he was now forced to speak the truth. 'Our man in Bath was carrying a note that could have been from the sniper himself.'

'What did it say?'

No way out of this now. 'Only two words—"You're next."'

She gasped.

Diamond added at once, 'We don't know for sure if it refers to the shooting.'

'How could it?' Her eyes threatened panic at the possibility and Diamond wished he could have spared her this. 'No,' she said, 'I'm certain Ossy would have told me if he was sent anything like that. Anyway, he was the first to be shot. He wouldn't have been sent a note like that.'

'Not those words.'

She was far from satisfied. 'Did the other man, the one who was shot in Radstock, receive a note?'

'If he did, it hasn't been found. Like I said, we follow up every lead, however unpromising.' He backtracked again, shamelessly. 'One note out of three isn't significant. Don't let anything I've said undermine you. You're doing brilliantly. Ossy would be proud.'

Hollow words.

He left soon after. He'd learned things he hadn't expected, potentially crucial, but he felt only contempt for himself. Behind her brave stance, Juliet Hart had been rocked by what she'd just learnt, and he was responsible. He'd messed up big time with Emma Tasker and this hadn't gone any better.

A widow too far?

Right. So right.

CHAPTER SEVENTEEN

His phone went, offering him a choice of traffic offences: use the mobile while driving or stop and block a passing point in the narrow Somerset lane. He pulled over. He'd met nothing for some way, so he reckoned this was the better option.

'Yes?'

'Diamond, where the fuck are you?'

'Is that you, Jack?' As if anyone else spoke to him like that.

'I said—'

'Heard you. I'm on the way in.' True. He was more than halfway back from Wells.

'Do you know what time it is? I've been trying to reach you at Manvers Street. Some of us are at work this morning and we've struck gold.'

He yawned. He wasn't in gold rush mode. 'Tell me more.'

'I can do better. Meet me in twenty minutes at Avoncliff railway station and I'll show you.'

'Can we make that forty?'

'Are you still in your fucking pit?'

'Would I tell you if I was? See you at twelve thirty.' He switched off.

Whatever Gull had discovered it would need to be good to outweigh this morning's find. Ossy Hart and Stan Richmond both involved in folklore and with a prospect of film money in the offing. True, Ossy had by then retired from his role as the Sailor's Horse, but the lure of thousands of dollars had revived his interest, even if he'd dismissed it as bullshit.

Big money brings its own temptations.

Next question: did Harry Tasker, boring old Harry who did nothing but pound the beat and go fishing according to his wife, get a sniff of the money? Did he have a passing interest in local customs that Emma had failed to mention?

And if any of this was true, why did all three get murdered?

Another session with Emma Tasker beckoned, and Diamond didn't relish it. Good thing Stan Richmond hadn't also left a widow to be interviewed. Be thankful for small mercies.

He looked in at the incident room and was told three times over that Jack Gull had been trying to reach him.

'Don't suppose he told you what it was about,' he said to Ingeborg.

'No, guv, except it was urgent.'

'Always is with Jack. Makes him feel important.'

The tension from yesterday's team meeting hadn't all evaporated, but at least they were on speaking terms.

'Did he ask where I was?'

'We didn't know,' Keith Halliwell said, and it felt like a dig.

'I was in Wells.' He gave them the gist of what Juliet Hart had told him about the Minehead May Day ritual, adding only one comment. 'And that, my friends, is how Martin Hart came to be known as Ossy.'

Usually the idea of one of the force up to something eccentric was sure to provoke some laughs. This morning's response was a few bemused looks.

'Does it make any difference?' John Leaman

asked in his habitual downbeat tone. 'This all happened before he joined the police.'

'The film offer was the new factor,' Ingeborg said, sharp to the point as always. 'And he was tempted, by the sound of things.'

Leaman was unmoved. 'But it didn't come to anything.'

She gave an impatient sigh. 'It came up shortly before he was shot and it was big bucks. We all know about trying to survive on a police salary.'

'Are you saying this led to him being murdered?'

She turned to Diamond. 'Is that what you're thinking, guv?'

After yesterday's dust-up, Diamond wasn't being drawn. 'It's a new angle, that's all.'

Ingeborg wouldn't leave it. 'Okay, let's talk about Stan Richmond. He was into folklore, too. He'd written articles. Do you think the film man went to him for advice?'

'I simply don't know.'

'It's worth checking if he ever wrote anything on the Minehead hobby horses.'

'Could be.'

'Shall I?'

'If you want.' He couldn't have sounded more neutral. Secretly, he was pleased. 'Has anything else come up that I should know about?'

'On your desk, from personnel,' Leaman said with a look laden with reproach. 'About thirty pages of names . . . including all of ours.'

That explained the coolness. Yesterday evening he'd gone ahead and asked Headquarters for the printout. No one here would have printed it for him.

He opened the office door and glanced at his

in-tray. The paperwork was spilling out of it. Most would be junk. Headquarters had a whole department called communications and they justified their existence by making sure everyone was made to feel wanted on an hourly basis. They'd found out he didn't bother much with emails, so they deluged him with paper. Georgina the ACC (who had probably arranged it) was always leaving him memos. As well as all of that, there were the usual letters the postman had brought, bunched and held in place with an elastic band. Another with no stamp and just *Detective Diamond—PERSONAL* on the envelope must have been delivered by hand. And there was the sheaf of A4 sheets listing all those names. Thanks to Jack Gull he didn't have time to start on any of it.

*   *   *

Avoncliff station, Gull's choice of meeting place, hardly deserved its name. It was that rare thing on the railways, a request stop on the main line between Southampton and Bristol. If you wanted to board a train you were instructed to put out your hand and wave at the driver. There were no train announcements, no display boards and no staff. But it had existed for over a century and the locals would make sure it continued.

One useful facility the station did have was a small car park and Gull was waiting there when Diamond drove in ten minutes late.

'This had better be good,' he said as he reached for the walking stick and heaved himself out. 'The drive down was hairy.'

'Sod that,' Gull said. 'Can you walk?'

'Not a problem.' He looked around. 'Where to? Are you keeping me in suspense?'

'Not for long. We're going to follow the railway for a few hundred yards. Are you up for it?'

'I just said.' Much more of this and he would be peppering his own speech with obscenities.

'Let's go, then.' Gull had got to know this little area pretty well, taking the soft option last night while Diamond had been overseeing the hunt for the sniper between Westwood and Bradford on Avon. All action now, he headed under the massive Victorian aqueduct that carried the canal over the railway and also served as a passenger bridge. 'Keep up,' he called back. 'It isn't far.'

Sandwiched between the River Avon and the railway was an overgrown, uneven footpath, not easy to manage with a dodgy leg. Gull was already some distance ahead. Diamond had to raise his voice to be heard. 'So you took a stroll while you were guarding the aqueduct?'

'I sent one of the plods on a recce. He made the find. It was too dark to check out yesterday. I had a look for myself this morning.'

Diamond plodded on, managing with the help of the stick. The leg was on the mend, he decided.

Gull stopped to wait for him. 'This stretch is known as Melancholy Walk. I think I know why.'

'Tell me, then.'

'If you're feeling sorry for yourself you've got the choice of lying on the railway or jumping in the river.'

'Charming.'

He pointed. 'You can see it up ahead. That stone building half-covered in creepers.'

They walked the last stretch in silence and up to

a solid, squat concrete block on the railway side of the path.

'Christ knows what it's for,' Gull said.

'It's a World War Two pillbox,' Diamond told him, looking at the narrow, elongated space in the front wall, about chest-high, meant for aiming guns. 'They built hundreds of these in 1940, when the German invasion was expected.'

'Before my time.'

Before Diamond's, too, but suddenly the roles were reversed and he was enjoying himself as the one in the know. 'All along here was the stop-line, the most important one in Britain. Churchill wanted a way of slowing up the Panzer tanks, so he asked General Ironside—nice name, that—to build a series of defensive lines northwards from the coast. Pillboxes, stone bollards, trenches, barbed wire. Ironside made good use of what was already in place, and this stretch was perfect: the river and the canal are barriers for miles. The GHQ line, as it was known, ran all the way from Bristol to Kent. There are pillboxes at regular intervals.'

'How do you know this stuff?'

'I live nearby. You find things out.'

'Well, clever-clogs, you don't know what's inside. Be my guest.'

Diamond walked round to the back, found the narrow, open doorway, stooped and went in. The light wasn't good and the smell reminded him of a rugby changing-room after a match. He could make out the dark shape of a bedroll stretched across the end, with a six-pack of beer beside it and some empty cans. There was food also, a half-eaten loaf, apples and the remains of a cooked chicken. A newspaper was tucked between the wall and the bedroll.

'Yesterday's *Mirror*,' Gull said, coming in behind him. 'He was here as recently as that.'

'You think it's our man?'

'Someone sleeping rough, isn't it? We've left it like this for when he comes back. I've taken one of the empties to get some prints.'

'No gun.'

'He's smart, isn't he? Either he's got it with him or it's somewhere nearby.'

'The motorbike as well?'

Gull preferred not to think about the motorbike. In truth, it was probably parked in a street somewhere.

Diamond glanced at the folded newspaper. Part of a banner headline was visible: SNIPER: NOW IT'S –. Every national daily was reporting the shootings. Because the paper happened to be face up, nothing could be assumed about the recent inmate of the pillbox.

'These places get used sometimes by people sleeping rough.'

'Rough is what he is,' Gull said. 'We know he passed at least one night in Becky Addy Wood. The bugger's on the run and dossing down wherever he can.'

'You think he's moved on, do you?'

'He wouldn't leave his bedding here, or the food. He'll be back and I'm laying on a welcome.'

'If you're right and he's got the gun with him, that may not be such a good idea.'

'Get real, Diamond. I've got armed police in hiding all around us. You wouldn't have noticed.'

True. He hadn't spotted them.

'With orders to shoot on sight?'

'No, they'll close in after he comes back.'

'Is that wise? This thing was purpose-built for defence. From in here he could take out several more coppers.'

Gull thought about that, obviously decided it was true and then glared back. 'What's your suggestion, then?'

'Ambush him before he can get inside. He'll be trapped between the railway and the river.'

This silenced the head of the Serial Crimes Unit.

'Or you could let him go in and then bung in some tear gas. By the sound of it, you need a better game plan. If I were you, I'd think it over, but not in here. I'm getting out in case he's on his way.'

In truth, Diamond found it hard to believe that the sniper—if that was who had spent the night here—would return in broad daylight. But he'd satisfied his curiosity. He limped back to the car park, leaving Gull to work out the new strategy with his shock troops.

*   *   *

Back with CID, he asked for the latest on Ken Lockton. No change, the hospital had told Keith Halliwell. The patient remained unconscious, in the critical care unit. Christina, the sympathetic PCSO, was still with the family.

Diamond had never known such an atmosphere in his workplace. Bath CID had become the Slough of Despond. A lot of it was down to him and his inept performance yesterday, but there was still a pervading air of gloom. The murder of a colleague on duty and the near-murder of another had poleaxed everyone. The angry mood of the first day had given way to this grim resignation. Generally humour has a way of breaking through the most harrowing of investigations, if only for sanity's sake. Right now, a light remark seemed like a betrayal. The usual currency of so-called wit was unfit for use.

The only way to get through this was to focus on the job in hand. You knuckled down and did whatever you could to bring the killer to justice.

He walked into his office and closed the door. That heaving in-tray waited on his desk. First, he phoned Emma Tasker. The call was picked up by the Good Samaritan from next door, who'd survived longer as comforter than anyone could have expected. Her voice showed the strain. She said they hadn't long been back from the undertaker, fixing the funeral, and she doubted if Emma would come to the phone. He said it wasn't necessary. He just wanted Emma to know she could expect another visit from the big thug from Bath Central this afternoon around three.

'Are those the exact words you want me to use?' the neighbour asked.

'She'll understand.'

'She won't like it.'

'She'll have to lump it, then. And speaking of lumps . . .'

'What's that?'

'It's milk and two sugars for me.'

He cradled the phone, set aside the morning's mail for later and started leafing through those lists of personnel from three police stations. Not just the current staffs, but years of them, including people transferred and retired. The job of finding matching names was likely to take hours. For a start, he crossed out the three victims and Ken Lockton and his own CID team. If he couldn't eliminate them as suspects he might as well jack in the job. But upwards of a thousand remained. They weren't even alphabetical. They were listed in order of taking up duties.

He'd been at the task about twenty minutes when there was a knock and Ingeborg came in. He bent forward to fold his arms protectively over the lists, a reflex action. Clumsy as ever, he found he'd tipped several sheets on the floor. He reached for the walking stick, but Ingeborg stooped to pick them up.

She couldn't help seeing what they were. 'How are you getting on with this, guv?'

'Barely started.'

'I bet you've already found a bunch of Smiths.'

'Well, I'd expect to.'

'Smith . . . my surname.'

He'd been slow to spot this attempt at a peace offering. 'Oh, I get you,' he said finally. 'No, I'm not lining up my own team as possible suspects.' He leaned back in the chair. The need to be furtive was well over. 'What did you want?'

'I found a website called Fairs, Feast-days and Frolics and you can download hundreds of articles on folklore and customs. Stan Richmond definitely wrote about the hobby horses.'

'Did he, by God?'

'Several places have them. Padstow in Cornwall, Combe Martin in Devon—'

He raised a finger. 'Do I need to know this?'

'I thought you'd be interested.'

'I'd rather you got to the point.'

Her lips tightened. 'You could download the

piece if you want.' She knew damned well he wouldn't.

'You've obviously digested it,' he said.

She nodded.

'So what were the tasty bits?' He watched her wince a little.

'It's clear that he visited Minehead at some point and spoke to people on the hobby horse committee.'

'When was this?'

'The article was dated 2008.'

'No chance he interviewed Ossy Hart, I suppose?'

'Ossy was living in Wells by that time. I guess Stan could have caught up with him there if he wanted to talk about what it's like acting the Sailor's Horse, but he doesn't mention him by name, or list him in the acknowledgements.'

'If I've learned anything from all these years of sleuthing, Inge, it's that nothing comes easy. At least you've found proof of what we suspected—that Stan Richmond knew about the hobby horses.'

'I'll get you a printout if you want.'

'That would help.' He reached for the lists again.

She stepped to the door, hesitated and turned her head, in Lieutenant Columbo mode. 'One other thing, guv.'

'What's that?'

'Shouldn't we be tracing that film man, Cubby, or whatever his real name is?'

'If we knew his real name, yes,' he said. 'Anything you can do to find him would be helpful.'

She smiled. 'Anything? Like a trip to Hollywood?'

'That might be hard to explain to our

paymasters.'

'Is there any proof that Cubby also made a cash offer to Stan Richmond?'

'Not yet. It's starting to sound possible.'

'And Harry Tasker? What if he met this guy?'

'That's something I hope to find out from his widow. I'm seeing her shortly.'

'Again? People are going to start talking.'

'Get outta here.' But it did him good to know someone on the team still had a spark of humour.

* * *

The sight of Bath's last gasholder didn't do much for his morale when he drove up and parked across the road from Onega Terrace. Unsightly and outmoded, the great drum of gas seemed to sum up his self-image. He was about to cross the road when a sudden barrage of sound came from behind him. He stepped back and a motorbike that had just started up from a parking place a few cars away zoomed past and away towards the city. The rider was in black, just as the motorcyclist in the woods had been.

Don't get paranoid, he told himself. There are thousands of these things on the roads and they're not all out to get you.

The large neighbour opened Emma's front door, took one look at him and said, 'Right, I'm off home.'

'What's this called—respite?' he said as she pushed past.

'Man, I've earned it. You can go in.'

He found the angry widow in the living room kneeling on the floor. 'Watch where you're walking with those great plod feet,' she said and he saw that the carpet was littered with CDs. 'I'm supposed to choose the music for the committal, as they call it. Harry wasn't a believer, so I don't want any of that so-called sacred music. When I told them, they said it was up to me. Pick a favourite piece for a send-off, they said. Fat chance of finding anything here. We bought these for easy listening, not a cremation.'

He let his gaze travel the width of the carpet, taking stock of the Taskers' collection. Most of it would be called retro: big bands, crooners, even skiffle. Difficult to find a farewell piece among that lot. 'I Did It My Way' was supposed to be the most popular choice for funerals, but didn't sound right for a murder victim. He gave some thought to the few facts he knew about Harry's life and an idea came to him. 'You may think this is in poor taste.'

'Try me.'

'I see you have some Louis Armstrong here. There's an old Satchmo number with Bing Crosby called "Gone Fishin'".'

Her deep brown eyes locked with his and seemed appalled. Then they slipped aside briefly and came back to him with a gleam of understanding. '"Gone Fishing"?' The start of a smile lit up her face. 'That'll do nicely. He's gone for sure and if he's got any choice, fishing is what he'll be doing.' She stood up. 'You can have that tea. Is my neighbour Betty seeing to it?'

'She went home for a bit.'

'Lazy cow. I'll have to make it myself. Tidy up the discs, would you? I won't be long.'

Left alone in the room, he made a show of poking the CDs with his foot into a smaller area near the fireplace. He wasn't going to risk kneeling. That done, he inspected the few paperbacks displayed on a built-in unit along one wall. No new insights here. Several by Stephen King and John Grisham, the *Police and Constabulary Almanac for 2009*, the *Observer Book of Freshwater Fish* and *The Good Guys Wear Black*, by Steve Collins. He picked up the last. It was subtitled *The True-Life Heroes of Britain's Armed Police*. Inside were photo illustrations of various SO19 raids. All-action. Not his scene. He replaced it.

Emma returned with a mug of tea in each hand. 'It was two sugars?'

A distinct improvement in relations, courtesy of Louis Armstrong. 'Thanks. I was looking at your books.'

'His, not mine. If you want any, take them. No point in me keeping them.'

'That wasn't why I mentioned it. I was thinking we don't know much about Harry except his fishing and his TV viewing.'

'Why do you want to know?' She sat in an armchair and gestured to him to do the same.

'Oddly enough, I know more about the other guys who were shot. Harry was one of our own.'

'Typical, isn't it?' she said, back on her familiar tack. 'He was just a number and a uniform.'

'That's not been my experience.'

'You got lucky, then.'

'I did my stint in uniform. I started in the Met a long time ago.'

'That lot? We were always hearing horror stories of them. We were country cops in Cornwall at the start. That's where we met, Harry and I.'

He'd forgotten she was originally in the force

with her husband. 'Which part of Cornwall?'

'Helston.'

His brain dredged up something Ingeborg had tried to tell him about town customs and traditions. 'My geography isn't up to much. Is that anywhere near Padstow?'

She shook her head. 'Padstow's a good forty miles away, on the north coast. Why do you ask?'

'It was a long shot.' Stupid bloody expression to use, he thought, the moment he'd said it. He'd never been noted for discretion. By some miracle the words got past her, so he followed them up fast. 'I was trying to find some connection between the three officers who were killed.'

'The only connection is the sonofabitch who shot them.'

'There is that note you found.'

'The "You're next" thing? Are you taking that seriously?'

'I can't ignore it.'

'That would mean Harry was a marked man and probably the others as well. Did they get notes?'

'We haven't found any.'

'They could have thrown them away. Why did you ask me about Padstow just now? Was one of the others from Padstow?'

'No.' This was as good an opening as he was likely to get. 'But there is a possible link between the first two victims, Ossy Hart and Stan Richmond. It may amount to nothing. When you said you served in Cornwall, I remembered that the town of Padstow has a hobby horse ceremony.'

'What?' All the good work of the past ten minutes went for nothing. She glared as if she'd caught him stealing underwear.

'The locals call it 'obby 'oss,' he said.

'Now you've lost me altogether.'

'Hold on.' He launched into an explanation: the origin of Ossy's name and the Minehead May Day celebration and the fact that Stan Richmond devoted his spare time to the study of such things.

She still looked at him as if he was talking bilge, so he threw in the added ingredient of the film man and thousands of dollars. Now it was all out in the open and he felt only the chill of her stare.

'I don't know if I've understood you,' she said finally, 'but you seem to be suggesting they were shot because of this horsing around in Minehead. Is that it?'

'It's an incomplete theory,' he said, wishing already that he'd kept it to himself.

'You're hoping I'm about to say something that will make sense of it all?'

'I'm not expecting anything.'

'You won't get anything. The reason they were shot—all three of them—is that some evil bastard hates the police and wants to kill as many as he can. While you waste time on weird theories, he's no doubt lining up the next one.'

'We're actively pursuing him, ma'am,' he said, thinking of Jack Gull and his armed police on watch in Avoncliff. 'It's not just down to me.'

'I should hope not. In the state you're in, you couldn't actively pursue the last man out at closing time.'

There wasn't much point in continuing. He reached for his stick and stood up. 'Thanks for the tea. I'll be in touch.'

'Do me a favour,' she said.

'What's that?' He prepared for one more

crushing putdown.

'Come to the funeral on Thursday.'

His voice shrilled in surprise. 'Me?'

'I don't know any of the Manvers Street lot except you. A few of Harry's relief are coming, but they're only names to me.'

'I hardly knew him myself.'

'You thought of "Gone Fishin'". Saved me hours of headache. The least I can do is ask you to be there. And you don't suffocate me with sympathy. Come for my sake. Three p.m. at Haycombe.'

Haycombe wouldn't be easy. He'd been to the same crematorium for Steph's funeral. But for all her carapace of toughness, this woman was in mourning, and he knew what that was like.

'All right. I will.'

'And join us after, for a drink and some snacks,' she added.

'Okay.'

She came to the door with him. 'All that hobby horse stuff is bunk. Don't waste time on it.'

CHAPTER EIGHTEEN

On the drive back, he had a Eureka moment. Ask for another list.

So had he finally flipped?

Not at all. The list would contain the names of all officers from Wells, Radstock and Bath who had completed a firearms course. If the sniper was, indeed, a policeman, he must have been trained to use a gun.

Neat. If this worked, the thousand-odd names in

those earlier lists could go to the shredder.

Back in the 1980s when Diamond had joined the Met, as many as fifteen per cent of the force had gone through a five-day course at the range and were dubbed authorised firearms officers. After certain well-publicised fiascos in the last decades of the twentieth century arising from under-trained armed police, the policy had changed. Since 2004 the National Police Firearms Training Curriculum ensured that the training was much more rigorous and intensive. An initial course lasted thirty-five days and those who passed were required to complete two days' training every month and requalify four times a year.

An AFO was now a specialist. And they were all on record.

Better start on home ground, he decided. Back in Manvers Street, he asked for the Bath Central names. Fourteen in all.

He didn't know them all personally. Even after serving here for so long, he couldn't keep up with the staff changes outside CID. But he knew who to ask, the key people in each section.

The problem wasn't who to ask, it was what. 'Has PC Plod the firearms officer been acting strangely of late? Talking to himself? Looking over his shoulder? Writing two-word notes on slips of paper?' Questions of this sort could rapidly turn the whole place into a hotbed of rumour and recrimination. The word witch-hunt had already been used in CID.

His enquiries had to continue alone. He couldn't even risk asking for help from the civilian staff. Face it, Diamond, he told himself, you'll have to exercise the mouse.

He started by accessing the duty rosters for the last twelve weeks. You'd think old stuff like that was over and forgotten, but in the computer age everything can be retrieved. Straight away he eliminated eight of the fourteen AFOs. Two had been on protection duty for some minor royal in Bristol at the time of the Wells shooting and three on the night shift in Bath. Another three couldn't possibly have been in Radstock when Stan Richmond was shot because they were at Portishead on the two-day rifle refresher course.

Down to six already.

He turned to the rosters for last Saturday night. Of those remaining, one had been off sick all week with a broken arm and three more on night duty and accounted for as part of the armed response unit which had actually attended the scene in Walcot Street when the shout came.

That left two from the original fourteen: a Sergeant Stillman and a PC Gaunt. Theoretically, either could have been at all three scenes.

The first name was familiar.

He didn't have to dredge deeply in his memory. Stillman was the sergeant who had accompanied Ken Lockton on the morning after the shooting. He'd driven Lockton from Walcot Street to the Paragon and gone through the house to the garden where they'd found the rifle resting against the railing overlooking the scene of the shooting.

If Stillman had been with Lockton that night he couldn't have shot Harry Tasker.

Or could he?

Assumptions sometimes need to be challenged. Diamond sat back in the chair and closed his eyes in concentration. This was the kind of problem he had a knack of unravelling.

The only version of the events in the garden was Stillman's. The sergeant had surprised everyone by turning up two hours after the shooting saying he'd fallen asleep in his patrol car after being told to move it out of sight by Ken Lockton. But what if Stillman had been lying? Could he have clobbered Lockton himself? And done it to cover up the fact that he'd earlier shot Harry Tasker?

Hair-raising possibilities. They had to be explored. Stillman's whole story was odd. He'd apparently been on patrol in his car, heard the shout about the shooting in Walcot Street and driven there. Was he alone then? The usual arrangement was that patrolling officers at night worked in pairs.

Then—according to his story—he'd been spotted by Lockton and ordered to drive him up to the Paragon, which in itself was strange, because it would have been quicker to use the steps. The pair had been admitted to the house by the blonde, Sherry Meredith. That much was true. She'd testified to it.

There was only Stillman's word for the rest of what happened. The next undeniable event was that the firearms unit broke into the garden and found Lockton face down and unconscious from a serious head injury. The sniper's gun was gone.

Sergeant Stillman needed to be questioned, and soon. He was on duty, Diamond learned from the control room, but in a patrol car north of the city on Lansdown. His shift was due to end within the hour.

'Shall I tell him to report to you, sir?' the operator asked.

‘Absolutely not.’ There were ways of doing things and Diamond’s way was not to announce them ahead of time.

He turned his attention to the other authorised firearms officer of potential interest, PC Gaunt. But it turned out that Gaunt couldn’t possibly have murdered Harry Tasker. On Saturday afternoon his wife had gone into labour and at 3.20 p.m. in the Royal United Hospital he’d become the proud father of twin girls. Under the Partners Staying Overnight scheme, he’d taken up night duty of another kind, in the maternity unit until 9 a.m. on Sunday.

* * *

Diamond was waiting for Stillman when he drove into the yard where the police vehicles parked.

The sergeant turned as pale as his shirt. ‘Something up, sir?’

‘It is if you insist on calling me “sir”. A few things need clearing up. We can do it in one of the interview rooms. Saves going upstairs to my office.’

The eyes showed Stillman didn’t fancy being treated like a suspect. ‘I don’t mind the stairs.’

‘But I do,’ Diamond said, pointing to the stick. He could be informal and still assert his authority.

They used interview room two. No caution, no tape running, but not lacking in tension, and Diamond’s first question didn’t lessen it.

‘How well did you know Harry Tasker?’

Stillman blinked rapidly several times. ‘Quite well, I suppose. He’d been around a long time and so had I.’

‘What did you make of him? Nice guy?’

'He was okay.' Not a thumping endorsement.

'You can be frank,' Diamond said, picking up on the lack of enthusiasm. 'It's not easy to speak ill of the dead, especially after what happened, but we're on a murder investigation here. I'm looking for honest impressions of the man.'

'There isn't much I can say. We didn't have a lot in common.'

'Was he good at the job?'

Stillman hesitated. 'He put in the hours all right.'

'Not always the same thing.'

'I meant he didn't skive off, like some do.'

'This isn't a test of your loyalty, sergeant. If there was a problem with the man, I need to know. I'm sensing something wasn't right.'

'I wouldn't call it a problem.'

'What did it amount to?'

'Nothing more than gossip, really.'

'From him?'

'About him.' Stillman had an expressive face, and the mental anguish was spreading over his features like spilt paint.

'Come on.'

'Harry didn't take kindly to change. If someone called in sick and the beats had to be rearranged, he wasn't at all happy. He liked to be given his duties for the week and stick to them. He kicked up so much that we tended to ask other people to switch.'

'What was the gossip you mentioned?'

A downward look. He drew a line along the table with his finger as if to tell himself that he'd already said too much about his dead colleague.

Diamond wasn't stopping there. Tittle-tattle it may be, but it was going to come out. The stakes were too serious for reticence. He sat back with arms folded and insisted with his eyes.

In a battle of wills, Stillman was always going to lose. 'No one ever proved it, but they said he made arrangements.'

'Arrangements?'

'Meeting certain people.' Stillman looked away. 'This is all speculation.'

'He was on the take?'

'That's what the whisper was, but we weren't sure how, or who was involved, or how much.'

If true, this was a new and depressing sidelight on the murder victim. Every police force has its bad apples. How galling if Harry Tasker, hailed everywhere as the brave victim of the sniper, had been rotten to the core.

'Let me try and get this clear,' Diamond said as if he wasn't used to plumbing depths like this. 'You're saying some of his fellow officers suspected he was using his official position to solicit bribes.'

The last word was too strong for Stillman. 'I wouldn't go as far as that. Like I said, it was only talk. There wasn't any proof.'

'Didn't anyone investigate while he was alive?'

'It never got that serious. I mean, it could have been nothing more than turning a blind eye to under-age drinking in return for an occasional pint.'

'Equally it could have been taking backhanders from drug dealers.'

'Or nothing at all, Mr Diamond. It could be just innuendo. I'm uncomfortable with this.'

'So am I. Let's continue.' For the present, he chose to say nothing about someone of sergeant rank who knew of the gossip and failed to act on it. 'We'll turn to the events of last Sunday morning.

You were on patrol in your car when the all-units call came that there was a shooting in Walcot Street. Is that right?'

Stillman's voice showed he was relieved to move on, even at the cost of having his own conduct examined. 'I was keeping an eye on a group of youths in Corn Street. It didn't take me long to answer the shout. I wasn't the first, but I was at the scene before the first ambulance.'

'You were alone in the car?'

The spasm of blinking afflicted him again. 'Er, that's correct.'

'Didn't you have an oppo?'

'I did not.'

'That's the norm on patrol. Why were you alone?'

'My partner had to finish early. A domestic problem. I'm experienced. I can cope with most situations.'

'Who was he?'

'My partner? I'd rather not say.'

'You're not getting the option, sergeant.'

He shook his head.

'The name,' Diamond said.

Stillman fingered the back of his neck. 'He's a good guy. We've done a lot together. I really don't want to drop him in it. It has no bearing on what happened after.'

'I can easily find out.'

He sighed. 'His name is Charlie Hunt. He was with me most of the night. We did the usual Saturday night stuff around the clubs and pubs. After the nightclubs emptied it went quiet like it always does. The thing is, Charlie's a married man and his wife is disabled. She has one of those horrible wasting diseases. She needs a lot of attention and doesn't like being alone in the house at night. I dropped him off somewhere near and I was aiming to finish the turn alone.'

'Have you done this before?'

He shrugged. 'It's not right, I know, guv, but can you overlook it on this occasion?'

'I'll still need to speak to him.'

'Why?'

'To verify what you just told me. It's for your benefit. You see, until and unless Ken Lockton comes out of his coma, there's no corroboration for your version of events.'

Stillman said after a long pause, 'Don't you believe me?'

'You're an authorised firearms officer. Is that correct?'

More frantic blinking. 'You don't seriously think I'm the sniper?'

'I have a duty to keep an open mind about everyone, even a serving officer with a blameless record.'

Abruptly the eyes opened wide in a horrified stare. 'I couldn't have shot him. I was in Corn Street when it happened.'

'And because you were alone, I've only got your word for it. Any other patrol officer attending the scene would have someone to back his version of events.'

Stillman shook his head, apparently in disbelief.

'From what you told me the morning of the shooting, Ken Lockton saw you at the scene in Walcot Street and told you to drive him up to the Paragon.'

'That was after he worked out where the shots

came from. He was the duty inspector that night so he became the SIO. He knew me quite well.'

'Why did he need the car? Why not use the steps?'

'I, em, can't say.'

'But you have a theory.'

A sigh. 'What difference does my opinion make?'

'Come off it, sergeant. You're uniquely placed to say what was going on.'

'Well, I got the idea Ken felt important. He wanted to be driven. He and I were sergeants together for quite some time before he got promoted.'

'He was lording it over you?'

'I wouldn't put it in those terms. There was more to it. I think he wanted company in case the sniper was still up there in the garden.'

'Sensible. But then you say he sent you away.'

'That was after we found the gun and decided the sniper might be coming back for it.'

'Two of you would have been better at making the arrest.'

'Yes, but Ken wanted the car moved away from the front of the house. It would have alerted the sniper.'

'True.'

'And he made it very clear to me that I wasn't to come back.'

'Why was that?'

'He thought he could make the arrest on his own.'

'Big mistake,' Diamond said. 'Do you think the sniper was hiding in the garden all the time?'

'That's possible. You saw the height of those weeds.'

For all his jumpiness, Stillman had been pretty convincing. His nervousness at the beginning could have been down to fear of being found out after he gave his partner unofficial time off.

'Let's fast forward,' Diamond said. 'You slept in the car for a couple of hours and then woke up and found out about Lockton being clobbered and taken to hospital. Must have been a hairy moment for you.'

'Extremely.'

'You did the right thing reporting to me and telling all. If I remember correctly, I advised you to go home and get some proper sleep. Is that what you did?'

He nodded.

'So you weren't among the AFOs who were present in Becky Addy Wood the same day?'

'Absolutely not.'

'Or on the night shift?'

'No.'

'Don't get me wrong,' Diamond said in his bull-in-a-china-shop mode, 'but doesn't the training of an AFO include some orienteering and living rough?'

The man may have been punch drunk by this stage. He showed no sign of alarm. 'It does, but I've never had cause to put any of that into practice in real life.'

'I should hope not, because the sniper is an expert at both.'

Now Stillman blushed deeply. A blush is not necessarily proof of guilt, Diamond knew. It could have been caused by the sergeant's realisation that he was firmly in the frame.

* * *

DC Paul Gilbert came into the incident room as wide-eyed as if he'd spotted the Loch Ness monster in the Roman Bath. 'Guess what the boss is up to.'

It was mid-afternoon and most of the team were present, collating information and dealing with witness statements.

Everyone looked up. Not enough had been happening in CID since that uncomfortable meeting yesterday. They'd not seen much of Peter Diamond. They wouldn't have admitted it, but some were actually missing him.

Halliwell spoke first. 'Fill us in, then.'

'He's downstairs with that sergeant who fell asleep in his car.'

'Steve Stillman? What's so special about that?' John Leaman asked.

'Using interview room two?' Gilbert said, refusing to be downed. 'The word from Jenny in the control room is that he was waiting in the yard to meet Stillman's patrol car when he came off duty. They went in looking as if World War Three had broken out, both of them.'

'Going over his story again, I expect,' Leaman said.

Halliwell said in support, 'It's no big deal, using an interview room to talk to a fellow officer. My guess is he didn't want us to hear about it in case we get the idea he's picking us off one by one. It would have looked bad if he'd come up here with Stillman in tow.'

'He's made up his mind the sniper is in-house,' Gilbert said.

'He'd better think again, then,' Ingeborg said

from her side of the room. 'In-house he is not. The report has come in from forensics. It's on my screen now. The guy living rough in the woods is definitely the sniper.'

'How do they know?'

'Matching shoeprints. There was a good set in the pillbox at Avoncliff. They're a perfect match with another set taken from the tree house at the Wells shooting.'

'That's it, then,' Leaman said. 'Who's going to tell the boss?'

'What's more, there were more of the same along the countryside walk where the sniper was almost caught last night.'

'Shoeprints aren't as reliable as fingerprints,' Halliwell said. 'I've heard of mistakes being made with shoe evidence.'

Gilbert said, 'He's bright enough not to have touched anything except the gun.'

'It's not just the make of shoe he was wearing,' Ingeborg said. 'It's the wear on the shoes, all those little grooves and nicks. They're in no doubt.'

'Pity we don't have a national database for shoeprints, like we do for fingerprints,' Halliwell said.

'Now you're being facetious,' Ingeborg said. 'This is good evidence. No way is he in-house, as Paul suggested, not in any sense. He's very much out in the open and he can't be one of ours, living rough like that. There's no reason for a cop to go on the run.'

'Are you going to tell the guv'nor?' Leaman asked her.

'I'll have to, won't I?'

'I'd like to see his face.'

'We'll all see it when he comes upstairs.'

He did, several minutes later, all smiles. 'Afternoon, people,' he said, and before Ingeborg or anyone else could speak he told them he'd just had a profitable session with Sergeant Stillman. The word 'session' made it sound like a chat over a glass of beer. He was more buoyant than he'd been all week. 'Things are starting to emerge,' he said, 'things some of us may find difficult to deal with. Keep this strictly to yourselves for the present. There was gossip—and it may be no more than that—about Harry Tasker, to the effect that he was on the take.'

Ingeborg took a sharp, indignant breath. 'That's so mean, regardless of whether it's true. The poor man is dead and his own fellow officers are slagging him off?'

'Which is why we're going to deal with it discreetly.'

'I don't think we should deal with it at all.'

'Worthy sentiments, Inge, but you're wrong. It's got to be investigated. We may have found the motive for Harry's murder. If he was demanding pay-offs from people up to no good, he was playing with fire.'

'You said it's only gossip.'

'And sometimes gossip is true. Harry was one of the longest-serving beat constables and he thought he was entitled to special treatment. He was very protective of his own beat, unwilling to switch with anyone else.'

'That's to be expected. He knew it better.'

'Agreed, but there is another construction.'

Halliwell said, 'He didn't want anyone else finding out?'

'Correct. Well, Harry's dead, and he can't object any more. I want two of you on that beat tonight, meeting people, finding what they know.'

'Tonight?' Ingeborg said.

'Around ten, when the lowlife come up to feed. I'll tee it up with the beat manager. This is a job for you, Paul. And Inge.'

'Me?' she said. She obviously had other plans for the evening. In Diamond's murder squad, you could never count on anything.

'You're quick to spot evasion. Walk the same beat Harry did, call at the same pubs and clubs and get a sense of whether he ever demanded backhanders in return for protection, or silence or information.'

'What if Jack Gull makes an arrest before then? Some forensic results are in that I think you ought to see.'

'We'll still be stumped for a motive. This could be it. Meanwhile I'll talk to our contacts at Wells and Radstock and see if by any chance the earlier victims were on the take.'

* * *

A little later, Keith Halliwell stepped into Diamond's office. The big man was studying yet another list, this time of officers who had served with Harry Tasker in the past and also had firearms experience. Guiltily, he turned it face down.

'Do you seriously rate Sergeant Stillman as a suspect, guv?'

'Why? Is there something else I should know about him?'

'He's a good guy. If a volunteer is wanted, he

puts up his hand. Doesn't mind doing an extra shift to help out. They're saying in uniform that he was dog tired on Sunday morning when he fell asleep in the car.'

'It's no excuse, as you and I know, Keith.'

'No one thinks he could have shot Harry.'

'He's an AFO. He knows how to handle an assault rifle. I want to find out next if he was issued with one recently.'

Halliwell sighed softly. 'He'd need a motive.'

'He wasn't Harry's best pal, I can tell you that.'

'Harry was an awkward cuss, guv. Didn't get along too well with anyone in uniform. You can't blame Stillman for being cool about him.'

'I'm not blaming anyone at this stage,' Diamond said. 'There's more to come out, I'm sure. This is in confidence, Keith. I've been going over lists of firearms officers from way back, people who served with Harry and the other victims. Prior to 2004, as we know, you could do a five-day course and plenty did. It looked good on your record. So there's a fair number of names.'

'Anyone we know?'

'Harry, for one.'

'Harry did the course?'

'When he was based at Helston. One of twenty-three names supplied by Devon and Cornwall Constabulary, PC Tasker. He could have upgraded here and done the five-week course at Portishead, but he never did. He wasn't ambitious any more.'

'Unlike certain other people?'

Diamond gave him a sharp look. 'Who do you mean?'

'Ken Lockton, for one. If he hadn't gone it alone,

we might have caught the sniper.'

'I wasn't going to say that.'

'Guv, did Ingeborg show you that forensic report?'

'On the shoe marks found at Avoncliff? She handed me a copy, true. She didn't have much to say. She's not a happy bunny.'

'But this new evidence seems to wrap it up.'

'Yes?' He couldn't have made the word sound any more negative. 'We still don't know who the sniper is.'

'True, but this is a definite link with the killing at Wells.'

'Keith, I've been in this game too long to use the word "definite" about anything. It's new information, I grant you.'

Sensing that Diamond's pride was on the line, Halliwell didn't push the argument any further. He cleared his throat. 'About tonight, guv.'

'All these years and I thought you'd never ask.'

Halliwell did his best to humour the boss by smiling. 'I'm thinking about young Gilbert and Ingeborg walking Harry Tasker's beat. They said nothing to me about this, but is it safe, do you think?'

Diamond frowned. 'They're grown-ups. They're cops.'

'I know, but Harry was murdered on that beat.'

'He was in uniform and so were the other victims. If the sniper wants more blood, he's not going to kill coppers in plain clothes. He'll move on to some other town and target another poor blighter on the beat. That's the pattern, Keith. He doesn't vary it. To come back to your question. Yes, those babes are going to be safe.'

CHAPTER NINETEEN

'I feel like a traitor, doing this,' Ingeborg said to Paul Gilbert. 'It's muckraking, that's what it is, and it's so much worse because Harry is dead. He can't defend his reputation.'

'That's for sure.'

'I've got a lot of respect for the guv'nor, as you know, but this time he's screwed up.'

'There is one thing about it.'

'Tell me,' she said in a world-weary tone. 'I'm all ears.'

'Up to now, he's been saying the sniper could be one of us, a cop. If I understand him right, he's come round to thinking it could be an outsider after all. You and I are trying to find out if Harry was bent, right?'

She sighed. 'I get you. If it turns out to be true, and Harry was shot because he was on the take, the killer has to be some lowlife he was threatening.'

'And that's got to be preferred to one of us.'

Ingeborg didn't appear any happier. 'It still leaves us doing a filthy job. Why can't he see what everyone else does—that there's an evil guy out there who is killing cops and doesn't care who they are?'

They'd reached George Street, into the second hour of their trek around the beat that Harry Tasker had done so often that he'd claimed it as his own. Finding people willing to speak was easier than they'd expected. Most had heard about the murder and a few had actually met Harry. No one had so far said a word against him.

Gilbert, too, had doubts, but more about the practicality of the task. 'Even if Harry bent the rules a bit, who's going to tell us? As soon we mention he's the lad who was murdered, they only want to say nice things about him.'

'I've written some of them down, ready to quote back at you-know-who,' Ingeborg said. '"An old-fashioned bobby, like you lot used to be." "Firm, but fair." "Good with the teenagers." None of that squares with what Mr D suggested.'

'But are they sincere, or are they telling us what they think we want to hear?'

Ingeborg flicked some hair back from her shoulder. 'Not much we can do about that.' She wasn't usually so resigned. The tug of loyalties was getting to her.

Gilbert decided it was up to him to suggest a change of plan. 'Two of us together is a bit heavy. Listen, why don't I stand back and watch you from across the street? People might speak more freely to you if you're on your own.'

'I shouldn't think so.'

'The blokes will.'

'Go on. Pull the other one.'

'I mean it, Inge. Let's give it a go. See those two?' He was looking across the street at the bouncers outside Moles, Bath's oldest nightclub. 'It's a fair bet they spoke to Harry at some time.'

She still didn't like the suggestion. 'I won't be popular with the queue. They'll think I'm trying to sweet-talk my way in.'

'The guys on the door will know you're serious as soon as you show them Harry's picture. I'll watch from over here.'

There was sense in what he was saying. She gave

way with a sigh, adding, 'At the next place, it's your turn.'

'Okay, but I don't have your advantages.'

'Bollocks.'

'Knickers.'

She raised a smile, gave him a dig in the ribs and crossed the street. In the timeline of popular music, Moles, at over thirty years old, was not quite as venerable as the Rolling Stones, but it had had some biggish licks. Its small stage had hosted The Cure, Primal Scream, Tears for Fears, Radiohead, Blur and Oasis as bands on their way up the charts. Ingeborg's visits didn't go back that far, but she was a regular and knew the interior nearly as well as the CID room. Even so, bouncers tend to change and neither of these two recognised her.

'Hi, guys.' She gave them her playful smile and a sight of her warrant card. 'Just checking that it's all okay tonight.'

'What's all this?' the bigger of the two asked. 'You expecting bovver on Cheese night?'

She laughed. The Big Cheese was a midweek institution here, cheap drinks and cheesy tunes everyone knew the words to. Trouble was rare. 'I'm trying to get some background on the officer who was shot last weekend.' She held up Harry's picture. 'Did you know him?'

'Poor sod, yes. He'd stop and have a word sometimes.'

'What about? Last night's TV?'

'No, darling. He was doing his job, telling us to keep a lookout for drugs and that.'

'And were you able to help?'

He shook his head. 'We know who the bad lads are, anyway. They don't get in when we're on.'

'You wish!'

'Like that one across the street making out he's nothing to do with you. He's got bad lad written all over him.'

She didn't turn to look at Paul, but the comment amused her. She'd save it up for later. 'I can tell you're smart. Harry would have looked to you two for the inside story.'

The one who hadn't spoken, shorter, wider and with more tattoos, said, 'He didn't need no inside story. This was his manor.'

'He controlled it, you mean?'

'He had his methods.'

The taller one's T-shirt tightened against his pecs. 'The lady doesn't want to know that.'

'Pardon me, the lady does,' Ingeborg said, alerted.

He shook his head. 'We're not in the business of shopping people, 'specially dead people.'

'You wouldn't be shopping anyone. You might be helping to find his killer.'

'Some chance.'

'And if you withhold information, you could have blood on your hands.'

The wider and shorter of the pair looked concerned and said, 'You could try asking in the Porter next door.'

He was talking about the pub where patrons tanked up before using the club. It was said to be owned by Moles.

'Who would I ask?'

'You could start with a black guy called Anderson if he's there.'

The tall one cut in and actually put out an arm to ease his mate aside. 'Leave it.' To Ingeborg he said,

'Anderson doesn't know a thing. My mate is talking through his arse.'

'But I'm listening.'

'Lady, you're wasting your fucking time, and ours.'

Ingeborg would be the judge of that. She'd heard of Anderson before. He was well known in Walcot. She returned to Paul Gilbert and told him she'd learned nothing concrete from those two, but there were hints of illicit goings on. His turn had come now and he might get lucky.

The Porter had a history of retailing liquor going back almost two hundred years. Much extended since it originally opened in Miles's Buildings, it was a favourite pub of students and the young, a warren of a place, always noisy, busy and reeking of beer. On popular nights like this one, the clientele spilled out on to the alley that separated the pub from Moles.

'Try downstairs in the cellar bar,' she told Gilbert. 'A tall black guy called Anderson may know something. He's well up with what goes on.'

'Anderson who?'

'Jakes. Surname Jakes. No one has ever pinned any major crime on him. But be careful. Make it clear you're not accusing him personally of anything. I'll be waiting in the front bar at street level.'

'What's the angle here?'

'Try under-age drinkers. Anderson is a grown-up. Harry must have been round here checking a few times.'

Gilbert pushed his way through the crowd, descended the stairs and found an even bigger crush in the vaults. Joining a group would be no problem.

It was like rush-hour on the London underground, but darker and noisier. All the cubicles along the walls were taken. Getting anywhere near the bar would be a major achievement.

'D'you mind?' a redhead said regardless of the fact that she'd just backed into him. He'd pressed his hand against her to prevent her four-inch heels impaling one of his feet. True, he'd felt the curve of warm flesh under the smooth silk of a miniskirt. People had been arrested for less, but in this situation it was inevitable.

'Sorry.'

She squirmed around to face him and now the contact was breast to chest. Fumes of some musky perfume wafted from her cleavage. She looked about fifteen, if that.

'Do I know you?'

'Paul.'

'Polly. You've split me up from my friends.'

'Sorry.'

'Don't keep saying that. Be nice to me.'

That stumped him. 'Er, what do you suggest?'

'What do I suggest?' she mimicked his voice. 'It's no use offering me a drink, is it? You'd never find me again in this crowd. Got anything else on you?' She showed him the tip of her tongue and curled it upwards.

'Sorry, no.'

A sharp, stricken sigh. 'Are you here for the comedy, Paul?'

'Is there any?'

'Some pathetic stand-up any minute now. If you haven't come for that, what are you doing here, apart from groping me?'

The truth had to emerge at some stage. 'I'm a

police officer looking for information.'

She thought that was hilarious. 'Oh, yeah? Why aren't you in uniform?'

'I'm CID.'

'K—I—D, more like. Prove it, then.'

'I would if I could reach my warrant card in my inside pocket.'

'Nice try! Put that groping hand of yours anywhere near my boobs and I'll knee you in the balls, I warn you. You're not really one of the plod, are you?' She gasped. 'Christ, I know who you are. You're the comic trying to reach the stage. My big mouth. I wasn't being personal just now, honest.'

'No, I really am a cop. Are you in a job, or still at school?'

'What's it to you? Do you fancy schoolgirls?' It was obvious she didn't believe him.

'Seriously.'

'Seriously, he says. Next thing he's going to ask me how old I am and tell me I'm nicked.'

'Relax. I was hoping to speak to a black guy. Anderson. Have you heard of him?'

His serious tone was making an impression on Polly at last. 'Heard of him? I've met him. He isn't under-age. You won't nick him for that.'

'Is he here tonight?'

She shook her head. 'He doesn't come in on Cheese night. He's more into hip-hop and breaks.'

'Where would he be tonight?'

'That's anyone's guess. I still don't think you're a cop.'

'That's all right, then,' Gilbert said. 'I must be good at it.'

Her voice changed. She became more confrontational. 'Looking for Anderson, yeah? Like has he noticed anyone selling e? If he goes yes, find out who and tell me, 'cause I'm down to my last one. I'm leaving you, Paul the funny man. Thing is, you don't amuse me one bit.' She squeezed herself to the left and was gone, forcing Gilbert hard against the back of a large guy smelling of tobacco and black leather, a back that flexed ominously.

'Sorry, mate,' Gilbert said into a mangled ear.

'Piss off, then.'

'Sure.' He edged away and with steady shoving—but keeping his hands at his sides—forged a route back to the stairs. Up there, he could breathe again.

Ingeborg had the best of this arrangement. She'd managed to find a barstool and was holding a tonic with ice and lemon. 'Any joy?'

'It's the black hole of Calcutta down there. Anderson isn't in tonight. Can I have a sip of that?'

She passed him the glass. 'I showed Harry's picture to the barmaid. She says we're wasting our time.'

'Tell me something new.'

'Well, there may be something.'

He waited, and she made him wait a little longer.

'When she isn't working here, the barmaid spends most of her time surfing the internet—the poor benighted girl—and she says we ought to look at some of the stuff out there.'

'You do already, don't you?'

'Useful stuff. I don't bother reading blogs. People have been blogging about the sniper, ninety-nine per cent rubbish, of course, but she reckons she's seen one that looks as if it's being posted by someone local who's worried about her friend's partner, who sounds like a nutcase, and possibly dangerous. Might be worth a look.'

'You reckon?'

'She's given me the link.'

'Cool. Do they use their real name?'

'Let's find out if it's any use first. I'll take a look tomorrow—if I haven't resigned by then.'

* * *

Deep in the Limpley Stoke valley, Peter Diamond had joined the stake-out. Jack Gull had stayed on watch at Avoncliff for five hours without any result and had phoned Bath Central and demanded some relief. Diamond had asked why DI Polehampton couldn't take over, and Gull had muttered something about wanting a safe pair of hands, before adding quickly that Polehampton was making an important contribution liaising with the Wiltshire police. Diamond had said his hands might be safe, but he couldn't answer for his feet. Gull had said the firearms team would take care of any action. They simply needed someone to shout, 'Go, go, go!' when the moment came. Privately Diamond thought he'd shout it anyway if the sniper hadn't shown up by midnight.

He didn't fancy another night in the open, but he was a realist. This was the place to be. It would be dereliction of duty to ignore the forensic evidence linking the Avoncliff squatter to the murder of Ossy Hart in Wells. The matching of shoeprints from both locations made this stake-out central to the investigation.

The novelty of trying out night-vision binoculars soon lost its appeal.

He was flat on his stomach on a mound of gravel. The stone chippings had obviously been dumped there by the railway company for use as ballast in laying sleepers and maintaining the track. The line from Chippenham to Westbury ran straight through the valley and was the backdrop to his view of the pillbox, in front of the embankment. Heaped together, the gravel was moderately high and formed a convenient lookout post about fifty yards off. The mound must have been there some years. Enough grass and weed had seeded itself between the stones to provide effective cover.

Ideal, he thought, except it was bloody uncomfortable.

'This is worse than a bed of nails,' he complained to the sergeant from the firearms unit who was with him. 'It's all right for you in all that bulletproof gear. I'm not dressed for this.'

Not a syllable of response. In truth there wasn't much the sergeant could say by way of sympathy. If Diamond had thought about protection, he'd have called at Manvers Street and collected the kit. Because he didn't see himself as an action man and had no intention of becoming one, he'd driven straight here and was still in his day clothes. He'd made a point—and now he was suffering from a thousand points he hadn't bargained for.

'What time did you arrive?' he asked the sergeant.

A finger to the lips. Then, after the point was made, six fingers raised.

It was already after eleven. Diamond modulated his voice. 'What's your name?'

'Andy Gillibrand, sir.'

'Guv will do. And are you from my lot, or Wilts?'

'Wilts, guv.'

'Aren't you getting cramp by now? I'm sure I

would.'

The answer came in a whisper. 'We move about from time to time. I've swapped positions with one of the lads up at the railway station.'

'They'll get the first sight of him up there and radio us, will they? Radio communications open at all times?'

'That's the theory—if he comes from that direction.'

'If he comes at all.'

Sergeant Gillibrand plucked at his ear. 'I wasn't going to say that.'

'If he has any suspicion we're here, he'll stay away. He's rather good at giving us the slip.'

'We've got to assume he'll come.'

'And how many are we?'

'Right now? With you, thirteen.'

'Is that enough?'

'Should be, if we play it right. We're well spread out.'

Silence resumed. Silence and suffering. No way could he relax on this heap of gravel. The ache in his leg had been overtaken by what felt like piranha bites all over his flesh. Who knows, he told himself, trying to be positive, it may work like acupuncture and cure me altogether. Put your mind on other things, Diamond. Get a grip on what's been happening.

Plenty had.

In the scramble that had been his day, this was his first chance to get things in perspective. A mass of information had come to light since this morning when he'd got up early to drive to Wells. The challenge was to find how much of it was germane to the investigation. Certainly visiting the scene of the first shooting had been worthwhile. If he'd harboured any doubts that the sniper had planned the shootings to the last detail, they'd been dispelled. That tree house with the view across the street and the easy escape route was a brilliant location.

The first real surprise of the day had been Ossy Hart's widow. Juliet Hart had defied expectation with her robust way of coping with her bereavement. She was resolute in her cheerfulness. True, she'd had almost three months to come to terms with the shock. At first he'd thought her out of order, then impressive, then a little weird. He wondered how brittle her bravery was. She'd made up her mind that there had been no personal intent in the murder of Ossy. That telling statement—'It was the uniform, wasn't it?'—had been flung at him like a challenge. How could he dare suggest that the killing was anything other than random? He'd told her about the 'You're next' note and ducked out of saying any more. If he'd floated his theory about the sniper targeting certain individuals starting with her husband, she would very likely have snapped.

And yet ironically it was Juliet Hart who had started him on the promising new line of enquiry. He might have dismissed the hobby horse connection as hokum were it not for the big bucks said to have been dangled by the American film man. This wasn't some documentary for television that was being proposed. It was a Hollywood action movie. He could remember some of the set-piece chases through carnivals in the Bond films. Everyone knew the millions that went into modern feature films. But was the money real, or just talk? A film in development, or some kind of confidence trick?

He'd speculated on a link with the second victim, the folklore specialist, PC Richmond, and within hours it had been confirmed.

Ingeborg and her surfing of the web had added substance: the evidence that Stan Richmond had made a study of the Minehead hobby horse celebration. There was a strong chance he would have been approached by the same film man and offered money as a consultant.

Two murdered police officers, each with a strong link to the same ritual. But nothing so far tied in with Harry Tasker. His widow Emma had dismissed any connection out of hand. Different as she was from the eerily cheerful Juliet Hart, this lady's theory of the shooting amounted to the same: 'Some evil bastard hates the police and wants to kill as many as he can.' She'd refused to believe that the 'You're next' note meant Harry was a marked man.

A movement from the sergeant, hands gripping the gun and taking aim, jerked Diamond back to the gravel heap.

'What is it?'

He could have saved his breath.

Better not distract the guy, he thought.

By degrees, Sergeant Gillibrand relaxed enough to reply. 'Wildlife,' he muttered finally.

'Plenty of badgers hereabouts,' Diamond said from personal knowledge.

'That was a small deer.' The sergeant rested the gun on its side, black and chunky, not much over two feet in length.

'We could have had venison for supper.'

No answer.

'Are those things heavy?'

'Almost three kilos, guv.'

'What's that in words I understand?'

'Over six pounds.'

'It's a G36, is it? Same as the sniper uses?'

'So they tell us. Want to feel the weight?'

'No thanks,' Diamond said. 'I'll take your word for it. Guns aren't my thing.'

Unexpectedly, this got the sergeant going at last. 'Anyone could learn to use this in ten minutes. The mechanism is dead simple. You've got a thirty-round curved magazine.' The sergeant patted the boxlike lower section with his hand. 'Basically, the rifle is gas-operated and fires from a closed rotary bolt. When you want to line up the target there's an optical sight with 1.5 magnification and for conditions like this you clip in the night-sight as well. Get the red dot on your target and squeeze the trigger. Simple as that.'

The specifications didn't interest Diamond. People did. 'The press keep telling us the sniper is a brilliant marksman. Are you saying he doesn't need to be?'

'My mother could fire one of these things.'

'Get away.'

'Honest. The sight system makes it a doddle.'

'If it's that easy, why is the firearms course such a big deal?'

'You have to know how to assemble the gun, load it, clean it, carry it safely, and there's a load of other stuff apart from the sessions at the range, like land navigation by day and night and constructing and using hides. It's all about confidence and discipline.'

'Confidence, I can do,' Diamond said.

The sergeant had enough tact not to ask about

discipline. 'Don't you have a handgun on you?'

'It's all I can do to handle this stick.'

The exchange stopped there. The two men didn't have much in common. Diamond's thoughts moved on to another of the day's discoveries—the fact that Sergeant Stillman was an authorised firearms officer. How much confidence and discipline had he exhibited? Not much of the latter. Here was an officer who, against regulations, had given his partner time off during a patrol; and who had slept in his car at a major emergency. Yet it was thanks to Stillman that the question of Harry Tasker's alleged dirty dealings had come up. Taking the uncharitable view of Stillman, he may have traded this titbit in the hope that his own failings would be overlooked. The question had to be asked: had he invented it all? If so, Ingeborg and young Gilbert would be better employed at this minute catching up on their sleep.

Thinking of Stillman brought back the sequence of events immediately after the shooting. The 999 call from the student, Damon Richards, who lived over the shop in Walcot Street: impossible for him to have fired the shots from there. He was in the clear. But the residents of the house in the Paragon couldn't be so easily eliminated as suspects. In all the emphasis on the fugitive in the woods, they'd almost slipped out of the frame. He wondered if any of them had colluded in the crime by letting the sniper into the house. They didn't have to be gun-toting killers themselves, but they could have harboured one. More was needed on their backgrounds. Even that elderly couple, the Murphys, could have hated the police enough to be part of a conspiracy. The blonde, Sherry Meredith, and the civil servant on the top floor, Sean Willis, had appeared to say enough to clear them of active involvement, but aiding and abetting the killer was not out of the question.

Mental note: check those tenants again.

The sergeant hitched himself up on his elbows. 'Nearly midnight.'

'That's nothing. He keeps late hours,' Diamond said. 'He's probably stuffing himself in an all-night kebab shop.'

'Mind if I take a leak?'

'Be my guest, but not just here, eh?'

'I won't be long.' Gillibrand picked up the gun.

'Do you need that?'

'It's the golden rule. Have it with you at all times.'

'Don't shoot yourself in the foot, then. Or worse.'

Left alone, Diamond tried the night-vision binoculars again. They were not unlike standard field glasses, but with a single elongated front lens. A proximity sensor turned them on when they were lifted to the viewing position, saving battery life. He focused on the pillbox and used the digital control to intensify the image.

All was still except some hogweed stirring slightly in the breeze. Everything was in weird green hues and he had the impression he was looking into a fish-tank badly in need of cleaning. The concrete structure appeared as eau-de-Nil with a horizontal stripe as dark as spinach, the oversized letterbox allowing the occupants to fire from a well-defended position. Seventy years since the pillbox was built and it could never have been used for its intended purpose. No doubt it had become a play place from time to time for adventurous kids and an occasional shelter for hikers and rough sleepers.

Behind him sounded the faint crunch of steps on the gravel. You couldn't walk on this stuff in silence. It amused him that Gillibrand had made such a fuss about speaking aloud and then announced to the world with his police-issue boots that he was off for a jimmy riddle.

He continued to focus on the pillbox. Had anyone actually looked inside tonight? he wondered. He wasn't wholly confident that Jack Gull would have thought to check. Was it possible that the sniper had crept inside earlier and was sleeping peacefully while the armed police kept their vigil outside? Stranger things had happened.

Sometimes you got a gut feeling about the presence of a fugitive. To be fair, the little building wasn't giving out vibes that it was occupied. Diamond doubted if anyone was inside. But then he also doubted whether the sniper would put in an appearance at all.

The crunch of gravel got louder, then stopped.

What was the man doing now—zipping up?

Diamond removed the binoculars from his face and everything appeared several shades darker than it had before. He turned to the right expecting Gillibrand to join him.

It didn't happen.

Instead, there was the rasp of an indrawn breath and then he was hit with the full force of a falling body. He'd felt nothing like it since his days playing rugby, and rugby wasn't played on mounds of railway ballast. He was crushed, winded, pained. This wasn't an accident. It was an attack.

His face was hard against the sharp points of stone and his attacker had a hand on his head, forcing it further in. A weight heavier than his own was bearing down on his upper body. The assault was so sudden that he was virtually overpowered before he could fight back. He tried turning more to the right to shift the weight and succeeded only in scraping his ribs against the gravel.

Excruciating.

This was no place for a wrestling match. The stones shifted when he tried bracing his legs to get some leverage. Immediately he was trapped under the weight of his attacker's thighs. A pathetically uneven contest. Surprise had done for him. He tried wriggling and squirming, yet each movement brought a counter-move that locked him down, denying another attempt. He was wasting the little strength he had left.

What next?

The bullet in the head?

The fractured skull?

He could do nothing to avert either. He was down and out.

Incapable of moving, he could only wonder how this had happened. The sniper must have spotted the stake-out when returning towards the pillbox and decided to take out one more of the cops he despised. An easy target, an unarmed man, face down, defenceless.

He felt movement again. His right arm was grasped above the elbow and twisted behind his back and in the same action his neck was grabbed, the classic half-nelson, as good a way as any of disabling a man.

But it didn't end there. His attacker forced him further over to his right and groped for the other arm. Diamond at first trapped it under his own body. When that didn't succeed, he tried stretching it beyond reach.

No use. A longer arm than his own found his wrist and tugged it inwards and against his back.

Something odd happened then. Something very odd indeed. He was handcuffed.

First he felt the enclosing steel as his right wrist was clamped. Then the left was pulled across and applied to the second cuff. These were rigid cuffs, the sort the police themselves use, simple to operate with one hand.

Hot breath gusted into his right ear and a voice started speaking familiar words. 'You do not have to say anything. But it may harm your defence if you do not mention now something you later rely on in court. Anything you do say may be given in evidence.'

He'd been arrested.

CHAPTER TWENTY

'On your feet.'

'You're joking, of course,' Diamond said, still face down on the gravel heap.

'That's an order. Do it now.'

'What do you think this walking stick is for?'

A moment for thought. 'Sit up, then,' his attacker said. 'You can do that.'

Manacled as he was, he rolled over and succeeded in raising his back from the stones. He had difficulty seeing in this poor light. The voice had sounded strangely familiar, though, and the height of the standing figure silhouetted against the night sky confirmed the galling truth. 'Oh, Christ almighty!'

DI Polehampton of the Serial Crimes Unit was no less appalled. 'Stone the crows, I thought you were the sniper.'

'You thought wrong. Get me out of these cuffs, you wally.'

Polehampton was in full body armour, black coveralls with pockets galore. Diamond's confidence of an early release faded when he saw the man starting to frisk himself.

'Don't tell me you've lost the key.'

'It's here somewhere.' He kept locating new pockets and patting them. 'What were you doing lying there in your ordinary clothes?'

'I'm CID. That's what I wear, plain clothes.'

'I was expecting a man in combat gear. I was told one of the Wiltshire firearms team was here, not you.'

'Sergeant Gillibrand. He's on a comfort break.'

'Look, I'm frightfully sorry.'

'Save it, man. Just find the key and unlock the cuffs.'

Polehampton was round to his thigh pockets now in a process that was getting frantic, ripping Velcro apart with sounds that must have carried all the way to Avoncliff station. 'The view I had of you, lying face down, I just couldn't take a chance. I know the key is on me somewhere.'

'It had better be.'

'I hope I didn't hurt you.'

'Apart from causing facial scars that could be permanent, pushing my head against the gravel and destroying my sciatic nerve with some item of equipment you're wearing on your belt, you didn't trouble me in the least. Have you tried the back pockets?'

More ripping sounds ensued.

'Got it.'

'Thank God for that.'

Polehampton knelt behind Diamond and got to work on the handcuffs. 'I didn't know you were here. I thought Superintendent Gull was in charge.'

'He was until an hour ago. What's holding you up? My wrists are giving me hell.'

'Done.'

The cuffs snapped open. Diamond massaged his chafed flesh.

'If you don't mind, I'd better move on,' Polehampton said. 'There's more liaising to be done.'

'Is that what you call it?'

The irony was lost on Polehampton. 'Are you able to move?'

'No thanks to you.'

Left alone, Diamond checked for blood where his face had been forced against the gravel. To his surprise there didn't seem to be any. His wife Steph had once told him he had a tendency to over-dramatise injuries and ailments. He'd denied this, of course, while admitting to himself that there was a germ of truth there. Now he could almost see her smiling at this latest non-injury. A comforting thought. He massaged his bad leg. Pins and needles had set in. As the blood flow returned he expected the steady ache to come back, but it didn't. Was it possible that the wrestling match had effected a cure?

The gravel crunched again and Sergeant Gillibrand reappeared.

'I thought I heard sounds,' he said.

'More wildlife,' Diamond said.

* * *

In Walcot Street, Ingeborg and Paul Gilbert had reached the Bell, one of Bath's oldest pubs at some two hundred and fifty years, renowned for real ale and live music, and close to the point where Harry Tasker had been shot. They had spoken to a few more of Bath's night owls along the way without adding anything to the dossier on their dead colleague.

'Going in?' Gilbert said.

'What's on?' Ingeborg asked.

'Getting choosy, are we?'

'Jerk. Is it Anderson's kind of music is what I'm asking. It doesn't sound like hip-hop to me.'

'I'm starting to think Anderson is a red herring. And I need a drink.'

'We're not here to enjoy ourselves, DC Gilbert.'

'It's on me.'

Her eyes widened.

The music was definitely more folksy-rootsy than hip-hop and any tall black guy should have been obvious and was not, but Paul Gilbert was able to pick his pint of real ale from an abundant selection. The Bell's large interior had a well-used feel to it. A whiff of malt, a live band playing, a congenial atmosphere. The somewhat hippy clientele averaged fifteen years older than the crowd at the Porter.

Ingeborg had a spritzer and a packet of crisps. They worked their way through the crush to a games room at the back with table football and darts, far enough from the music to make conversation possible.

'We won't have much to report to the guv'nor,' Gilbert said.

'He can't say we didn't try.'

'Did we try enough?'

She said with a sharp note of disfavour, 'What's that supposed to mean?'

'Let's be honest, Inge. Your heart isn't in it, and neither is mine.'

She was silent for a while, then shed any pretence at irritation. 'True. I've never felt like this about a case before. I want the sniper off the streets, of course I do. I guess I want it on my terms, without rubbishing a dead colleague.'

'Leaving everyone's reputation okay?'

'Except the sniper's.'

'Him? He's scum. Goes without saying.'

'Am I asking too much?' she said. 'When Harry was murdered, I was shocked, of course, same as everyone. I looked at the papers next day, and thought there's something different here, the way it's being reported. For once the Old Bill are getting a good press. Outraged headlines that someone should kill a policeman. None of the flak we've got used to about clear-up rates and never being on the spot when you're needed and turning a blind eye to rampaging kids. They want us to catch this creep before he shoots another cop. But here at the coalface it doesn't feel like that. First the boss talks about our own people coming under suspicion and then he's suggesting Harry was bent. How's that going to play with the public if it ever gets out?'

'If it's true,' Gilbert said. 'Personally, I don't see

it.'

'The guv'nor does, and he's no mug.'

'Do you think he knows something he isn't telling us?'

She shook her head. 'He plays it straight. There'd be no point in keeping back information. But he's troubled. I can read him.'

'I wish I could.' He stared into the foam still settling in his glass. 'Was it his wife being murdered that turned him so grouchy? It couldn't have helped.'

'The truth is, he was like it before. He takes it personally when a case is difficult and he doesn't know how much it shows. When I was a crime reporter, I used to watch him do press conferences. The press boys baited him for sport. They liked to see him lose his rag. A big laugh, especially as they didn't have to work with him. There was a DI called Julie Hargreaves who was brilliant at deflecting questions. He relied on her a lot and I think she put up with a lot. Even she got to the end of her tether and put in for a transfer. He was gobsmacked.'

'Did she leave?'

'Left Bath, yes.'

'Is she still serving?'

Ingeborg nodded. 'She did very well career-wise, ending up at Headquarters. She's a DCI now. She was one of the interviewers when I applied for the job here. I remember her telling me it wouldn't be a bed of roses and by God she was right. But she also said I was lucky to be joining this team because it was the best-led in the county.'

'She meant him?'

Ingeborg nodded. 'And she was right about that, too. Watch him with Jack Gull, who's supposed to be the class act. There's no comparison.'

Gilbert yawned. 'I guess we'd better drink up and move on. Is it worth talking to any of this lot?'

'Didn't you ask the barman about Anderson?'

He blushed. 'Sorry. I was deciding which ale I wanted. Took all my concentration.'

'You could return the glasses and see if he's heard of him.'

He drained his and wiped his lips. 'That was something else. Okay, I'll give it a shot.'

Outside in Walcot Street a few minutes later, he was buoyant. 'Anderson has a regular steak dinner in the Hudson Bar and Grill up the street. This way.'

'I know the Hudson,' Ingeborg said, standing her ground. 'It's not cheap. A steak there sets you back twenty to thirty pounds.'

'So?'

'Anderson obviously eats well.'

'He's not the only one, by the sound of it.'

She laughed. 'I don't pay for steak dinners. I was taken there a couple of times. I knew it better as the Hat before it went upmarket. The Hat and Feather. A great pub with a DJ called Dave who was a local legend, the oldest in the biz. The trouble was that the brewers kept putting up the rent, so the pub was always changing hands. And it was a listed building even older than the Bell. At one stage there was a danger of the floor upstairs collapsing. Seeing as the stage was up there and that was where the dancing went on, it was a real headache for the publican.'

Ingeborg's memories of wilder times weren't going to help their quest. She seemed to want to linger outside the Bell. 'Let's go find him, then,'

Gilbert said.

'Where?'

'The Hudson.'

'I wouldn't bother,' she said. 'It'll be closed. It's after one a.m.'

He swore. He almost stamped his foot. 'I don't get it.'

'I think I do. Did you say you were police?'

'Well, yes.'

'You were being sent on a wild-goose chase.'

'Bloody hell. So where do we go now?' Gilbert asked.

'Isn't that obvious?'

'Not to me.'

'Wait and see.' She took a step back into the shadow of the building next door and tugged at Gilbert's arm for him to do the same.

They didn't have long to wait. A tall black man in a suit stepped out of the Bell and into the street speaking into a mobile phone, looked to right and left and waited at the kerb.

'I didn't see him in there,' Gilbert said, in awe of Ingeborg's foresight.

Immediately the sound of a car with speakers on full volume filled Walcot Street. A white Lexus came from nowhere and halted in the centre of the road. The speed of all this was worthy of a bank robbery except that robbers don't usually have Black Eyed Peas going at full belt. The nearside door was open and the man was in the act of getting in.

'Stop him,' Ingeborg said.

Gilbert didn't need telling. He had already sprinted forward. Just before the door slammed shut, he dived for the man's arm and got a grip.

The stitching on the sleeve gave way and a wedge of white was revealed at the shoulder. Gilbert's hand came within a microsecond of being crushed in the door.

The boom of the music stopped and the car window slid down. Gilbert was on his knees in the road.

The man said from inside the car, 'That will cost you. That was a Savile Row suit.'

Ingeborg caught up with Gilbert. 'Are you okay?'

'No problem,' he said.

'Is *he* okay?' the man said. 'He just destroyed my jacket.'

'Are you Anderson Jakes?' she said.

'Sure. And you're the fuzz. It will still cost you.'

'DCs Smith and Gilbert. We'd like a few words. Do you mind stepping out of the car?'

Anderson took time to think about his options. Meanwhile, Gilbert had got upright and was now standing directly in front of the car to prevent it from moving on—brave, but not necessarily wise.

'Turn off the engine,' Ingeborg told the driver. She couldn't see his face, just his black hands resting on the wheel.

It didn't happen.

'Tell him,' she said to Anderson with more insistence.

Anderson gave a nod and the driver obeyed.

'I was on my way home,' Anderson said as he emerged from the car. 'Can we keep this brief?' He was at least a foot taller than either of them and he moved as if he spent time in the gym.

Ingeborg had the initiative now and she intended to keep it. 'What were you doing in there? Not your kind of music.'

'Bar billiards. The only decent table in my neighbourhood.'

'I didn't see you playing.'

He shrugged and the wedge of white increased in size. 'Changed my mind, didn't I? There was an unpleasant smell in there . . . of pigs.'

She ignored the taunt. She wanted co-operation. She was trying to think where best to take him. 'You say you want to keep it short. Tell your driver to pull into the side of the street and wait for you.'

This relaxed Anderson a little. He nodded to the driver. Gilbert stepped around the car and joined the other two.

'We'll take a short walk up the street,' Ingeborg said, still reassuring. 'This isn't about you. It's about the officer who was shot on Saturday night. Harry Tasker. You knew him, didn't you?'

They started a slow stroll in the direction of the city centre.

'I had no dealings with Harry,' Anderson said.

'We were told you might know about some of the people he spoke to on his beat.'

'Small fry. Kids, mostly,' he said. 'They're the ones need keeping in order, right?'

'Students, you mean?'

'Younger than that, sixteen, seventeen. Should be at home, doing their school work instead of making trouble, graffiti and that.'

'There's not a lot of graffiti here.'

'Like I say, Constable Harry kept them in line.'

'Are there any he didn't keep in line, the over-twenties maybe? You know why I'm asking, Anderson? Some crazy person was way out of order taking a shot at him.'

He went silent again. His heels had metal tips

that clipped on the paving stones. Club XL was on the left, probably the last place Harry Tasker had visited before he was shot. Like most of Bath's nightclubs, it occupied an old building. In this case a carved stone over the entrance said ESTD 1798. Established as a *nightclub*? The security man on the door gave Anderson a nod that was more respect than just recognition.

'This is your manor, isn't it?' Ingeborg pressed him. 'What's going on? Walcot is swarming with cops and pressmen. You don't want that kind of attention.'

'If I knew who shot the cop, I'd tell you,' he said. 'I've asked around. Nobody knows.'

'We're not suggesting you know,' Gilbert said, picking up on Ingeborg's approach. 'We're looking for help. Was there anyone who could have felt threatened by Harry?'

'I'm not a mind reader.'

'Try.'

'I told you, man. He was looking out for small fry, juveniles. He had the sense not to mess with grown-ups like me.'

'Any juveniles in particular?'

'I keep my distance.'

'Sensible,' Ingeborg chimed in. 'As a grown-up it can't be any pleasure being questioned about their misdemeanours.'

'You said it, lady.'

'At the same time, being a man of some influence in the community, you must have taken an interest. Were there any juveniles giving Harry a hard time?'

Anderson shook his head.

'Looking at it another way,' she said. 'Was Harry

giving any of the kids a hard time?'

He clearly enjoyed that. His gold teeth glinted in the street lighting.

'What exactly was going on?' Ingeborg pressed him. This was all against her resolve to stay loyal to a brother officer, but there was something in Anderson's smile. The truth had to come out if it was buried. 'Some kind of scam?'

'Your word, lady, not mine,' Anderson said.

'Was Harry threatening the teenagers?'

'Whatever he did, it worked.'

'Until Saturday, when he was shot. I need to know more, Anderson. We're investigating murder, not some dodgy arrangement with tearaway kids.'

'I can't tell you who topped him, or why.'

'You'd better tell me about the scam.'

'It was small beer. Harry knew what the kids were up to, who was dealing, who was stealing. He turned a blind eye mostly, and they paid him when he chose to look and caught them off-base.'

'Paid him cash?'

'Cash and kind. Not many kids have cash in hand.'

She felt an uprush of revulsion. 'What are you hinting at, Anderson? Give it to me straight.'

'Don't get me wrong, sister. I mean a stash of the stuff they were dealing in. His way of dealing with juveniles was confiscation.' He intoned every syllable of the last word like a line of rap. 'No harm in that.' He laughed. 'Confiscation.'

Ingeborg said in Harry's defence, 'You couldn't be more right. There's nothing wrong in that. His duty was to take possession.'

'Sure, and they wouldn't hear any more until the next time they were caught.'

That, certainly, was all against the rules. 'Are we talking drugs?'

'And any junk they lifted from the tourists. Bath is one big sweetshop and the sweets are mostly mobiles, cameras and nice designer bags.'

'He would confiscate these things—is that what you're saying?'

'Haven't I made that clear already?'

'It doesn't sound enough to justify murder.'

'Probably not.'

She had a strong sense that Anderson knew more and might be persuaded to reveal something in a different league from stolen phones. 'Is it possible Harry got into something major, something that put his life at risk?'

Anderson walked on for some seconds as if pondering the question. More likely, Ingeborg suspected, he was weighing the risk of opening up to the police. In the circles he moved in, there were definite no-nos and informing was high on the scale. Yet he seemed to be tempted.

'There is one kid, a rich kid,' he said finally. 'Likes to think he should have respect. What is it they say?—a rich man's joke is always funny. Wears all the latest gear, rides a five-grand Japanese bike. What he's got is folding stuff, any amount. He trades in larger items. Don't know if you'd call them major.'

'What items?'

He laughed. 'How would I know? He doesn't want money my black hands have touched.'

'Is he a racist, then?'

'Did I say that?'

'You say he wants respect,' Ingeborg said. 'Doesn't he get it?'

'A good name is better than wealth. Isn't that the truth?'

Ingeborg was getting impatient with the axioms. 'What's the link with Harry Tasker?'

'I heard that Harry would make a point of speaking to this youth. If the kid wasn't around, Harry would ask where to find him.'

'It sounds as if Harry had something on him.'

'Could be. If so, he was playing with fire.'

'Why?'

'Because the kid's daddy is Soldier Nuttall.'

Cyril 'Soldier' Nuttall was notorious in Bath. Three years ago, dissatisfied with right-wing politics, even its extreme forms, he had started a group known as Fight for Britain. Ostensibly a young men's fitness association linked with patriotism, it had militaristic overtones that appealed to thuggish elements up and down the country and alarmed people who saw it as a burgeoning fascist movement. Boot camps, drill, martial arts, target practice and the shooting of game were compulsory elements and so were cropped heads, tattoos and combat gear. But the FFB was cleverly led. Whenever its innate purpose was challenged, Nuttall pointed out that Britain was a free country and all the activities were legal and practised by some of the most respected people in the land. The fact that the membership was almost exclusively made up of young white males was said to be down to the indigenous thirst for adventure, fitness and companionship. Soldier Nuttall insisted that his nickname went back many years before the FFB was formed and in no way was he leading a private army. He wore the combat clothes and the boots and the tattoos with pride in Britain and its long tradition of self-improvement and 'get up and go'.

All of this was founded on his personal fortune. He was no fool financially. His millions and his mansion on Claverton Down had been acquired from astute property development. Cut-throat dealings had bought him a luxurious lifestyle and allowed him to promote his organisation and hire the best lawyers. Plenty of complaints had been levelled against him, but no charge had ever stuck.

Ingeborg didn't need to ask why Anderson was willing to stretch a point and inform on Soldier Nuttall's son. 'What's the boy's name?'

'Royston.'

'From what you're saying, Royston is a wheeler-dealer like his father.'

'Except he was born into money,' Anderson said. 'He never had to earn it.'

'And you say he rides a motorcycle?' She was thinking of the incident in Becky Addy Wood that had left Diamond limping.

'Sure.'

'Has he been around Walcot lately?'

'On and off.'

'You can be more precise than that. Have you seen him tonight?'

'Not tonight. Yesterday.'

They'd walked as far as the point where Harry had been shot. It was unmarked now, every trace of blood removed. As if by mutual consent, they stopped under the street light, but short of the place where the body had lain. Ingeborg glanced up at the garden where the shooting had come from, above the wall on the opposite side, as if staring at it might reveal the killer's identity.

'Does Royston live at home?'

'That's my understanding.'

'Is his father ever seen in Walcot?'

He vibrated his lips. 'Not Soldier. Not his scene.'

They parted there. Anderson turned and started the walk back to his chauffeur-driven car and the two police officers moved on, towards the police station. Ingeborg had mixed feelings. The information on Royston Nuttall could be the breakthrough and she looked forward to telling Diamond their mission had brought a result. But she wished to God it didn't muddy Harry Tasker's reputation.

CHAPTER TWENTY-ONE

'I'm moving.'

An executive statement. The mound of gravel had become increasingly uncomfortable. In fact it was just about insufferable for a man dressed normally as Diamond was, without padding. He had just reminded himself that in Gull's absence he was nominally the supremo here, in charge of the stake-out at the pillbox, even though the tactical decisions would be taken by the young man of inspector rank leading the firearms team.

'I'm moving,' he repeated to Sergeant Gillibrand beside him. 'Need to check some of the other positions.'

There was no objection from Gillibrand. He said nothing at all. The two men hadn't exactly bonded.

'Use your radio to tell the other units I'm doing the rounds. I don't want anyone thinking I'm the sniper.'

The relief of getting upright was marvellous. Parts of him that had gone numb were restored. He almost forgot to pick up his stick, the sensations were so good. He could probably have walked all the way to Avoncliff station unaided, but decided it was wise to have it with him. Heels sinking into the cascading shingle, he slid down the gravel mound the back way, making no more sound than Gillibrand had on his trip to the bushes.

Now he was mobile he wondered why he'd endured the prone position for so long. The thinking had been that he'd presented less of a target. But if you're face down on stone chippings there comes a time when safety considerations dwindle to nothing.

He could have borrowed those night-vision glasses, but they weren't of much use on the move. The moonlight came and went, and his eyes adjusted well. He could see enough of the ground at this minute to step out with confidence. Equally, he had to remember he would be visible to the sniper.

Was the killer of three police officers really holed up somewhere in this remote spot? He had his doubts. Even so, he stayed close to the river bank, as far from the footpath as possible. The firearms lads were posted at least fifty yards to his left with their guns pointing away from him.

The going was easy here, fairly flat, with nothing more difficult than a few waist-high clumps of meadowsweet to negotiate. The Avon had a tendency to flood in this section of the valley after heavy rain and it was squelchy in parts. But the ripple of the water close at hand meant he was safely south of the area targeted by the police marksmen. Closer to Avoncliff he would pick up the roar of the weir.

Despite what he'd said to Gillibrand he didn't really plan to check the firing positions. It would be folly to creep up behind an armed man. Polehampton might, but then Polehampton was Polehampton and even he might have learned something from the handcuffing episode.

No, the object of this move was purely to get his blood flowing again. He'd reached a stage on that gravel heap when he was incapable of thinking of anything except his own discomfort. This was bliss, inhaling the fresh night air. He patted the injured leg: virtually restored, he decided. He was favouring it a little from caution rather than necessity.

A sudden piercing shriek drilled a shock through him. Close, frighteningly close. He halted, tense, alert for danger.

Blood-curdling—but was it human in origin?

Then a skittering in the water told him he must have stepped close to a coot or a moorhen.

Better not stay so close to the bank, he told himself. There are sure to be other waterfowl and the screech must have been audible for some distance around. Advertising his presence wasn't in the plan. He veered left, around some reeds and found more of a path. He would follow it in confidence that the river ran parallel with the railway. Keep going for ten minutes or so and he should find himself reasonably close to Avoncliff station without disturbing the firearms teams.

That waterbird had shaken his nerves. All the pleasure of being on the move had gone. He was tense, primed for more disturbances. A mass of cloud had crossed the moon again. He was forced to take shorter steps, even though the path was clear of hazards.

He could definitely hear the faint swish of falling water now. The weir was some distance beyond the station, so he was making good progress. He stopped and listened. He didn't need to walk too far.

Then he heard a loud splash to his right.

Something pretty big had entered the water. More wildlife? The sound had been heavier than a bird would make. What else could have made it? Were there otters along this stretch of the Avon? He wasn't aware of any. Actually it had sounded heavier than an otter.

If the cause of the splash wasn't natural, what was it?

His heart thumped.

He hadn't gone more than a couple of steps when there was another sound, more alarming still, a grunt as of effort, chesty, heavy, close at hand. Some living creature far larger than an otter was nearby.

Maybe the splash had disturbed some mammal, a fox or a deer. Or was it the mammal that had leapt into the water?

Animal or human?

He soon knew.

The cloud cover shifted from the moon. A man with a backpack was up and running, not more than ten yards ahead of him.

'Hey, you!' Diamond yelled.

The runaway figure didn't react, except to go faster.

He shouted a time-honoured warning: 'Stop,

police.'

This didn't work either.

More from instinct than good sense, Diamond started running too. He was back in rugby-playing mode, a Met Police wing forward doing his damnedest to catch an opposition three-quarter in full flight. He'd never been the fastest man on the pitch. Power had been his forte more than speed and he'd added much weight since his playing days, so this couldn't last long.

In the urgency of the chase, his leg was functioning as it should. The problem was that the opposition was faster on its feet. There was no way of catching up. Nor could he get a decent view of the guy, who was little more than a black smudge now, fast disappearing.

Diamond stopped running and gulped in some air. Felt twinges in his thigh. A few visits to the fitness centre would have helped.

Up ahead, a gasp and a thud sounded across the landscape. Had someone else joined in?

Heavy-legged, he forced himself into a semblance of motion again, heading towards the source. It was impossible in the moonlight to make out precisely where the fugitive had got to. Not where Diamond expected. He appeared to have got clean away.

But he hadn't. The man was grounded, and suddenly Diamond could see him, in the act of getting up. He must have tripped and fallen.

When you get lucky, you need to make the most of it. He bore down on the runaway, who was now upright and starting to move off again, but with less agility. The tumble must have winded him, or caused an injury.

Diamond realised as he belted across the spongy turf that ridiculously he was still holding his walking stick. He was about to toss it aside when he had a thought that it could yet come in useful. He was definitely catching up, starting to move with more freedom, accelerating again. He urged himself on and reached a point a few yards short of his quarry.

Now use the bloody stick, he told himself.

His grip was halfway up the shaft. Still at full pelt, he extended his arm, dipped forward, and managed to hook the curved handle around the man's left leg above the ankle.

The man went over for a second time with another bellow of pain, or frustration. And this time, Diamond's full weight followed, a dive so committed that it absolutely required a soft landing. For a split second he was airborne. Then his shoulder crunched against firm flesh. He grasped for something to hold and found what must have been one of the shoulder straps of the backpack. The main thing now was to stay on top and let his body mass work for him.

The guy was wriggling like a beached fish. He couldn't escape from the middle-aged spread bearing down on him.

'I told you to stop,' Diamond said breathlessly into his ear. 'You're nicked.'

No response.

For the next minute or so, the struggle was frenzied. By degrees the resistance became intermittent. The trapped man would let up for a few seconds before making another attempt. He was strong, no question, and quite a bit younger than Diamond. But he was exhausting himself.

The main problem in Diamond's mind—apart

he'd got so far.

'What were you doing out here at night?'

Not a murmur.

You do not have to say anything, Diamond mentally intoned to himself from the official caution, and added his own corollary: but what's stopping you if you're innocent?

More minutes passed.

If nothing else, the bouts of struggling had stopped. Maybe the guy had exhausted himself. Or was he preparing for one almighty push for freedom?

Diamond tightened his grip, just in case.

He couldn't be sure how much more time passed before he thought he heard a movement nearby, no more, perhaps, than a rustle in the reeds. More of that wildlife? He wasn't certain. He strained to pick up another sound.

Getting nothing, he lifted his head and said, 'Anyone there?'

Amazingly, there was.

Brilliant lights dazzled him, and a voice blared through a loudhailer, 'Armed police! Don't move.'

CHAPTER TWENTY-TWO

'Is that it?' Jack Gull said.

In the yard at Bath Central police station, a van used for transporting prisoners had backed up to the entrance. The rear doors were open, but the grille remained in place. Alone inside, a slight, scruffy man, his clothes coated in mud, sat with his hands cuffed behind him. He looked dirtier, but otherwise no different from the drunks who are brought in any night of the week. Red-eyed, unshaven, not much over twenty, he stared past Gull as if he didn't exist. His expression wasn't defiant, or angry, or resigned. It was indifferent.

Anticlimax was about to ruin the night.

Gull had come in specially for his moment of triumph. Fireworks and a fanfare were in order. For while it was Peter Diamond who had detained the man, the major credit had to be chalked up to Supergull for setting up the operation. All the planning was down to the Serial Crimes Unit. As for Diamond, he'd been called in only as a stopgap. He wouldn't have played any part if Gull hadn't needed a break after five hours on watch. The silly arse hadn't even armed himself, or the arrest would have been routine instead of the pantomime it had become.

The tacky circumstances of the arrest did take a little of the glory away. One of the firearms team had gone to relieve himself behind the police line and thought he heard a distant voice down by the river. A small detachment had been sent to investigate and found a large man face down on the river bank. Only after a minute or so did someone spot the second man underneath. His struggles had turned the spongy turf into a mudbath and it was difficult to see where the mud ended and the man began. One man face down can be assumed to be blind drunk, ill or dead; two, in that position, looked like consenting adults. Only on close examination had it been discovered that this was a senior police officer in charge of a suspect.

'Who is he?' Gull asked the sergeant who had come in with the van.

'He hasn't said.'

'What did he say when we nicked him?'

'Nothing, guv. He hasn't spoken a word yet.'

'We'll soon alter that. Didn't Diamond get anything out of him?'

'He said not.'

'Prick.' It wasn't clear whether Gull was speaking of the prisoner or his esteemed colleague. 'Bring him in, then. Let's see what the custody sergeant gets out of him.'

He stood well back while the grille was unlocked. The suspect was plucked from the van by a couple of PCs not over-concerned about his safe progress down the steps and into the bowels of Manvers Street. As every prisoner discovers, descending from a police van while handcuffed isn't easy. He stumbled more than once on his way to the desk where a sergeant waited who had seen it all so many times that boredom had set in.

'Hold it. I don't want your filth all over my desk. Name?'

The prisoner said nothing.

'I need your name, sunshine.'

He wasn't even making eye contact.

'Do you hear what I'm saying? Give him a prod. See if he's awake.'

The prod had no result.

'You're not going to be difficult, are you?' the custody sergeant said. 'If I decide you're not in a fit state to be dealt with, I'm within my rights to put you in a cell until such time as you start acting sensibly. Let's try again.'

The try was unsuccessful.

'Has he been searched? Anything on him with his name on it?'

The sergeant who had brought the man in said no form of ID had been found.

All this procedure was too much for Jack Gull. His patience snapped. 'Take his fucking prints and get them checked. And we'll need his shoes as well, for forensics. What's he wearing? Are they trainers, or what?'

The prisoner's footwear was so covered in mud it was impossible to tell.

While the man was hustled away to have his shoes removed and hands washed for the fingerprinting, Gull said to the custody sergeant, 'I'm not taking any more shit from this fuckhead. He's given us enough already.'

'Leave it to me, guv. I'll deal with him.'

'Okay, I take the hint.'

'Will you tell the press we've nicked him?'

'You bet—and rub their noses in it. All the bollocks they've given us about no progress.'

'They're sure to ask who he is.'

'No problem. They won't expect to be told his fucking name, not until we've charged him. There's a man helping us with our enquiries, period.'

CHAPTER TWENTY-THREE

This morning I picked a moment to look through the invoice book. Every transaction is there, names and addresses of sender and recipient, the messages that go on the little cards, and how much the client paid and whether it was cash or card. Sally sometimes asks me to mind the shop while she slips out for ten minutes to buy two takeout cappuccinos at the shop up the street.

This was my opportunity.

It's stuffed with famous names and intimate messages, that little book. You could sell it to one of the Sunday papers for a small fortune.

Forgive me, angel, the blonde bitch is history now.

Roses are red, violets are blue, Billy is hot and he's lusting for you.

See you—all of you—in the penthouse tonight.

I won't reveal the senders' names, but you'll have heard of them, believe me. I was dying to read on, but if I got too interested, Sally would be back with the cappuccinos before I found what I wanted. I was looking for one delivery on a particular Saturday in June because I remembered it was my birthday and I had a date that evening and wanted to get the job done in time to get to the hairdresser's.

I thumbed through the pages and found it. *26 June. Corsage, pink rose. Buttonhole, red car. To Mr John Smith, 48 Blahblah Avenue. £5.50 paid cash.*

John Smith?

The others were going to jump all over me.

I was so blown away that this was his real name that I still had the book open in my hands when Sally came back holding two coffees.

I froze.

She was like, 'Have you taken an order?'

I snapped the book shut and felt myself go bright red. 'No, I was trying to remember the name of one of our clients in Blahblah Avenue.'

'John Smith?'

'That's him.'

Sally, bless her, was as calm as a midwife. 'Nice man. Always buys his wife something to pin on her frock. Well, I assume they're married. They act as if they are.'

And I'm, 'You know them, then?'

'Not really.'

'Do they come in together?'

'Not in the shop. I've seen them somewhere. Where was it? A Christmas concert in the Guildhall, I think. She's rather gorgeous, tall, dark-haired, in her thirties.'

Sounds awfully like the go-between I watched in the pub, I was thinking.

And Sally went, 'What's your interest in them?'

I dug deep and made up an answer. 'A friend happened to mention a charming couple she knows who live in Blahblah Avenue and I was curious to know if the man was our client. Stupid of me. I couldn't remember his name.'

'It's forgettable, being so common.'

'How right you are.'

'If you've finished with the book, would you put it back in the drawer?'

This is as near as Sally has ever got to a rebuke.

'Of course.'

My insides clenched with shame. I couldn't wish for a sweeter, more considerate boss and I'd disappointed her.

* * *

And now I've fallen out with my friends as well. My shameful scene with the invoice book troubled me more than I can say. I spent most of today wrestling with my conscience, asking myself what could have possessed me to be so sneaky. It was like reading someone else's diary.

When we met this evening in one of the city's many pubs I bought the drinks and then told the other two I wanted out.

Anita was onto me at once. 'Out from what?'

'The sleuthing thing. It started as a game, but it's got too serious for me. The fun has gone out of it.'

'Because you recognized my picture of Heathrow man?'

'Actually, yes.'

'You know exactly who he is, don't you?' She was in my face and looked ready to scratch it. The jolliest people can turn into monsters very quickly. 'That stuff about not knowing his name isn't true.'

'Hold on, Anita,' I went. 'I'm not dishonest. If I'd remembered the name I'd have told you at once. What I'm saying is that now I know he uses the shop I'm not willing to put my job at risk.'

'Yet you were happy enough to go along with the game when it was my job on the line.'

'You volunteered the story. We'd never have heard about city break man if you hadn't told us.'

'Yes, and I've got a whole lot more to lose than you have. I'm the branch manager. You're only a van-driver, sunshine.' With her Egyptian look she was like Cleopatra dealing with a

Nubian slave.

'It's still my job and there's trust involved in it.' I dredged up a smile in spite of all the mean stuff being said. 'I don't want to stop being friends or meeting you. I'm pulling out of the sleuthing, that's all.'

'Quite a turnaround after we all agreed it gives us a cause to take on together. What do you say, Vicky?'

Vicky shrugged. 'It's up to Ishtar, I guess.'

Anita wasn't letting her off with a wishy-washy answer like that. 'Don't you cop out as well. We're all involved. From what I understood, it's given you a new lease of life. When you get a bit low—as we all do from time to time—this is a whole different project to get stuck into.'

'That's true,' Vicky went. 'I need something outside myself.'

'Nicely put.' Anita was pleased to have won a point.

'But it doesn't affect my job. I can understand where Ishy is coming from.' Poor Vicky, she was trying so hard to keep the peace.

'Why should it affect her job?' Anita went. 'She doesn't work with the guy. She only delivers a bloody buttonhole once in a while. That's no big deal.'

'Excuse me,' I put in. 'I'll be the judge of that. Loyalty matters to me.'

'What about loyalty to Vicky and me, your sleuthing sisters? Doesn't that count for anything?'

I could see this ending in a catfight and I didn't want that. 'It was a bit of fun. It's come to an end for me. That's all.'

Anita refused to let go. 'Let me tell you something about this bit of fun, as you call it. This bit of fun is making a difference to someone's life, someone not a million miles from here. Vicky, why don't you tell Ishtar what you told me?'

Vicky swayed back as if she'd been hit.

'Go on,' Anita commanded her. 'She's your friend. She's not going to broadcast it all over town.'

Vicky swallowed hard and suddenly it was like a tap had been turned on. 'Things are not going well with Tim,' she went in a low voice, looking down, avoiding eye contact. 'It's been difficult for some time. I try and talk to him and he ignores me. He can look straight through me. I don't know if anyone close to you has ever done that. It's chilling, like you've become a ghost. Over the last three months there's been a massive change in him. He never smiles and jokes like he used to. We sleep in separate rooms. Well, we have for some time. Originally it was because he was working late and wanted to sleep on in the mornings and we were disturbing each other. We both needed our seven or eight hours of sleep so we came to this arrangement. But he doesn't have a job any more and he still sleeps alone. He uses his room like a bed sit. He's got a computer in there and a portable TV. He'll go in there of an evening and I don't see him at all. He's put a lock on the door and I have to knock if I want to speak to him and sometimes he doesn't bother to open it. He'll talk to me through the closed door. It makes life very hard.'

'I'm sure,' I told her, my heart going out to her. 'What about meals?'

'He doesn't want me to cook for him. He lives out of tins mostly and eats in his room.'

'It sounds as if he needs help.'

'Not from his own wife,' she went and was close to tears.

'How do you manage for money?'

'He pays the rent and the main bills. Well, you pay them, in a way, as taxpayers. He's on the social now. I buy the food and my clothes. It works out about right.'

'You buy his tins?'

'I know what he eats and drinks.'

'Speaking of drink . . .'

'He's not alcoholic. He doesn't touch it at all, or drugs. And there isn't another woman, I feel sure of that. He's never been one for playing around.' She paused and glanced away. 'Actually he has quite a low sex drive.'

I remembered her wish to have children. Will she ever have any now?

'Could it be gambling behind this? You can do that alone on the computer.'

'It crossed my mind, but he pays the bills on time. We don't get the red ones. There's something else,' she added. 'Sometimes he'll go out at night. I hear him creep out and lock his bedroom after him. He's back before dawn. I don't know what he's doing.'

'Have you asked him?'

She shook her head. 'I don't like to.'

'Forgive me, Vicky, but are you totally sure there isn't another woman?'

'I can't be a hundred per cent certain, but I

think I'd get an inkling and I don't. All I can feel is the unhappiness coming from him. Bitterness. Not towards me. He ignores me.'

Anita folded her arms and turned to me. 'You see now why she needs something else to take her out of herself? The sleuthing sisters does it nicely.'

I wasn't really listening. I knew she wanted to press home how inconsiderate I am, and how Vicky's situation was heaps worse than my own. That's Anita's steam-rollering style, and I don't blame her for it. No, I was still coming to terms with what I'd been hearing, this sad, dysfunctional marriage and what could lie at the root of such misery.

I probed gently. 'What was his job?'

Vicky didn't seem to mind talking now. 'Originally he was in the army. Ten or eleven years. He got to be a sergeant.'

'You were an army wife?'

'Yes, and it worked quite well until he got posted to Iraq. I stayed home, of course. The war changed his feelings about the army. Instead of signing on again, he resigned. With his savings he bought a second-hand car and started up as a taxi-driver in (she mentions another city twenty miles from here), but he lost his licence.'

'Why? Why did he lose his licence?'

She sighed. 'It was such a shame. He was doing really well with the taxi business. Working hard and making good money. Then one night he got a call to pick up a group of teenagers from a party at a house somewhere out in the country. When he got there and saw the state of them, he refused. They'd obviously been drinking heavily and were rowdy and abusive and two of them were vomiting. A driver isn't forced to take people. Tim took a pride in his car and always kept it spotless. He drove off and left them. But something dreadful happened. The sick ones got worse and the others called an ambulance and they were taken to hospital, but one of them died.'

'Died? How ghastly.'

'It turned out that the two who were sick had eaten some seafood that caused acute food poisoning. Tim had to give evidence at the inquest and a doctor said they could have saved the girl if she'd been taken to the hospital earlier.'

Anita went, 'Meaning if Tim had picked them up as planned?'

And I was like, 'He wasn't to know that. He wasn't supposed to be taking them to the hospital.'

'That's right,' Vicky went, 'but the way it was reported in the press, he was the villain in all this, not the people who served up toxic food or the friends who behaved so unpleasantly. Tim was the scapegoat, the cabdriver who refused to pick up a critically ill young girl. It was written up in the local paper three weeks running on some pretext or another. There was a lot of bad feeling in the city. You see, the girl who died was a policeman's daughter, only fifteen.'

'You'd think the policeman would have picked her up.'

'He was on duty. Anyway, soon after the inquest was in the papers, Tim started getting stopped by the police for things they never usually check: tyres, emissions, a dodgy brake light, mud covering the number plate, so-called speeding when he was just on the limit. It became obvious it was a campaign to get his licence taken away. And that's what happened in quite a short time. We can't say for certain that some of the things that went wrong—like low tyre pressures—were caused deliberately, but we're very suspicious. He got in trouble several times over and in the end he lost his licence to drive a taxi.'

'That's so unfair. Him an ex-soldier, too.'

'And people treated us like shit—neighbours, shopkeepers. They'd all read the papers. The only ones who were sympathetic were other cabdrivers. They know it could easily have been them. But they couldn't do anything to help. We decided to leave. That's why we moved here.'

'And he's been unemployed since?'

'He had to sell the car, so he can't do taxi work. He rides a motorbike now.'

Anita gave me a Mother Superior look. 'Hearing what Vicky goes through puts our little enterprise into perspective.' She turned back to Vicky. 'It's light relief, isn't it, my pet?'

There was no response from Vicky. I could see it had been a huge effort for her to talk about her problem.

The tension between us was unbearable. I felt it was up to me to end it and I knew how. 'All right, I'll tell you the name of Heathrow man. It's John Smith. And now you know as much as I do.'

Anita began to laugh. 'You're kidding.'

'I checked the invoice book this morning.'

Vicky blinked several times, as if snapping out of a trance. 'John Smith? That's amazing. So what are we going to do about him?'

CHAPTER TWENTY-FOUR

In the morning Peter Diamond put in a later appearance than usual. The word had spread in CID that he'd personally arrested the Somerset Sniper overnight, but it hadn't been the triumph it might have been. At the scene, the capture had been messy. Back at the nick, he owed the team an apology. Almost every line of enquiry he'd initiated had been shown as mistaken. No one was going to forget that his focus had been closer to home. They hadn't missed the irony that he, of all people, had nicked a man who by all accounts wasn't a serving officer, an ex-officer or even a civilian employed by the police.

So it wasn't going to be a case of round to the pub, lads, we nailed this together. No one knew what the big man's mood would be.

He looked none the worse for his wrestling match on the riverbank—except for what he was wearing: a houndstooth sports jacket with leather elbow patches, grey flannel trousers and crepe-soled canvas shoes. God only knew where he stored such relics. There was a distinct smell of mothballs. His movement was ponderous, as if every muscle was stiff, yet he wasn't carrying the stick and the limp had gone as he passed through the CID room on the way to his office.

Actually he sounded energised. 'Morning,

people. Ingeborg and Paul, I need to hear from you about last night.' He left the door open.

Looks were exchanged. It seemed to be business as usual, regardless that the main suspect was under arrest in the cells downstairs.

'What did you come up with?'

In his office, Ingeborg played along, assisted by Paul Gilbert, with a short account of their walkthrough of Harry Tasker's beat, how they'd got the tip that Anderson Jakes might have information and where they'd tracked him down and what he had to tell them about Harry's possible dealings with Soldier Nuttall's son, Royston.

'It's all academic now,' she added. 'In view of the arrest last night, we don't need to pursue this.'

'Why not?' Diamond said.

'It's dirty linen, isn't it?'

'Don't talk to me about dirty linen. Both my suits are at the cleaner's.'

'Guv, no one wants bad stuff like this to come out, even if it's true. Harry's funeral is on Thursday.'

'I thought I made myself clear at the meeting the other day. If Harry was up to no good, it has to come out. Nothing is off limits.'

'But we've got a man in custody.'

'Has he confessed, then?'

'Not yet. I don't think they've got much out of him.'

Paul Gilbert added, 'He seems to be claiming the right to silence. But they've sent his shoes to forensics and taken his prints and we'll soon know if he's the killer.'

'Shows how much you know about forensics,' Diamond said. 'Don't hold your breath.'

Gilbert gave a queasy smile.

'He's within his rights not to say anything.' Diamond's mouth curved in a way that wasn't charitable. 'He's Jack Gull's catch. Well, more or less. Jack always believed the guy in the woods is the killer and that's who we nicked and now he can go to town on him. We're pursuing our own line of enquiry. This Royston sounds like someone we should speak to. Where does he hang out?'

Suppressing a sharp, intolerant sigh, Ingeborg said, 'Claverton Down. He lives with his father.'

'Soldier Nuttall?'

'Right.' The triple nod she gave said it all about Nuttall's reputation.

'Is the kid employed?'

'It seems not. He's a young man of independent means, thanks to his father. A bit of a wheeler-dealer, according to Anderson. What he deals in wasn't made clear, except it's a cut above what most of the others handle.'

'Sounds like hard drugs. And he's a night bird, obviously. This morning might be a good time to find him at home.'

A little of the colour drained from Ingeborg's cheeks. 'You want us to go to the house?'

'It's a lot easier than trailing around the streets at night. I'd better come with you.'

'I can handle it,' she said quickly.

'Put it another way. I need to come with you. When there's a suspicion a police officer was corrupt, I have a duty to get involved.'

She eyed him warily, suspicious that he was being over-protective. 'What about Paul?'

'It won't take three of us.' He turned to Gilbert. 'Have a quiet word with the PCSOs who share that city beat with Harry Tasker. If he was on the take as we now suspect, they'll surely have heard a whisper.'

Before leaving the office, he eyed the overflowing in-tray. The morning's mail had been heaped on top of yesterday's. With care, so as not to spill everything on the floor, he extracted those sheets listing the personnel at Wells, Radstock and Bath. He held them over the waste-paper bin. And then some inner prompting made him hesitate. He stuffed them into his top drawer. On the way out, he turned to Keith Halliwell and casually asked him to deal with the mail. Opening letters was all too boring for a man of action.

* * *

Down at Avoncliff, three of Avon and Somerset's underwater search unit were following up Diamond's report of a loud splash in the river. A rigid inflatable boat was secured with lines from the bank and the first diver and his attendant were aboard and ready to start.

'What exactly are we looking for here?' the constable in the scuba diving suit asked before taking the plunge.

'Mr Diamond said it was heavier than a bird and lighter than a body,' the sergeant in charge said from the riverbank. 'Think of it as a lucky dip.'

'If it was a branch off a tree it will have floated away.'

'And we wouldn't want to find it, would we? He thinks it was an object slung in the water by the guy they arrested last night.'

'The sniper? Maybe it's his gun.'

'That would be the top result. I suggest you stop going on about it and go down and have a look.'

The diver nodded, adjusted his mask and tipped off the side of the dinghy.

He wasn't down for long.

He bobbed to the surface and gave a thumb-down sign.

'What's wrong?' the sergeant asked.

The diver pushed up his visor. 'Visibility almost nil. Do we have the sonar equipment?'

Their grey USU van was nearby. The operation was halted for a while.

Even with sonar, and after several dives, nothing seemed to be down there.

The sergeant studied his map and said to the diver's assistant, 'I hope this is the right stretch of river. They could have left a cone here to help us.'

'They like to test us out.'

The diver submerged again. He took much longer

'Not a bad spot,' the sergeant said, looking at the wooded hills surrounding them. 'There's a good pub a short walk from here. Do you know the Inn at Freshford? Nice old place with a packhorse bridge. If he doesn't surface soon, I'll be off there for a pint.'

Then the water churned and the diver's head and shoulders came to the surface.

'Got something?' the sergeant said.

He poured the water from his find and held it up: a motorcycle helmet, black and shiny. 'Hasn't been down there long,' he said. 'It's in good nick. Why would anyone want to chuck this away?'

* * *

Diamond continued to function as if he was high on caffeine. 'Jack's done us a bloody good turn,' he said to Ingeborg as she drove out of the police station in her shiny Ford Ka. 'All the media interest is going to be on the man he's holding. We can come and go as we like.'

'Isn't he the sniper, then?'

'I honestly don't know. All I can tell you for sure is he tried damned hard to get away.'

'Wasn't he armed?'

'They looked in the rucksack and all he was carrying were a few apples and a cut loaf.'

'Money?'

'A few quid in his trouser pocket.'

'What was he doing by the river?'

'Same as me, I expect. Trying to avoid being picked off by one of Jack's sharpshooters.'

'So you think he knew the stake-out was in place?'

'Most likely. If he is the sniper, he's been smart avoiding arrest all these weeks. He's not going to blow it by being too obvious.'

'And if it isn't him?' Ingeborg said as she steered left and they crossed the Avon at Churchill Bridge and approached one of Isambard Kingdom Brunel's oddest indulgences, his railway viaduct disguised as a castle wall.

'It will have been some ne'er-do-well out late. Didn't stop him spotting one or other of the firearms team and steering a wide berth. Do you know where Soldier Nuttall lives?'

'I must have passed the gate a hundred times,' she said, not wanting to be patronised. She moved out to overtake a farm vehicle. 'There's something else I ought to tell you, guv. Last night when we were doing the rounds and questioning people, someone told me about a blog she'd been looking at. Sounds as if it's posted by some woman who reckons a friend's partner has been acting suspiciously.'

'In what way?'

'Staying out all night, secretive, refusing to answer questions.'

'Male?'

'Yes.'

'Not uncommon,' he said. 'It's known as playing away.'

She gave him a world-weary look.

'How does it help us?' he asked.

'It appears they live in Bath. The blog never says so, but when you read it carefully, there's enough to tell you she's located here. I visited the site this morning and I'm satisfied it can't be anywhere else. This guy is obviously up to no good and the woman is terrified.'

'Not just a wandering husband?'

'It's got the feel of something much more serious.'

'Get in touch with the blogger, then.'

'I wish we could. She's taken good care she can't be traced. I guess she feels freer to write whatever she likes.'

'Can't be traced? I don't follow you. We've got hackers who can break into anything.'

'Not this. It's a site that uses an elaborate relay system, bouncing anything that's posted on it from point to point until no one can get back to the source. Intelligence agencies use it to disseminate their own information, but they've never succeeded in cracking it.'

He gave a nod of approval. 'In a way it's heartening to hear there's something computers can't do—until you realise it's been set up by a bloody computer.'

'People are involved as well. Do you want to look at it when we get back?'

'I'd better. We can't neglect anything.' His head turned. 'Hey, did you notice that—an old-fashioned sweetshop with big glass jars in the window?' He'd spotted the display in Widcombe Parade, along Claverton Street, in a row of shops with traditional fronts that supposedly imparted a 'village' feel to them.

After a pause, Ingeborg said, 'You don't do much shopping, do you, guv?'

'Why?'

'They're opening everywhere, old sweetshops, every town on the tourist map, anyway. Don't ask me why. I don't bother with them.'

'Sweet enough?'

She didn't say so, but she found the comment about as cringe-making as the outfit he was wearing.

Widcombe Hill morphs into Claverton Down Road a mile out of the city and then loops around the contour and doubles back. At almost the farthest point out, Ingeborg swung the little car into a space in front of a set of closed iron gates.

'This is it.'

A straight drive between lawns led to a large three-storey building. Block-like in shape, the house had an institutional look, rows of windows as regular as a prison. But it was heavily clad in some climbing plant like wisteria that had established such a good hold it reached to the eaves.

'Wouldn't be my choice,' Diamond said.

She shrugged. 'Up here, the air's easier to breathe than it is in Bath through most of the summer. Prime location and plenty of land. I bet you wouldn't get much change out of ten million.'

'Let's see how we get in.'

A notice on the gatepost informed them: *Callers strictly by appointment. Video surveillance in operation. High voltage protection. Guard dogs patrolling.*

'And a hundred thousand welcomes,' Diamond said. He pressed the entryphone button and put his head close to the mesh. Nothing happened and the gates stayed shut.

'Maybe you should say something into it,' Ingeborg suggested.

'Like: Open up, it's the Old Bill?'

'I was thinking more along the lines of: Special call for Mr Royston Nuttall with something to his advantage.'

'You try, then. You've obviously got the patter and you'll look better on the video.'

She tried and those assets made no difference.

Diamond inspected the perimeter wall. It was brick-built, all of eight feet high and topped with what looked like a triple electric cable strung along its length. He ruled out climbing. 'The gates look as if they might open with a little persuasion.' He gripped the left side and pushed. The base was anchored to a grooved arc in the ground, but there was some movement higher up. 'I could squeeze through, at a pinch.'

From nowhere obvious, a black Dobermann flung itself at the gate, all teeth and snarling.

Diamond withdrew his fingers just in time. 'Not such a great idea.'

Ingeborg produced her mobile. 'Shall we try phoning the house?'

'I have a feeling they're ex-directory, but no harm in trying.'

No joy.

'If it wasn't for the dog, we could get in,' he said.

'I know how to deal with the dog,' Ingeborg said.

'Shoot it?'

She told him her plan.

'I'm willing to try,' he said.

They got in the car and drove back to the shops at Widcombe Parade. In the traditional sweetshop they asked for aniseed balls and a strong tin to put them in. 'It acts like catnip except it's dogs who go for it,' Ingeborg told him. 'He'll be far more interested in these than your fingers.'

* * *

Beside the river, the sergeant was looking at his watch. The search was taking longer than he'd estimated. He'd sent for reinforcements and now had two men underwater and they'd moved a short distance downstream. Closer to the pub, but not close enough for his liking. He'd call a halt soon.

He didn't have long to wait. One head surfaced and then another. They didn't appear to have brought anything up. The searching of river bottoms can be unrewarding. Mud and reeds make it difficult.

'No joy?' he shouted, with joy of his own in mind.

'It's okay, we hit the jackpot this time,' one of the constables said, 'but we're going to need lifting gear.'

'For Christ's sake—what is it?'

'A bloody great motorbike.'

* * *

Diamond and Ingeborg returned up the hill and tried the conventional entryphone once again and still got no response. Ingeborg opened the tin and tipped out one of the aniseed balls just out of the Dobermann's reach at the far end of the gate. The dog was there at once, muzzle through the bars, sniffing strongly. Ingeborg put down two more, taking care not to handle them. One rolled close enough for the dog to twist its head sideways and scoop up. The sweet was crunched in those powerful jaws. 'That should improve his breath.'

'Will it improve his behaviour?' Diamond said.

'Why not give it a go and see?'

Tentatively, he put his shoulder to the gate. The dog paid no attention, fully absorbed with the challenge of reaching the remaining aniseed balls. Diamond increased the pressure, forced a space and squeezed through. On the other side, with the Dobermann for company, he said, 'Hurry up. I don't fancy standing here for long.'

Ingeborg eased herself through and they walked at a quick rate up the tiled drive towards the house, leaving the dog to work on its tantalising problem.

'It all seems strangely quiet,' Ingeborg said. 'The lawns are well mown. They must have staff.'

'Part-time, I'd say. It's low-maintenance, grass and trees. Not a single flowerbed.'

As they approached the front, Diamond pointed to more cameras. 'Before we declare ourselves, let's see what else there is.' He'd spotted some outbuildings to the right of the main house. An open-sided barn contained two motor-mowers, a four-by-four, a red Porsche and a powerful-looking motorbike. Behind it were a woodshed and a couple of locked buildings that probably contained tools.

'Would that be the bike that ran you down?' Ingeborg asked.

'It was all too sudden. I wouldn't know.'

'Might be worth getting a print of the tyres.'

'What with?'

'Later, then. Fancy a swim?' Ingeborg said, moving on. Shimmering in the sunlight, tiled blue, green and gold, and enclosed by Romanesque columns, the pool looked more California than Claverton Down. It was at least thirty metres by twenty and deep enough to have a springboard. At the far end was a whirlpool and a building that probably housed a sauna.

'An hour on one of those recliners with a beer would do me the most good,' he said. 'What's over there—a games room?' Behind the house and some distance away he had seen a long, low wooden building with shingle roofing. 'No, it's a firing range. Let's go over.'

A private range fitted in with the ethos of Fight for Britain. And this one was on a military scale. The target lines on gently rising ground were set at what must have been four hundred metres and backed with sandbags. A higher set of butts was at about six hundred metres.

The covered stand where the shooting was done had a gate on a latch and a safety notice. Diamond and Ingeborg let themselves in. It was wide enough to take up to ten guns. The flooring was coconut matting on Astroturf over what felt like a concrete base. Clearly it was well maintained. They weren't stepping on used cartridge casings. Diamond paced the length of it, weighing the significance of the find. You didn't expect a military-style range in private grounds. As far as he was aware, it was legal provided that the weapons were licensed, but he doubted if anyone except the owner and his private army knew the scale of this place. The remote location meant no neighbour was likely to be disturbed by the gunfire.

'Guv, have you seen these?'

Ingeborg had been rummaging at the back of the stand. She picked up a large cardboard target with the usual black circles on a white background—usual, except that this one was mounted on a life-size silhouette of a police officer with helmet.

His blood ran cold for a moment. 'Nasty.'

He knew you could buy targets of hate figures like Bin Laden. This was a variation he hadn't seen. And he doubted if it could be prosecuted.

Turning away, he stared into the distance, imagining up to ten of the target figures spread across the landscape at six hundred metres. If it wasn't so sinister in the light of the recent killings, the sight of all those helmets might seem comical. He could imagine Soldier Nuttall's recruits thinking it funny.

Silent now, he moved forward a short way. Beyond the matting the Astroturf extended for about thirty metres before the real grass took over. When he stepped on it there was a difference in sound, a drumming effect. He brought his foot down more heavily. 'Must be hollow underneath.

Give me a hand,' he said to Ingeborg.

They found the edge and rolled the Astroturf back like a carpet to reveal some board panels. 'Let's have one of these up.'

The panel was about two metres square and took some lifting, but Diamond was insistent and they prised it up and hefted it aside. Below was a deep cavity.

'Storage space?' Ingeborg said.

'I wonder how deep it is.' He squatted, perched himself on the edge and dangled his legs. 'I can see a wall ladder here. I'm going down.'

'Careful,' Ingeborg said. 'You could get injured again.'

He turned, got a foot on one of the rungs and started to descend. 'A torch would be useful.'

'Don't know where we'll get one unless I go back to the car,' Ingeborg said.

'I'd rather you kept guard. There was a time when I'd have carried a cigarette lighter.'

He continued down until his head was below the opening. 'Strange. I've come to the bottom of the ladder and it hasn't connected with the floor.' Then the explanation dawned. 'I know what this is. The walls are tiled. It's another swimming pool—empty fortunately—and this must be the deep end.'

'Better leave it,' Ingeborg said.

'Can't be all that deep. They don't make private pools really deep.' He began lowering his handhold until he was in a crouched position on the lowest rung. Then he hung his right leg below the ladder and just made contact with the floor. 'As I thought. Not so far down.' He let himself down completely. It was a relief to stand upright. His suspect leg had started aching. 'Could you roll back the turf a little more and give me some extra light?'

'It's back as far as it will go,' she called down.

'Hold on. There's some flex hanging here. I think I've found a light switch.' He pressed it and got the flicker of strip lighting that presently came on fully and showed him the entire area. 'Would you believe it?'

'What's down there?' Ingeborg asked.

'This is the armoury.'

He'd not seen so much weaponry in one place. There must have been fifteen purpose-built wooden racks ranged across the width of the pool, each stacked with rifles and sub-machine guns. He was no expert, but everyone has seen the ubiquitous Kalashnikov on film and in print and he was pretty certain there were military weapons from other East European countries and Germany, all systematically clipped into place and grouped by type. It had the look of an efficient, well-maintained arsenal.

He was staggered by the find, here in Claverton, less than a mile from Manvers Street. No private citizen should own a sub-machine gun. Plenty did illegally, of course. The international trade was huge. At one time the KGB was giving them away to foment terrorism. But he'd always thought Bath was the most unlikely place to attract illicit arms. He didn't doubt that it was shotgun territory. Countrymen liked their sport. Weapons like these were something else.

'Guv, are you coming up?' Ingeborg called down.

'Give me a moment more.' He was checking the extent of the collection, pacing between the racks and counting. He also needed time to think how to deal with this. There were new priorities now. What had started as a house call to speak to a seventeen-year-old about suspected drug dealing had turned into a major illegal arms find that could see Soldier Nuttall put away for years.

'Guv, time's going on.'

Finally he returned to the ladder and switched out the light. As he hauled himself up the rungs he said to Ingeborg, 'You should see it. Mind-blowing.'

'I'll take your word for it. We're over-running.'

'I know. If this was James Bond, you can bet someone would have crept up on us by now with a gun and caught us red-handed.'

'Why do you think I was calling out?'

'There isn't anyone, is there?'

'It could still happen. We're not equipped for heroics.'

'Looking at what's down there, we'll need the SAS to raid this place. It's huge. More than seventy high-velocity rifles, and they're not for shooting grouse, believe me.' He climbed out of the space and with Ingeborg's assistance replaced the board and rolled the Astroturf into place. 'See?' he said. 'Exactly as we found it. Bond could learn a thing or two from me.'

* * *

The motorbike in the river had been a rewarding discovery in more ways than one, for it made a break necessary while a truck with a lifting mechanism was called out from Bath. The underwater searchers had now returned from their late pub lunch and were filling the time making a further survey of the stretch where all the action had taken place the previous night. Besides the motorcycle helmet and the bike they'd found some rusty farm tools, a bucket and some bottles.

The staff in the incident room at Bath sounded excited about the bike. They informed the search party about the motorcyclist in Becky Addy Wood who had almost run over Peter Diamond. The evidence was stacking up nicely, according to Jack Gull, the head of the Serial Crimes Unit, although he put it in more colourful language.

Gull was lost for words of any description when they called him twenty minutes later. One of the search team had just emerged from the water holding the day's star discovery, a Heckler and Koch G36 assault rifle.

CHAPTER TWENTY-FIVE

'Shall we get out while we can?' Ingeborg said.

'Why?'

She looked at Diamond as if the reason was all too obvious. 'We've stepped into something really big, that's why.'

'Have we?' He tilted his canvas shoe and looked down. 'The revenge of the Dobermann?' Even when faced with this urgent decision he couldn't resist a poke at Ingeborg's intensity.

'You know what I mean, guv. We're courting disaster here.'

'We came to meet Royston, in case you're forgetting.'

Trying to stay patient with her boss, but showing the effort, she said, 'We've got nothing for certain on him. It's all hearsay up to now. After what you just discovered under the firing range, shouldn't we change plans and get the hell out?'

'It crossed my mind too, I don't mind telling you, Inge.'

'But what?'

'But the case against Royston has been ratcheted up by this. He has easy access to a whole armoury of assault rifles. If it's true that Harry Tasker was leaning on Royston, giving him grief, it doesn't take a genius to work out what may have happened.'

'And the others, in Wells and Radstock?'

'Right now I'm thinking mainly of what happened in Walcot Street, but there is another angle. You saw the target you found, the policeman figure. Royston could have been trophy-hunting, to put it crudely. We have a duty to find out.'

She nodded, reluctant still, but forced to accept his advocacy. 'All right, but let me phone Headquarters now and tell them about all those guns.'

'Absolutely not. Wait until we're through. I don't want some high-up ordering us to return to base.'

More at cross purposes than ever, they covered the open ground to the house in silence, each troubled, yet knowing they must prepare for confrontation.

Then Diamond said, 'We're being watched. Third window from the right. I saw a movement. Keep going.'

'He'll know we've been at the range.'

'Hopefully he won't know everything.'

Leaving the grassed area, they reached the tiled surround of the house. 'Front door this time,' Diamond said. 'Are you still up with your shorthand? I want a note of whatever's said.'

'I'm carrying a mini-recorder.' In an afterthought she added, 'Don't ask where.'

'Good thinking. Make sure it's switched on.'

The front door looked as solid as the door of a jumbo jet. No bell, no letter-flap, no means of announcing their arrival.

'What are we meant to do, rap with our knuckles?' Ingeborg said.

'They know we're here,' he said with a glance at the security camera above their heads. 'The question is will they let us in?'

The sound of bolts being released answered that. The door swung inwards.

'Who the hell are you?' The speaker was in a bathrobe and flipflops. He didn't seem to be wearing anything else. Dense tattoos down each side of his neck looked as if they were an extension of the robe, like a stand-up collar. In his late forties, broad-shouldered, with shaven head, but bristly face and hostile grey unblinking eyes, he plainly wasn't overjoyed to have callers. And, to be fair, Diamond's get-up—like a character out of a Whitehall farce—didn't encourage respect. 'How did you get through the bloody gate?'

'My colleague has a way with dogs,' Diamond said, held up his ID and gave their ranks and names. 'Would you be Mr Nuttall senior?'

'If you're any use at your job, I don't have to answer that. What's it about?'

'May we discuss it inside?'

'I want to know what there is to discuss.'

'Your son Royston.'

'Him?' The eyes narrowed. 'What's he been up to this time?'

'We're investigating the murder of PC Tasker in

Walcot Street last weekend.'

Soldier Nuttall rocked back as if avoiding a punch. 'You won't pin that on my boy.'

'Is he at home?'

'In bed. He keeps late hours. What's all this about, then?'

'Would you ask him to get up and answer some questions?'

'Is that all it is—questions?'

Diamond nodded.

Soldier Nuttall snatched a mobile phone off a table behind the door and pressed a key. Several seconds passed. Then: 'Roy, get down here quick. The fuzz have come calling.' With that, he stepped aside and let them in.

The hallway was large enough to be called an entrance court. A full-size stone lion dominated on a plinth in the centre, jaws forever open in a silent roar. Hanging above it was a large flag of St George. Beyond was a flight of marble stairs that wouldn't have looked out of place at Buckingham Palace.

'You'd better come in here.' He led them into what appeared to be a military briefing-room with ordnance survey maps and photos of uniformed groups on the walls and a huge table with about twenty chairs around it. There was a screen and some kind of projector.

'The games room?' Diamond said.

'Why do you say that?'

'War games.'

'Nothing done in here is games,' Nuttall said. 'What were you doing poking around my firing range?'

'Just that—poking around,' Diamond said. 'We

couldn't make ourselves heard at the door so we went looking for you. Saw those targets you use. Not nice.'

'What's wrong with them?'

'Taking shots at policemen?'

'Chipboard policemen. It's harmless. You've got to see the funny side,' Nuttall said without smiling.

'Funny, is it?'

'It's a free country. I can do what I like in private.'

'If it's legal. It looks like a military range. You wouldn't get a licence for the assault rifles the army use.'

He gave Diamond a long look before answering, 'We do things properly in my organisation.'

'Fight for Britain?'

'That's our name, yes. Do I have to explain that it doesn't mean violence? You can fight for your rights, and sometimes you need to in this ineptly led country. You can fight for your health, your future, your right to live in peace. Everything we do is lawful, or they'd have clapped me behind bars years ago.'

This could have been a nice moment to raise the matter of the hidden arsenal, but Diamond had something else on his mind.

'When you phoned your son just now,' he said, 'did you get an answer? I heard what you said. I didn't hear his end of the conversation.'

Nuttall frowned and walked over to the doorway. 'He said something. He ought to be down by now.' He stepped out into the hall and yelled, 'Royston, get your arse down here double-quick.'

Diamond murmured to Ingeborg, 'Could have scarpered.'

She nodded.

They heard Nuttall's flipflops slapping the stairs as he stomped up them shouting his son's name.

'I'm going after him,' Diamond said.

'Both of us are, guv.'

Large as this house was, it was easy following the owner through it. The uncarpeted corridors acted like soundboxes. Nuttall had stopped at a door on the middle level and was rattling the handle when Diamond and Ingeborg caught up. He didn't seem to mind that they'd followed him. He was fully focused on his unresponsive son.

'If you don't open this sodding door, son, I'll kick it in and you can pay for the repair.'

Not with those flipflops, you won't, Diamond thought.

Nothing was heard from Royston.

'I'm not messing. It's up to you.' Nuttall stepped away, opened the door opposite, went inside and staggered out carrying an entire bedside cabinet and heaved it at Royston's door. The panel above the door handle burst inwards and Nuttall had to be nimble to avoid the cupboard bouncing off and hitting his feet. He thrust his arm through the hole and turned the key. High-stepping over the cupboard, he went in.

'Bloody hell.'

Diamond and Ingeborg followed him in. The interior was typical of any adolescent's bedroom in its clutter of clothes, shoes and magazines scattered across the carpet. A huge built-in wardrobe dominated one wall and was stuffed with what were obviously expensive clothes, among them a rail filled with studded leather jackets. The walls were covered with posters of pop groups, motorcycles and body-builders flexing their muscles. Two guitars were propped against a keyboard. A quilt with the red cross of St George was on the bed. But Royston wasn't.

Soldier Nuttall was at the open window, leaning out. 'He must have climbed down the wall.'

Diamond joined him and looked out. 'Down the creeper, anyway.' The branches of the wisteria, some as thick as drainpipes, would certainly have given enough support. Down on the ground there was no sign of a teenager. The bare lawns and the driveway stretched for a long distance. 'Can he get the front gate to open?'

'He's got a remote, same as me,' Nuttall said.

'There must be a way to override it.'

'Downstairs.'

'Better do it now.'

Nuttall swung around and practically shoved Ingeborg aside in his eagerness to take up the suggestion. He was over the barrier of the cupboard, through the door and heading towards the stairs like a bat out of hell. Exactly why he was so keen to stop his son escaping wasn't clear. Possibly, Diamond thought, having Royston in the line of fire was preferable to being questioned about the activities of Fight for Britain. The man had been visibly shaken at being asked about military weapons.

'Search the room for anything dodgy,' Diamond told Ingeborg. 'I'm going after him.'

Downstairs, Nuttall was in the hall, hitting the digits of a control panel mounted on the wall just inside the front door. 'I've locked everything,' he said. 'No one can get in or out.'

'Can you tell if the front gate was open in the last

few minutes?'

'It wasn't. Definitely.'

'He's still in the grounds, then.'

'He'll have gone for his bike,' Nuttall said.

'Where the Porsche is?'

'Christ—I'll kill him if he uses that.'

'Shall we check?'

Outside, Nuttall kicked off the flipflops and sprinted across the lawn towards the open barn, with Diamond doing his insufficient best to keep up. Royston wasn't in sight, but as Nuttall got closer the sound of barking started and the Dobermann raced towards him. He stooped and grabbed it by the collar and held on.

Diamond approached with caution.

'The dog won't go for you,' Nuttall said. 'It's a guard dog, but I won't let go of it. I feed the brute, so it knows me. But if it was sniffing here, the boy must be somewhere around.'

'Does it know Royston?'

'Yeah, but he doesn't feed it. If he steps outside when the dog's on guard, it'll have him.'

'Let's see if there's anything left of him,' Diamond said.

They approached the collection of vehicles. The motorbike was still in place and so was the Porsche.

The dog started growling, straining to be free and showing its teeth.

'I'm going to let go of it,' Nuttall said.

'Is that wise?'

'Stay real close and it won't touch you.'

Not liking this one bit, Diamond pra-
nudged shoulders with Nuttall on his free s-
instant it was released, the Dobermann
the Porsche and prowled around it, c

snarl.

'He's inside, the scumbag,' Nuttall said. 'He was going to use my motor.' He charged forward and flung open the door.

A youth was cowering on the rear seat.

The dog leapt inside and sank its teeth into the sleeve of the boy's bomber jacket. Nuttall grabbed it by the collar and tugged, trying to haul it off. He only succeeded at the cost of a slice of leather that remained in the closed jaws.

'Get outta there!' Nuttall shouted at his son.

The dog had moved a short way off and was lying down, content to chew the leather.

Royston looked anxiously to see where the dog was and then emerged from the car, a tall, pale young man who had gone through the adolescent growth spurt and hadn't yet put on much flesh or muscle. There was a slight resemblance to his father in the flat nose and puddle-brown eyes, but he didn't have the military grooming. A mop of thick, dark hair drooped over his shoulders and he hadn't shaved in some time. He was shaking, either from the experience with the dog or fear of what would happen next.

He said in a rush of words, 'Dad, I wasn't trying to take the car, honest. I haven't got the key, have I? You left it unlocked. It was the only place I could find to get away from the dog. You've got to believe me. I didn't know it was anywhere near the house. It would have gone for my throat. I was desperate.'

'Get inside the house, you pillock,' Nuttall said. 'We'll sort this later. This gentleman is a cop and he can have you for evading arrest if he wants. I'm not going to stop him.'

'What does he want me for?'

'Do as I say. In the briefing room. At the double.'

Royston wasn't of a mind to argue. He turned and walked swiftly towards the house.

'He won't run off again,' Nuttall said to Diamond.

Diamond nodded his thanks. 'He was probably making a dash for the motorbike. Does it belong to him?'

'Yeah.'

'Powerful. A present from you?'

A shake of the head. 'He paid for it on the never-never. I brought him up to value things. I'll say this for him: he's no scrounger.'

'If you don't mind, I'd prefer to speak to him without you in the room. He's not being arrested. We want his help as a possible witness.'

'Suit yourself. I'll put the dog in its pen.'

A double favour—better than Diamond could have hoped for. The man was only too relieved to be asked to keep his distance. It hardened Diamond's opinion that Nuttall was more concerned about the hidden armoury than whatever trouble his own son might be in.

Back in the house, Ingeborg met Diamond at the door. He raised his eyebrows—a silent question.

'A wad of banknotes,' she said in a voice pitched low. 'A grand or more, at a guess. Plenty of expensive clothes, some soft porn magazines and CDs and a small quantity of party drugs.'

'Personal use?'

'I reckon.'

'Are you switched on?'

'Aren't I always?'

'The mini-recorder.'

'Ah.' She touched a point deep in her cleavage. 'I

am now.'

They went into the briefing room.

Royston was sitting at the far end of the long table, arms folded in such a way that one hand covered the hole in his sleeve, as if he'd resolved not to reveal any weak point. He'd got a little colour back. It was likely that after being mauled by a Dobermann everything else paled into insignificance, including a grilling from the police.

Diamond established the boy's identity as well as confirming theirs, then said, 'This is about the murder of PC Tasker in Walcot Street last weekend. You know about it, I'm sure.'

'What do you mean—know about it?' Royston said, shooting him a defiant look. 'I know sod all.'

'You heard about it.'

He shrugged. 'Everyone did.'

'And you're often in Walcot Street, doing the pubs and clubs?'

'It's a free country,' he said, echoing his father's comment when justifying shooting at targets of policemen. Plainly this interview wasn't going to be an easy ride, but at least the boy wasn't playing dumb.

'How old are you?'

'Come on,' he said, getting more confident. 'You're not going to do me for under-age drinking. Seventeen, and never touched a drop.' He grinned, inviting a challenge.

'You met Harry Tasker more than once.'

'So did loads of others. Walcot was his beat. He was always down there trying to get us to talk. Community policing, innit?'

'Sometimes he caught people doing stuff they shouldn't,' Diamond said. 'Did he ever catch you?'

'What—drugs and that?' Royston said, cool, as if prepared for this line of questioning. 'Never. Not me.'

'Other people?'

He shrugged. 'Not for me to say.'

'I was told you know a lot about what goes on.'

'Doesn't mean I do it.'

'You're not saying you never do drugs, are you, Royston?'

Ingeborg said, 'We know different. There are some in your room.'

He glanced at her as if he'd only just noticed she was there, then frowned and shifted position on the chair. 'I've never been nicked or anything.'

'So you've got a clean record,' Diamond said. 'Was that thanks to Harry Tasker?'

'No comment.' He knew the jargon. But who was to say whether he'd learned it from watching TV or more direct experience?

'Let's be frank with each other. Harry made it his business to find out what was going on. You do some wheeling and dealing in the Walcot Street area. You're known for it.'

'Not drugs,' Royston said firmly.

'You make a good income. You bought the bike with your own money. Is it all paid off yet?'

'The bike? Yeah. It's mine.' There was more than a hint of self-congratulation.

'Several grand. How do you do it?'

'Business, innit? You buy cheap and sell at a profit.'

'What are you selling? What's the commodity?'

'Anything I can shift.'

'Where do you get it?'

A tinge more colour came to his face. 'All over.

Bristol, Bath. London sometimes.'

'Wells?'

He shook his head.

'Radstock?'

His lip curled and he looked away, as if the question didn't even merit an answer.

'You're not being very open, Royston. Should we ask your father?'

'He ain't interested.' Said swiftly, and without any sign of alarm.

'In that case we'll have to look more closely at PC Tasker's notes.' In the same even tone, Diamond expanded on this white lie. 'Did you know he kept a detailed record of everything he observed on his beat?'

'I bet,' he said with scorn, but there was a frisson of concern.

'How do you think we got on to you?'

Royston shifted in the chair again. 'You can't do me for anything. I could blow the whistle on your lot.'

'Really?' Diamond said. 'Why haven't you done it already?'

No answer.

'I think PC Tasker was wise to everything you get up to, Royston, and you were scared shitless. He could have nicked you whenever he wanted, but he chose to hold off. I want you to tell me why.'

'You've got it wrong.'

'Was it because of who you are?'

'What are you talking about—my old man? No way.'

'You're not short of money.'

'Which I earn,' Royston put in quickly.

'Around the pubs and clubs?'

'It's legit. Like I said, I sell at a profit. It's investment. I make money, buy more stuff and sell it on. That's called trading, right? I'm a trader.'

'Trading in what?'

'All kinds of stuff. It changes. You need to know what's high-tone, right? Could be some flash new mobile one week, a bit of bling the next. The trick is to stay ahead of the game.'

'Mobiles and bits of bling aren't going to make you all that rich. I was told you're in a bigger league than that. Larger items.'

He almost purred. 'Who told you that?'

'Never mind. Is it true?'

'I've put a few things people's way.'

'Don't piss me about, Royston. What items?'

'Guitars. I can clear a good profit on a Japanese acoustic and still save money for my customer.'

The terminology tripped off his tongue slickly enough to carry conviction. Diamond followed up at once. 'Ever traded in firearms?'

Royston shook his head, almost too quickly. 'I'm not stupid.'

'You know about guns. Your father trains people to use them.'

'And I know about the law, and all.'

'How does your business go down with your father?'

'I told you. Doesn't give a toss.'

'Are you a paid-up member of Fight for Britain?'

He flicked the ends of the long hair upwards. 'Don't make me laugh.'

'I dare say you've used the firing range at some time. We were looking at it earlier. Impressive.'

'I've had a go, yeah. Why shouldn't I?'

'Any good, are you?'

'Average.'

'Got your own gun?'

'I know what you're on about,' Royston said. 'Just because my old man has a firing range, it doesn't mean I shot the copper. No, I'm not interested in shooting. I wouldn't want one of my own.'

'There are plenty on the premises here.'

'So?' He stayed nonchalant.

'So it's important for you to convince us you didn't borrow one of those guns on the night of the shooting. Were you in Bath on Saturday night?'

'It doesn't mean shit if I was.'

'Were you?'

'Sure—and so were hundreds of other kids.'

'In the Walcot area?'

'Some of the time. I was on the move. I don't stay in one place long. I'm doing business, in case you forgot.'

'Where were you at four on Sunday morning?'

'Back here. It's all gone quiet by then.'

'Is there any way you can prove that? How did you travel—taxi?'

A shake of the head. 'Used my bike. I leave it in Beehive Yard.'

'Off Walcot Street? So that's where you ended up, close to where the shooting happened?'

He was unmoved. 'There was no shooting when I was there.'

'When you got home, was your father still up?'

'No.'

'Did you make any phone calls, use the computer? Don't look at me like that. I'm trying to help you prove what you're saying.'

'I crashed out.'

'Until when?'

Now his voice rose. The pressure was getting to him. 'Jesus, I don't know. Late.'

'Next day—Sunday—what did you do?'

'It's a blur, man. Sundays always are.'

'Think carefully, Royston. This is important. Did you go out at any time on Sunday?'

He squeezed his eyes as if trying to see through that morning-after blur. 'I might've.'

'Not good enough,' Diamond said. 'Did you use your motorbike?'

'I always use the bike to get about.'

'Try and remember. Did you drive out to Bradford on Avon?'

'Why would I go there?'

'You tell me. There was a sighting of a motocyclist in Becky Addy Wood, near Bradford, on Sunday. Could that have been you?'

'No chance,' he said at once and with finality.

'It's well known to motorcyclists. They do motocross there. Scrambling. Do you do that?' It was a trick question from Diamond, the offer of an explanation for being there.

Royston wasn't buying. 'With my machine? You're crazy.'

'Recently cleaned, by the look of it,' Diamond said.

'That's no crime. If you had a bike like that, you'd take a pride in it.'

This had not been as productive as Diamond would have liked. The boy had flinched a few times, when told (untruthfully) that Harry Tasker kept a written record of his beat patrols, when asked where he acquired his items for trading, and whether he'd ever dealt in firearms, but he'd put up an able defence.

* * *

They left the official way. The front gate opened for them.

'What did you make of him?' Diamond asked Ingeborg when they were on the road again.

'Royston? Smart for seventeen. Cool, but scared underneath. There's definitely something he doesn't want us to find out, but I'm not sure if it's as serious as murder.'

'How about the father?'

'He's capable of killing. I'm sure of that.'

'He's got the firepower, as we now know,' Diamond said. 'The underground armoury has got to be reported. I'm afraid it's going to look as if the boy blew the whistle on his father.'

'Won't Nuttall get arrested and put away before he can do anything about it?'

'You can put someone like him away, but you can't stop ugly things from happening. He has plenty of followers.'

Ingeborg took in a long breath. 'Would he put out a contract on his own son?'

'It's not impossible. I didn't detect much love between them.'

They were driving down Widcombe Hill where the road narrows before it joins the A36 south of the railway station.

'So will you report what you found?' Ingeborg asked.

'All those guns? Of course.'

'Now?'

'Soon as we get back.'

CHAPTER TWENTY-SIX

Jack Gull was in the incident room with DI Polehampton peering at mugshots on a computer screen.

'Family history?' Diamond said as he walked in.

'Piss off, Peter,' Gull said without looking up.

'What's this about, then?'

It was Polehampton who answered. 'Looking for a match with our friend in the cells.'

'Hasn't he told you who he is?'

'He's still playing dumb, unfortunately.'

Still with his gaze on the screen, Gull said, 'So here we are checking every sad fuck arrested for possession of firearms over the past five years.'

'You've got his prints. You must have checked the PNC.'

'Nothing matches. He's not in the system.'

'So why bother with this lot?'

'No system is infallible, that's why, not even the Police National Computer.'

'You must be desperate.'

'Did he say anything to you when you were lying on top of him?'

'Not a word,' Diamond said. 'Maybe he is mute.'

'Maybe he was enjoying it.'

Polehampton laughed. Diamond did not.

'Seriously, Jack, he could be handicapped.'

'No chance. He can make sounds all right. He's a fucking teddy bear. Jump on him and he squeaks.'

'Is that what you tried—jumping on him?'

'Would I do that?' Gull said, turning to look at Diamond. He did a double take at what he saw and then grinned broadly. 'Jesus Christ, are you auditioning for *Midsomer Murders* dressed like that?'

'Both my suits are at the cleaner's. I hope you haven't used violence on this man.'

'He's got a voice for sure. Squeaks, but won't squeal—yet.'

'Some teddy bears talk if you treat them right.'

'Okay, Mr Nice, you try.'

Diamond shook his head. 'He's yours.'

'But you nicked him.'

'Only when he made a run for it. I wasn't sure if he was the guy we were looking for. I'm still not certain.'

'You can be now.' With relish, Gull told him about the finds in the river at Avoncliff. 'He's your demon motorcyclist, Peter. When the search closed in he dumped the bike and helmet in the river. He kept the gun for longer. Decided to get rid of it when he spotted the stake-out around his bolt-hole. That must have been the splash you heard.'

This all made sense. Difficult to see it any other way. The confidence was draining from Diamond. 'Where is it now?'

'The G36? Already gone for ballistic testing. They'll dry it out and get it firing again, no problem. These are army guns built for battlefield conditions.'

'You're not serious about wanting me to see him?'

Gull's tone changed abruptly. 'He's the Somerset Sniper, for Christ's sake. He shot your man in Walcot Street. He ran you down and put you in hospital. You should be on your fucking knees begging for a session with him.'

'Do the forensics match up?'

'You bet they do. His prints were taken last night when he was brought in and we got an eighteen-point match.' In fingerprint scoring, this was an inner ring. Sixteen points of similarity would be enough for the courts.

'A match with what?'

'The beer can in the pillbox. Every fucking thing he's handled. And the shoeprints match up too. The trainers he was wearing last night were definitely the same ones the sniper wore in that garden at Wells. It's not just the tread pattern on the soles. The wear marks make a shoe impression unique, all the cuts and scratches in the rubber.'

Diamond said in a spat of annoyance all his own, 'You don't have to lecture me on shoe evidence, Jack. I wasn't born yesterday.'

'It means we've got the bastard bang to rights.'

There was no denying the boast if the forensics were that good. Up to now, there had been doubt whether the man Diamond had caught at Avoncliff was the same individual who had slept in the pillbox. But you can't argue with quality fingerprint and shoe evidence. Diamond had obviously got his thinking wrong, hopelessly wrong. Instead of treating the case as an out-and-out manhunt, as Gull had, he'd tried to be clever, divining motives that didn't exist and looking for suspects close to home. In the process he'd misread the signs and alienated his team. Self-reproach bore down on him like a tsunami.

Bullheaded in defeat, unwilling to cede Gull the triumph, he said, 'But you don't know who he is.'

'We'll find out.'

'Or why he did it.'

'Obvious. He's down on cops. You want to see the look in his eyes.'

'Have you told the press?'

'Put out the usual short statement last night—"a man arrested and helping us with our enquiries". You can't keep a news story like this under wraps.' Gull flexed his arms. 'I'll have to face the hacks again in the next hour. Then of course they'll be screaming for a name.'

'Didn't he have anything on him?'

'Some loose change, that's all.'

'You'll have taken his DNA?'

'Nothing like it in the database.'

'Any scarring, tattoos, vaccination marks?'

'Bit of a birthmark on the right hip. Fat lot of use that is if no one ever sees it. No other marks.'

'Teeth?'

'I'm not going down that route. Tracing dental records is bloody impossible unless you know which dentist to ask. One day we'll all be computerised and then it'll be child's play. That's a long way off.'

'It's down to old-fashioned persuasion, then?'

'Down to you, mate, and your winning ways. Give me a shout when he's ready to talk.' Gull returned to the images on the computer.

Diamond started walking towards his office. 'I can give it a go. First I'd better get through to Portishead.'

'Headquarters?' Gull was all ears again, staring over the screen at Diamond. 'What for? I'm your Headquarters man. You've got me.'

'It's too big for you.'

'Bollocks to that. Your uncle Jack's in charge.'

'Not this time.'

He told them both about Soldier Nuttall's

underground gunroom. His account of it grew a bit in the telling and impressed them mightily, but didn't have any bearing on the sniper investigation. Having something positive to show for the man-hours spent pursuing the wrong villains was scant consolation for the mistakes Diamond had made.

'Fair enough, you'd better pass the info on to someone who can act on it,' Gull had to concede finally, and then recouped some self-importance by stressing his inside knowledge of Headquarters. 'Ask for the Head of Operations. My good friend Danny can organise a raid. Doesn't mean you have to be part of it. Tell them I need you here. They can find the fucking guns without your help.'

* * *

In ten minutes the chastened Peter Diamond was in the interview room with the Somerset Sniper facing him across the table. Keith Halliwell had joined him and the tape was running. This was being done strictly to the code of practice of the Police and Criminal Evidence Act even though the official caution had to start with the unhelpful directive, 'You do not have to say anything unless you wish to do so.' How many hundreds of occasions had Diamond spoken those words without expecting them to be taken literally? Suspects always had something to say, even if it was only, 'No comment.'

This one had already sat silent through several hours of interview time. For his fortitude he had a cut lip and some swelling above and below his bloodshot right eye. No doubt Jack Gull would say he must have tripped on his way to the cells. As the prisoner wasn't talking, he couldn't give his own version.

He was handcuffed and dressed in the white overall provided for suspects whose clothes have been taken away for examination. Of course the stupid-looking outfit can also puncture the self-esteem of a cocky criminal. Pale, thin-faced and unshaven, with deep-set, staring brown eyes, this one didn't appear to care. He looked about twenty-five, but days on the run can put years on a man. He could have been as young as eighteen. Red-raw hands, the lines ingrained with dirt, presumably from living rough. Fingernails chewed to the quick.

'Staying silent isn't going to help you,' Diamond told him in a reasonable tone. 'The evidence we have is overwhelming. Your shoeprints match those found at the scene at Wells where PC Hart was killed. We've recovered the murder weapon from the river. There's no chance you'll walk out of here.'

He got no reaction except the steady, contemptuous stare.

'So I'll tell you what happens next. After twenty-four hours we get an extension from a senior officer. That's a mere formality. I could issue it myself. After thirty-six, we apply to a magistrate for a warrant of further detention. Another thirty-six. Unless we charge you before that.'

The prisoner seemed indifferent to what was being said. All Diamond was getting from him was hostility. Understandable.

'In case you don't recognise me,' Diamond went on, 'I'm the one who caught up with you last night. You may think it was rough, being pressed like a piece of ironing under a man my size for twenty minutes or whatever it was. What you may not realise is that I'm also the unfortunate who was standing in your way when you revved up your motorbike and rode out of Becky Addy Wood. Knocked me sideways, put me in casualty. That's why I was forced to use a walking stick, the same stick I felled you with last night. So there was a little bit of justice in the end.'

Not a glimmer of comprehension. For appreciation, Diamond had to turn to Halliwell. This was all depressingly one-sided.

'The bike and the helmet were hooked out of the river today. I'm assuming he stole them from somewhere.'

Halliwell gave a nod. Even he was stuck for a comment.

Back to the suspect. 'What shall we call you?' Diamond tried. 'It doesn't have to be your real name, if you're coy about that. John? Bill? Andy? Fancy any of those? We're Keith and Peter, so it had better not be one of our names. I see you as a Bill. William. Wasn't there someone called William the Silent?'

'I've heard of that,' Halliwell said, to show support.

'And there was William Tell,' Diamond added. 'Definitely not the name for you. Tell—geddit?'

Some eye contact would have helped. The man had stopped staring and was cultivating indifference, looking at a spot on the table midway between them. He'd had time to practise this act.

Diamond made yet another start, low-key this time, touching on matters that might get through and elicit a response as basic as the flicker of an eye or a twitch of the lips. Find a telling point and work on it. 'There's a lot you can tell us when you decide to speak, as you will, sooner or later. What is it about the police that you hate? Some bad experience in the past? You don't seem to have form. Your fingerprints are new to the system. They're checking the faces in criminal records, just in case, but it would appear you're a first offender. So what possessed you? These officers you shot couldn't have been known to you. They died because they happened to walk by when you were lying in wait with your G36 rifle. Don't you think their people—their loved ones—are entitled to know why?'

Evidently not.

'Where the policemen fell, members of the public leave flowers, notes, soft toys even. One word gets written in large letters again and again, in Wells, in Radstock and here in Bath. "WHY?".' He paused, allowing it to sink in. 'The shootings happened. That's fact. Can't alter it now. Don't you think you owe us an explanation? I don't get the impression you're mad. You thought this through stage by stage, choosing your position, your timing, your escape. If the killings were meant to be some kind of gesture, a protest against the way this country is policed, or whatever, it's futile unless you explain the thinking behind it.'

The prisoner swayed back a fraction, barely enough to be noticed, and then resumed the hunched position. For Diamond, the movement was encouragement. 'Am I making myself clear? The thing is, *you* haven't made yourself clear at all.' He waited again, watching for a response and getting none. He was forced to resume. 'Your actions are going to be misinterpreted. Did you know that? I bet it's happening on the internet as I speak, extremist groups claiming you as one of their own, every bunch of nutters intent on undermining the system. You did the shooting and they take the credit. That's how it works these days.' He stopped, sensing how strident he was sounding.

He glanced at Keith Halliwell. He, too, was starting to look as if he'd stopped listening.

This wasn't working.

'Things get out of proportion if you don't make yourself clear. I'll give you an example from my own experience. When PC Tasker was shot in Walcot Street in the small hours of Sunday morning, my first reaction like everyone else's was that this was your work. The Somerset Sniper claims another victim. It was just like the shootings in Wells and Radstock, well planned, but random. The victim had to be a cop, yes, but which cop didn't matter. Easy to pick one off at night walking his beat. Everyone said the identity of the victim was immaterial to you as long as he was a bobby in uniform.'

He waited, still hopeful of a nod or a shake of the head. Getting nothing, he resumed. 'Being an obstinate sod as I am, I wanted to test this theory. Was it really as simple as that? I made enquiries about the officers killed in Wells and Radstock. Went down to Wells and talked to PC Hart's widow and one of my team did some research in Radstock. A strange connection emerged. Ossy Hart came originally from Minehead and used to take the leading role in a street event they have there each midsummer. Centuries old, it is. He'd be dressed as a hobby horse and parade the streets collecting for charity. He was the best horse anyone could remember. Not a pantomime horse. More of a token horse decked out with ostrich feathers and ribbons. Of course it had to stop when he joined the police and got posted to Wells. But there was talk of the event being filmed for some kind of action scene in a Hollywood movie. Some film man came to see him shortly before he was killed offering big bucks if he would reprise the role. Now here's the link. The officer you shot in Radstock, PC Richmond, had an interest in old customs and was one of the leading experts. He wrote an internet article about the Minehead hobby horse, and it's not impossible he was seen and hired by the same film company who were offering to make Ossy Hart a rich man. Now can you see why I started to get interested? There was a common interest and the chance of money, silly money.' He paused again.

The prisoner looked mentally a million miles away from the Minehead hobby horse. Halliwell had a glazed look, too.

Undaunted, Diamond started again. Although this was beginning to sound increasingly like a confession, it was crystallising his own thoughts. Set out like this, the process sounded logical. 'After finding this out, I went to see the widow of the third victim, PC Tasker, just to find out if her late husband had ever had anything to do with the hobby horse ritual. He hadn't. Quite a blow, that. I was forced to accept that coincidences happen and they're no more than that. In short, I was up the proverbial gum tree. I'd wasted precious time on a theory that didn't hold water. The killings had to have been random after all. But I did learn something from Emma Tasker that I still can't explain. Among Harry Tasker's personal items returned to her after the shooting was a scrap of paper with the words "You're next". It threw me into confusion again. Here was another challenge to the theory of random killings. It seemed someone had been out to get him and wanted him to know. Taunting him. What else could it mean?' He let the question linger for a moment and then put his hand forward and touched the prisoner on the arm.

It was the lightest of touches, but it brought a sharp response. The man jerked away and braced himself as if preparing to head-butt Diamond. Or spit in his face. But at least there was eye contact.

'I asked you a question,' Diamond said, remaining calm. 'What else could it mean? The shooting of Harry Tasker wasn't random. If the note meant anything at all, he was singled out, warned and slaughtered deliberately. Am I right?'

The prisoner's angry brown eyes were still locked with Diamond's. Not a word was spoken. Then he lowered his head and the moment passed.

So was it only the touch of the hand, and not the words, that had prompted the reaction?

Apparently.

'The note sent me down a route I didn't want to take,' Diamond began again. 'Because he was a marked man, as I saw it, I looked for a reason. Who's going to have a grudge against an ordinary copper? The people who know him best—his workmates. I started looking here in Bath Central for a suspect. A police officer or someone employed here. Bad mistake. A sure way to make myself unpopular. Okay, I discovered that PC Tasker didn't always follow the rules. He had his own way of keeping law and order on his beat and some might say it was rough justice. Maybe after all it was someone from the criminal class who bore that grudge. But I didn't find anything that justified murdering him. And now you're in the frame, I've had to face it. I'm wrong again. The shootings really were random. Harry Tasker died for no more reason than being on the duty roster. He happened to be on nights when you were lying in wait with your rifle. Simple as that. Mind, the fact that it wasn't personal makes it even more despicable.'

He stopped speaking. He'd said as much as he wanted to say. No form of persuasion in his repertoire was going to work.

On an impulse, he snapped his fingers. The prisoner blinked.

'You're not deaf, then.' To Halliwell, who had also jerked in his chair, he said, 'Still awake, I see.'

Halliwell drew himself up, ready to leave.

Diamond made a restraining gesture with his levelled hand. 'Do you know if Jack Gull tried any foreign languages?'

'I doubt if Mr Gull knows any, guv.'

'That's probably true, and the English he knows isn't exactly the Queen's. If this guy is a foreign national, we're supposed to find an interpreter and his consulate has to be informed.'

Unexpectedly the prisoner became animated again, shaking his head and making sweeping movements with his handcuffed arms.

'Hey, fellow,' Diamond said, 'what's this about? What did I say wrong? Interpreter? Consulate?'

If anything, the negative gestures redoubled.

'You understood something I said,' Diamond said. 'What's your name? Where are you from?'

Too much to expect. But at least some form of communication was established. The man was watching Diamond and listening intently.

'Whoever he is,' Diamond said to Halliwell, 'he isn't keen on his government knowing about it. I'm wondering if we have an asylum seeker here.'

'Funny way to seek asylum, murdering three policemen,' Halliwell said.

'But worth following up.'

The prisoner was returned to the cells. Diamond learned from the custody sergeant that several languages had been tried on the clam-like young man and brought no response.

'Well, it took a long time, but he made one thing clear to us,' Diamond said. 'If he's on the run from his country it may explain why he's saying nothing.'

Jack Gull was called to the custody suite.

'It's becoming clear he's a foreigner without much English,' Diamond said, 'but there's more to it. Even if you don't follow the language, you co-operate. You'd understand when you're being asked your name. Why is he withholding his identity?'

'He's a fucking killer giving nothing away, that's why,' Gull said.

'He could be more scared of his own people than he is of British justice. What if he arrived here like plenty of illegals have, in a container lorry, and is on the run?'

'Doesn't explain how he gets hold of a G36 and why he goes on a killing spree,' Gull said.

'All right, suppose he was rounded up soon after arriving and sent to a detention centre to be repatriated.'

'Removal centre,' Polehampton said. 'They

changed the name. The words "detention centre" were thought to be offensive.'

'Strike a light, what are we coming to?' Diamond said. 'To my ear, "removal centre" sounds a whole lot more sinister. Call it what you will, he'd mix with all sorts there. Some of them would know where a weapon can be bought. And we've all heard of break-outs and detainees escaping.'

'He'll have been photographed and fingerprinted if he was detained,' Gull said. 'That's compulsory. He would have shown up when we ran the check.'

'It's still worth checking on recent breakouts. Didn't a bunch of people escape from one of those places last year?'

'I'll get on to the UK Border Agency, see if they can throw any light. But no one has explained to me why he shoots cops.'

'Did you look into his eyes?'

'How could I not?'

Diamond didn't say so, but there are some things a senior detective has to work out for himself.

* * *

'One thing nobody has mentioned is what happens when we charge this guy,' Keith Halliwell said in the incident room.

Diamond frowned. 'What do you mean?'

'If he still withholds his name, what's the legal position? Can we actually charge an unknown man?'

'Fair point. I'd need to think about that.'

'And if he isn't charged, and the custody clock runs out, are we compelled to release him?'

'No way. We can't let a serial killer walk free

when we know the forensic evidence is watertight.'

'You say that, guv, but is it lawful?'

'Off-hand, I can't say. It's been a heavy day. Do me a favour, Keith.'

'What's that?'

'Don't mention this to John Leaman. Or Ingeborg.' He stifled a yawn. 'I'm bushed. With the killer under lock and key, I think we can safely get an early night.'

'I'll second that.' Halliwell switched his computer to the sleep function. 'There was good news from the hospital this afternoon. Ken Lockton has recovered consciousness. They think he'll make a full recovery.'

'Thank God for that.' Diamond hesitated. 'I hardly dare ask.'

'Does he remember what happened? No, guv. No memory at all. Concussion does that sometimes.'

'Too much to expect. We don't get many breaks, do we, Keith?'

'There is one thing before you go. I dealt with the mail as you asked.'

'What do you want—a pat on the back?'

Halliwell grinned. That would be a rare event.

'I haven't looked into my office,' Diamond said. 'No problems, I hope.'

'All very straightforward, guv. Three-quarters of it was junk, and the rest I could cope with.'

'What's the thing you wanted to mention, then?'

'It's on your desk. An envelope marked "personal". I didn't like to open it.'

'In case it was from an old flame of mine? More junk, I expect. Or someone wanting money.' He remembered seeing the envelope the previous day.

'I'll pick it up, then.'

He went through to the office.

His desk hadn't looked so tidy for at least a week. Just that one letter remained in the in-tray. He picked it up. *Detective Diamond—PERSONAL*. The sender didn't seem to know his rank or initials. The white self-seal envelope had obviously been put through a printer.

He opened it and withdrew the slip of paper it contained.

Short and to the point: *YOU'RE NEXT*.

CHAPTER TWENTY-SEVEN

He invited Paloma over. If he didn't speak to someone outside the CID fishbowl, he wouldn't get much sleep. In case she got the idea that romance was in prospect, he warned her it was cheese and cream crackers and there was a reason why he didn't want to go out for a meal.

She arrived with a bottle of kaolin and morphine. 'I heard what you were saying, and I think I know what this is about,' she told him. 'This is an old-fashioned remedy and really effective.'

'I don't have diarrhoea,' he said. 'I prefer to eat in tonight, that's all. I've opened a bottle of Merlot. I'm touched by your kind thought, but mine has a better flavour than yours.'

'Mine may have a better kick,' she said.

'And it could still come in useful,' he said.

She had also called at the cleaner's and collected the first of his two suits. He was going to need it in the morning.

He showed her the 'You're next' note and a shiver went through her. She didn't need telling about the similar one found in Harry Tasker's card-wallet. They'd discussed it when he was feeling bruised after the team meeting a couple of days before.

'But I heard on the car radio that you arrested someone.'

'We have,' he said, 'and all the evidence shows he's the sniper. This looks to me like a practical joke.'

She was appalled. 'Joke?'

'Black humour. It's a police thing. No one is immune from it. I dish it out sometimes and I must expect it back.'

'Well, I don't remotely understand what's funny about it,' Paloma said, 'but if that's all it is, some kind of joke, can't you make a show of laughing it off?'

'That was my first reaction.'

'And?'

'And I'd like to. The difficulty is that there's a small chance it's genuine, sent by the same individual who sent the note Harry Tasker received. As the SIO, I'm bound to take it seriously and treat it as evidence.'

'That's what your joker intends.'

'Probably.'

'Does it look the same as the first note?'

'Just about identical. The only difference is that there was no envelope with Harry's note. He may have destroyed it. The slip of paper is the same size, the wording is the same and so is the font. Easy to copy, of course. They've all seen it.'

'If it's meant as a joke, can you be certain it

came from inside the police station? Calling you Detective Diamond instead of your proper rank is odd. Would one of your own team address you like that?'

'Normally, no. As a way of bamboozling me, I wouldn't put it past them.'

'Could some bloody-minded member of the public have sent it?'

'The first note hasn't been made public—except to you.'

She smiled faintly. 'I'm innocent. I have better ways of winding you up. Why is it being kept a secret?'

'Sometimes we keep information back so as to have something known only to the killer and ourselves. My team have seen the first note and so have Jack Gull and his deputy, a mental giant called Polehampton. The "Detective Diamond" bit looks like an attempt to divert suspicion—as if it must be from the killer himself, always assuming the killer is an outsider.'

'And it can't be from the killer because he's in custody.'

'Since early this morning, yes.' He felt his skin flush as he revealed the flaw in his logic. 'But I have to tell you that the letter was on my desk unopened for most of yesterday. I saw it myself and didn't open it. The last forty-eight hours are a blur.'

Paloma took a moment for thought. 'He was still at liberty when the letter arrived on your desk?'

'He knew we were on his trail by then. It's hard to believe he would have come to Bath Central police station and delivered a death threat by hand. I'm ninety-nine per cent certain it's a hoax.'

'The first note wasn't a hoax,' she said. 'The

threat was carried out.'

He remained sceptical. 'I'm not even sure if that first note was what it seemed. There may have been some innocent explanation for those two words, like a reminder to Harry from his mates to stand a round of drinks. We talked about this in CID. This was the team meeting I told you about. Made me about as popular as a birdwatcher on a nudist beach.'

'Haven't they got over that by now?'

'I still sense some soreness. You see, it was the note that acted as the catalyst, my suspicion that some police officer could have written it. If they're taking revenge, this is a neat way of doing it.'

'"Neat" is not the word I'd use.' She took a sip of the wine. 'Bear with me, Peter, and please look it this another way—the one per cent chance that the note isn't a hoax. Have you spoken yet to the man you arrested?'

'Plenty. The problem is he's saying nothing in return. We suspect he's a foreigner with a poor command of English.'

'I doubt if he wrote the note, then. You need to be up with the language to use the apostrophe correctly. Plenty of native speakers get it wrong. Your average foreigner would leave it out altogether and spell it Y-O-U-R.'

He raised his thumb. 'Good thinking. You've disposed of the one per cent. It looks certain this is just to teach me a lesson.'

'Do they know you've opened it?'

'The team? They will now. Keith Halliwell made sure I looked at it before I left the office.'

She tilted her head in surprise. 'You've often said Keith is your main support. Would he play a mean trick on you?'

He weighed the question. Already he was thankful he'd invited her over to help him get the incident into perspective. 'Put like that, I'm less sure. I've known Keith longer than anyone. I'd say it's unlikely—except . . .' He stopped and cast his mind back. 'Except that he was leading the protest at the meeting, that is until Ingeborg took over and said I was ordering a witch-hunt. It was an issue of principle for Keith, standing up for his colleagues. Right at the end I asked him to supply me with a list of police personnel from the three stations and he virtually refused, said I was putting him in an impossible position. I backed down and said I'd do it myself. In all our years together I've never known him to defy me. I could see how deep it went.'

'If it affected him like that,' Paloma said, 'I can't believe for a moment he'd take revenge with a practical joke. He'll be as bruised as you are. It's obvious he has a high regard for you.'

'I've always thought of him as rock solid.'

'And he is. You've got to see that, Peter. He was right. You did put him in an impossible position. It's a good thing you had the sense to climb down. Things have improved since, haven't they?'

'By degrees. We're back to normal, just about.'

'Did he actually watch you in the act of opening the envelope?'

Diamond shook his head. 'I was alone in my office. He didn't see my reaction and neither did anyone else.'

'You said Ingeborg was angry. Is she capable of setting you up?'

'Well capable. She knows my weak points.'

'The female of the species . . .'

He shook his head. 'But I can't see her doing it. She'll criticise me openly, tell me I'm off message, but there's a tipping point and Ingeborg has never gone past it. I trust her. I trust them all, or they wouldn't be in the team.'

'John Leaman?'

'He's a one-track man, incapable of twisted thinking.'

'Twisted it certainly is,' Paloma said. 'And cruel. What's it meant to achieve?'

'At the very least, me dosing myself with kaolin and morphine.'

She wasn't letting him laugh off the danger. 'Have you ever thought why the first note was sent to Harry Tasker?'

'It's a kind of bravado on the part of the killer. Serial killers sometimes get an extra kick from announcing their crimes in advance. Jack the Ripper is supposed to have done it.'

'I thought most of the Jack the Ripper letters were sent by people cashing in on the publicity, like the man who sent the Yorkshire Ripper tape.'

He was impressed. 'You've done your homework on serial killers.' Another remark he wished he could take back.

A silence developed between them.

Finally Paloma looked at his plate. 'I don't think you've eaten any of the cheese and biscuits yet.'

'Not much appetite.'

'Peter, you *are* worried by this.'

He made a sweeping gesture in dismissal and then thought better of it, deciding he owed her an honest answer. 'Well, I'll tell you. I'm not entirely sure that the man we are holding killed all three of the victims. The case has had huge publicity. Any police killing does. I've had a suspicion all week that the shootings weren't random. Now I believe Harry Tasker may have been shot by someone else, a killer who wants his crime to be lumped in with the Somerset Sniper.'

'But it's the same gun for all three, isn't it?'

'The same kind of gun, same kind of ammunition. A Heckler and Koch G36, firing 45mm cartridges. They're standard issue in the police. See the way my mind is working?'

'Someone in the police had a grudge against Harry and saw this as an opportunity to kill him and have the crime credited to someone else?'

'Exactly.'

'Is this G36 a prohibited weapon?'

'God, yes.'

'You'd have to be a firearms officer to own one?'

'You wouldn't own it. They're police property.'

'Does anyone else use them? What about the army?'

'No, but they're widely used in Europe. It's the standard service rifle of the German army, among others.'

'Do you see what I'm getting at?' she said. 'There must be some being traded in the criminal world.'

'That goes without saying. The G36 has been around since the early nineties. Not as long as the Kalashnikov, the AK47, but you can get them illegally. I've seen one that was used in an armed hold-up in Bristol. I didn't think they were knocking around in Bath until today, when I visited a house and found a whole secret armoury of AK47s, G36s and much more. Big shock.'

Her eyes widened. 'In Bath? Where was that?'

'I'd better not say. We haven't recovered them

yet.'

'Not a policeman's house?'

He smiled. 'No.'

'The guns are out there, then,' Paloma said. 'That's all I'm saying—that the weapon used to kill Harry Tasker may not have been a police weapon.'

'We'll know shortly. A G36 was recovered this afternoon from the river close to where our suspect was arrested.'

She brought her hands together in approval. 'Can it be identified as the gun that killed all three?'

'When it's cleaned up. The ballistics experts will do a test firing, discharging bullets into a test-firing chamber. The rifling inside the gun creates marks called striations along the side that are as good as fingerprints. Under a microscope they can be compared with the bullets found at the murder scenes.'

'You said we'll know shortly. How soon is shortly?'

'Always longer than you hope for.'

'And then you can be certain?'

A silence followed. Diamond was pondering new possibilities.

Paloma gave a sudden cry of surprise. Raffles the cat had crept into the room and jumped on her lap. He'd belonged to Stephanie and enjoyed female company. After letting her feel the weight of his paws on her thighs, he settled into a comfortable position, anticipating he wouldn't be disturbed for some time.

Diamond was so deep in thought he hadn't heard Paloma's cry or noticed the cat. 'I may have made a wrong assumption about the gun.'

Paloma frowned. 'Go on.'

'Everything happened in a matter of hours, the shooting of Harry followed by the report of a gunman in Becky Addy Wood. It was easy to assume that the two incidents were related and the gun being carried in Becky Addy belonged to Harry's murderer. But if my theory is right, and Harry was shot by whoever wrote that note, this is going to need a rethink.'

'Can't you tell your forensics people this is an emergency?'

'They still take the same amount of time.'

'Meanwhile, you're at risk of being killed.'

'That's why we're eating in tonight.'

'Peter, you shouldn't make light of it. I don't think you should leave the house until these tests are confirmed one way or the other.'

'I can't take time off.'

'How will you travel to work tomorrow?'

'Car, as usual.'

'That's crazy. He could be lying in wait. We'll go in my car, with you out of sight, lying on the back seat.'

He laughed.

'I'm staying the night,' she said in a tone that brooked no argument.

'If that's the outcome,' he said, 'I'll settle for the back seat.'

'It's nothing to do with you,' she said glancing down at her lap. 'Raffles isn't moving off my lap. His decision.'

CHAPTER TWENTY-EIGHT

'I don't want anyone to see me like this,' Diamond said from his position lying along the back seat.

'They won't. That's why we're doing it,' Paloma said as she drove down the Lower Bristol Road into Bath. She knew when to be firm with him. 'Last night you were perfectly okay with it.'

'Yes, but this is now.'

'We're just passing another cemetery on our right.'

'Point taken.' He was dressed for a funeral, but not his own. They had discussed whether he should take the risk of attending Harry Tasker's funeral. Diamond had insisted he would be there, after giving his word to Harry's widow. It wasn't as if he'd be standing in the open around a grave. The cremation would be in a small indoor chapel, surely too enclosed for a sniper to take a shot at him and escape.

He had decided to treat the latest 'You're next' note seriously and take care, but say nothing about it until the ballistic test results came in. Then he would be better placed to judge whether the note was a hoax. He'd know for sure if the rifle recovered from the river had been used for any or all of the shootings. Then it would become clear whether the killer of all three victims was in custody.

'Crossing the river now,' Paloma continued her commentary. 'Soon be in Manvers Street.'

'I may sound ungrateful,' he said. 'I want you to know I appreciate this. You don't have to drive right inside the nick. Just drop me in the street.'

Paloma smiled to herself. The police parking area was a yard at the heart of the building enclosed by walls several storeys high and scores of windows. 'Fine. We'll do as you say.' Her voice softened. 'Please take extra care today. It matters to me, you know.'

He thanked her. The car halted and he got out and was crossing the pavement without appearing to hurry when she surprised him by sounding the horn twice as she rejoined the traffic. He tensed, looked round and wagged a finger. But she was already gone.

Inside on the stairs, he met John Wigfull, a blast from the past. Now a civilian responsible for publicity and press relations, Wigfull had once been his deputy and they had never got on. JW was someone well capable of setting him up. Diamond wondered how much he knew about the present investigation. 'Morning, John.'

The cordialities had to be exchanged, whatever each was thinking. Wigfull's Lord Kitchener moustache had always masked his true sentiments. 'Morning, Peter. You're looking sombre.'

'Harry's funeral later,' Diamond said.

'I thought his widow didn't want us there.'

'She made an exception of me.'

'You? I can't think why. He wasn't CID.'

'I'm the man on the case, that's why.'

'Better stick to the case and keep your head down, then.'

Diamond grasped Wigfull's sleeve before he moved on. 'What do you mean by that?'

'You'll find out. I think some heavy artillery is coming your way.'

Keep calm, Diamond told himself. It's an expression of speech. It doesn't have to mean that he knows anything about the note. 'Artillery from who?'

'The assistant chief constable, no less.' With that, Wigfull moved on, leaving Diamond reassured that Wigfull wasn't talking about gunfire, but wondering what new infliction to expect from Georgina. If the ACC was on the warpath, it was serious. She'd kept her distance all week.

Keith Halliwell gave his usual warm, 'How you doing, guv?' in the incident room and confirmed that Diamond was summoned upstairs. There was no indication what it was about.

* * *

He found Georgina staring out of her top-floor window, hands behind her back wringing the neck of an invisible chicken, an ominous sign. The window looked out on to Manvers Street, where he'd stepped out of the car. As usual Georgina was in uniform. She was one of the few female officers who always wore a skirt.

Without turning to face him, she said, 'Is your mobile switched off?'

He delved into his pocket. 'It is,' he said. 'It won't go off.'

'I guessed as much. I've been trying to reach you all morning.'

'I just got in.'

'I know,' she said. 'Is something the matter with your car?'

'A friend gave me a lift in.'

She about-turned and practically clicked her

heels. Her look travelled up and down his clothes. 'Why are you dressed like that?'

'Harry Tasker's funeral this afternoon, ma'am.'

'I thought it was a family affair, with none of us invited.'

'Mrs Tasker made an exception in my case. Some lads from uniform are going as well, I believe.'

'It seems to me,' Georgina said with a sniff, 'that I'm the last to be informed about anything in this place.'

He still wasn't sure what could have triggered this hostility. His mind raced through the possibilities. Clearly she was in a state about something he'd kept from her.

She gestured to him to sit in the upright chair facing her. Then she lowered herself into a swivel armchair. Having checked that the hem of the skirt was as close to her knees as possible, she started. 'Yesterday afternoon, you phoned Headquarters.'

The light dawned. A large bee called Protocol lived in Georgina's bonnet. 'Correct, ma'am.'

'Without a word to me.'

His confidence returned. He was at an advantage here. Play this straight, he thought, and I'm on a winner. She doesn't know the full story of the secret gunroom. 'It was a matter of some urgency, ma'am. As you know, I've been working closely with a Headquarters man, Detective Superintendent Jack Gull, head of the Serial Crimes Unit. I informed him about the call and he was in agreement, so I got on with it. Should have notified you as well, I see that now.'

'The first I heard of it was a call from Headquarters relayed to me at home this morning before eight o'clock.'

'At home before eight? That's a liberty,' Diamond said with an effort to sound compassionate.

'They referred to a tip-off you gave them. I knew nothing of this.'

He heaped more sympathy on her. 'Lines of communication loused up again. I'm sorry if I'm to blame, ma'am. My enquiries into the sniper case took me to Soldier Nuttall's property on Claverton Down. He's the nutcase with the private army, Fight for Freedom.'

Georgina said in a frigid tone, 'You don't have to tell me about Cyril Nuttall. I know him, and "nutcase" isn't a word I'd use.'

A warning light went on in Diamond's head. 'Is he a friend of yours?'

'Hardly. He owns the property I lease.'

Wheels within wheels, Diamond thought. She's worried about her tenure. Well, Georgina, my dear, some things have to take priority over your living arrangements. Prepare to hit the ceiling when you hear what your head of CID discovered here in cosy old Bath. 'His son Royston showed up on the radar. I visited the house with one of my team with the intention of interviewing the lad. No one was about when we arrived so I took the opportunity to look around. There was a rifle range, which didn't surprise me, knowing Nuttall's reputation, and below it—hidden under boards in a former swimming pool—I discovered a secret armoury. A large collection of assault rifles. These weren't sporting guns, ma'am, they were high-velocity killing machines, AK47s, G36s and MP5s. It was obvious they had to be reported at the first opportunity.' He paused for effect and folded his arms. 'That was my tip-off to HQ.'

'So they informed me at 7.55 this morning,' she said in a voice every bit as measured as his. 'Acting on this tip-off of yours, a major operation was mounted, a pre-dawn raid on Mr Nuttall's house and grounds.'

'I'm glad to hear it,' Diamond said, but that inner voice was telling him not to celebrate yet. Georgina wasn't as impressed as she should have been. Something must have gone wrong with the raid. Had some idiot fired a live round?

Georgina was telling the story now. 'Thirty trained officers from Bristol in full body armour with dogs. Once inside, they split into two groups. Half of them stormed the main house while the other half located the swimming pool and took it over. Cyril Nuttall and his son were roused at gunpoint.'

'The guns were still there, weren't they?' Diamond said, baffled by the strong tone of disapproval in Georgina's account.

'Oh, yes, just as you described.'

'At least seventy assault rifles of various makes?'

'Yes,' Georgina said. She made a long, alarming pause before adding, 'And no.'

'I don't follow you.'

'Seventy *replica* assault rifles. They're fakes, made in China. Not one of them is capable of being fired.'

If Georgina had leapt over her desk and gone for his throat he couldn't have been more surprised. 'Never.'

'You'd better believe it, Peter. This is a major cock-up. I've had my ear chewed by the Head of Operations. A raid like this doesn't come cheap, you know, and highly trained officers aren't amused at being bussed to Claverton in the small hours to pick up a load of plastic toys.'

'They looked real to me.'

Georgina exhaled sharply. 'The whole point of replicas is that they're made to look real. They're constructed with minute attention to detail. Even the weight and balance match the original. But the fact remains that they are not the genuine article. It was a wild-goose chase, a total shambles.'

'Aren't imitation guns still illegal?' he said, clutching at straws.

'Not on private property they're not. Brandish one in the street and you're committing an offence, but these are strictly for use in war games within the walls of Mr Nuttall's estate. He's entitled to own them and play soldiers with them and so are his members, so long as they don't venture outside.'

He clutched the back of his neck in despair. Nothing was going right.

Georgina was relentless. 'Because of you, I've spent most of the morning grovelling. Headquarters are incandescent. Cyril Nuttall has been on to me several times threatening legal action for invasion of privacy, damage to property and wrongful arrest.'

'Damage? What damage?'

'His wrought-iron gates were bulldozed and his front door was battered in. He puts the cost at over two thousand pounds.'

'Didn't they find anything incriminating? He must have some real guns on the premises to use on the range.'

'All legal and licensed and properly stored. He's squeaky clean and we're up to our necks in ordure.

Thank you very much, Peter.'

* * *

An embarrassing story can't be suppressed. All of Manvers Street knew of it. Downstairs in the incident room, everyone was waiting for Diamond to show his face again. Jack Gull was grinning from ear to ear.

'Here comes the man of the moment. Looking for a new job, Peter? Something in plastics?'

Ignoring them all, Diamond stepped across the room to his office and closed the door, careful not to slam it and let them know how he felt. The only way he knew of surmounting the ridicule was to apply himself to the unanswered questions that remained. He reached for the phone and got the number of the forensic science company who were examining the rifle recovered from the river.

'Any results on the G36 yet?'

'Who is this?' the voice on the line asked.

'Peter Diamond, Bath CID. I'm the SIO on the sniper enquiry.'

'Diamond. Aren't you the chap who set up the dawn raid on Soldier Nuttall's plastic gun collection?'

His knuckles went white squeezing the phone. 'How the hell did you hear about that?'

'I had Jack Gull pestering me for results only ten minutes ago. Amusing story. Look, we've worked miracles already cleaning up the gun and we've done some test firings, but we haven't finished analysing them. We understand the urgency, the custody clock ticking and all that. We'll let you know as soon as we have anything definite. You'll be pleased to hear one thing.'

'What's that?'

'It's a real gun. Not one of your plastic jobs.'

He could hear faint giggling before he ended the call.

Stay positive.

He opened the door and asked Ingeborg to come in.

'What's happening with the man in custody?' he asked her. He wasn't going to ask Gull and present him with the opening for yet another clever dick remark.

At least Ingeborg was straight-faced. 'He still hasn't said a word yet. Your theory that he's an illegal immigrant is looking good.'

'There must be a link with Westwood or Avoncliff or Bradford on Avon. Else why would he have holed up there?'

'Jack Gull says it was close to Bath and handy for the third shooting.'

'I don't buy that,' Diamond said. 'Have they traced the owner of the motorcycle?'

Alert as always, Ingeborg had already checked with the DVLC at Swansea. 'His name is Hamish Macintosh.'

'Doesn't sound like an asylum seeker.' His mouth twitched into a smile. 'Unless he escaped from Scotland.'

She still couldn't rise to a shaft of humour from Diamond. 'He's from Shepton Mallet. I've spoken to him on the phone. He lives in a thatched cottage there. The bike was stolen some time in the last five months from the stone shed at the back, along with his helmet and leathers. Hamish was away in Argentina on an engineering job and didn't report it missing until he got back a few days ago.'

'Shepton Mallet is right in our territory, right in the sniper's territory, come to that. How do you start a motorbike without a key?'

'They use pigtail leads to bypass the ignition. It worked well for the thief because the bike was taxed and registered and no one knew it was stolen property.'

Diamond began fleshing out his theory with this new information. 'Wells, Radstock, Shepton Mallet—three towns south-west of here and no more than ten miles from each other. This is where our friends the profilers with their criminal maps would be getting excited. He was operating within quite a small area.'

'Avoncliff where he was caught isn't far off from those places, fifteen miles at most.'

'You're right, Inge. Bradford on Avon, Becky Addy Wood—all very local. A motorbike would be useful to any criminal. Fast, easy to manoeuvre, even over rough ground, and he was well disguised in the helmet.'

'I haven't seen him,' Ingeborg said. 'Is it obvious he's a foreigner?'

'Not at all. He could pass for British. You can't go by appearances.'

She lifted an eyebrow. 'But you're very confident he's an illegal?'

'From how he reacted when I mentioned a consulate, yes.'

'He won't be from one of the EU countries, then. Could he have escaped from a detention centre? Some do.'

He shook his head. 'I've already been over that with Jack Gull. Everyone who goes into one of those places is photographed and fingerprinted. He'd be in the system and he isn't.'

'So he probably arrived in a container and is anxious not to be caught. Why start shooting policemen when you want to keep a low profile?'

'I'll say this. The guy we're holding appears to be hyped up, angry and fearful at the same time.'

'Angry at being roughed up by Jack Gull?'

'Much more than that.'

'Angry at being reeled in?'

'That's part of it, I'm sure. And fearful of being sent back. He got very agitated when I said his consulate must be informed. He doesn't expect sympathy from his own government.'

'Perhaps he committed crimes there.'

'Could be. Or it's just that they're repressive. Someone like that, desperate not to be picked up by the police, decides to arm himself. He's served in the army in his own country and knows how to use a gun, so he buys one from someone in the criminal underworld, in Bristol, say, where we know there's a trade in weapons. He steals the bike and starts to feel more confident. He's got wheels and he's got an assault rifle. It's a short jump from defending yourself to going on the offensive. He hates the police so he begins murdering us.'

'That's an awful lot to infer from one angry guy in custody.'

He gave a smile that admitted as much. 'Lost faith in my powers of reasoning, have you?'

'I don't know about reasoning,' she said. 'If I put up a theory like that, you'd be saying unkind things about feminine intuition.'

'Never.'

'How about the West Country connection?'

'Here's an idea I've been mulling over,' he said. 'There was a lot in the papers last year about private colleges that offer a route into Britain for illegal immigrants. I wouldn't mind checking whether any such colleges exist in and around Bradford on Avon.'

'What you're saying is that you wouldn't mind *me* doing a check,' she said.

'What a good idea.'

* * *

Three-quarters of an hour later came the call he'd been waiting for—from the forensics company conducting the ballistics tests.

'You wanted the results from the test firing of the G36 rifle found in the river near Avoncliff yesterday.'

'Don't I just.'

'It's definitely the murder weapon. The bullets discharged in the test-firing chamber have been examined microscopically now and compared with those found at the crime scenes. As you know, the rifling along the sides of the bullets is like a fingerprint, unique to each weapon. The standard is that at least three identical patterns be found. We have better than that.'

'Nice work.'

'But . . .'

'There's always a "but" with you people. Tell me, then.'

'The match is with the used bullets recovered from Wells and Radstock. The bullets from the Bath scene are too deformed to be of any use. However, you did send us a cartridge casing from

Bath.'

'Correct.'

'Automatic weapons have mechanisms that eject the spent cartridge case and place the new bullet in the firing chamber. The process leaves scratches and marks on the side of the casing that are just as individual, just as reliable.'

Why do scientists always insist on telling you more than you need to know? Impatiently, Diamond said, 'And?'

'The casing found in Bath was ejected from a different weapon.'

'Different? Not a G36?'

'You're misunderstanding me. Still a G36, but a different G36.'

'Are you certain of this?'

'Totally. We compared the Bath casing with the ones from the test firing and they don't match. The gun from the river wasn't used to murder PC Tasker.'

* * *

He didn't spend long brooding on the results. Surprising as they would seem to most of those working on the case, they chimed with the hypothesis he'd been working towards: two gunmen. Jack Gull had to be brought up to date and so had the rest of the team.

He braved the mockers in the incident room.

Gull's response was predictable—and satisfying. 'Why the fuck did they tell you first? I'm the CIO. I'm the head of the Serial Crimes Unit.'

'I wouldn't worry about it, Jack,' Diamond said. 'No one's after your job, unless Polehampton is, and they didn't call him, they called me.'

'The custody clock is running down. I'm going to have to ask a magistrate for a warrant of further detention.'

'Yes. Don't miss out on that.'

'Ballistics must have got it wrong, anyway,' Gull said. 'The sniper won't have used more than one gun. A gunman treats his weapon like another limb. It's part of him.'

'He slung it in the river.'

'Only when he knew we had him by the short and curlies. It's got to be the same gun he used for the Walcot Street shooting. Got to be. He's had it with him ever since.'

Across the incident room, John Leaman looked up and gave Diamond a slight smile. On the first day he'd cautioned Gull against assuming the same gun had been used for all three shootings.

'Will you take some advice from me?' Diamond said to Gull.

'Let's hear it and I'll tell you.'

'Keep things simple. Concentrate on what we know for certain. The gun we found was definitely used for the shootings in Wells and Radstock. It was in the river at Avoncliff where we arrested the guy we're holding in the cells. We're confident he's the sniper.'

'I know all this. All I want is a fucking confession.'

'And you won't get it until you find what language he speaks. Here's a tip. When I was with him he clearly didn't understand what I was saying, but when I used the word "consulate", he went bananas. Some words are the same in different languages, like "le weekend" in French. I think you should look for a language that has the same word for consulate, or consul.'

'I'm a detective, not a fucking linguist.'

'Ask a fucking linguist, then.'

Even Jack Gull was forced to grin. 'It could be one of those words that's the same in dozens of languages.'

Diamond held up a finger. 'Yes, but I haven't finished. Like I said, the mention of the word really upset the suspect. My sense is that he comes from a state that treats its people harshly. He doesn't want his government getting involved. He'd rather answer to our law than his own.'

'Are you thinking of the old Soviet bloc? He looks European.'

'Could be, and I wouldn't discount the Middle East. Some of those people could easily pass for Europeans.'

'I'll give it a whirl. What are you doing next?'

'I've got a funeral to attend.'

But the funeral wasn't until 3 p.m. Diamond had other lines of enquiry he wasn't revealing to Gull at this juncture.

'Guv.'

The quiet, yet insistent, call from across the room was timely. A chance to leave Gull to wrestle with the linguistic problem.

Diamond shimmied between the desks to where Ingeborg was sitting back, adjusting her blonde ponytail, eyes on the computer screen.

'What is it?' he asked.

'You asked me to check private colleges in and around Bradford on Avon. There's one here known as the West Wiltshire Higher Education Institute. It was under investigation last summer and closed down.'

'What for?'

'Enrolling more foreign students than they could possibly cater for. It was an immigration scam. They got accepted for courses, obtained student visas and then disappeared into the underground economy. The government has been trying to crack down. Across the country ninety thousand were taken on last year by educational establishments that don't have the "highly trusted" status the Ministry of Education is trying to insist on.'

'When you say "foreign", you mean from outside the European Union?'

'Yes. Iraq, Iran, Somalia, Algeria. Shall I go on?'

'Tell me about this college they shut down. Where was it?'

'Off the Bath Road at the top of the town. Just a large house as far as I can make out.'

'You mean Bradford on Avon?'

She nodded. 'They had capacity for fifty and they enrolled five times that number over the course of a year. They were crafty. They had what they called an induction course that lasted a couple of weeks and then off-site work experience to acquire better language skills. Many of the students couldn't speak any English when they arrived.'

'And I suppose the work experience was low-paid casual labour?'

'You bet. In theory they were supposed to return to study full time when they'd got enough language skills, but they wouldn't learn much English picking fruit and digging potatoes. You can see why the college lost track of most of them. It was a huge turnover.'

Diamond didn't need much more persuading.

'But they'd learn about the local terrain. This is just what I was looking for, Inge, and the best explanation yet for how the sniper might have got to know Becky Addy Wood and Avoncliff. His student visa has no currency any more and he doesn't have the language skills to integrate into the system. His world has collapsed. He knows it's only a matter of time before he's arrested and banged up in one of those removal centres. He's living rough, stealing stuff to get by, but he has the bike and he has the gun. He's angry, vulnerable, terrified. He resolves to take the fight to the opposition, take revenge on the police. The rest we know.'

'Want me to do more checking?' Ingeborg asked.

'It would be nice if there's a record of the students they took on.'

'I doubt if they kept one. Or if they did, they would have destroyed the evidence.'

'There must have been some evidence of malpractice if the college was closed down. Wiltshire Police may know something. It's worth trying.'

'I'll get on to them.'

'Before you do,' Diamond said, 'we were talking the other day about the blog you found.'

She turned to face him, all attentiveness. Clearly she thought he'd dismissed the blog as yet another piece of computer nonsense. 'I can't claim credit for that. The barmaid at the Porter found it and told me.'

'Still worth a look?'

'Definitely.'

'Could you bring it up on the computer in my office?'

'Not a problem. You'll have at least four postings to read, but they won't take long.'

In front of his screen, working the keyboard, Ingeborg said, 'This is interesting. There's a fifth.'

CHAPTER TWENTY-NINE

So much has happened since my last blog that I hardly know where to begin. You remember I risked my job by turning snoop and looking at the order book for the client I recognized as Heathrow man. I was on the point of pulling out of the whole shebang until it became clear how crucially Vicky needed the distraction. Against my better judgment I passed John Smith's name on to my two friends. Vicky was at breaking point, poor lamb. Her husband Tim has been behaving more oddly than city break man and Heathrow man together. My guess is that his problem stems from the Iraq War. Post-traumatic stress, they call it, don't they? On top of that came the bad luck of losing his taxi business in such cruel circumstances. Sometimes people just need time and space to get over their troubles and I hope this is the case with Tim. I don't like to think what he gets up to when he leaves the house at nights. Well, to be honest I've been thinking about it a lot. Maybe he just walks the streets to clear his head of depression. I hope that's all it is, for Vicky's sake. She's so certain he isn't visiting some other woman that I have to believe her. What else can he be doing? When he left the army, did he smuggle out anything as a souvenir? Don't go there, I keep saying to myself. Don't go there.

Now we know where Heathrow man lives we're better placed to find out more about him. I was willing to do some local research, but this time Vicky volunteered, saying she hadn't contributed much up to now. Fine, I thought. The more she gets involved the better for her peace of mind. Compared to her difficulties at home this is child's play. So Anita and I left her to it.

She delivered.

We met in the department store the next afternoon and Vicky looked a million times better than when I'd last seen her. For one thing she'd dressed in brighter, trendier clothes with a beautiful blue floaty scarf over a lemon-coloured top that she insisted she'd found in Help the Aged. A tight black skirt and suede boots completed the outfit. With her gorgeous looks and that amazing black hair she was radiant. And eager to tell us what she'd discovered.

'After we spoke yesterday, I went to the house, just to see for myself, thinking John Smith is still away in Amsterdam so it ought to be safe to look round. While I was standing on the opposite side of the street, I had a piece of good luck. A woman drove up in a Volvo and got out with some shopping and went inside number 48, leaving the car on the drive. I don't think she noticed me.'

I couldn't stop myself interrupting. 'What was she like—dark, shoulder-length hair, grey suit?'

'Yes.'

'Could so easily be the woman city break man

met in the pub. I wonder if they're married.'

Vicky nodded. 'I've never seen her before, so I can't say, but from your description it's well possible. At the time I was more interested in the car, thinking maybe it belonged to him and his wife was using it while he was away. I crossed the road and took a closer look and found I was right. There was a parking permit next to the tax disc on the windscreen. It said J.Smith.'

'Nice detective work,' Anita went. 'A permit for where?'

'The city museum.'

Anita blinked and pulled a face. 'He's a pointy-head? And I thought he looked quite dishy.'

I gave a shrug. 'He could be both. Why not?'

Vicky picked up her story. She was dead keen to tell it. 'I decided to go up there in the morning and see what else I could find out. I took the whole day off work. I've never been in the museum before.'

'I have,' Anita went. 'School trip, years ago. Full of bones and fossils. No refreshments. Not my thing at all.' She was definitely a little jealous of Vicky finding out things.

'That's what I was expecting, and to tell the truth it is like that, most of it, but there's a Roman room, as you'd expect, with bits of pottery and some jewellery. I was the only visitor for the first hour and a half.'

Anita rolled her eyes. 'You stayed as long as that?'

'I was sleuthing, wasn't I? I needed to talk to someone and find out for sure if John Smith worked there. In the end I found the word

CURATOR on a door upstairs and I was looking at it, trying to think what to do next, when a woman came out of a door opposite and offered to help. I had to think quickly and I put on a foreign accent and asked what a curator does. She was a chatty sort and said it was a fancy name for the head keeper of the museum. He was her boss, but unfortunately he was away for a couple of days.'

'Aha,' Anita went. 'Away where?'

'In Cornwall. He has a cottage there and likes to escape sometimes.'

'A bloody long way from Amsterdam.'

'But we kept talking. She said she was the finds liaison officer, another fancy name. She'd put FLO on her door and since that day everyone called her Flo. Her job was created to deal with all the stuff being found with those metal detector things people use in fields and on beaches. As you know, this area is stuffed with historical remains and the detector brigade are coming into the museum every week with objects they've picked up. Anything gold or silver and more than three hundred years old has to be reported because of something called the Treasure Act. She said she thought when she saw me that I might have brought in some artefact.'

'Better than being mistaken for one,' Anita went. 'We're none of us getting any younger. Did you find out if John Smith works there?'

'Yes—and he's her boss, the curator.'

We straightened up like meerkats.

Anita was frowning. 'But he's in Cornwall.'

'That's what he told her. We know better,

don't we?' Vicky's eyes were like newly minted coins. 'John Smith doesn't want it known he's in Amsterdam.'

'What's he up to, then?'

'I think I've worked it out. I talked some more to this young woman, whose real name is Francesca, and she was telling me how exciting it can be when people get in touch. She never knows from one day to the next what will turn up. The best thing of all is a hoard. That's when they discover something like a pot of Roman coins, up to fifty thousand of them. She'll get called out to see them at the site. She arranges for them to be properly excavated by experts and then they're brought back here in stages before being sent to the British Museum to be washed and evaluated.'

'And is John Smith involved in any of this?' I asked, already thinking I could see where this was going.

Vicky flashed a big smile at me. 'You've got it. There's a huge safe in his office in the museum and he makes sure the finds are locked away securely before being taken to London.'

'Whose job is it to record the finds?'

'The British Museum. They have conservators who wash them and separate them. It's specialised work. Coins get stuck hard together over time. Some of them can be really rare and worth a lot of money and you probably know what I'm thinking.'

We did. By now we were all thinking along the same lines. It would be all too easy for a dishonest curator to pick out some special items that never get sent to London. The metal detectorist has no idea how many coins or objects there are in a hoard, and the British Museum staff only get to see what arrives there.

I was the one who said it. 'These short trips to European cities could be John Smith selling coins and other finds to foreign collectors. It would explain why he never makes the booking himself and why his wife collects the tickets from city break man. Vicky, you're brilliant. I think you've sussed it.'

Anita had been listening to this with awe. 'A profitable little scam. How do we prove it?'

'With help from Francesca,' Vicky went. 'She's very knowledgable and I think she may have her suspicions already. If certain rare Roman coins are starting to be traded in Europe she'll be alerted. When we tell her about the city breaks Anita has been arranging, she can check the dates Smith is supposed to have spent in Cornwall.'

'Proving he's on the take is going to be difficult,' Anita insisted.

'Not at all,' Vicky went. She'd had longer to think about this than Anita and me. 'Next time John Smith arranges another city break, we do what you did before, tip off the girls at the check-in and they can speak to the customs men. He'll be caught with the goods on him. Whatever he says, you can't export stuff like that without a licence.'

I was like, 'Brilliant.'

Even Anita gave her a hug.

It's so nice that we've all played a part and Vicky has brought it to fruition.

The sleuthing sisters will shortly wrap up their

first case.

So what's next?

CHAPTER THIRTY

He was so wrapped up in the blog that he didn't notice Ingeborg enter his office until she spoke.

'Guv.'

'Mm?'

'A result.'

'What's that?'

'I managed to contact the inspector who investigated the bogus college at Bradford on Avon.'

'You did?' For a moment he was floundering. Then the bogus college clicked into place, possibly the alma mater of the silent man in the cells. This could be the chance to prove the suspect was an illegal immigrant on a student visa. 'What did you find out?'

'The case came to trial at the end of last year and there was a successful prosecution. As we expected, the principal had shredded all the enrolment records, but he was still convicted and jailed for six years. They found some of the so-called students and got them to testify. But countless others disappeared off the radar.'

'Interesting.'

'And there's something else. More than half of them were Iranian. He had some kind of arrangement with Tehran.'

'Iran?' He leaned back in his chair. 'That would explain a lot. If you escaped from there you wouldn't want to be sent back. What do you think they do to defectors?'

The way Ingeborg scrunched the front of her T-shirt was answer enough.

Diamond drummed his fingers on the desktop. 'What we need now is a Persian–English dictionary.'

'You want to look up the word "consul"?' she said. 'We can do it on the internet.'

He shook his head in awe or despair at the limitless uses of the web while Ingeborg leaned across him and worked the keys. In seconds she had a website that allowed you to type in an English word and get the Persian, or Farsi, equivalent. 'Consul' produced some Persian script and the pronunciation 'Konsul'.

'Spot on,' Diamond said. 'Now we can tell Gull which fucking interpreter he needs.'

Ingeborg blinked. She'd missed the earlier exchange.

Without more comment Diamond moved on. 'I finished reading the blogs.'

She locked in at once. She was staking her reputation on the account of the three sleuths being germane to the case. 'What do you think?'

Under her earnest gaze, he couldn't resist being playful. 'I think you and I are in the right job. Sleuthing is cool.'

'Do you agree it must be about Bath?'

'Seems so.'

Her voice was charged with urgency as she told him, 'It can't be anywhere else, guv. I picked up any number of local references. She says somewhere that they're living in the West Country and several times calls the place a city. The department store they met in sounds exactly like Jolly's—the restaurant on the first floor, the cream teas with miniature scones, even the placing of the loos upstairs next to the hairdressing salon. It could all be coincidence, you may be thinking, but the details add up. When she comes out of the store and follows city break man she goes up the hill, as you would up Milsom Street.'

'To cut this short,' he said, 'I think you'll find that in blog number three she mentions delivering red roses to a lady in the Royal Crescent. There aren't many West Country cities with that address.'

She gave a little cry of delight. And now he felt the heat of her enthusiasm. 'You *have* read it carefully.' She hesitated on the brink of the next question. 'What do you think, guv? Is it a load of hooey?'

'You mean how seriously should we take it? I'm not about to arrest the museum curator, if that's what you're asking.'

'You know very well that's not what I'm asking.'

'Tim, the weird husband?'

'That may not be his real name. Well, I'm sure it can't be. She says at the beginning she changed the names.'

'Whoever he is, if he's real, he ticks some of our boxes,' he said. 'In the army on active service, so he knows how to use a rifle. Lived in a city twenty miles down the road. Must be Wells. Drove a taxi, so he had wheels. Is held responsible for the teenager's death.'

'The policeman's daughter's death,' she put in.

'True, which is why he is harassed by the Wells police, or believes he is, so he moves here and starts going out at nights and being secretive and moody. There's not much doubt that these women think he could be the sniper. Motive, opportunity and possibly the means as well if somehow he managed to hang on to his service rifle after being discharged.' He leaned back in the chair and linked his hands around the back of his neck. He'd indulged Ingeborg enough. 'But we arrested the sniper and he's sitting in the cells. We have the weapon and we have the shoeprint evidence. Is there any point in looking for Tim?'

Her large, eager eyes were fixed on his. 'You tell me. You're the boss.'

'Here's a question for you, Inge, as a computer buff. All that stuff in the first blog about making it untraceable by bouncing the text around the internet through a series of volunteers—is that true?'

'I'm sure it is. She over-simplifies, but the principle is correct. It's known as the onion method. The text is encrypted and goes through a series of proxy handlers. Each one can tell where it comes from and where to send it, but that's all they know, and all they'll ever know.'

'Then we'd have an impossible job trying to find out who wrote this thing and who the people are?'

'Through the internet, yes.'

'So the mighty computer does have its limitations?' He rubbed his hands. 'We'd have to find these sleuthing ladies through old-fashioned detective work, picking up clues about where they live. I'm almost inclined to start—just to get one over technology.' He smiled. 'But I'm not going to. We'd be wasting precious time.'

Ingeborg stared at him in disbelief, if not defiance. 'So you think it's all one big red herring?'

'Don't you?'

She didn't get a chance to answer. The phone on Diamond's desk rang. The desk sergeant was asking for him urgently. A clear note of alarm was in the voice.

* * *

This might have been the interview to duck. There was a definite prospect of a blow-up, if not a punch-up, even within the police station. But avoidance never crossed Diamond's mind. The case had come to a critical point.

'In room one, sir. He's in quite a state.'

Diamond found Soldier Nuttall in combat clothes and desert boots, pacing the small room, speaking agitatedly into his mobile. Seeing that he was no longer alone, he switched off.

'You took your time,' he told Diamond. 'I want a straight answer from you. No bullshit. Are you, or are you not, holding my boy?'

'Holding Royston?' He spread his hands. 'I am not.'

'Don't mess with me, Diamond. If it isn't you, one of your lot has got him. Where is he? I want him released.'

'I've no idea what you're talking about.'

'He's only seventeen, you know. You can't do this. I know the law. If you detain a juvenile, you must inform the appropriate adult—that's me—of the reason why you're holding him and his whereabouts. And I have the right to see him immediately.'

'Didn't you hear me?' Diamond said. 'He's not here.'

'Some other nick, then.'

'I don't think so. I've heard nothing about an arrest.'

'You'd better check, hadn't you?'

'I will. What makes you think he's under arrest?'

'He didn't come home last night, hasn't been in touch, hasn't texted, phoned, whatever.'

'Do you have any reason to think he might have been picked up by the police?'

A wary look settled on the hawkish features. 'Why do you say that?'

'Because of what you're saying.'

'I won't be tricked, you know. I know my rights. You people are going to pay heavily for damaging my property for no good reason. You'll be hearing from my solicitor. Nothing will alter that.'

'I didn't mention your property,' Diamond said, keen to move on. 'I thought you were here about your son. When did you last see Royston?'

'Yesterday, after your visit. You insisted on speaking to him alone and I don't know what was said. That was against the law.'

'Don't lecture me on the law, Mr Nuttall. He wasn't under arrest or in detention. I made that clear to you. Let's cool off a bit and see what can be done. Did you speak to him after I left your house?'

'What do you take me for? I'm his father. I'm responsible for him. Of course I bloody did.'

'And did you accuse him of anything?'

'Everything under the sun.'

'Really?'

'I wanted to know why you lot came calling. Isn't that the duty of a father? If he'd been caught drinking, or doing drugs, or making a nuisance of himself, I needed to know.'

A new slant on Soldier Nuttall: the responsible parent.

'Did he admit to anything?' Diamond asked.

'If he did, would I blab it to a cop? I'm not simple.'

'Let's put it another way, then. How did he seem to take it?'

'Take what?'

'Being questioned by his father. I need to know what frame of mind he was in. If he's run away from home, is it because you frightened him?'

'Him? He's a bloody teenager, spoiling for a fight.'

'That wasn't the way I saw him, cowering on the back seat of your car.'

'I loosed the dog, didn't I? You'd be cowering if one of them brutes was trying to rip your throat out. Royston was brought up tough. He can take a bollocking from me.'

'Then I don't see what the problem is.'

'He's a missing child, that's the problem.'

'Big child.'

'Under eighteen.'

'It's not unusual for a kid his age to take umbrage at something and go off on his own for a night, or a couple of nights.'

'I want him found. That's your job.'

'One of my jobs. Now that you've reported it, I'll get the word out. Did he take his motorbike?'

'That's gone, yes.'

'Does he have money?'

'Plenty.'

'He wouldn't be armed, would he?'

A suspicious glare. 'What with?'

'I was told you possess a number of licensed

weapons, and I mean real ones that fire. Have you checked them today? If any are missing, you must certainly let me know.'

The mention of weapons seemed to take all of the steam out of Nuttall. It was suddenly as if he wanted to be out of there and taking Diamond's advice. 'You'll tell me right away if you see anything of him?'

'Certainly.'

'He may look like a man, but he's just a kid really.'

'We've both been that age,' Diamond said as if he was a headmaster being merciful to an anxious parent. 'Leave it to us, Mr Nuttall.'

Left alone in the interview room, he asked himself why this bizarre scene had taken place. Why was a little Hitler like Nuttall demanding help from the police? It was obvious he wasn't really troubled over Royston's welfare. His own welfare was under threat. But he was unwilling to disclose the reason. First he had believed Royston was in custody. A serious issue, then, a criminal matter, else why did he assume that the boy was being held? Was he alarmed by what his offspring would disclose?

Learning that Royston wasn't being held should have come as good news to Nuttall and obviously didn't. He wanted him rounded up, and quickly. It seemed the lad was a loose cannon, capable of doing real damage. Did it go back to what had been said between father and son? By his own admission Nuttall had laid into Royston and accused him of everything under the sun. One of the charges must have stuck. Under interrogation or at liberty, the errant teenager was a direct threat to his father's well-defended reputation.

But in what way?

He returned upstairs. The statements from yesterday, every word transcribed from Ingeborg's hidden tape-recorder, were threatening to slip from the top of the tower of paper rising from his in-tray. He plucked them off and read Royston's answers again and delved lower in the stack and found the report Paul Gilbert had written of the night touring Harry Tasker's beat—Moles, the Porter, the Bell, Walcot Street and Club XL. The find of the night had been Anderson Jakes, the man who had put them on to Royston.

Then it became clear.

After reading precisely what Anderson Jakes had told Paul and Ingeborg, Diamond worked out how, where, when and why the boy would be found.

But he was in no mood for self-congratulation. There was an urgent need to revisit the crime scene.

He stepped out of his office. The incident room had gone quiet. Jack Gull, he learned, was trying to get hold of an interpreter who spoke Persian. Ingeborg, still preoccupied with the blog, was putting markers on a map of the city. Polehampton had gone to have a word with the custody sergeant. John Leaman and Keith Halliwell were together at the window, looking down into the street.

'What's going on?' he asked them.

'Come and see.'

He joined them in time to see Polehampton heading purposefully up Manvers Street towards the station. 'Where's he off to?'

'The pub on the corner, the Royal, for another quick one. He needs it every two hours. It's the strain of working with Gull.'

At any other time, he might have been amused. Today, he had too much on his mind. 'I'm slipping out for a while myself. I need to go back to the crime scene as a matter of urgency.'

* * *

Paloma wouldn't approve after the trouble she'd taken to protect him from being shot, but this had to be done. The streets of Bath were thronged as midday approached and he reasoned it would be crazy for anyone to loose off a round of ammunition. No potential killer could have anticipated him leaving the police station at this moment. Mingling with the shoppers and the tourists, he took the most direct route around Orange Grove and along the High Street past the Guildhall and the Podium, all well-populated places at this hour, then left at St Michael's and up the steep rise of Broad Street and right at the top towards Bladud Buildings and the Paragon.

It was difficult to conceive of anyone planning the shooting of Harry Tasker without prior knowledge of the layout of the Paragon. The terrace of twenty-one houses as elegant as any corporation-built property in Britain stood in a gentle curve that followed the road's contour rather than being designed as a crescent. All were similar in style, difficult to tell apart except for a few with window boxes on the first-floor sills. From the front there was no sense that you were on the edge of a precipitous slope with vaulted basements overlooking Walcot Street.

He was angry with himself for taking so long to tumble to the obvious. All the pressure of pursuing the man in the woods had stopped him thinking straight. Finally, he'd worked it out. Whoever murdered Harry must have visited the Paragon house before. They had to know the set-up.

The residents had some explaining to do.

He eyed the bell-push panel and the handwritten names: S. Willis, MA, Mr & Mrs D. Murphy and Sherry Meredith. The fourth bell, for the unoccupied basement, had no name against it. After a moment's thought, he pressed the third. Sherry Meredith worked in the cosmetics department in Jolly's, only a short walk away, and it was just possible she came home in her lunch break.

'Hi, who is it?' said the shrill voice on the entryphone.

He smiled. His guardian angel was doing the biz today. 'Peter Diamond, Detective Superintendent.'

'I'm sorry, I don't buy anything at the door.' The line disconnected. She couldn't have been listening properly.

He tried again, twice. He'd kick the door in, if necessary.

At the third attempt, she came on again and said, 'Please go away.'

'Police,' he said, 'about the murder.'

After a pause, she said, 'Why didn't you say so? Push the door.'

Trying to give the appearance of calm, he stepped inside. Sherry Meredith, exquisitely made up, was halfway along the passage holding a door open, a yoghurt pot in one hand, a teaspoon in the other. 'You'll have to be really quick. I'm due back at work in fifteen minutes and I can't run in these heels.'

She showed him into the flat. Decorated in

primary colours, blue and yellow, it had shelves with collections of pottery figures, rabbits along one wall, Disney characters and fairies another. 'I'd invite you to sit down, but there really isn't time,' she said. 'I'll be in awful trouble if I'm late back.'

Diamond shrugged. 'So we'll get down to it. We talked before about what happened early Sunday morning. I need to know more about you and your background. I expect you have plenty of boyfriends.'

The false eyelashes did some rapid work. 'As many as I want. But one at a time.'

'Not going steady, then?'

'It's funny. I always start off thinking I am.'

'Where do you meet them—nightclubs?'

'Mostly, yes.' The blue eyes widened. 'How did you know that?'

'It's my job. Have you ever dated a policeman?'

She was open-mouthed. 'I don't wish to be rude, but I'm only twenty. Aren't you a bit senior for me?'

He remembered how tricky it was to interview her. 'I'm not talking about myself. This is an investigation. Would you answer the question, please.'

She appeared to decide he wasn't, after all, chatting her up. 'A policeman? I'm not sure.'

'You must know.'

'With some guys I never find out the jobs they have. We talk about other stuff—if we talk about anything at all. The bands we like, and that. Some of them like to get physical straight away. I've discovered it's best to stay clear of the silent ones.'

'There's a lad called Royston,' Diamond said. 'Younger than you, but mature in looks. He's often around the clubs. Ever met him?'

'I don't think so. Cute name. I'd remember it.'
'How about Anderson, a black guy?'
'Everyone's heard of Anderson,' she said. 'He's cool. But he's never shown any interest in me. Why are you asking me about these guys?'
'I need to know who has visited here.'
Her mouth formed a perfect O. 'I don't bring them home. If I spend the night with them it's never here. I wouldn't want that. I mean, they might ask to use my bathroom.'
'It's a case of his place, or his place?'
She giggled. 'That sums it up.'
'You're telling me you haven't entertained a man here in the past year?'
'Only my dad and he brings a blow-up bed.'
He believed her. He doubted if she had the ability to lie. 'I'll be frank with you, Sherry. What I need to know is who could have visited this house with a view to planning the murder of PC Tasker.'
'Not Daddy,' she said. 'He's a parish councillor.'
'No, not him. Do you remember any other visitors?'
'To me?'
'To anyone in the house.'
'They could be visiting upstairs, I guess. It's a quiet house. The Murphys have friends in on Friday evenings. I think they play bridge. They've been coming for years. They're all about eighty.'
'And the man on the top floor?'
'Mr Willis with the ponytail? He's younger and he has a lady caller I've met at the door a couple of times. Thick dark hair and too shy to smile. I know she has a key because she lets herself in at night sometimes. She's really quiet, but some of the stairs creak, so I hear her. I don't mind. It's romantic.

She's gone before morning. I can't believe she'd murder anyone.'

'He must have other visitors.'

'Well, I don't see all the comings and goings. I'm at work most of the day.'

'So is he. He's a civil servant. Have you ever seen him carrying a gun?'

'Lordy, no.'

'He belongs to a gun club.'

'Never. Who would have thought it?'

'His shooting friends could come calling.'

'With guns?'

'Probably not. Just socially.'

'They're very quiet if they do. I don't hear anything.' She looked at her watch. 'I have to go. I don't want to lose my job.'

'You can tell your supervisor you were being interviewed by the police.'

'I don't think I will.'

He allowed her to leave, but he remained in the building. After she'd closed the door behind her, he went upstairs and tried the Murphys' door. They didn't answer his knock. He went up another flight and found Willis wasn't at home either.

But he had the opportunity of another look inside the basement flat, which was unlocked. Forensics had been through on the first day, so he didn't expect to find a vital missing clue. Yet it was helpful to stroll through the rooms imagining how the killer could have passed several hours waiting to go into the garden and position the rifle for the shooting of Harry Tasker.

The garden, when he ventured outside, he found transformed. It had been levelled of those tall weeds, so he couldn't easily picture the second phase of the crime, the attack on Ken Lockton. Somewhere here, or inside the flat, the carefully executed plan went wrong. The killer had almost been caught red-handed—or with the G36 in hand—when Lockton arrived with Sergeant Stillman. Then it was a case of lying low, waiting for an opportunity to escape. Lockton had dismissed Stillman and gone to the front door with him. The sniper had retrieved the rifle, skulked in the undergrowth until the chance came to make a dent in Lockton's head with the stock. In the minutes that followed, nobody else came and the chance of escape was possible and ultimately simple.

Well planned? There had been a plan, certainly, but luck must have played a part as well. He walked to the railings and looked down into Walcot Street, busy with the lunchtime crowd. Difficult to visualise the same street at 4 a.m. on Sunday with just a lone policeman almost at the end of his beat, passing under the lamplight.

Calculating and cold-blooded.

Diamond gave a soft sigh for the death of his brother officer and the way he'd been ambushed.

* * *

Back in the nick, the desk sergeant told him he was wanted in the interview suite.

'Wanted who by?'

'Mr Gull. The interpreter arrived.'

He glanced at his watch. Not much time.

In interview room two, Gull greeted him with, 'Been out to lunch? All I have time for is a fucking sandwich.'

'Is that better than egg mayo?'

from staying on top—was what to do next. The advantage was his for the present. He could hold this position for some time and he would need to, because he wasn't carrying handcuffs. He hadn't expected to make an arrest tonight. He didn't even have a personal radio on him. All those young policemen in full kit had cuffs with them, but were they within hailing distance?

Doubtful. And he didn't want to give encouragement to his prisoner at this stage of the arrest.

He took stock.

If he allowed the man to stand up, the balance of power changed. He could be up and running again, with a good chance of getting clean away.

Another bout of wriggling came to an end.

'What's your name?' Diamond asked.

Silence.

'Suit yourself. This can't be comfortable and it could go on some time.'

He was talking to himself as much as the prisoner. There was no logical reason why anyone should come to his assistance. The firearms team were intent on watching the footpath leading to the pillbox. They wouldn't even give a glance in this direction. And he doubted if he could make them hear.

There were arm-locks he could try, but he hadn't much confidence he could keep a man under arrest who was so evidently fitter and younger. He didn't even know if he could still get upright. The chase may have finally done for his dodgy leg. Just about every fibre of his body was aching.

Yet he had a duty to hold out. This squirming piece of bone and muscle could be a triple killer.

Help was urgently needed. He took a deep breath and shouted with all the voice he could raise, 'Over here! By the river!' But he was so low to the turf that he knew the sound hadn't carried any distance at all.

Of course no one shouted back. Anyway, they were in whispering mode, like Sergeant Gillibrand.

'Diamond here,' he yelled. 'Someone get over here, for God's sake!'

The only immediate result was a heave from the prisoner that almost toppled him. The guy was strong.

A doubt crept into Diamond's mind. What if this was not the sniper, but some hapless person who had happened to be out late walking by the river? He'd run away when challenged and tried to break free when arrested, but that was the only sure thing against him. Alone in the dark, pursued by someone in plain clothes purporting to be a police officer, mightn't anyone have made a run for it?

And what if he actually was the lowlife who had been sleeping in the pillbox? Was that the clincher? Plenty of people lived and slept rough through choice or circumstance. Diamond hadn't ever been fully convinced by Jack Gull's theory that the killer was at large in Avoncliff.

Gull would point out that the shoeprints collected from the pillbox matched the prints found in Wells. He'd need more than that to get a conviction. He hadn't yet found the murder weapon.

'Are you going to tell me who you are?' he asked again.

An unshaven cheek rasped Diamond's face as the head jerked away, the closest thing to an answer

The joke was lost on Gull. 'Pull up a chair.'

'I may have to leave shortly. You can't turn up late to a funeral.'

As usual, Gull was oblivious of Diamond's needs. 'This is Polly. She's English.'

The reason he'd said so was because the young woman seated opposite was wearing the hijab. She looked young and confident.

'Married to an Iranian living here,' she explained.

Gull was impatient to begin. 'I've filled her in on the background.'

The prisoner was brought in, his bored expression suggesting he was resigned to yet another unproductive session. But the hours in custody had improved his appearance. The red-raw look from living outdoors had toned down to a passably healthy glow and a few hours' sleep had made his eyes brighter and less sunken. He looked younger, closer to twenty than twenty-five. The whole face lit up when he saw Polly and she said something to him in Persian.

Miracle of miracles, he spoke some words back.

'He is Iranian,' she said, 'from Tehran.'

Jack Gull didn't have the grace to acknowledge that Diamond and his team had done their homework and got it right. There wasn't even a glance Diamond's way. 'We'd better issue the caution, then.'

Polly was well organised. She had a card ready in her hand with the words in the Persian language. Then she introduced Gull and Diamond.

'And is he going to tell us his name?' Diamond asked in the spirit of the Chinese proverb that when heaven drops a date, open your mouth.

She turned back to the prisoner and, wonder of wonders, got another response.

'Hossain Farhadi, student,' she was able to tell them.

Was this the breakthrough, tight lips willing to loosen up at last?

'Student of which college?'

Polly listened to Farhadi's answer and translated. 'West Wiltshire Higher Education Institute, Bradford on Avon.'

Diamond felt the kind of lift you get from champagne.

'As we already worked out,' Gull said. 'Does he know the college was closed down?'

Presently Polly was able to say, 'Yes, and he and many other students who had come to England in good faith were left with nowhere to study. He tried other colleges and they wouldn't consider him without a better knowledge of English.'

'Tough tittie,' Gull said.

Polly paused, while Farhadi said more.

'He couldn't return to Iran. He'd fled his homeland for political reasons. People disappear, are imprisoned, tortured and executed. The secret police took away two of his brothers and one of his friends three years ago and he hasn't seen them since. He expected he would be safe in England.'

'Pity England wasn't safe from him,' Gull muttered to Diamond.

The prisoner said some more and the translation followed.

'He was on an official student visa and even though the college closed he intended to return to education later. So he was determined to stay at any cost. With the help of some other Iranians he obtained work as a casual labourer on farms mainly in west Wiltshire and Somerset. It was the kind of work he'd been doing as part of his education.'

'Education, my arse,' Gull said.

'I don't believe he knew it was a con,' Polly said.

'You're being paid to translate, not give an opinion.'

Diamond said, 'Be fair, Jack. She's telling us the sense of what he's said to her.'

Hossain Farhadi had started up again.

Polly translated. 'He worked hard for many months and earned enough money to live. He gave up trying to find another course because he needed to put in the hours of work to pay for his food and rent. Then one day he was picking potatoes in the field and the police arrived. He and some others ran off and managed to hide, but several others were put in vans and driven away. He was told by his friends that they would be taken to something called—' she hesitated and looked across at Gull for help—'an extermination centre?'

'What the fuck . . .?'

'Removal,' Diamond said, 'a removal centre.'

Polly shrugged. 'In his country this means something more sinister. He was afraid of being taken to such a place. He is still terrified you'll take him there.'

'Is he simple-minded?' Gull asked her. 'We don't do that. Someone must have told him about deportation.'

'That alarms him, too.'

'He can forget about that,' Gull said.

'Can I tell him?'

'Tell him we'll hear what he's got to say and then decide where to send him.'

The prisoner started speaking again and the English version followed.

'The remaining students decided their best chance was to split up and go their separate ways. Some went to London, some to the Midlands. He decided to stay in the only part of the country he knew, the west, but on his own, survival was even more difficult. He'd lost his job and couldn't communicate.'

'He took to stealing?' Diamond said.

'The motorbike,' Gull said. 'Is he admitting to nicking that?'

'Do you want me to ask him?' Polly said, more to Diamond than Gull.

Diamond nodded. It could open the gate to the bigger charges.

They could see Farhadi frown as the question was put to him.

Gull took a photo of the bike from the folder in front of him and passed it across the table.

Farhadi took one glance and nodded. Then he continued speaking, but in shorter, more impassioned statements that Polly rendered into English in her even tone, as straightforwardly as if she was reading out instructions on assembling flat-pack furniture.

'He knew he was on the run from the police. His student visa was no longer valid, so he got rid of it with his passport. He didn't want to be identified. He was angry because he had done nothing wrong.'

'Worked in the black economy and stole a fucking motorbike. Nothing wrong there?' Gull said.

He didn't get an answer, presumably because Polly treated the remark as rhetorical.

'He believed he had only a few days of liberty left, and he could expect to spend the rest of his life behind bars.'

'Too fucking right,' Gull said.

'He is thinking of prison in Iran. The penal system there is very harsh.'

Gull turned to Diamond and said through his teeth, 'I can see where this is heading and I don't buy it, don't buy it at all.'

Farhadi was already making his next point, stabbing the air with his hands.

Polly translated in the same steady tone, 'He was living rough, a fugitive, a wanted man, surviving on what he could find or scavenge, sleeping in barns and outhouses, constantly expecting the police to arrest him. He has a deep-seated fear of men in uniform.'

'I think I'm going to throw up,' Gull said.

Diamond said, 'Let him speak, Jack. He's doing our work for us.'

Another rush of words followed.

'For a time he was in other towns, south of here, but eventually he came back to the place he knows best, where the college was. He knew the police were closing in. He had a couple of narrow escapes before you finally arrested him.'

Farhadi had stopped speaking. Polly waited and only got a nod that seemed to say, 'End of story.'

The prisoner folded his arms and sat back.

If he thought he had finished, he was being optimistic.

'Let's rewind a bit,' Gull said. 'We recovered the bike from the river. We also recovered this.' He pushed a photo of the assault rifle across the table.

Farhadi tensed and his facial muscles rippled.

He was silent for a few seconds, as if weighing his options. Then he spoke more words that Polly turned into English.

'He had money in his old lodgings, saved from the farm labouring, and he decided to arm himself. He'd learned to shoot during military service. He was a qualified marksman. He bought the gun from an illegal trader in Bath.'

'Your patch,' Gull said to Diamond. He turned to Polly. 'Ask him if he wants to tell us how he used the gun. No, let's go for broke. Tell him we have ballistic evidence that this gun—his gun—was used to murder police officers, the first in Wells twelve weeks ago.'

Up to now, Farhadi had given little away, but as Polly translated, the first signs of alarm showed in his eyes. He glanced down, seeking the right words to explain his actions. When he finally spoke, the gravity of what he was accused of came through in the voice.

Polly's rendering was, of course, free of all that, except in the sense of the words. 'His original plan was to defend himself when the police came for him. He was sleeping rough, with the loaded gun beside him. But the more he considered his situation, the more he realised he was likely to be killed in a shoot-out.'

'Twisted thinking,' Gull said.

'He says the combination of being alone and on the run, forced to break the law to get food, often being hungry and too afraid to get much sleep, affected his brain. He became paranoid.'

'His word?' Diamond asked Polly.

She reddened. 'All of this is as accurate as I can make it. Paranoid is the expression he uses. I can ask him again to be certain.'

There was another short exchange before she said, 'He confirms it. He was having nightmares about the police. He believed they were everywhere, watching him through spy cameras, setting traps, waiting to ambush him. It all built up in his brain and became unbearable, usually at night.'

'This is breaking me up,' Gull said with a yawn.

Farhadi's explanation had moved on to a new level. 'When the night terrors reached a particular point of crisis, he believed there would be no release until he used the gun to shoot one of his tormentors. This would be a way of striking back when everything was targeted at him. At first he thought it might be enough just to get a police officer in his sights without pulling the trigger. He would plan the shooting with great care and the sense of power might satisfy.'

The two detectives were compelled to wait while the process of translation was renewed.

'He found a place in Wells that suited his plan, a tree house. Two nights he took aim at a passing policeman and resisted firing a shot. But the impulse was overwhelming and on the third occasion he pulled the trigger.'

Gull slapped his hand several times on the table. He'd got his confession.

'He got away and left Wells for good, but he needed to find another town where there were bins to search for food. He came to Radstock and for a short time he survived quite well. Then the terrors undermined him again. He felt compelled to use the gun a second time, and he did.'

'For the hell of it, or what?' Gull said, becoming

angrier now that guilt was admitted.

Polly put this into some form of words for Farhadi and got a response.

'He experienced the same build-up of extreme anxiety that he believed could only be assuaged by shooting another policeman. He wishes to make clear that he didn't know either of his victims. They were uniformed police and the idea alone was driving him, inhabiting his brain.'

'*Either* of his victims?' Gull repeated.

'He told us about two,' Polly said.

'I heard what he told us, but we all know there are three. He shot Harry Tasker right here in Bath.'

In response to Polly's enquiry, Farhadi shrugged and made another short statement.

Polly told Gull, 'He denies this. He shot two policemen, two only, in Wells and Radstock, and nobody in this city. He was living in Becky Addy Wood and Avoncliff, not Bath. He came here because he was at college in Bradford on Avon and knows the locality.'

'Bullshit,' Gull said. 'Listen, chum, I don't serve in this dump. I'm from Headquarters. You'll get no sympathy from me this way. You're a piece of crap whether you killed two of us, or three. Might as well fess up.'

But Farhadi was insistent when it was put to him again.

'Fucking liar,' Gull said.

Then Diamond said, 'Actually, I believe him.'

CHAPTER THIRTY-ONE

Before leaving, Diamond instructed Keith Halliwell to take a small surveillance team to keep watch on Emma Tasker's house while she was at the funeral.

'Are you expecting a break-in?' Halliwell asked, appalled. 'What kind of sick bastard would plan something like that?'

'Get with it, Keith,' Diamond said as one who had heard and seen it all before. 'That's one of the oldest tricks in the book. Weddings and funerals. They know the house is empty at this time, so they take their opportunity. I don't want it happening today. Take Ingeborg and Paul Gilbert and stay out of sight.'

'If anyone tries it, we'll come down hard, don't worry.'

'Hold on.' The lofty tone changed rather suddenly. 'I'm not suggesting violence. It could be just a neighbour pushing a sympathy card through the door.'

* * *

He was at Haycombe crematorium a few minutes before the hearse arrived. He stood with the three uniformed police who had served with Harry. They told Diamond that more would certainly have come, but Emma had insisted she wanted three only. About fifteen other people had gathered outside. They all looked grim-faced. He found himself thinking his suggestion of 'Gone Fishin'' for Harry's send-off may not have been such a good one.

'You're invited to the Hop Pole after the service,' a man who seemed to be family told the police group. 'It's on the Upper Bristol Road, quite close to the house.'

'We know it, thanks,' Diamond said. In some ways, he thought, a couple of strong drinks *before* a funeral wouldn't come amiss. This would be the first he'd attended since Steph had died. He'd felt numb that day. The main service had been in the Abbey, a large affair with almost four hundred in attendance. The close family had been driven here for the committal.

This would not be easy to get through.

The hearse glided through the cemetery towards the entrance followed by a red Fiat Panda. Everyone stood respectfully while the undertaker and his team attended to the coffin. Emma emerged from the Panda in a black trouser suit with a blue shirt. She'd been driven by Betty, the neighbour Diamond had met on his second visit to the house. Actually, Betty looked more like the principal mourner, in a long fur-trimmed coat, black tights and a hat large enough for everyone to shelter under if it rained. They followed the coffin into the chapel.

Apparently Harry had not been religious. The last rites were overseen by a dapper little man Diamond recognised and couldn't place who admitted in his opening remarks that he'd never met 'our much-lamented friend,' which sounded like a contradiction in terms. On hearing the voice Diamond remembered arresting the man the previous summer for selling fake Rolex watches outside the Roman Baths. It seemed he had a second career officiating at non-religious committals.

Someone had prepared a short account of Harry's life that the watch salesman read out in a suitably uplifting voice. He reminded the mourners that Harry had met the love of his life, Emma, while they were both serving in the police. There was a lot about the selfless dedication of the force that was gratifying to hear. Better still from Diamond's point of view, the tribute went on to say how much Harry had enjoyed his fishing. Surely some of those present would make the connection when the music started.

At the front with her large-hatted neighbour, Emma controlled her emotions. She wasn't the sort to break down and weep. Hands clasped in front of her, she gazed steadily ahead.

'And now we have a few moments for quiet reflection on Harry's life before we take leave of him.' In a lapse of decorum, the salesman turned his arm to glance at his watch.

The genuine article? You bet it is, Diamond thought.

He couldn't help noticing that the salesman had a CD in his other hand. Had he forgotten to hand it to whoever managed the music? He could see the man's eyes widen as he sensed his mistake. In the nick of time he stepped to one side and passed the disc to the undertaker.

After a silence that threatened to go on too long, the curtains started to close around the coffin and the first chords of music filled the chapel.

But the tune didn't sound right.

'Lazy bones,' came Satchmo's voice.

They'd got the wrong track.

Heads turned. People shifted awkwardly in the

pews. The music stopped and the curtains went into reverse.

Finally, 'Gone Fishin'' took over.

* * *

Keeping watch on Emma's house was more of a challenge than Keith Halliwell had anticipated. The small terrace stood at a right angle to the Upper Bristol Road and the only approach was a narrow passage along the front with a six-foot wall along the left side. Anyone standing there would be as obvious as a bull on a bowling green. The unmarked police car had slotted into a space across the road, but the view from there was side-on.

'Better split up and keep radio contact,' he told the other two. 'I suggest you take the far end of the terrace, Inge. As for you, Paul, find a vantage point somewhere on the gasworks side, at the back.'

'Do we have any idea who to expect?' Paul Gilbert said.

Ingeborg rolled her eyes. 'If you don't, I do. Why do you think you and I were chosen for this?'

Paul stayed silent, not caring to reveal his ignorance.

'Be ready for anyone,' Halliwell said. 'Soon as they show up and seem interested in the place, we radio each other.'

'Do we let them break in?'

He nodded. 'Grab them in the act.'

'I thought the first duty of a police officer is to prevent crime taking place,' Ingeborg said.

'Not this time, kiddo.'

They split up.

Halliwell looked at his watch. Down at

Haycombe, the funeral would be under way. He preferred doing this.

A blur of heavy vehicles moved past the window, some of them rocking the car. As one of the main arteries into Bath, this was not the ideal residential area. There was an army recruitment place and a fitness centre, the Hop Pole pub and an Argos with its own car park. Further along on the north side was Victoria Park, with its play area, but a line of tall conifers behind wire fencing blocked out the light where the car was parked.

Halliwell guessed anyone planning a break-in was likely to approach the terrace from the south, using Midland Road. He made sure his radio was switched on. He'd give the others a few more minutes to take up positions before getting in contact.

Two joggers approached from the Bath direction and passed the terrace without a sideways glance.

Halliwell spoke into the phone. 'All set?'

'I'm in place,' Ingeborg answered.

'Me, too,' Paul said.

'Anyone suspicious, sing out.'

The radio went quiet again. More HGVs thundered past. Halliwell wished he could have had a pound for each minute he'd spent on police duty waiting for something to happen. He'd buy an Aston Martin on the proceeds.

His phone beeped.

'Yes?'

'How's it going?' Diamond, straight to it, as always.

'Nothing happened yet, guv. How's it with you?'

'Funeral's over. We're outside looking at the flowers right now. Then we move off to the Hop

Pole.'

'Lucky you.'

'It's tough at the top. Stay sharp and be gentle.'

Confused by the last remark, Halliwell pocketed the phone and heard what he took to be another lorry coming close, but it wasn't. This was a motorcycle, a powerful machine, coming to a stop in a space a couple of parked cars away. The rider, in black leathers and dark helmet, lowered the kickstand, swung his leg over and pulled up the visor to check the road. Then he crossed, heading straight for Onega Terrace.

'Stand by,' Halliwell said into his radio. 'Guy on a motorbike just arrived. Heading your way on foot.'

In all that gear, the figure could have been anyone of average height and build. Definitely male, Halliwell decided. He watched the approach to the access path, saw the motorcyclist stop in front of Emma's house. The gardens were so short that there was not much chance of privacy for the residents. It was easy to see the interiors through the bay windows unless there were blinds or curtains in place. Equally, anyone inside would notice a visitor approaching.

Sometimes you get a feeling whether a house is inhabited or not. It's an instinct cultivated by door-to-door salesmen and burglars. The motorcyclist, whatever his purpose, seemed to have made up his mind. He didn't break in. He didn't need to. He lifted the doormat, looked underneath and picked something up.

'Give me strength, you couldn't make it up,' Halliwell said to himself as the visitor put the key in the door and gained entry. 'Why are people so bloody obvious? A police family, too.'

The others had to be informed, and fast. He said into the radio, 'She keeps a spare key under the mat. He's found it and gone inside.'

'What do we do now?' Ingeborg asked. 'Is that technically a break-in?'

Technically, it wasn't. In theory the intruder could be there by invitation, a friend or family member, but there wasn't time to analyse the situation. 'We close off the exits at front and back. Get as near as you can without being obvious and stop him when he comes out.' Halliwell left the car and crossed the road. He would cover the obvious escape route, the end of the access path. Ingeborg would be at the far end and Paul would take the back door.

A minute passed.

Two minutes.

Confusing thoughts rushed through Halliwell's head. Maybe this was just someone who had turned up too late for the funeral and decided to wait in the house for Emma's return. He could be making himself at home, sitting in front of the TV or helping himself to a cup of tea. On the other hand, he might be ransacking the house, looking for whatever bits of jewellery Emma possessed.

The house was only a box of a place. Shouldn't take long to search. Any self-respecting thief would go through it in under ten minutes.

There would come a point when the only sensible option was to ring the doorbell and see if anyone came.

Not yet.

He spoke into the radio. 'Paul, where are you?'

'Back of the house, right up against the wall by the back door. He can't see me.'

'Can you hear anything inside?'

'Traffic's too noisy.'

'We'll give it three more and then I'll ring the bell. Inge, are you all set?'

'All set. Wait, the door's opening. He's coming out, coming your way.'

This was it, then. Up to now, Halliwell had been out of sight, using the cover of the end-terrace house. He stepped on to the path and saw the black figure of the motorcyclist striding towards him, having removed the helmet and carrying it in his left hand. Halliwell didn't recognise him. He was just a youth, but he could be dangerous.

In his right hand was a black plastic sack wrapped around an object with an ominous shape.

'Hold it,' Halliwell said. 'Police.'

The youth dropped the helmet and it skeetered across the path. But he held on to the object in the sack. He ripped open enough of the sack to reveal the barrel of the automatic rifle Halliwell had suspected was inside. He gripped it in the firing position.

Halliwell's flesh prickled. 'Drop it,' he shouted.

The young man spun on his heels and dashed in the other direction, towards Ingeborg.

'He's got a gun,' Halliwell yelled, to warn her. He jammed the radio to his mouth. 'Paul, get round the front.' He was already sprinting up the path in pursuit, regardless that the gunman could swing around and fill him with bullets. There was no escape, nowhere to duck and dodge. This was death alley.

The next moves happened in a split-second that—to Halliwell's adrenalin-charged brain—appeared like a slow-motion sequence. The gunman reached the low wall at the end of the path and vaulted over. Ingeborg, crouching out of sight, made a grab for his leg. They crashed to the ground and the gun flew from his hand. Ingeborg held on and the pair of them rolled over and over.

Halliwell leapt over the wall just as Paul Gilbert appeared around the side of the house. Together, they flung themselves on to the struggling man and forced his arms behind his back. Halliwell handcuffed him.

'You okay?' he asked Ingeborg.

'I think so.' She hauled herself up and tightened the blonde ponytail. 'You know who this is?'

'Never seen him before.'

'Soldier Nuttall's son, Royston—and that's a real G36, not one of their plastic jobs.'

'Don't handle it, then.' Halliwell took a pen from his pocket and looped it under the skeletonised frame of the stock. 'Let's get him back to the car.'

Royston wasn't the menacing figure he'd seemed when he arrived. He was shivering like a nervous pup. They walked him back and retrieved the helmet on the way.

'The guv'nor was expecting him to break in, I reckon,' Gilbert said.

'If he did, he could have warned us about the gun,' Halliwell said.

In the car, Royston was still shaking. 'Are you going to bang me up in the cells?'

'That isn't up to us,' Halliwell said.

'I don't mind if you do,' he said.

Halliwell pretended not to be baffled by this reaction. 'That's all right, then.'

'Long as you don't tell my old man.'

So that was the reason for the panic.

'I expect we will,' Halliwell said. 'He's very concerned about you. He was in this morning asking us to find you.'

In what came out sounding like a whimper, Royston said, 'I want protection from him. I don't want to go home.'

'Right now, son, you're in no position to dictate terms.'

Halliwell decided he'd better report the arrest to Diamond. He stepped out of the car and used his mobile. 'Guv.'

'Yep.'

'Is this a good moment?'

'Not bad. I'm in the Hop Pole with a glass in my hand.'

'We pinched Royston Nuttall coming out of the Tasker house.'

Diamond didn't sound unduly surprised. 'Nice work. He was sure to surface at some time. No one got hurt, I hope.'

'We're okay. He was carrying a rifle.' Halliwell felt like adding, 'And you could have warned us what to expect.' Only he wasn't totally certain Diamond had known in advance.

'That'll be the murder weapon.'

'I thought we already found the murder weapon in the river.'

'This is the one that did for Harry Tasker. Treat it carefully. I expect it's been wiped of prints, but you never know.'

'I don't think I follow you.'

'It's a G36 assault rifle, isn't it?'

'Yes.'

'It was hidden inside the house and the funeral was Royston's chance to get it back.'

'Get it back?'

'It belongs to his father. That's why Soldier Nuttall was round at the station this morning. He wasn't worried about Royston. He wanted the gun back.'

'I thought all his guns were imitation.'

'A major player like Nuttall isn't satisfied with plastic. He has some of the real things squirrelled away inside that house. Okay, the search squad didn't find anything when they raided the place, but that was because Royston had borrowed the G36 some time ago. What better to raise a tough teenager's street cred than a genuine firearm? He took it into Walcot to impress his friends around the pubs. Unluckily for him, Harry Tasker got to hear about this gun being shown to all and sundry. Harry caught up with the kid and took it off him. In the words of Anderson Jakes, Harry practised what he like doing best—confiscation. He took charge of the gun. But Harry didn't bring it back to the station. He took it home.'

'I'm with you now, guv. I shouldn't speak ill of the dead, least of all today, but we all knew Harry was working some kind of racket.'

'Yes, and he knew Soldier Nuttall would throw a fit if he found out, so he had Royston by the short and curlies. He could demand money whenever he ran into him, the same as he collected hush money from other kids he'd caught misbehaving. It's not surprising Harry was so insistent that no one else walked that beat.'

'I guess the raid alerted Nuttall and made him check his personal firearms.'

'For sure. Royston panicked and fled the house. He'd already got the idea that with Harry dead he might have a chance to get the gun back. He was watching the Tasker house the other day when I visited Emma. I was almost knocked over by a motorbike revving up and racing away.'

'For a second time.'

'Right, but different bike and different rider. It had to be Royston this time and he was bound to work out that the funeral—with Emma out of the way—was the ideal time to get inside and collect his dad's property.'

'You don't think he's Harry's killer?'

'Royston? No, I don't. Tell me something. You said you pinched Royston, but you didn't say where. Did you go inside the house?'

'No. We waited for him to come out. He didn't break in, you see. The key was under the doormat.'

'Handy.'

'Stupid, we thought. Asking for trouble.'

Diamond didn't want to get into that kind of debate. 'Look, I've got to go now. Keep the kid under arrest. He won't object. He's safer with us than he is if we let him go.'

Halliwell had discovered that much from Royston himself. He was still listening to Diamond, but his attention had been drawn across the street, to Emma's house. 'Hold on, guv. Something's happening here. A bloke just walked up the path to the house. He seems to have a key and he's letting himself in.'

'D'you know him?'

'Christ, yes, I do. We interviewed him at the Paragon. It's Sean Willis, the smart-arse civil servant in the top flat who belongs to the gun club.'

CHAPTER THIRTY-TWO

The Hop Pole, Emma's choice for the refreshments after the funeral, was only a few hundred yards along the Upper Bristol Road from Onega Terrace. It was her local, and she couldn't have found a better one. The dark-panelled bar was Victorian in style, comfortable and not noisy. From there you moved through a restaurant created out of a skittle alley to the real glory of the place, a secluded beer garden ideal for summer drinking, with vines around the perimeter and threading upwards into well-placed gazebos. This was where the mourners had gathered in sunshine, becoming relaxed by the minute as the more formal part of the day became a memory.

Diamond pocketed his phone and helped himself to a warm sausage roll. The business end of the investigation was working out as he had expected, some compensation for his wrong assumptions earlier. Royston had surfaced at the Tasker house while the funeral was in progress. The murder weapon was now in police hands. It could be test-fired and used in evidence. Sean Willis had declared his intent by arriving at the house with a key. He'd always seemed a character with a secret.

The family member who was acting as host appeared with a plate of sandwiches. 'You know it's a free bar?'

'I do,' Diamond said, 'but I'm limiting myself.'

'Diet?'

'Duty, actually.'

'But you'll have a sandwich?'

'Thanks.' He took two. 'Are you related to Harry?'

'I'm Gordon, married to one of his sisters, Agnes—going round with the spring rolls. Sad occasion. I believe you caught the son of a bitch who did this.'

'Not yet,' Diamond said.

'Oh?' Gordon's eyebrows popped up. 'I heard he was in the cells. Some foreigner shooting you chaps more or less at random, just because you represent law and order.'

'He shot the other two, not Harry.'

Gordon almost dropped the sandwiches. 'How on earth can that be?'

'Everyone assumed all three crimes were by the same hand, me included, for a time. It's what we were meant to think, that the so-called Somerset Sniper shot Harry as well. Harry wasn't shot at random. It was deliberate.'

'And you know who did this?'

'We do. And an arrest is expected shortly.' He turned his head to check who was still there. 'Have you seen my colleagues, the three guys in uniform?'

'They had to leave, unfortunately. Something about duties.'

'Ah.' A little of Diamond's laid-back manner ebbed away.

'They had a drink and a bite to eat. You're not rushing off too, I hope?'

'Not yet, but I must make a phone call.'

'I'll leave you to it, then.' Gordon appeared glad he had the plate in his hand as a reason to move away. You meet some strange people at funerals.

A minute later, Diamond spotted the neighbour Betty's enormous black hat and went over to where she was standing with Emma. 'Excellent choice of pub,' he said. 'Do you use it much?'

The question was addressed more to Emma than Betty. 'Not often. Harry wasn't one for going out, as I told you.'

Betty then used what was becoming her catch-phrase. 'I'm off.'

Emma said quickly, 'There's no need.'

'There is, dear,' Betty told her. 'A pressing need, to put it delicately.' She left at speed.

With Emma to himself, Diamond said, 'Nearly over, then.'

She remained in control. 'Just about.' Then she gave him an opening for a polite leave-taking. 'It was good of you to come.'

Leaving wasn't in his plans. 'I wondered why you invited me. Aside from the obvious fact that I'm charming enough to make a success of any occasion, however sad, what could I possibly contribute? I've worked it out.'

'You'd better tell me,' she said, but her gaze was elsewhere.

'As I'm here, I can't possibly be somewhere else—keeping watch on your house.'

'Is that so?' she said with only a slight show of interest.

'In the force we look after our own, as I don't have to tell you,' he said. 'It's one of those sad reflections on humanity that people's homes sometimes get broken into while they are out at events such as this. I couldn't keep an eye on your place myself, so I sent a few of my team.'

She frowned slightly. 'To my house?'

'You needn't worry,' he said. 'All's well. They've been in touch. You had a visitor, but apparently he was expected. He knew where to find the front door key. Under the mat, right? Young Royston let himself in, picked up something belonging to him and left.'

Emma didn't comment.

'One of the many items Harry confiscated in the course of duty. Your husband had his own unofficial way of keeping the streets safe.'

She appeared unmoved.

'You made an arrangement with the boy, didn't you?' Diamond went on. 'Royston had been pestering you ever since he knew Harry was no more. I saw him near your house on Tuesday when you asked me over. He almost knocked me down making his escape on the motorbike. Decent of you to put his mind at rest. His father is a scary man and of course the rifle belonged to his father. And it suited you to send it back to where it belonged. A neat solution.'

Now Emma said with more of her old thrust, 'This is neither the time nor the place.'

'There's never a time or place,' he said, matching her steel. 'The funeral's over. We've taken leave of Harry in a civilised way. You're ex-police yourself. You know I have a job to do.'

But Emma wasn't interested in hearing any more. She shook her head so violently that the thick, black hair briefly covered her face. Then she took a sidestep and darted past him at a rate he hadn't expected, around a table of startled mourners and out through the gate at the bottom of the garden.

Diamond could have used those three officers who had left early. Alone, he wasn't sure he could cope. Pursuing Emma would be next to impossible.

There wasn't time to get on the phone for reinforcements. He'd already lost sight of her.

But it struck him that one thing was in his favour. She'd get no further than the river. Wide and deep, it flowed parallel to the road. Going after her might, after all, be worth it. A few hundred yards, no more.

He crossed the garden at the best speed he could, followed her through the gate, across rough ground below the Argos car park, and saw her veer towards the right.

Why that direction?

He'd miscalculated.

The iron bridge.

A narrow, one-way track called Midland Road snaked down to the river and provided a crossing. It was used mainly by vehicles heading south to the Lower Bristol Road.

To chase, or not to chase? For the present his damaged leg was holding him up. He couldn't rely on it.

Ahead, Emma had reached the brick wall that separated the open ground from Midland Road. It looked high for her, but she was agile. At the second attempt she drew herself up, clambered over and dropped out of sight.

Diamond lumbered after her, taking shallow breaths. He actually caught up a little while she was scaling the wall. Being taller, he reckoned he'd find it less of a barrier. He attacked it at his best speed, grabbed the top, hauled himself up and over, making sure as he dropped that he didn't land on the sore leg.

She'd already put more space between them and she was still running strongly. Catching her would be a lost cause once she was across the river. The iron bridge came up sooner than he expected. Dry-mouthed and gasping, he watched her dash under the first arched strut without looking back, her dark hair rising and falling.

What now? Phone for reinforcements? Wave down a car? Any more delay and she'd be out of sight again. The Lower Bristol Road gave her options of side streets that made any pursuit pointless. He was forced to flog himself harder and try and keep her in sight.

He reached the bridge and trudged across at the best speed he could. He remembered that on the opposite side of the river the road made a sharp left turn. She was about to vanish from view.

Then chance threw in a different possibility. A silver van ahead of Emma braked and signalled as if to go right.

Right? The turn was left. What was going on?

Emma hesitated, and at first Diamond thought the driver was stopping to pick her up. He was wrong. On the right side, a gate had opened in the tall metal fence at the angle of the bend and the van was driving through. Emma had seen the opportunity of following it off the road and into the large yard beyond.

That was her choice. She nipped through that gate faster than the van.

As Diamond approached, someone was in the act of slamming it shut.

'Leave it,' he shouted with as much voice as he had left.

He came to a juddering halt when the gate slammed in his face. It was a barrier built with security in mind, set into ten-foot fencing and topped with barbed wire. The man on the other side was threading through a chain and padlock.

'Police,' Diamond said in a gasp. 'Open up again.' He felt for his ID and shoved it at the mesh barrier.

After an unendurable pause for thought, the gatekeeper allowed Diamond through.

By this time, Emma was not in sight.

He stood in uncertainty, wondering if she had turned sharp right and doubled back to the river. From there she could scramble down the steep bank to a narrow footpath.

He covered the few yards to check. No one was down there. She hadn't chosen this escape route. So where was she?

Again he took stock of his surroundings. Then his heart pumped in his chest as if it was ready to burst out. So intent had he been on watching Emma run away from him that he'd missed the biggest thing in view inside this compound, the thing nobody could fail to miss: the gasholder. The enormous buff-coloured cylinder in its rusty iron framework dominated the scene this side of the Avon. In the heyday of the Bath Gas, Light and Coke Company, the fuel had been brought up the river in barges and three gasholders had stood expanding and contracting to meet the demands of the entire city.

He had spotted a movement near the base. A small figure in black was on the lowest section of the iron surround moving up a diagonal traverse that was evidently a set of steps.

He broke into a stiff-legged run again, powered by the knowledge that this was the end of the line for Emma. She had trapped herself. He would catch her now.

Then his confidence plunged again. The yard containing the gasholder and some brick buildings was enclosed by yet more metal fencing. So much security. How the hell had she got through? As he got closer he saw the gate open to admit the same silver van that had passed through the other entrance. Gratefully he hobbled through.

At the base of the gasholder steps, he took out his phone.

John Leaman answered.

'Emma Tasker is climbing up the gasholder in Twerton. Don't ask. Get a patrol here fast.'

He grasped the handrail and looked up. She had already scaled the first level and was on the narrow landing staring down at him.

'It's all over, Emma,' he shouted up. 'Better come down.'

Her response was to run to the next staircase and start on the next set of steps. What was she thinking of?

With a chilling certainty, he knew. She meant to throw herself off.

He had no other choice than to follow, if only to reason with her. The steps were a severe test for his knees after all the running. He toiled upwards to the first landing.

'Emma, this is crazy,' he yelled. 'You're going nowhere.'

Altogether there were four staircases and three landings. She stopped halfway up and turned again to watch him.

He continued upwards. And so did Emma. She made it to the second landing and dashed straight to the next staircase.

Soon she would reach the exposed section above the top tier of the great metal cylinder. The gasholder itself was about one-third below capacity. The supporting framework rose much higher, into space.

And she was still climbing.

Far from certain if he had a head for heights like this, Diamond continued to mount the steps, even when he could only see daylight instead of solid metal through the spaces between. Three landings up, he gripped the handrail and drew breath. She was about to go up the final set of steps. No doubt there was a panoramic view of Bath from up here. He didn't care to see it. He tried to focus on what his feet were doing.

There came a point more than a hundred feet up when even Emma sensed that this ascent was finite. A few steps short of the crown of the entire structure, she came to a halt. Diamond was following slowly now and he hadn't faltered, but he made sure he stopped a safe distance from her feet.

Down at ground level he hadn't been conscious of any wind at all. Up here, it tugged at his clothes and rasped his face.

Even with the rushing in his eardrums, he thought it possible to exchange words, extraordinary as the situation would be. He needed to get his breath first, and find a way of keeping Emma from panicking.

No threat. No confrontation. Get her talking.

Finally he managed to say, 'You should have brought the three sleuths up here.'

'I didn't think of it,' she said.

He was encouraged that she was willing to speak at all.

'You read the blog, then?' she said. 'Someone told you about it?'

'They did.'

'What do you think?' She was keen to get an opinion on her imaginative effort. She wanted praise.

'Compulsive reading once I got into it,' he said. 'You must have started writing it some time before Harry was shot.'

'At least a week.'

Which left no question that the murder was premeditated, but he chose not to say so at this juncture. 'You've got a lively imagination. It was clever, the way you wove in the clues about Bath and Wells and Radstock towards the end. I soon cottoned on that the real story you wanted to get across was about Tim, pointing the finger at a fictitious man.'

'He wasn't entirely fiction,' she said.

'All right, there were elements of Harry in the character, the non-communication and so on, but Harry wasn't ex-army and the only outings he had at night were when he was on beat duty. You wanted us to read the blog and think Tim was the Somerset Sniper.'

'Did I?'

How bizarre is this? he thought, trying to analyse a work of fiction on a rusty old staircase a hundred feet off the ground. But his show of interest seemed to be working. She'd invested a lot in the blog and this was her chance to find out how well she'd succeeded. Keep talking, he told himself. Pitch it calmly and she may not think about jumping.

'So let's sum up the real situation. When we first met and I informed you Harry was dead, you were straight with me, remarkably straight. You let me know it was a failed marriage. He was a non-communicator with no ambition and when he was off work he slumped in front of the telly or went fishing. You convinced me you were an honest, hard-done-by woman. It didn't cross my mind that you had a lover, not until much later. I only twigged when I spoke to one of his neighbours, the blonde on the ground floor. She told me Sean Willis had a night visitor sometimes. Was that while Harry was on the night shift?'

After he'd spoken, he knew it sounded a cheap remark. He wasn't surprised she didn't answer.

A huge flock of starlings was spiralling just a short way off in the flat, grey sky. They twisted into the shape of an hour-glass.

He tried again. 'You wanted an escape from Harry and when you started seeing Willis, your home life seemed even more pointless. You're not going to deny the affair? Only a short while ago I was told by my team that he called at your house.'

She said, 'Sean? You're bluffing.'

'To comfort you after the funeral, I guess. Obviously he couldn't be there at your side in front of everyone, so he waited for it to be over. He let himself in with his own key.'

'He didn't!' Her voice piped in disapproval.

'And if he had a key to your place, it's reasonable to assume you have a key to his—the house in the Paragon. Where did you first meet him—at the rifle range in Devizes?'

She said, 'Let's get one thing clear. Sean had nothing to do with Harry's death.'

'But that's how you met?'

'Yes.'

'You'd learned to shoot when you served in the police. In those days it was a five-day course to get qualified as a firearms officer and lots of us did it.'

She snapped, 'How do you know that?'

'It's listed. You know what the police are like. Everything goes on record. I asked for the list of firearms officers at Helston while you were on the strength. It said PC Tasker, which at first I took to be Harry. That's the sort of sexist I am, assuming only men are interested in using guns.'

'Harry's sport was fishing, not shooting,' she said, as good as admitting she'd done the course. She was proud of her skill with the rifle.

'After leaving the police, you had a less adventurous life teaching infants. Harry had his own hobby at the weekends, so you went back to shooting at targets and found a new friend as well. You were keen, keen enough to make trips all the way to Devizes.'

'There's no gun club in Bath.'

'How did you get there? Not on your pushbike?'

'Other people offered me lifts. Several came from Bath.'

'Including Willis?'

'He was one of them, yes. Sean knows nothing about any of this,' she insisted.

'I'm not suggesting he does. Let's talk about Harry. He had his own way of controlling youth crime. Confiscation, as one of our sources put it. He'd take away illegal goods and demand hush money. Did you know about that?'

She shrugged. 'Make a guess.'

'We haven't searched your house, but I'm sure we'll find a stash in the loft or under the floorboards. Harry's biggest prize was Soldier

Nuttall's sniper rifle, unwisely borrowed by his son Royston to impress his friends. You found the gun and the temptation was too much. Harry had supplied you with the means of your freedom, the same make of rifle the Somerset Sniper was known to use.'

'It wasn't as cold-blooded as that,' she said. 'Several things came on top of each other.'

He waited for her to expand on this, but she chose not to. 'I know what some of them are,' he said. 'There was all the stuff in the media about the sniper shooting policemen. Wives of policemen all over the West Country worried sick that their men would get the next bullet. You, I imagine, thought along different lines.'

Her mouth twitched into a quick, faint smile.

'You knew Harry's beat took him along Walcot Street, below the Paragon. Last Saturday night you let yourself into the house with the gun and waited in the empty garden flat and most of what happened went according to plan. You picked off Harry with your second shot. You meant to make your getaway at once, but there was a delay.'

'That damned alarm went off,' she said. 'I was afraid someone in the house would look out and see me in the garden, so I crouched down among the weeds. I lost one of the cartridge cases and panicked a bit. The sniper never leaves them behind. It would give you the chance to prove I used a different rifle. I don't know how long I was scrabbling around, trying to find it. Then I noticed Sean's blinds were raised. He had no idea I was there. I couldn't go back through the basement flat and risk running into him. I had to give him time to go back to bed. I hadn't reckoned on some of your lot getting there so soon. I was hiding behind the nettles. The police noticed the gun where I'd left it, but then they went away for a minute and only one came back.'

'You picked up the gun and cracked him over the head with it. Almost a double murder.'

'He'll be all right, won't he?' she asked without much concern.

'Decent of you to enquire. He'll survive. Whether he's brain damaged, I don't know. How did you eventually make your escape?'

'The way I came. On my pushbike.'

He was in awe. 'Where was it?'

'In the street opposite.'

'You cycled through the streets at night with the murder weapon?'

'It's a short ride, under a mile, even taking the quiet route along Royal Avenue, and the gun folds up and fits into the saddlebag.'

'After which you played the angry widow, sat back and watched events unfold.'

'More or less,' Emma said.

'Right. "More or less" means you weren't as passive as it appeared. You still did what you could to influence things. Top marks for the fake blog, inventing a whole different explanation.'

'So you weren't taken in?'

'Almost. Something didn't ring true. I felt this was an educated woman trying too hard to sound streetwise and trendy.'

'In what way?'

'Some of the conversations and how you handled them. "She was like . . ." and "She went . . ." I bet you don't say stuff like that to your own friends. It didn't chime with the rest, the university degree, teaching the piano and so forth.'

'It's the modern vernacular.'

'And only an educated woman would use a phrase like that. But I did fall for the "You're next" threats. They reinforced the idea of a series of shootings. I really thought someone in the police must have threatened Harry. I suppose you added the note to his card-case after it was returned to you.'

'Anything to deflect suspicion,' she said.

'Including the one you sent me?'

'That was meant,' she said in the same calm tone of acceptance and then without warning switched to a shrill note of frenzy. 'Because you're next, Detective bloody Diamond, of course you're next, else why would I have brought you all the way up here?'

With that, she braced herself and leapt off.

Directly below her, Diamond had the split-second warning of what she was about to do, but there was no escape.

The full weight of her body hurtled towards him.

Her feet caught his left shoulder and swung him to the right. In that infinitesimal moment of grace the instinct for self-preservation had made him grip the handrail hard and pull himself closer. Even so, his left arm was jerked off the rail and he careered backwards and lost his footing. He dangled in space, only the fingers of one hand stopping him falling to his death. By kicking out frantically he got his left foot between two steps and hauled himself back to connect with the staircase and hold on.

Only Emma knew whether her leap was intended to be suicidal. Certainly she meant to take Diamond with her. She fell no further than the landing, hitting it with a thud that sounded hideous and final, but was not. She lay groaning on the narrow platform.

Diamond was fortunate. His only injury was to his dignity. His trousers had ripped wide open at the back.

The rescue effort was not long in coming. Emma, with both legs broken, had to be winched down on a stretcher. She was still conscious when Diamond was helped off the steps. She saw him and said, 'You think you're lucky, and you are, bloody lucky, but when this comes to court I'm denying everything. You've got it all to prove.'

* * *

English law has its unique way of dealing with offenders. When the cases finally came to court, Soldier Nuttall was given a suspended sentence of six months for possession of an unlicensed weapon. Emma Tasker was found guilty of murder and given the mandatory life sentence, but at the lowest end of the scale thanks to a spirited defence. She would be out some years before the expiry of the fifteen-year term. Hossain Farhadi, the Somerset Sniper, was also found guilty of murder and told that the life sentence in his case meant at least thirty years. He seemed to regard this as salvation. Jack Gull hailed it as a triumph for the Serial Crimes Unit.

The bruises healed in Bath CID. Diamond was soon back on good terms with his team. One afternoon he was called to Georgina's office. She was looking benevolent for once. 'I have good news, Peter. This is in confidence. Ingeborg's promotion to sergeant is approved.'

'That *is* good,' he said, delighted, 'and not before time.'

But where there's good news, there is usually bad as well.

'Headquarters have been looking at your budget report. I'm afraid you've overspent again.'

'I don't think so, ma'am,' he said.

'I had to bump up the figures a bit before they went in.'

'Oh?'

'We were sent the invoice for a replacement suit.'

'Not by me,' he said. 'I ripped a perfectly good pair of trousers on that gasholder thing, and I can't wear the jacket without them. I've never claimed for clothing.'

'You wouldn't get it,' Georgina said.

'Who's got the nerve to claim for a suit?'

'Mr Anderson Jakes. He said one of your officers was responsible. I didn't want it itemised for the accountants to question, so it's gone through as extra overtime.'

'How was it damaged?'

'Unfortunately it came apart at the shoulder seam.'

'That's repairable, ma'am.'

'Apparently not. The more expensive the suit, the less likely it is that a repair will pass muster. This is a bespoke Savile Row suit costing over a thousand pounds.'

He was outraged. 'A grand? My suits cost a hundred and forty-nine.'

Georgina passed no comment.